DIARY
OF A
BAD BOY

USA TODAY BESTSELLING AUTHOR
MEGHAN QUINN

Published by Hot-Lanta Publishing, LLC

Copyright 2019

Cover Design By: RBA Designs

Cover Model: Cormac Murphy

Photo Credit: Sylvie Rosokoff

This book is licensed for your personal enjoyment only. This book may not be re-sold or given away to other people. If you would like to share this book with another person, please purchase an additional copy for each person. If you're reading this book and did not purchase it, or it was not purchased for your use only, then please return it and purchase your own copy. Thank you for respecting the hard work of this author.

No part of this book may be reproduced in any form or by any electronic or mechanical means, including information storage and retrieval systems, without written permission from the author, except for the use of brief quotations in a book review. To obtain permission to excerpt portions of the text, please contact the author at meghan.quinn.author@gmail.com

All characters in this book are fiction and figments of the author's imagination.

www.authormeghanquinn.com

Copyright © 2019 Meghan Quinn

All rights reserved.

PROLOGUE

Dear Diary,
    Fuck, it sounds like I'm a hopelessly besotted teenage girl with heart beams spewing from her hormonal eyes. Yeah, there is no fucking way I can write Dear Diary. I need a different name. Something manly, something with giant balls, something that will scare away any little punk who tries to read this. Let me think on that.

    And yeah, I fucking wrote besotted. I might be a whiskey-slinging party boy with the luck of a four-leaf clover, but I'm also a goddamn gentleman. A gentleman who occasionally writes words like besotted.

    Unfortunately, this "gentleman" got himself into a wee bit of trouble. I blame it on the Irish temper and the tawdry hoodlums who thought they could get in my face while I was flirting with a fine-as-hell lass. But I guess the court system looks down upon punching someone in the nose while still expertly holding a tumbler of whiskey—didn't spill a goddamn drop.

    Thank fuck for a good lawyer. Well, I thought he was good until I realized what I had to do instead of jail time. Eighty hours of community service and anger management therapy sessions with Dr. Stick Up Her Ass, who requires me to write in this godforsaken diary about my . . . feelings.

    Guess what I'm feeling?

    Horny. Thirsty. And in the mood for a hot dog.

And that's as much as you're going to get out of me, Diary. Sorry if you were expecting a grand confession of childhood dilemmas or an outpouring of hysterical and exasperating diatribe. Not going to happen. Not with me.

Until our next unwanted engagement,
Roark

CHAPTER ONE

SUTTON

"It's late."

"It's eleven thirty in New York City, so that's early," Maddie says, tugging on my arm. "Come on, live a little."

I scan the dark streets, my dad's warning about being a single girl in the city running on repeat in my head. "I don't know, I think I should get home."

I've lived in the city for two years now and have yet to be out this late on my own. Grad school and studying will do that to you. Also, the pure fear of being scooped up by a human trafficker—thanks, Dad—instills enough fear inside me to never go past my front door any time after nine at night.

But I'm supposed to be celebrating today, at least that's what Maddie told me. After two solid years of doing nothing but studying, I graduated with a master's in philanthropy, and I'm about to start my new job . . . working for my dad.

I know what you're thinking—nepotism at its finest. And maybe . . . BUT I also earned the position, interning under the director of operations for four years. For free. I spent four years working my butt off—twenty hours every week—proving to the team I'm not just Foster Green's daughter, but a valuable attribute to Gaining Goals, a non-profit foundation founded by my father, the four-time All-Pro quarterback for the New York Steel.

And all that hard work paid off when Whitney Horan hired me as public relations manager.

"You're not going home. What happened to experiencing life? Remember that little New Year's resolution you made?"

This is why I shouldn't share anything too personal with Maddie. She always holds me to it. Although, I guess that's what a best friend does. Also . . . she found my New Year's resolutions on a notepad on my kitchen counter. At first, she admired the different colored pens I used for each resolution—five in total—and then memorized each and every one of them. Maddie and I met our freshman year in college, and she is the yin to my yang. Where I am more reserved, she's outgoing and adventurous, an attribute I wish I possessed. But I would never tell her that.

"I don't think staying out past eleven thirty defines living life."

"It sure as hell does." She loops her arm through mine, our puffy jackets clashing together to form one huge ball of warmth. "This is the beginning of living life. We did your thing and saw a Broadway musical, now we're going to do my thing."

"What's your *thing*?" I ask hesitantly.

"Getting a hot dog." Maddie hails a cab and rattles off the intersection of two streets like a true New Yorker.

"A hot dog? That's living life?"

"Yes, and didn't you say you wanted to try all the iconic food of New York?"

Darn it, another resolution, although that resolution has been my favorite and the easiest to accomplish so far, going around the city and trying all the different food the urban jungle is known for. But along with that resolution came a gym membership, one I've used quite often.

"I do want to try *all the food*," I answer, biting on my lip.

"That's why we're going to Gray's Papaya to get some famous hot dogs and mango juice."

Thoughtfully, I ask, "Isn't that the hot dog place in *You've Got Mail?*"

"And *Fools Rush In*," Maddie adds. "If Matthew Perry is so fond of it, so am I. And from what reviewers have been saying, you're supposed to get the dogs dressed in mustard and their famous onions. So get ready, we're about to have dragon breath."

"Oh, I can't wait." I chuckle.

Maddie elbows me in the side. "See, there you go, you're getting into the spirit. Midnight hot dogs, what could go wrong?"

Famous last words.

∽

Okay, this place is cute: white subway tile plastered on the walls, paper pineapples and bananas dangling from the ceiling, and mirrors hanging from the waist up so you can watch yourself enjoying your hot dogs at the tiny counters provided. It's quaint and smells like heaven.

And if there was anything Maddie and I instantly bonded over, it was our love for hot dogs. We have no shame in buying one from a street vendor and eating it on our way to class. So even though I'm a little reserved, this is kind of fun.

"Look at all those wieners," Maddie shouts as she steps up to the grill. "Thinner than I expected, but I'm not one to mock girth as long as they do the job. Am I right, Sutton?"

The guys behind the grill chuckle as my face heats up. I hold up my fingers and shyly say, "Two hot dogs, please. Mustard and onions." I reach for my wallet when Maddie stops me.

"Two each please." She turns to me and says, "It's on me," as if it's no big deal, even though I'm the one who paid for her Broadway ticket.

I glance toward the dollar-fifty price tag and then back at her. "Are you sure you can handle that?"

"Hey now, don't get sassy with me." Muttering softly, she says, "I'm not the one with a father who plays professional football."

True.

I put my wallet back in my purse and give her a side hug. "Thanks for the hot dogs."

"Anything for my girl."

Our hot dogs are delivered on rickety paper plates, which we take to the small counter in front of the mirror. Our drinks follow closely behind.

Inspecting the dog, I lift it up to my mouth right before Maddie stops me. "What are you doing? We need to document this. Hot dog selfie. Come on, Sutton."

Maddie and her selfies . . .

Playing along, I hold up my dog with hers and smile into the mirror as she uses her phone to take a picture of our reflection.

The door blows open and in walk two guys: one wearing a suit and tie, the other in black jeans, white shirt, black jacket, and a beanie hanging loosely on his head. His green eyes connect with mine in the mirror as a small smirk pulls across his lips.

"What's up, Miguel?" he says in an Irish lilt that quickly gains my attention. "Got some dogs for me, man?"

"No," the guy behind the grill playfully says. "I don't serve hot dogs to guys who put ketchup on them."

The man in the tie eyes his friend. "You put ketchup on your hot dog?"

"It's good." The guy shrugs and pulls out a twenty. "Four hot dogs, two with ketchup, two with"—he gestures to his friend—"what do ya want?"

"Mustard and relish."

From over her shoulder, Maddie scoffs. "Don't you know you're supposed to get mustard and onions on these beauties? Ketchup and relish are for heathens."

Slowly, the Irishman turns toward us, a tilt to his head. "Who made you the hot dog police, lady?"

Proudly, Maddie says, "I did. If anything, I have experience. I know my wieners and how to make sure they taste good in my mouth."

Oh, sweet Jesus. How can she come out with something so laced with sexual innuendo so easily? See? Yin to my yang. Although, I am mortified. I adjust my winter hat on my head and tug on Maddie's arm just as more men filter into the small hot dog shop. Whispering, I say, "Don't tell people how to eat their hot dogs."

"I'm not telling them; I'm just letting them know they're wrong."

"Miguel, five dogs and coconut juice," a man in a blue faux-fur jacket and droopy pants says, nodding at the grill master.

The space seems to be getting smaller and smaller, and for some reason the hairs on the back of my neck start to rise as Faux Fur—that's what I'm calling him—eyes Irish up and down.

Miguel hands the ill-dressed hot dogs to Irish and the man in the tie, giving him a head nod before addressing Faux Fur and his friend.

Wanting to get out of this small space, I turn to take a bite of my hot dog when Maddie says, "I need to retake our picture. I look dead in the last one. This lighting is terrible. Maybe if I back up—"

"Maddie, watch out."

But I'm too late. She bumps into the Irishman whose hot dog grazes the man in the faux-fur jacket. Jerking his arm to the side with disgust, Faux Fur glances in the mirror to check for stains. Out of sheer curiosity, I take a look as well only to find the tiniest fleck of ketchup on the jacket. A quick swipe of the finger would do the trick, but the guy in the jacket thinks otherwise. "You're going to pay for this, you motherfucker," he hisses. Frantically, the man searches his sleeve while Irish sits back and chews his hot dog, not a care in the world passing over his features.

"Are you fookin' kiddin' me?" he asks, his accent heavy. "It's a fake, man. Here's twenty bucks." He reaches into his pocket. "Go buy another at the pagoda on the corner."

Oh boy, that didn't seem like the right move. I back up, a little nervous as Faux Fur spins—fire rolling from his eyes—and launches himself at the Irishman, who tosses his hot dogs in the air and powers forward as well. In a matter of seconds, all hell breaks loose and the two go at it, fists flying, shirts being torn, legs being kicked out from one another.

What is happening?

This is crazy.

Over hot dogs.

"Oh God," I screech as they move toward us, backing Maddie and me into a corner. Like the voyeur she is, Maddie's eyes never leave the brawl as she chews on her hot dog, fully invested in the fight, while my heart practically beats out of my throat, terror eclipsing me.

Curses are being thrown, cell phones, including mine, scatter across the floor, and the man in the tie reaches for his friend, trying to tear the two apart.

"Roark, leave it," he shouts, as both guys roll over the dropped dogs. There will be ketchup on the jacket now.

"We're going to die, we're going to die," I mutter, burying my head into Maddie's shoulder.

"Ouch, that one is going to hurt," Maddie says, attention still fixed on the fight. "The Irish guy took a jab straight to the eye."

Oh, that's what that crunch sound was.

"Oooo." Maddie jolts backward. "Irish just pummeled jacket guy in the jaw."

"I don't need the play-by-play. Just get me out of here."

"Take it outside," Miguel yells over the grill.

For some reason, the two listen to Miguel and roll outside, but not before knocking over a small high-top table and some of the signs in their path. From the reflection in the mirror, I watch tie guy bend to grab his friend's cell phone while still holding his hot dog, his face clearly annoyed. He doesn't look particularly surprised. Maybe this isn't the first time he's had to deal with his friend fighting.

And I can believe that, given Irish went from zero to sixty in only a few seconds. I've never seen anything escalate that quickly, and I've watched a lot of football over the years.

Still beating the crap out of each other outside, I turn to Maddie, who has a huge smile on her face. "Wasn't that exhilarating?"

Blinks.

"Are you insane? We could have been stabbed."

She waves me off and goes back to her phone where she takes a selfie of herself, hot dog in her mouth. She chews and then says, "There were no knives involved. Just some good old-fashioned street fighting."

"We need to get out of here." I don't bother with my hot dogs, entirely too freaked out to even consider eating them now. I pull on Maddie's arm, who waves bye to Miguel and, luckily, flags down the first taxi she sees.

Once we're settled in the vehicle and I've given the cab driver my address, I lean back on the seat and let out a long, scared breath. I take a few seconds to gather myself, my hands shaking, my nerves completely shot. What on earth would cause someone to launch into a fight with so little provocation? It was almost . . . animalistic.

"This is exactly why I don't stay out past nine. We could have been seriously hurt."

"Look at this picture," Maddie says, leaning over. "You look hot in it."

For the love of God.

Entirely uninterested, I don't spare her screen a glance. "Maddie, how can you be calm after what just happened?"

She groans and sighs, eating the last of her hot dog. "Can you take a chill pill, Sutton? We're fine. If anything, you should be thanking me. You just experienced a touch of culture. Wasn't that fun?" She hands over my phone she must have picked up and says, "You dropped this."

"Thank you," I quietly say while looking out the window. "And

I think I could do without that touch of culture. I'm fine with my life."

"Have it your way, but I've never felt more alive."

I guess that can happen when you're faced with a near-death experience.

And yes, I might be over exaggerating about the near-death thing, but that was seriously scary. The guys were out of control. One wrong swing and we could have been clocked in the head. Given how many hours of football I've logged over the years, I really shouldn't be so squeamish. But it's probably why I am. I've seen the head injuries resulting from fights on the field, so I'm not interested in seeing much of the same when I'm out buying a hot dog on a celebratory night.

Peering down at my phone in the dark, I try to unlock it, but it asks for a password.

What?

I got this phone today and haven't had time to activate any facial ID or enter a password. I bring the phone up into the light and examine it. Black case . . .

"Oh crap!"

"What?" Maddie asks, leaning over. "Did you break a nail in your attempt to climb inside my jacket?"

Funny.

"*No.* This isn't my phone."

"Seriously?" Maddie takes a look at it, flips it around. "Are you sure?"

I nod. "I had a purple case, but this is black."

"Well, would you look at that." She examines a picture, blowing it up with her two fingers, "I bet it's the Irish guy's phone."

Of course, it is. Just my luck.

"Could this night get any worse?"

I pace the small space of my studio apartment, staring at the phone on my nightstand, willing it to ring. Maddie tried calling my phone several times but no one picked up, and since it was late, she wanted to get home. She told me she'd keep calling.

You would think Irish would have called by now since my phone doesn't have a passcode on it.

Which . . . God, why didn't I set that up at the store? Oh yeah, because it took an hour to update my phone, and I didn't want to be late to the musical. Little did I know I was going to lose my phone during a fistfight in a freaking hot dog shop.

Twelve thirty, and there is no way I'm going to be able to sleep, not when my heart is still racing from the fight. My mind is whirling with everything the guy can get into with my phone.

"Ugh," I groan, trying to recollect the pictures I have stored. No naked shots, I know that for sure. But selfies? You take at least ten until you have the right shot. I have so many selfies on that phone it's going to look like I'm vain.

The phone buzzes on the nightstand and I run to it, my heart rate kicking up once again when I see my number flash across it.

Fumbling for a second, I answer and hold the phone up to my ear. "Hello?"

"Who's this?" An Irish accent comes through the other end. Yup, Maddie was right, he ended up with my phone.

"Um, this is Sutton. I think you have my phone."

"Yeah, no shit," he groans. "How the hell did I get it?"

I don't understand why he's being so rude. It's not necessary when he's the one who ruined my night by mouthing off to the faux-fur guy.

"Well, you rudely bashed into me and my friend during your little hot dog fight and knocked my phone from my hand. Your friend must have picked up the wrong one."

"Fucking Rath," he mutters. "Where do you live?"

"Do you really think I'm going to tell you that? I just watched you punch the crap out of a guy over ketchup. You don't seem like an upstanding citizen I'd want to hand over my address to."

"I meant what borough. Christ."

Oh, that makes more sense.

"Brooklyn."

Another low groan.

"Of course. You seemed like a Brooklyn girl."

"What's that supposed to mean?"

Ignoring my question, he says, "I'm in no form to hike it out there tonight, but we can meet up tomorrow to trade, in a neutral place since I don't want you seeing where I live."

How dare he? As if I really want to know where he rests his hot-tempered head at night. "It's probably Jersey."

Did I say that out loud?

"Ya think I live in fookin' Jersey?" Lord, does this man have a short fuse.

"Where do you propose we meet?" I ask, ignoring his question.

He unhappily groans into the phone. "No idea. Fuck. I have a headache." Well, probably because he took fists to the head tonight. "I have meetings all day tomorrow, but can ya meet in the morning."

"What time?"

"Seven."

Seven? I can do seven, but can he? I can't possibly imagine this guy, who was just in a New York City brawl, recovering from brutal fists and what seemed like excessive alcohol intake, as a morning person.

"Uh, yeah. I can do seven. Where?"

"Bain on Pan on Fifth. I need a goddamn pastry tomorrow morning."

That makes me giggle. "Okay." I chew on my lip, a little nervous. "Uh, can you be careful with my phone? It's brand new."

"Not smart leaving a brand-new phone on the floor, don't ya think?"

"I didn't leave it on the floor. You knocked it out of my hand and then your friend took it."

"Uh huh," he answers, sounding entirely bored. "Whatever, lass. Just be there tomorrow morning, okay?"

Someone has a stick up his ass.

"I will be."

"Oh, and if ya need to use my phone, my passcode is 111111. There's a folder in my photo album of some of my favorite nudes I've gotten over the years. Help yourself."

Ew, is he serious? I hold out the phone from my ear as if it's diseased. It probably is.

"I think I'll pass."

"Your loss. Tomorrow, seven, don't be late. I have shit to do."

"I'll be there," I say with a stern tone. "And please don't search through my phone. Be respectful of my privacy."

"Aye, too late, lass. You take a lot of selfies."

I don't think I've ever disliked a person this much, this fast.

"That's private."

"Not anymore. See you tomorrow."

Then he hangs up. I look down at the phone, my anger building in the pit of my stomach. I can't believe he went through my pictures. Who does that?

My finger hovers over the number one on his screen, wanting to do my own exploration, curious who this man is and what drives him to be such a giant . . . asshole.

But I'm better than that. My dad taught me to be better than that. So instead, I unlock his phone and go straight to the clock where I set a wake-up alarm. I'll be damned if I show up late tomorrow morning.

CHAPTER TWO

Dear Melvin,

Eh, Melvin doesn't sit well with me for your diary name. Melvin seems more like a guy who licks his pencil before writing in an answer to his on-going crossword puzzle he can't solve, but acts like he's on the verge of a breakthrough. Nah, I don't want to write to fucking Melvin.

I don't want to write at all, but guess who has "homework"? This sorry motherfucker. So here I am, a glass of whiskey in my right hand and completely fucking nude.

Yup, my dick is peering up at you, asking what the hell I'm doing writing to some pansy-ass named Melvin instead of jacking off to the pictures of the girl on the phone.

Wide blue eyes, naturally platinum-blonde hair, big-ass tits, she's a goddamn wet dream. And that voice of hers? A hint of southern charm and sweet molasses dripping from her plump lips.

Those lips would look amazing wrapped around my cock, that's for damn sure.

But I have morals—not many, but I have 'em—and whacking my cock to a selfie isn't necessarily a low moment I want to log away as a memory. So, I turned to you, Melvin, and just like that, my erection deflated like a fizzled-out balloon animal.

Poof.

Gone.
Thanks, pal.
Roark

∽

ROARK

"Christ." I roll out of bed, my head still pounding, my mouth dry, and my dick hard as a rock. I press my palm to my eye to wipe the sleep away when a sharp pain ricochets through my head. "Ah hell," I mutter, as I recall last night's events.

Hot dogs before clubbing. That's all I wanted—a hot dog with ketchup—and I wound up rolling around in a puddle of New York City scum with a blue faux-fur-covered dick trying to beat the shit out of me. Too bad for him, I'm numb to any kind of punch at this point. Well, numb until the next morning.

But I welcome the pain. It makes me feel like I'm alive at least.

Standing from my bed, I stretch my hands over my head. Light from the expanse of windows filters into my room, lighting the path to my bathroom.

As I pass the mirror, I glance at my reflection and wince. Deep shades of purple and blue circle my eye and a red abrasion sits just below it. The douche got in a good hit with a ring on his finger. I'll give him that.

I lean against the wall in front of the toilet and take a long piss, my head resting against my arm for support from the incessant pounding. Flushing, I turn toward the bottle on the counter and bring the cool glass to my lips, taking a long swig of whiskey. No better way to start the morning than with a shot of pure Irish blood right down my throat.

The burn doesn't even hit me anymore.

I start my shower and press against the bathroom counter, the cold surface cutting over my bare ass, taking some of my sleepiness away.

I take one more swig and then set the bottle on the counter before hopping in the shower. The warm water hits me, soothing my aching bones that were roughed up last night. By no means was the other guy the winner of our brawl, but I'll admit, I underestimated him. He was tougher than I thought and a lot quicker on his feet. It's why my ribs are sore this morning. He got in a few blows before my drunk ass was able to spring to my feet and defend myself again.

Leaning against the tile, I soap up one hand and drift it over my body to soap up the contours and divots in my abs, then run it gingerly across my ribs and move on to my pecs. I flick each nipple, because why the hell not, and then I run my hand to my dick where I tug on the hardened length.

Fuck that feels good.

I press my forearm against the tile of the shower, letting the water roll down my back as I glide my hand up and down my cock, seeking the release I wasn't granted last night. I was supposed to meet up with Candace at the club, but since I had a small detour, I was out of commission—not by my choosing. I'm sure Candace wouldn't have made out with my goddamn bloody face. I don't have very high standards when it comes to fucking, so taking her wouldn't have been an issue on my end, but I spared her the encounter. Fuck. I wonder if Miss Brooklyn Hottie received a text or two on my phone last night. The thought makes me laugh. And now I have *Sutton* on my mind. Gorgeous, perky-tits Sutton.

Pumping harder, I roll my hand over the head of my cock. My breathing starts to pick up as blood pools to the center of my body. I spread my feet a little more and run my hand down to the root where I grip my balls for a few seconds and then drag my hand back up, this time, squeezing harder.

Fuck.

Me.

My hand moves faster now, my erratic breaths aching my bruised ribs. Just a few more strokes.

I groan, my grip growing impossibly tight as my balls seize and I lean forward to release onto the tile of the shower floor.

Christ. I needed that.

I finish washing myself, scrubbing my hair and leaving it a wild mess as I hop out of the shower and turn on the heat lamp above me before wrapping my towel around my body. The worst part about taking a shower is being fucking cold when you get out. When I made my first million, the first thing I did was install the heat lamp. It cost me a few hundred dollars, but in that moment, I knew I'd made it in life. All the rich fucks had heat lamps in their bathrooms. Me being one of them now.

A buzzing sounds off in my bedroom, but I ignore it as I take one more swig of whiskey to dull the aching pain coursing through my bones and then brush my teeth. Mint and whiskey, lucky I don't mind the combination.

The elevator to my penthouse dings. I should be alarmed, but I'm surprised I got a shower in before he showed up. He's usually earlier than this.

"Roark," Rath, one of my best friends, calls out. "Where are you?"

"Bathroom," I shout over a mouthful of toothpaste.

Rath appears in the doorway, wearing his signature navy-blue suit and tan Berluti dress shoes. The smartest of my friends, he's a take-no-prisoners asshole in the business room, has zero time for any relationships unless it's with his phone, and he really fucking loves pastries.

Like, hides them in his office for bad days.

I sometimes dip into his stash whenever I'm hungover and in the need of a fix . . . which is often.

He gives me a once-over. "Glad to see you're not dead."

I spit. "It's going to take a lot more than a guy in a douchey jacket to kill me."

The buzzing sounds off again.

"Are you going to take your meetings today?"

I scrub my tongue and then spit, rinsing my mouth with a splash of water. "Yeah, why wouldn't I?"

"I don't know, maybe because you look like you got run over by a taxi."

I glance in the mirror at my black eye. "My clients have seen worse, like they really give a fuck. As long as I'm making them money, that's all they care about."

"If I were an athlete, I wouldn't want you as my sports agent."

I straighten and tap Rath's cheek. "Good thing you were blessed with zero ability to shoot a ball in a basket then, huh?"

I move to my closet where I pluck a pair of jeans from the shelf, not bothering with underwear, I drop the towel and slip my jeans on.

"What about your probation?"

"What about it?" I tuck everything in and zip up the front of my pants.

"You can't get in a fucking fight, Roark. If you violate your probation, you can be tossed in jail."

Yup, that's how my lawyer spelled it out for me, and I would love to say I actually tried last night to hold back my temper, but who am I fucking kidding? I didn't. I was looking for trouble, felt the need to get into it with someone, and it's why I was such a dick.

When I have an itch, I need to scratch it, and after a shitty day, I wanted nothing more than to get into it with someone.

"The dude wouldn't have pressed charges, because he had his own shit to worry about."

"That doesn't matter," Rath says, most likely wondering why he became friends with me. When you're in a fraternity together and see each other get slapped on the bare ass like a brand-new baby by every brother, you form an unfortunate, special bond. "Dude, you're the top sports agent in fucking New York. You have a waiting list clamoring to sign up with you. Don't throw it away on a goddamn ketchup stain."

He does have a point. Always the smart one.

"Yeah, fine." I drag my hand over my face. "I'll try harder."

"Or how about you just don't get into fights. The last punch you delivered made that guy ralph on the sidewalk."

I chuckle. Ralph, what a fucking way to say puke. "You know what I always wondered about?"

Annoyed, Rath bites out, "What?"

"What kind of violent retching did Ralph go through to grant him the title of puke king?"

The furrow in Rath's brow eases as a small smile passes over his lips. "No idea, but I'm just glad I'm not Ralph." My phone buzzes again. "Are you going to answer that?"

"My clients know I'll call them back when I'm available."

"Uh . . . dude, do you not remember ending up with that girl's phone last night?"

"What ph—" Oh motherfucker. I jog to the phone on my nightstand with the purple case and answer the call. "Hello."

"Hello?" Fuck, she sounds annoyed.

"Hey there, lass."

"Are you kidding me right now? Do you know what time it is?"

I sit on my bed, getting ready for her lecture. "Must be late for something from the bitchy tone in your voice."

"Excuse me? Did you just call me a bitch?"

"No. I said bitchy tone. Totally different."

"You are two hours late. I've been sitting at this restaurant waiting for you to bring back my phone."

"Oh yeah." I push my hand through my wet hair. "I slept in. Sorry about that, lass."

"Are you . . . I can't . . . you told me to be here at seven sharp, and you slept in?"

I shrug even though she can't see me. "I had some drinks last night. I can't be held accountable for what I said."

"You . . . you are so rude."

"Whoa, look out, she's slingin' the insults." I lean back on one hand.

There's silence on the other end of the phone, and even though

I don't know this girl and have a fuzzy recollection of what she looks like from browsing her pictures, I can imagine her counting to ten.

Finally, "You know, I've been very kind answering your non-stop calls and telling people that you are without your phone but will get back to them—"

"Why not let it go to voicemail? That way I can actually hear what they have to say."

"Well . . ." She pauses and I chuckle. "I thought it was polite since your phone wouldn't stop ringing."

"Being polite isn't on my radar, and I already have a secretary, so don't answer the calls."

"Would it hurt you to say thank you?"

"No, but I'm not thankful, so it would be wasted words."

She huffs. "You're a jerk. I'm . . . I'm going to toss your phone in the trash can."

"Suit yourself, I'm fine with using yours. Plus the selfies you took are an added bonus."

"Stop looking at my pictures." I smile to myself, but when I look up at Rath, his arms are crossed over his chest, and he shakes his head at me. "Can we please set up another meeting? I really need my phone back."

"Sure thing, lass." I scratch the stubble on my cheek. "How does next Tuesday work?"

"Next Tuesday?" she asks, outraged. "Next Tuesday does not work. How about in the next hour?"

"Ah, I'm naked and not decent. It's going to take me at least two hours to put pants on. I do have a black eye, ya know. Hard to see." She doesn't need to know I'm already halfway dressed.

I have no idea why I'm being such a dick to this girl. Honestly, I kind of like the anger in her voice, the fiery sparks being flung my way.

"It's not my fault you got in a fight over ketchup."

"Don't judge. I didn't judge you and the duck-lip photos in your phone."

"I'm going to kick you square in the balls."

"You're not making me want to meet up with you anytime soon."

Blowing out a frustrated breath, she says, "Just tell me a freaking time . . . today. Not next Tuesday."

I glance at my nightstand clock and think about it. "Tonight, eight, at Marlo."

"Marlo, I don't know—"

I hang up and toss the phone on the bed, exhausted.

"You're a dick," Rath says with a roll of his eyes.

I can't stop the chuckle that bubbles out of me. "I know. But it's my nature."

Standing from the bed, I walk to the bathroom and peer into the mirror, checking my eye out again. It looks even worse now that I'm more awake.

"How many black eyes is that for you?" Rath asks, leaning on the doorway.

"Too many to count."

∽

Sutton: *I can't believe you just hung up on me.*

Sutton: *I have no idea what this Marlo place is.*

Sutton: *Hello? If you're not going to answer my calls, at least text me back.*

Sutton: *Seriously, I will call the police for stealing phone.*

Sutton: *Why are you the worst human ever?*

Roark: *Some of us have to work and can't spend our entire day taking selfies.*

Sutton: *I don't take that many! Why did you hang up on me?*

Roark: *Had to take a piss and didn't want you to listen in.*

Sutton: *You are so vulgar.*

Roark: *Because I said piss? I could say way worse.*

Sutton: *Spare me. Just tell me where this place is that we need to meet.*

Roark: It's called Google Maps.
Sutton: I tried, and I couldn't find it.
Roark: Did you put in Marlowhit?
Sutton: What? No, you just said Marlo.
Roark: You're exhausting. Marlowhit is a club. I put your name on the list as phone girl. Just tell the bouncer you have Roark's phone, and he'll show you in.
Sutton: Can't you meet me outside?
Roark: I can, but I don't want to. See you at eight. Don't be late.
Sutton: You don't be late!

∼

Sutton: Sending a reminder, you're supposed to meet me in an hour.
Sutton: Text me back to let me know you are good for eight.
Sutton: Are we still on for eight?
Sutton: Thirty minutes, please text me!
Roark: Something came up. Can't meet tonight.
Sutton: What? You can't be serious. The exchange will take ten seconds, what possibly could have come up?
Roark: My dick. Met a girl. Rain check.
Sutton: You can't possibly be serious.
Roark: Sex is way more important.
Sutton: Pick up the phone.
Sutton: I will call you all night.
Sutton: You're such a . . . ugh, you're an asshole.

CHAPTER THREE

Dear Terrance,
 Terry. Can I call you Terry? What about T-dawg? Are you a fan?

I'm not.

It's a work in progress.

I'm going to be honest with you, because that's what this is about, right? Being honest with one another? Well, I had every intention of meeting up with that girl yesterday, I really did, but then Carmella came up to me with a sultry look on her face and intentions to make me come when she sat on my lap. I really had no choice.

There was no way I could deny my dick another missed opportunity, so I took it.

Do I feel a little bad?

Maybe.

But it's not like the girl doesn't have a phone to contact people for emergencies. She has mine. So one more day isn't going to kill her.

That's what I thought until I woke up to Carmella's tit in my hand and twenty murderous text messages waiting for me from Miss Impatient.

Don't worry, I soothed my terrified soul with Carmella's tit in my mouth.

I feel much better.

Thanks, T-man.
Roark

SUTTON

"I hate life." I flop down on the table, my little backpack crashing onto the table top.

"Hey, watch it," Maddie says, picking up her coffee and holding it away as she studies me. "I'm guessing you didn't get your phone back?"

"No, he cancelled on me last night as I was trying to battle the bouncer to get into the club."

"What do you mean?" She sips from her cup, peering at me.

"The d-bag said I would be on the list to get in, but when I got there, the bouncer said there was no one on the list under 'phone girl' and if I was going to try to sneak in, I should be more creative with my name, because no one would believe me otherwise."

Maddie snorts and then covers her mouth. "That's kind of funny."

"It wasn't." I angrily slam the table. "It wasn't funny, especially once the line behind me started mocking me as I made the walk of shame down the sidewalk. I don't think I've ever met a bigger jerk in my entire life."

"What about Joseph Aphern? Remember him from freshman year? He kept stealing your pens in that British lit class."

"This guy is way worse than Joseph. It's like he takes joy in keeping my phone away from me. What happened to Good Samaritans? Are we so jaded as a society that we can't simply return a girl's phone?"

"To be fair," Maddie says with a tilt of her head, "he is attempting to give it back, just in his own time."

"In his time, exactly." I toss his phone on the table, multiple missed calls gone unanswered, texts from random women plugged into his phone under descriptions rather than names. "It's so rude, and look at all these missed correspondences." I scoot the phone toward Maddie who picks it up.

"Who says correspondence?" Maddie scrunches her nose and then thumbs through the home screen, taking in all the notifications. "My, my, my. I wonder who Brunette Mole Tit is. Oh, and look at this—Redhead Screams Loud."

"There's also Redhead Long Tits, Blonde Crazy Eyes, and Green Eyes Sucks Hard."

Maddie chuckles. "Green Eyes Sucks Hard sounds like a good time."

"They're all labeled like that in his phone. Can't he get their names? Is that too much trouble?"

"Well, after the trouble you've gone through with him, I'm going to assume gathering a name might very well be too difficult for him."

I slouch on the table and let out a long breath. "I can't stand the guy, and I don't even know him. But don't worry, he said if I needed something to look at, I could paw through the naked pics on his phone."

Maddie's eyes go wide as she fumbles with the phone. "He has naked pics on here? Does he have a big penis? I feel like he would."

"Not naked pics of himself." Although I can't be sure. "Naked selfies from girls."

"What? Seriously?" Maddie lays the phone on the table and opens the photo album.

"What are you doing?" I try to take the phone away but she swats at my hand.

"I'm just checking . . . Oh my God, he does have naked pics in here." Her head springs up and a wicked gleam crosses her face. "Do you know what you should do?"

"Am I going to like this?"

"I think you will. Let's send your friend a little threatening text. Really get his attention."

I prop my chin on my hand. "Do you really think we can get his attention?"

"Oh yeah."

She types away and then holds the phone out to me to read her *already sent* text message.

Sutton: *[Picture of naked blonde] You have two options, either meet me at the Starbucks on 58th at noon today, or all your precious pics are going to be deleted from your phone.*

I laugh and look up at Maddie. "Oh, that's good. Do you think it's going to work?"

"One hundred percent." She sits back with her cup of coffee. "He's going to be putty in your hands."

Sutton: *Did you see my text message?*
Sutton: *It's 11, an hour away from deleting every naked picture on your phone.*
Sutton: *Don't think I won't do it. Because I will. I will delete it all.*
Sutton: *Hello???*
Roark: *Christ, woman. Just delete it. I have everything backed up in the cloud. But if it makes you feel vengeful, go ahead and delete.*
Sutton: *You're so infuriating! Why won't you just meet me?*
Roark: *Some of us have to work.*
Sutton: *I work! And how can you possibly work when I have your phone?*
Roark: *I have an office. My life isn't all in one device.*
Sutton: *You have an office? That's hard to believe. What do you do? Pimp out all the girls on your phone?*
Roark: *I'm detecting a hint of jealousy.*
Sutton: *You wish.*
Roark: *Nah, couldn't really care less.*
Sutton: *Will you just tell me when we can meet?*
Sutton: *Hello?*

"I really don't think there are any more decent men in this city." I stroke Louise, my cat, on the back. "Because if there were, I wouldn't have to deal with the constant buzzing of this godforsaken phone, and I would have mine back. He's making me lose my mind. Really lose it, Louise. I yelled at a taxi driver today, and I never do that, but I was so fed up I took my anger out on the poor man and told him he needed to wash his seats. Granted, they were very dirty seats and could stand a rinse down, but I didn't have to embarrass the man like that, call him out on the hygiene of his ride."

I press my hand to my head and take a deep breath.

"I also snipped at the girl at Starbucks when she asked what my name was for the order and then she called out Sully instead of Sutton. I snagged the cup from her with great force and almost popped the lid right off with my grip. In the wake of my wrath, I plowed through the store, still phoneless."

I pop a snap pea into my mouth.

"And you know what? I think I was rude to the librarian today too. When I asked where the Kendra Elliot books were and she had no idea what I was talking about, I huffed and told her I would find them myself. That was rude. I knew it at the time, but I couldn't help it. This Irish bloke has me questioning my sanity."

I pick up my water and take a sip. "Jealous. Is he insane? How on earth could he think I was jealous of the naked women on his phone? I'm more skivvied out that he's a manwhore, and there must be a million diseases on the phone I've been carting around the last few days."

Louise rubs her head against my hand.

"And would it kill him to be a little more polite? He must know how to say please and thank you, given all the women that seem to pop in and out of his life."

I slouch on my bed in my small studio apartment and stare at the exquisitely carved white ceilings. When I found this apartment in Park Slope, I knew I had to have it because of all the old New York City architecture and history. Even though my kitchen, bedroom, dining room, and living room are all within a two-foot radius, I still had to have it. And it's done well for Louise and me. Two girls, living it up in Brooklyn, chasing our dreams of snap peas and water on a Friday night. Look out, world.

Who am I kidding? This guy is not going to contact me tonight when it's a prime partying night. Midnight on a Friday? He's probably knee-deep in booze, with a girl sitting on each of his legs.

Very accurate.

I pop another green bean in my mouth.

Probably has a V-neck T-shirt on. All douchebags wear V-necks.

I wince.

That wasn't a very nice thought. My dad taught me better than that.

But . . . he's probably wearing a V-neck and showing off his man chest. That's what douchebags do, show off their man-cleave.

Okay, that is the last time I'll call him that.

Sighing, I lean my head against Louise, her purr growing louder. "You know—"

The phone buzzes next to me and I see my number flash across the screen. Gah, miracles do happen. Maybe he wants to meet up. That would just tickle me pink.

But then again . . . I glance at my kitty jam-jams. Oy, I'm not dressed for a phone switch, although, who really cares at this point. All I'm worried about is getting my phone back and shedding myself of this irritating man.

Roark: *What are you wearing?*

Is he freaking serious right now?

Did I read that correctly?

The nerve of this man.

An abundance of anger lights up my veins, sending a furious blush straight to my cheeks as I pound out a response.

Sutton: *How dare you ask me that? You've been nothing but a* *complete jerk to me, holding my phone hostage, and skipping meeting after meeting. You can't act like we're friends now, you pompous idiot.*

There.

That should do it. With a smile, I set the phone down, satisfied with my response.

Until he texts back.

Roark: *I'm going to take that as you're wearing a full-on onesie with kittens chasing yarn on it.*

Mouth dropping, I scan my pajamas, wondering how on earth he knew . . .

My freaking photos.

Sutton: *Stop looking through my phone. That's so rude.*

Roark: *Ah, just perusing, lass. I might have sent a few to my friend for safe keeping.*

Sutton: *That is a huge invasion of privacy and I will sue. **Pounds fist** I will sue.*

Roark: *If you were good at text messaging, you wouldn't have to put asterisk around your actions. You would be able to convey it using just your words.*

Sutton: *Are you really giving me text messaging lessons right now? Do you really think that's a smart idea?*

Roark: *I mean . . . I can call you if that's more convenient. Really dive deep. You can take notes.*

Sutton: *Give me my phone back!!!!!!!!!*

Roark: *One exclamation would have sufficed, but you would know that if you let me teach you proper texting protocol.*

Sutton: *I hate you.*

Roark: *Whoa, that's a strong statement.*

Sutton: *And I mean it.*

Roark: *You know what happens when you throw words like that out in the universe, right?*

Sutton: *Oh, so you're going to get all philosophical on me?*

Steaming, I sink into my bed, spanning out on the length. Louise hops up on my stomach and makes herself comfortable. In my head, I like to believe she's trying to comfort me, when in reality I know she's only seeking warmth on this chilly February night. I love my apartment so much, but it's old, which means there are chilly drafts seeping through the cracks and crevices of the windows and doors.

Roark: *So much hostility. Maybe if you actually relaxed, you would be able to enjoy life.*

Sutton: *I enjoy life just fine. Thank you.*

Roark: *Yeah? When was the last time you had sex?*

I blink a few times, reading his question over and over. Well . . . that's none of his damn business. Even though it's been so freaking long.

Two years I think. Yeah . . . two. With Kent my senior year of college, the same night he broke up with me. What a gentleman. After he got what he wanted—and I mean he only got what he wanted—he up and left, saying he was leaving the country and didn't plan on keeping a long-distance relationship. A month later, I saw him working at a Starbucks.

Turning back to the phone, unsure why I'm still engaging with this man—maybe because I'm worried if I don't, he'll never give me back my phone.

Sutton: *I don't see how any of that is your business.*

Roark: *It's not.*

Well, at least he's honest—that's a little refreshing.

Roark: *But I still want to know.*

Of course.

Sutton: *We are getting off topic. When can I get my phone?*

The dots that were bouncing back and forth on the screen, indicating he was typing a response, stop.

And then there is silence.

Why? Why is this something he's avoiding? I don't get it. Does he enjoy tormenting women? Is it a favorite pastime of his? What could he possibly want with my phone?

"Louise, I very well might lose my mind. And then what happens to you? I would say you can go live with my dad on his ranch, but I don't think he'll treat you like the princess you are. He would stick you outside with the rest of the cats, and you would have to fend for yourself." I scratch the side of her head. "You're too pretty to be a barn cat."

Blowing out a long sigh, I swing toward the light on my nightstand and turn it off just as my phone rings. I look down, seeing my number.

He better be calling about a location—and he better be serious about it—or I might punch something.

"Hello?"

He sighs. "Hey, lass." I hate to admit it, I *really* don't want to admit it at all, but his Irish accent . . . it's sexy. Okay, there, it's out in the open. There is no denying it, hearing his voice over the phone does something to my insides, lighting them up in a weird way that sends shivers down my spine.

All from one word . . . *lass*.

"What do you want?"

He chuckles. "Ya seem a little uptight."

"Maybe because you still have my phone."

"Is that all you want to talk about?"

I drape my arm over my eyes, counting to five. What does my father always say to me? You can catch more flies with honey, something like that. Maybe I'm going about this all wrong. This guy seems to be someone who gets what he wants when it comes to women, so maybe I need to flirt a little to get my phone back.

The only problem with that? I really don't know how to flirt.

Even when Kent and I were dating, he said I was terrible at it. But at this point, I will do just about anything, so if it means flirting, then so be it.

"I guess not," I swallow hard, hating myself. "What do you want to talk about, big boy?" I ask in what I like to believe is my best sultry voice.

And instead of a response, there is silence, and not the good kind of silence. I weirded him out, I know it. Heck, I weirded myself out. *Big boy?* Where did that come from?

I blame Maddie.

Oh God. If Maddie heard what I said she'd have choked on her own saliva from laughing too hard.

"Did you just call me big boy?" he finally asks after letting my words awkwardly settle between us.

"I mean . . . do you not like that?" I wince. Kill me now. Put me out of my misery. *Maybe Louise could shift and smother me.*

"Just from the pics and texting you back and forth, you don't seem to be one to get high but . . . are you high?"

"No," I groan. "Just forget it. I was trying to be nice so I could get my phone. And since you seem to be a ladies' man, I thought maybe you wanted to be called that. But it was stupid. Forget it happened."

He chuckles and the gritty sound of it spreads goosebumps up and down my arm. "If you want to call me big boy, feel free."

"I really, really don't."

"Fair enough. Can I have a nickname for you?"

"No," I answer quickly, my nice demeanor faltering. "I don't think we'll know each other long enough to earn nicknames."

"Ah, now that hurts me. And here I thought we were forming an everlasting bond."

"Sorry to disappoint."

"We're not going to be friends after this?"

"Whenever *this* ends, which I hope is tomorrow, I don't think we will. We seem to have different ways of looking at life—"

"How so?" he asks, a challenge in his voice.

He can't possibly be that obtuse. From my pictures alone, he should know I'm a goody two shoes. I do everything by the book, and even though I might take a lot of selfies, they are always sweet, never sexy, because I'm not that girl. Never will be.

"I don't want to insult you, so I think we should just set up a time to meet tomorrow."

"My day is full of meetings," he answers tersely, as if I already insulted him. *Even on a Saturday?*

"Just tell me where I can find you and I'll do all the work."

"No," he answers matter-of-factly. "My clients are high-profile, so their privacy is important. I can't have you barging into any of my meetings."

High-profile? What does he do? I want to ask but decide better of it. The less I know about this guy, the better, because I'm already attracted to his voice. I want to keep my opinion of his personality at an all-time high of annoyance. Finding out that he saves endangered animals and his clients are people like Leonardo DiCaprio and Ellen DeGeneres would be detrimental.

An animal saver with that voice and those eyes—I mean, no, not those eyes, I don't care about his eyes—it wouldn't be good. None of it would be good.

"What about at another club? Maybe you can hold off on hooking up with someone before I get there. Is that possible?"

"Can't make promises. I'll text you tomorrow. Night, lass."

"Wait, no—"

He hung up.

Ugh, son of a mother freaking beach.

Why did I even bother to try flirting? *"Can't make promises."* Roark whatever his last name is, is a selfish jerk, and this game is over. I should have locked the phone down when he first stood me up. I don't know this guy. Well, what I do know I don't like. Tomorrow I'll go back to where I bought my phone, cancel the service, have a new SIM issued. Done. Mr. Sexy Irish will be out of my life forever, and *my* life will go on. Maybe I'll just throw his phone in the trash for the crap he's put me through. Ha. Beat that, Irish.

CHAPTER FOUR

Dear Big Boy,
 Sutton might not be able to pull it off, but I have to admit, it rolls off my tongue nicely. Although, I don't want my diary getting the wrong idea, so I'm going to keep searching for a name.

 Why am I torturing this girl you ask?

 Well, I wouldn't necessarily call it torturing, more like entertaining her. From the pictures in her phone, it looks like she needs a little more excitement in her life, and why not be the one to give that to her, at least for a little bit.

 If my therapist got wind of this, she'd probably have some very strong opinions on the matter, something like being a dick your whole life will get you nowhere—I'm sure she would say it in a much more sophisticated way, but you get the idea.

 And maybe I am trying to find pleasure in ways other than a woman spread out on my bed. Maybe I enjoy the banter, and maybe I like hearing her sweet voice over the phone. There's nothing wrong with that. She'll get her phone . . . when I'm ready to give it back.

 Roark

SUTTON

"What do you think of your new office?" Whitney asks, standing in my doorway, her signature red coffee cup in hand.

Hands on my desk, a huge smile on my face, I say, "I absolutely love it."

Whitney scans the space and shakes her head. "You're in what used to be the janitor's closet."

"I know." I chuckle as the lemon cleaning supplies singe my nose hairs. "But it's better than nothing."

"We'll get you into something new soon. This is just temporary until construction is completed."

"Seriously, this is great. Thank you. The added plant really gives the space life."

Whitney chuckles. "You mean the dilapidated fake plant Millie found on the twentieth-floor stairwell landing?"

"Is that where it came from?" I stare at its holey leaves and bent-but-not-broken branches. "Well, it was a good find."

"Always the positive one, that's why we love you." And I believe her. They could favor me, giving me a nice office instead of the janitor's closet, or they could have found a plant that wasn't dragged behind a tractor during planting season, but they didn't. They treated me like a regular employee, not the boss's daughter, and I appreciate that more than anything. "Once you're settled, I would love to go over your projects."

"I'm settled," I answer enthusiastically while standing. It's my first day and I might be a little overly excited but I can't help it. I worked hard to get to this position, and I can't wait to get started working with the foundation my dad created.

Chuckling, Whitney gives me a curt nod. "Okay, but let's go to my office so we have more space."

"Good idea." I pick up my notebook and pen, bring the phone—because who knows if he'll ever decide to return it—and follow

Whitney to her office. *Maybe after I sort out the phone at lunch, I'll be able to toss his in the trash anyway.*

Brilliant white with baby-blue accents, her office is gorgeous with wall-to-wall windows, pictures of the many boys and girls we've helped, and fresh flowers in scattered vases. That's one thing I know about Whitney, she loves fresh flowers.

"Take a seat." She gestures to the white chair across from her desk. She picks up a few files and pushes them toward me. "I have two projects for you. One is immediate, and the other will start with the season in September."

"Oh, okay." I pick up the folders and look through them as Whitney speaks.

"As you know, it's going to be your dad's farewell season with the Steel this fall, which means we have a lot of planning to do. As a new tradition, the teams in the league present players who've had a huge impact on the sport with farewell gifts. I'm putting you in charge of communicating with each team and securing their donation to Gaining Goals. Your dad made it quite clear he doesn't want any memorabilia, just donations to his charity."

"Yes, that makes sense. I can handle the organizing of that."

"And then the immediate thing is obviously the Gaining Goals camp at the ranch. We have all the kids picked. Six girls, six boys. You're, obviously, familiar with the camp and the grounds since you grew up there, so I thought you might like to head up the camp this year."

"Really?" I ask, a little shocked. Whitney is always in charge. Ever since my dad created the camp for kids to improve their skills while creating healthy goals for a lifetime, Whitney has been in charge, expertly putting on the camp without a flaw. I've been to many camps and watched her create a positive atmosphere with such ease that I don't think it's something I could replicate, but I'll give it my best shot.

I'm actually honored that she thinks I'm ready to take on such a big project, and all I want to do is gush and thank her, but Whitney is all business, so I listen intently instead.

"Yes, you'll be great for the project, and it will free up my time to do some other projects your dad has in the works."

"That's exciting. Retirement stuff?"

Whitney kindly smiles. "Yup, you know him, his mind is always turning with the next greatest idea."

"Used to drive my mom crazy," I answer with a sad smile. This coming fall will be the twenty-year anniversary of her death. She left this world way too early, leaving me motherless at the age of four. They got pregnant really young, at sixteen. I was a bit of an oops, but they never let me know it. They took on the challenge, worked together with the help of family, and raised me while Dad was able to pursue his dreams. Gammy and Gramps were an integral part of raising me, but Dad was there too, he was always there, especially when Mom passed at the age of twenty. "At least that's what Dad told me."

"I'm sure," Whitney says while clearing her throat. "Everything you're going to need to know is in those files and on the server you're familiar with. Do you have any questions?"

I shake my head. "Nope, I think I'm pretty good. I assisted with the last two camps, so this shouldn't be a problem."

"Perfect, and don't forget to sync your calendar to your phone."

"Yup, not a problem." I smile, even though I'm slowly dying inside. I need to get my phone back.

Today.

As I'm walking out the door, Whitney calls out, "And welcome to the team, Sutton. We're so excited to have you on board."

I smile over my shoulder. "I'm excited to be here."

And with that, I close the door behind me and hustle to the janitor's closet. It's time to end this. He's getting one more chance to do the right thing . . . at least that's what I tell myself.

Sutton: *Where are you? Want to grab a bite to eat?*

Roark: *Asking me out already? I thought it would take you a little longer. Guess I pegged you as a little too shy.*

Sutton: *Oh yup, that's what I'm doing. Please go out with me. I want to date you so hard.*

Roark: *You know, that sounds a lot like sarcasm.*

Sutton: *How would you know? I didn't use any asterisk to emphasize my actions.*

Roark: *Unnecessary.*

Sutton: *Just grab a bite with me.*

Roark: *I don't know. You seem very aggressive right now, a little crazy. I don't think I'm up for that.*

Sutton: *Do you want to make me cry? Is that what you're trying to do? Because I will cry. Right here, right now, I will cry.*

Roark: *It's a good thing I can't see you then.*

Sutton: *I'll blow up your phone with pictures of my tears.*

Roark: *Not surprised, since you're the selfie queen.*

Sutton: *I am going to kick you square in the balls.*

Roark: *Yeah? I like things a little frisky.*

Sutton: *Do you always have a comeback for everything?*

Roark: *Depends on my mood.*

Sutton: *Are you in the mood to meet me?*

Roark: *Nah, I have meetings all day. Sorry lass. Better luck tomorrow.*

Sutton: *Why the heck do you want to keep my phone? This is ridiculous.*

~

"I'm going to kill him, Maddie."

"This again?" she groans into the phone. "When are we going to stop talking about this whole phone thing?"

"When I get my phone back."

"Let me guess, he's not willing to trade today."

"No." I lean back in my chair. "Says he has meetings all day." I scroll through my email and click on my calendar, looking through my upcoming meetings.

"How can someone who punches another person over ketchup have that many meetings? He doesn't seem like the business type."

I click on the month, scrolling through everything. "I have no idea. He doesn't se—" I pause, a giant lightbulb clicking in my head. "Oh my God, Maddie."

"What?"

I go to the calendar app on the phone. And that's where I see my salvation.

Bingo.

"I have *his* entire schedule on his phone." I scroll through today. "He has a lunch meeting with an FG at Mirabelle's on Seventh. It's in thirty minutes." A huge smile spreads across my face.

"Well, what are you waiting for? Go."

∽

I shouldn't be nervous. I should be furious, stomping with angry steps, letting the world know I'm taking this day by the horns and making things happen.

But instead I'm standing outside the restaurant, nervously twitching, wondering if I can simply barge through those doors, interrupt this guy's meeting, and demand my phone back.

I'm ten minutes early, so I won't really interrupt his meeting. I'll just be a prelude to it, so it won't be too bad. But still, it makes me nervous.

What I hate most about this whole situation is realizing how much my polite southern charm has forced me to skip out on being ruthless. I don't think there's a ruthless bone in my body, and that's exactly why I'm having a hard time walking into the restaurant.

A cold breeze lifts my jacket, sending a deep chill right to my bones. Okay, I didn't dress to stand outside all day. Mustering my courage, I make my way inside, welcoming the warmth as I look around, trying to spot an irritable Irishman.

"Sutton Grace, what are you doing here?"

There is only one person on this planet who calls me that. It's the only voice that can calm the nerves running rampant through my body too.

I spin around and find my dad, standing and buttoning his suit jacket. His tall, broad frame makes the entry of the restaurant seem small, and his large hands that have gripped many footballs reach for mine.

"Dad, oh my gosh." I walk into his arms, reveling in his embrace.

"I tried to call you a couple times to tell you I'm in town. Are you really so busy with your new job that you can't find time for your old man?"

And this is exactly why I need my phone.

"No, someone else has my phone, it was accidently switched, and I'm here to get it back."

"Is this someone, you know . . . someone special?" My dad wiggles his eyebrows and in return I give him a giant eye-roll.

"No Dad, he is not—"

"Oh, it's a he," he drags out, shaking my shoulder. "Does he catch your eye?"

Yes, but I would never admit that. To anyone.

"Not even in the slightest."

"I don't know. I can contest that, lass."

Whipping around, Roark stands behind me, wearing a thick black jacket, hair tucked under a beanie, and a fading swab of purple under his eye.

Damn it, why do I have to be attracted to him?

"Roark, good to see you, man." My dad steps forward, lending out his hand.

Excuse me?

As if time stands still, I watch Roark and my dad exchange

handshakes that turn into a hug, followed by some teasing back and forth. My mind flies to his calendar, the initials hitting me right in the stomach.

FG.

Foster Green.

Good God, my dad is meeting with the guy who has held my phone hostage for the last few days.

"What happened to your eye? You didn't get in another fight, did you?" my dad asks, a hand on his hip, a worried look in his eyes.

As if I'm not standing there, Roark says, "Got twisted the other night and ran into a wall. Fucking almost took my head off."

Throwing his head back, my dad laughs and pats Roark on the back. "The old Irish tongue got ya, didn't it?"

"That's not what happened," I interject, surprised at myself. Both men turn toward me, a lift to my dad's brow, a mirthful look on Roark's face.

"Yeah, you have a different story, lass?" Roark folds his arms over his chest.

"Uh, yeah. A very different story, besides the drunk part."

"Wait a second"—my dad motions between us—"you know each other?"

"Unfortunately," I mutter. "He's the guy who stole my phone."

"Stole is a harsh word. Accidentally took, and it wasn't even me who took it, it was my friend."

"Oh, that's right." I nod. "That's because you were too busy pummeling some guy in the face over ketchup."

Grunting, my dad turns to Roark. "Pummeling?"

Uncomfortably, Roark shifts, and I can't help but wonder how the hell my dad knows Roark. Was Roark someone he helped over the years? One of my dad's charity cases? There have been quite a few men my dad has helped along the years, mentoring them and helping pull them out of a dark place. Roark seems like he could have been pulled from a dark place.

"I might have gotten in a fight."

Turning toward me, my dad says, "Will you excuse us, please?"

Awkwardly, I cringe and move toward Roark, knowing what it feels like to be on the receiving end of one of my dad's lectures. "I'll just grab my phone and be on my way."

I hold out my hand, but Roark doesn't move. Instead he keeps his eyes on my dad.

"Whatever you have to say, you can say in front of her. Don't really know her and won't see her again."

Brow creased now, my dad pulls me in by the shoulder. "Roark, this is my daughter, Sutton Grace Green."

"Your daughter?" Roark looks shocked, but only for a second, and then that cool façade slips over his Irish green eyes. "What a fucking coincidence."

"Yes, well." I wiggle my fingers, hand stretched out to him. "I'll take my phone and be on my way so you two can get back to your mentoring."

Rocking on his heels, Roark smiles at me, a devilish gleam in his eyes. "Mentor? I think you're mistaken, lass. Your dad isn't my mentor, he's my client."

"Client?" I look at my dad. "What could you possibly have hired this guy for? Bartending lessons? Oh God, please don't tell me he's going to be your wingman."

"What? No." Insulted, my dad says, "Why would you think that?"

"I don't know. I mean, you haven't dated in so long, I thought maybe you wanted some help now that you're in your final season."

He plays with the cufflinks on his dress shirt and says, "Trust me, I don't need assistance in dating." More than I wanted to know. "Roark is my agent."

"What?" I shout.

There is no way Roark is my dad's agent. The guy is irresponsible, a total disaster, and . . . young. Aren't agents supposed to be old with balding heads from running their hand through their hair for too many years?

I shake my head. "Stop playing with me. He's not your agent."

Stepping forward, Roark reaches his hand out to me and says, "Roark McCool, best agent in New York City."

I swat his hand away then turn back to my dad. "He's a joke. I can't believe you're using him. He got in a fight over ketchup, Dad. How is that professional?"

"Never said he had the best level of personal professionalism, but he's done more for me in the past two years than any agent ever has."

Ugh, if I think about all the endorsements and major contracts my dad has signed over the last few years, especially at his age of forty, I can see what he's talking about, but still . . . Roark is his agent?

"Dad, you can't be serious."

"As much as I love this conversation about your lack of confidence in me, I believe I have a meeting with your father." Roark gestures toward the hostess, but I cut him off before he can make a move.

"Just hand me my phone and I'll leave."

He shrugs. "Don't have it with me."

"What? Yes, you do." Without thinking, I reach toward him and dig my hands in the pockets of his jacket. "It has to be in here somewhere." I fling his jacket open looking for an inside pocket. When I come up short, I reach for his pants pockets, but a hand grasps my shoulder and pulls me away.

"Sutton Grace, stop feeling up the man in front of your father."

"No need to stop her." A full-on grin spreads across Roark's face. "I was enjoyin' it."

Ignoring both of them, I point at his pants. "Empty your pockets."

Eyes locked on me, he pulls his pockets inside out, revealing . . . nothing. "Son of a Ritz freaking cracker." I toss my hands up in the air. "Why on earth don't you have my phone?"

"Didn't need it for my meeting with your dad. Left it back at my place."

I pull on my hair, frustration eclipsing me. "I need it."

"You know, this is perfect actually," my dad says, "because I wanted you two to meet anyway." He gives Roark a serious look and points to him. "We'll have that private conversation a little bit later, but for now, how about we all sit down to eat? I'm starving, and I want to speak with both of you."

"What? Why?" I ask, but my questions go unanswered as my dad guides me with his hand at the small of my back.

What on earth could my dad possibly want to talk to Roark *and* me about? We have nothing to do with each other.

And why does Roark smirk every time we make eye contact?

And why does he smell like God blessed him with all the pheromones He had bottled up?

CHAPTER FIVE

Dear Gary,
    Do you know what song always plays on repeat when I hear the name Gary? That stupid fucking song Ron Howard sings as a young kid with a lisp in The Music Man. Gary Indiana, Gary Indiana, Gary Indiana, my home sweet home. Fucking little pint-sized Ron Howard.

Gary's not going to work out, because I can't be singing a goddamn showtune in my head day in and day out. Sorry, pal.

I have a meeting with Foster Green today and I'll be honest, I'm going to lie out my ass about my eye, because I know he'll have a fire lit under his ass if he finds out I was in another fight. And even though he's my client, I look up to the man. It's why I work hard for his wrinkly old ball sac.

I have a few options I can go with when it comes to the black eye. What do you think I should say?

Walking and texting, ran into a light post?

Yeah, kind of lame.

Old lady beat me in the face with her purse because she thought I was robbing her when in fact, I was helping her across the street?

Totally unbelievable, I know.

Then I'm going to go with an old classic: wasted off my ass and ran into a wall.

Always a winner. Once again, you were a trooper.

Thanks, Gar,
Roark

~

ROARK

I need another goddamn drink.
 Badly.
This one is getting low.

If I knew the girl with the cell phone was Foster Green's daughter, there is no way in hell I would have told her about the naked pictures in my phone.

I still would have given her a hard time, naturally—because that's the kind of dickhead I am—but the naked pictures I would have deemed too much.

And what are the goddamn odds?

And why is she so fucking gorgeous? She's prettier in real life with her platinum-blonde hair and wide blue eyes, all innocent looking but full of unreleased rage.

And her tits . . . Foster needs to tell her to lock those things up. Her shirt is way too low-cut. I keep catching myself as my eyes are like magnets to her nipples, trying to see right through the fabric of her shirt.

This little lunch date is uncomfortable for many reasons, and one big one is pressing against the zipper of my jeans.

If I knew I'd be this attracted to the girl, I might have returned the phone a little sooner and then taken her out . . . for a drink. I don't do dates.

"If you have any questions about the specials, just let me know," the waitress says, giving me a sly once-over before retreating, an extra sway in her hips.

Nice.

Uh, what were the specials? Between Sutton's tits and the waitress eye-fucking me, I don't know what happened over the last few minutes.

"The chef's salad sounds good, don't you think?" Foster asks. "But iceberg lettuce, I don't know."

Sutton leans over, a grin pulling at the corner of her lips. Sexy. "But Dad, the iceberg is of such high quality."

"With zero nutritional value. Might as well eat the guacamole burger and onion rings."

"Not even close to the same." Sutton gives her father a look.

He pats his stomach and says, "It's the off-season, Sutton Grace, which means your dad can eat whatever he wants."

Well, isn't this just fucking cute. Dad and daughter with playful banter. It's not nauseating at all.

And the asshole in me is tempted to make a snide comment about wanting to throw up after that little display of family ties, but I hold back because Foster Green is one of my biggest clients, and I want to keep him, especially given the endorsements I've been able to score him lately.

Instead, I sit back in my chair, bring my tumbler to my lips, and take a long swig, letting the amber liquid slide down my throat, coating me with numbness.

"What are you going to get, Roark?" Foster asks, peering at me over his menu.

I lift my tumbler in his direction and give it a little shake. "Drinking my lunch today."

A disapproving sound comes from his daughter that I ignore as I take another—*long*—chug from my drink. When I set down my empty tumbler, she sneers at me, clearly not on board with my lunch idea.

"Do you have a problem with my lunch, Sutton?" I ask, her name rolling off my tongue with ease.

Chin held high, eyes still trained on the menu, she says, "No problem. I just don't think it's very professional, but I guess you skipped right over being professional, didn't you?"

"I think your father would be concerned if I didn't have a drink at one of our meetings."

We both look toward him, and like the smart man he is, he lifts his menu, avoiding eye contact with both of us. Playing Switzerland. Foster Green has always been one of my more intelligent clients.

"Maybe try a meeting without it," Sutton suggests. "Get some fiber in your system."

"Fiber, when all they're serving is iceberg lettuce these days? Fuck that." I pick up the menu and spot the first thing under the pasta dishes. I set it back down. "I'll get the mac and cheese. Happy?"

"I couldn't care less. It's your choice."

"Couldn't care less?" I laugh. "You just lectured me about not drinking my lunch. I'm only getting mac and cheese so you'll stop judging me with that sneer in your lip."

She covers her mouth. "There is no sneer in my lip."

Foster leans to the side and speaks quietly, but not quietly enough. "There was a little sneer in your lip."

"Dad!"

"What?" He chuckles. "There was," he answers with a shrug and then sets down his menu. "Besides, you two are going to have to start getting along if you're going to work together."

That makes me sit up straight. "Work together?"

"What?" Sutton practically shouts, eyes wild.

The feeling is mutual, sweetheart.

Tamping his hands down to control our outburst, he says, "Let's order and then we can get to business." Turning toward me, he points at my tumbler and says, "That's your last drink for this meeting. Get some food, man."

With a smile tugging on her lips and a lift in her shoulders, Sutton proudly picks up her menu again and peruses it, acting as if she just bested me.

It's going to take a lot more than that to best me, lass.

And this is why I don't really eat food, or heavy meals for that matter.

Mac and cheese was such a bad idea. It feels like I just swallowed a brick of cheese. It's swirling around in my stomach with my whiskey in the worst way possible.

I'm bloated.

I want to pass out on this table, forehead into half-eaten plate.

And the burps. Christ. So many unflattering, what feels like beer burps that I've had to discretely hide because, heaven forbid, I let one out with Miss Manners sitting across from me. She might wilt in her chair.

"You look like you're ready to take a nap."

I glance at the all-black Gucci watch on my wrist, making a show of it, and say, "Well, we are closing in on my nap time."

Foster chuckles but Sutton doesn't look the slightest bit amused.

"I don't want to keep you too long, so I'll get to the point. I called this meeting not only to catch up with you, Roark, but to discuss the hours you have to put in."

"Hours?" Sutton asks.

"Community service hours," Foster clarifies and then turns to me. "Do you mind if I share with my daughter?"

"My life is an open book." I wave him off.

It really is. I couldn't care less about what people know about me. The more they know, the better actually, because maybe they'll get the hint I'm not looking for any new connections in life, and I'm perfectly fine with just my two best friends.

Want to know about my childhood? It was simple, boring. Raised in Ireland, had a father who didn't give two shits about me, and a strict Irish-Catholic mother who used—*and broke*—wooden spoons on me more times than I can count.

College, yeah, I'd tell you if I could remember. What I do know is I was part of a fraternity. I was drunk every day, threw up in trash cans around campus a lot of the time—I was *that* guy—and my social game was so damn good I ended up managing the careers of some of my close athlete friends straight out of college.

And now, I pull my head out of my ass when I need to do business, I land some of the biggest endorsement and contract deals in the sports field, and I party almost every goddamn night to get away from the rest of the world.

To forget.

It's a simple life, one I'm happy with.

And yeah, I might get in some fights, and I could have possibly gone to jail, but only because the hairy-backed, pointy nipple shithead I nailed in the jaw was too much of a pussy to punch me back. He called the cops and reported me.

I'm sure it won't be the last time it happens.

Clearing his throat, Foster turns to Sutton and says, "Roark got in a bar fight recently and rather that going to jail"—Sutton's eyes widen—"he's on probation, has to fulfill multiple hours of community service, and has to go to anger management courses."

She snorts. "And how's that going for you?"

I pluck a piece of lint off my black jeans. "The therapist and I are still getting to know each other."

"And since he's going to anger management and checking off that box—"

"Doesn't seem to be working since he clearly still loses it over the stupidest thing. Dad," Sutton says, "he got in a fight over ketchup."

"The dick was making a big deal over nothing and needed to be put in his place."

"You almost ran me over with your idiocy."

"Is that what this is really about?" I ask. "Were you scared?"

"Yes, I was scared. I was terrified. How did you know the guy didn't have a knife or a gun?"

I shrug. "You just know."

Sutton throws her hands in her air. "I can't believe this guy is your agent. Out of all the people, Dad, you picked the most ill-behaved, unprofessional, out-spoken guy on the planet."

"On the planet?" I lift my brow. "Wow, now that's quite the title." I pretend to write in my hand. "Making note of that for my résumé."

"Enough," Foster says, rubbing his hand over his forehead. "Christ, it's as if I have two children."

"Yes, exactly," Sutton points out. "I'm so glad you're finally realizing that. This man is a child."

Leaning forward, I nod at her. "He said *children*, plural, meaning you're acting petulant too."

"You are, Sutton Grace," Foster says. "And it's making me question if you're ready to work for the foundation."

"What?" she asks, panic searing through her eyes. "Dad, I worked my ass off and got a master's degree, even though it wasn't required for my position. That's more than I can say for him." She thumbs toward me, and though I can be even-cooled for the most part, all it takes is one person to flip my switch and I fly off the deep end.

She's tinkering with my switch.

"How do you know I haven't worked my ass off to get to where I am?" I counter.

She folds her arms across her chest. "Please. Did you even go to college?"

"He went to Yale," Foster says with a grin.

"Yale?" Sutton sits a little taller. "You went to Yale?"

"Yeah, I did, lass. And I fucking graduated with a three-point-eight GPA. Understanding economics was a bitch for me." And also, it was the early class, and I had a hell of a time trying to stay awake through it.

"Oh."

"Yeah, oh. From there, I managed Tyler Gaines, Henry Kumar, and Westin Hanks straight out of college. Made some mistakes, but then I created some huge opportunities. From there, my business grew. I have twenty employees who work under me, I represent more than fifty professional athletes including your father, and I have secured some of the biggest contracts in sports history. I make twenty percent—yeah, twenty because I'm that damn good—off every single athlete I manage. Your dad made over one hundred million dollars between his last contract and endorsement deals that I've landed him. Do the math."

She's silent, mulling it all over, so I continue. "I might drink like my ancestors and get myself into bloody trouble whenever I get my hands on it, but when push comes to shove, my job comes first, and I do a damn good job at it. So, before you go and judge me, know this: I know I'm a fuck-up socially, but when it comes to business, I'll talk my way through any contract, tripling the income of my client every goddamn time."

Finally, she lifts those bright blue, soul-searing eyes at me and says, "You could still stand to be more professional."

Jesus Christ.

Foster laughs out loud and pats Sutton on the back. "That's my girl. Raised with sweet southern charm."

Is that what society is calling retched witches now? Ladies with sweet southern charm? I beg to differ.

"And as much fun as I'm having watching you two spar, I need to go. But before I take off, I want both of you to know I spoke with Whitney and since I vouched as your sponsor, Roark, I've set up a way to meet all your community service requirements while helping me out as well."

I glance at Sutton whose mind looks like it's whirling a mile a minute, and before Foster can tell me what the plans are, she reaches out to him. "Dad, no."

"Sutton Grace."

"Please, Dad. I never ask you for anything, but please don't do this."

"You asked me last week for tickets to the Justin Timberlake concert."

I snort—loudly—which in returns grants me an evil eye from Sutton.

"Only because you were taking pictures with him at a game. I wasn't entirely serious."

Entirely . . . nice way of putting it.

"But seriously, Dad, I can't work with this man."

Work with me? Hold on a second. "Work with her?" I ask, pointing at the woman in question.

"Yes, you two will be working together on the Gaining Goals camp down at the ranch."

Sutton groans and I sit up straighter. "Down at the ranch? What does that mean?"

"It means you're going to be spending some time in Texas."

"Texas?"

"Yup, Texas." Foster stands and puts on his suit jacket while staring at the both of us. "I think it will do you both some good to get to know each other. The best way to shape our lives and add more culture to it is learning to understand others who might not be like us." He turns toward me and with a stern look says, "Don't let me down, Roark. You owe me this."

Fucking hell. Way to lay the guilt on thick. Although, he is right. I do owe Foster Green, as he did step in where others may have not. *Shit*.

Leaning down, he places a kiss on Sutton's head and then shakes my hand. "I've got the tab," he says before leaving us in our stunned and speechless state.

Texas? Working with Sutton? Working for free? Seems like Foster just set up my own personal hell.

When I look at Sutton, she's staring at me, worry and anger in her eyes. Before I can say anything, she says, "We have to get out of this."

How the young live in the clouds.

I might spend my days with a bottle in my hand, but I also know reality when it smacks me across the dick, and Foster Green just pulled down my pants and handed me a hefty dose of dick smacking. I heard finality in his voice. His mind is set, and there is no way either one of us are going to get out of our predicament without losing a valuable part of our jobs.

"It's cute how delusional you are." I fold my hands over my stomach.

"You don't have to be a condescending ass," she counters, wincing with the swear word. I shouldn't find that adorable, but unfortunately I do.

"Just telling you like it is. There is no way in hell your father is going to change his mind on this, so you better figure out a way we can work together without really having to work together."

"What do you mean?" she asks, sounding curious.

"You're the planner of the event. Just give me a task that grants me a shit ton of hours and lots and lots of miles away from you."

Hand on her hip, she says, "I can hardly see why you want to be away from me. It's not like I've done anything to you. You're the one who's kept my phone hostage."

"Yeah, and because of that, I've learned all your annoying tendencies, and I would like to stay as far away from them as possible."

She shakes her head in disbelief and stands from her chair. "You really are something else, Roark McCool."

"Why thank ya, lass." I smile proudly.

"That wasn't a compliment."

"Eh, I took it as one."

Fuming, she walks over to me and pulls on my sleeve. I swat her away, but she pulls on it again. "What the hell are ya doin'?"

"Encouraging you to stand. We're getting my phone, now."

"That's what you call encouraging? If you wanted to encourage me to stand, you would have held a bottle of whiskey between your tits, and I would be at your beck and call."

"Oh my God." She pulls her jacket close together. "Don't be so crude."

"Just giving you a little lesson on Roark, that's all." I stand, feeling heavier by the second. Cursing the mac and cheese, I swing my coat over my shoulders and punch my arms through the holes.

Looks like I'll be doing some goddamn cardio tonight, the devil's chore.

"I don't need a lesson. I need to make this as painless as possible." She secures her purse over her shoulder and pulls me by the jacket out of the restaurant and onto the chilly street.

"Christ," I mutter, buttoning up my jacket.

"Okay, take me to my phone."

"I don't have time," I lie, bouncing on my toes as the wind punches me in the face.

In defiance, she says, "Well, I'm going to be your shadow until I get it."

"Fine by me." I shrug and reach out to hail for a taxi. "Follow me all you want."

"I will," she says, sliding next to me, her small body lining up against mine. "And don't try to ditch me either. I'm going to be stuck to you like glue." This is going be fun . . . or epically bad.

CHAPTER SIX

Dear Ebenezer,
    I'm typing this into my phone—which I easily confiscated from Sutton when she wasn't looking—as I ride down the streets of New York, trying to look like I'm doing something.

I might have made an unnecessary big show about my job, and yeah, I worked semi-hard to get where I am today. I drank a lot, made friends, and know how to please the right people with tales from the land across the pond. But now that Sutton is watching my every move, I feel the need to act like I'm sending a shit ton of emails, when in reality, I'm a sad motherfucker making a journal entry I couldn't care less about.

And while we're on the topic of being a sad motherfucker, I really think Ebenezer is a terrible name. If there is one thing I know, no self-respecting lady is ever going to fuck a guy named Ebenezer. Sorry, pal, but facts are facts. You might have a giant dick but no one will ever see it.

Sorry your sex life sucks.
Roark

SUTTON

I wasn't kidding when I said I was going to be his shadow. I have not let this guy out of my sight and I refuse to give in until I get my phone, especially since he already took his back when I wasn't paying attention. Well, I might have been showboating a bit with it in my hand, trying to tease him in the taxi, so when he popped my hand up from underneath, knocking his phone away, I was caught off guard.

And when I reached for it, trying to steal it from his iron-clad grasp, I was instantly assaulted by his cologne, his wonderfully hypnotizing cologne. I failed and was put into a dizzy stupor for a few seconds before I recognized that my nose was planted into the sleeve of his coat, sniffing. When he asked what I was doing, I thankfully recovered quickly by saying I was sniffing him for drugs. Maybe slightly insulted—still can't read him well—he told me he might be a fuck-up, but he didn't do drugs.

He didn't seem like he did, but I didn't want to be caught sniffing his arm like a creepy stalker who finally got her captive alone in a small space.

"Where are we going now?" I ask, tapping my knee while looking out the window. "The post office was a real treat."

"Yeah, a fucking joy." He looks at his watch and smiles. I can tell there's something up his sleeve, and I want to know what it is. We've already been to his office, where we walked around the main floor, tapped the tops of cubes, and then walked back out. After that, we went to a juice place, and I watched as he downed two of those wheatgrass shot things, which was a total shock. We then went to a tailor where he was fitted for a suit, which might have done a little something to my insides, seeing this ultimate bad boy get fitted, the fabric stretching perfectly over his well-defined muscles. That was a hard hour for me, wanting to look anywhere but at him, and when he called me out for avoiding him in the mirror, I flushed even more. It didn't help that he stripped right in front of me, wearing nothing but black briefs.

Briefs!

What man just wears briefs these days?

A confident man, that's for sure. All I saw was his tight butt encased in black. I think that's what led to the arm sniffing.

Can't be sure.

The taxi stops—I'm surprised he uses public transportation given the amount of money he makes—and he quickly gives the cabbie some money and heads out the door. I stumble out the door, trying to keep up with him as he heads into a spa.

A spa?

When I catch up to him, I say, "What are you doing?"

He barely glances at me. "Getting a massage, what does it look like?"

Before I can answer, the receptionist says, "Mr. McCool, it's so nice to see you. Right this way."

Er, do I follow him? I mean, I told him I was going to be his shadow, but a massage? That seems rather personal. *You just saw him in his briefs. That wasn't personal?*

Then again, what if there is a back exit? That is not a chance I'm willing to risk. I am taking my phone back today, and that's the end of it.

Without giving it another thought, I catch up to him. I sense the humor in his voice when he says, "Had to think about that for a second, didn't ya?"

"Maybe a little." I bite on my lower lip.

He chuckles. "Well I'm glad you're seeing through on your promise. I'm impressed."

Impressed?

No, that does not make me happy. It really doesn't. I don't want his approval.

But . . . a little piece of me is maybe having the tiniest gleeful moment. It's stupid, and I tell that tiny part of myself to lock it up and be a professional, but . . .

Ugh, it's stupid.

The receptionist walks us through a door in the back where

there are two massage tables set up in the middle, and the lights are dimmed.

What is he up to?

"Would you like water for you and your guest, Mr. McCool?"

"I'm good. Sutton, ya want anything?"

"What? No." I shake my head, confused. "What's going on? I'm not your guest."

The receptionist leaves, letting us know that our masseuses will be with us shortly, leaving me alone in a dark room with Roark.

"I'm not getting a massage with you." Is he deluded? "And you seriously couldn't have rescheduled this? You said you didn't have time to get my phone. This seems like a luxury rather than a responsibility."

"I never said I had responsibilities to fulfill, just said I didn't have time. That was the truth. And if I'm going to get a massage, I'd rather pay for you to get one than have you sit in the corner and stare at me the whole time."

"I'm not getting a massage," I state firmly. Not cracking.

He shrugs off his jacket and reaches behind his head and pulls his shirt off.

Holy.

Hell.

Cords upon cords of muscle flex under the low lights in this barely lit room, his pecs clearly defined above his six-pack that ripples with his movements, and the V in his waist, sharply defined . . . How on earth can this man have such a good body with the amount of alcohol he drinks?

"Suit yourself, lass," he says, pulling my gaze away from his chest. "But from the looks of it, you need this massage more than I do." He undoes his jeans and pushes them to the floor, standing in only his briefs now. *Again. Lord, have mercy.*

I gulp.

His . . . oh God, his package is right there in front of me, all bulgy and . . . big. Sweet molasses, it's big.

"Get a good eyeful?" he asks, right before turning toward the table and peeling his underpants off, displaying his perfect butt.

I turn away, shielding my eyes, even though the image of his bare butt is imprinted in my memory, as if it were just stamped on the inner part of my eyelids, so every time I blink, I see it.

"What are you doing?" I ask, dumbfounded with his audacity to strip right in front of me.

"What does it look like? I'm not going to get massaged wearing clothes."

"You take off your underwear?"

"Yeah. Now get undressed." He reaches out and pats the table next to his. "It's time to pull the stick out of your arse." *The stick out of my ass?*

Insulted, I pull my jacket closer together. "I don't have a stick up my ass, nor am I undressing in front of you. And I'm not getting a couples massage with you either."

"Suit yourself. There's a chair in the corner you can stew in."

Huffing my discontent, I march over to the chair and remove my jacket before taking a seat. "How long is this massage?"

"Two hours."

"Two hours?" I shriek. "You have got to be kidding me."

"Nope, so enjoy your chair, lass. I hope it's comfortable."

Did I end up getting a massage? No. But did I take a nap on the second table while Roark was getting rubbed down? Yup.

After fifteen minutes of the serene music, essential oils, and a dark room, I had no choice but to give in and rest my head. I only wish I didn't fall into such a heavy sleep that Roark had to shake me by the shoulders to wake me up.

I also wish I didn't leave a drool stain on the floor from where I stuck my face through the head hole.

That was kind of embarrassing.

"You still have a red ring around your face," Roark points out while we're in the taxi headed to who knows where.

And there is nothing I can do about it. "It's my fair skin," I answer. "It will go away."

"Fair skin but grew up in Texas; how does that work?"

"Dipping yourself in sunscreen every day," I answer. "My gammy was adamant about making sure I was fully covered whenever I went outside."

He nods, but doesn't respond. Instead, he pulls his phone from his pocket and dials a number. I guess there goes our conversation.

It's late. We've hit nine at night, knowledge gained thanks to the taxi cab clock. We have to be heading to his place, right?

But when I hear his one-sided conversation with whoever is on the other line, I realize we are far from going to his place.

"Hey man. Yeah, I'm done. Are we hitting up Seventh Floor? Killer drinks tonight. Yeah, I'm headed there. Nah, haven't eaten, and don't plan on it." Of course he hasn't. Meanwhile, my lunch has already made it through me and I'm very much ready for another meal. "Yeah, see you in ten. Name is on the list, meet you in the back."

When he hangs up he sends off a text. I tap him on the shoulder with my index finger. "Uh, where do you think we're going?"

He doesn't look at me when he answers, "Seventh Floor. It's a nightclub."

I gathered as much.

"Can't you stop by your house quickly so I can get my phone? I'm sure you're not going to miss out on much partying." I am one more stop away from kicking this man in the family jewels, stealing his wallet, and buying myself a very nice dinner, accompanied by a trip to the cell phone store.

"Nope, have to meet a client."

"In a nightclub?" I ask, my voice borderline hysterical.

"Yup, it's where I met him first. I cater to my clients and how they like to conduct business."

"We're going to a nightclub, for business?" An hour at the most I figure. A meeting can't go much longer, especially in an environment like that.

"Of course not. I never go to a nightclub for *just a meeting*. You're going to be my wing*woman* tonight, Sutton."

Oh hell no.

"You know, that bouncer could have been nicer," I say over the loud music that's thumping in the center of my chest, shaking every bone in my body.

Roark gives me a once-over. "To him, you look like a nun."

"Because I'm wearing a jacket and scarf? I'm sorry for not wanting to be cold."

"I don't think he accepts your apology," Roark says, his mouth close to my ear, his hand on the small of my back as he guides me through the nightclub to the very back, past a curtain and into a roped-off space.

The music isn't as loud where I feel like my eardrums are about to rupture, but loud enough that if you wanted to dance, you wouldn't feel like a fool.

And believe me, I won't be dancing.

I give the space a once-over while Roark quickly pours himself a drink. "So, this is what a nightclub is like, huh?" I run a finger over the black leather couch. "Fancy."

Tumbler head close to his mouth, Roark peers at me. "Wait, you've never been in a nightclub?"

"No, never found a reason to be in one. I'm the good girl, and nightclubs aren't my thing. I've always found them very intimidating." He walks closer. "It's why I put it on my New Year's resolution list, because it scared me. I put all the things that scared me on there."

His brow lifts, and he scoots in even closer. "New Year's resolutions, huh? What else is on there?"

Feeling a little crowded, I take a step back. "That is none of your business."

"Let me guess, is one of them skinny dip?"

"No, Mr. Wise Ass. It's not."

He sips his drink, eyes still trained on me. "That's surprising. You seem like one of those bubbly, cotton-candy girls who would have that on a bucket list or something. Let me guess"—he scratches the side of his jaw—"one of your resolutions is trying anal?"

"Oh my God. No. What is wrong with you?"

He grins. "From your reaction, I'm going to guess you've never tried it."

"Yeah, and I plan on never giving it a second thought. That's not for me."

He nods, looking me up and down, then turns away. Has he had anal before? Honestly, I would be surprised if he hasn't from the way he seems so . . . seasoned. The mere thought of it skyrockets the heat in my body, forcing me to take off my jacket and scarf.

I set my belongings on the couch and eye the space. He catches my perusal and waves toward the decked-out tables full of freshly prepared food including shrimp cocktail and sliders, as well as the immaculate display of alcohol. "Help yourself, we're going to be here for a while."

"What do you mean a while?"

His back is toward me, his shoulders tightening the fabric of his shirt as he leans down and grips the short wall in front of him. He doesn't answer right away. I watch him survey the club and the partiers who seem to have started early. If there is one thing I know about nightclubs—which I know pretty much nothing—is nine o'clock is too early for people to start getting drunk and dancing. Which means . . . a while very well might be three hours.

Crap.

Finally, he turns around, sipping from his tumbler. Smacking his lips, he looks at me and says, "No idea when my client is going to get here."

"Wait, didn't you give him a time?"

He slowly nods, almost in a condescending way. "You can give them all the timeframes you want, but until they decide to show up, your meeting doesn't start."

Defeated, I lean against a pole and say, "You've got to be kidding me. This has been the most exhausting day of my life."

"Exhausting?" His brow creases. "You took a two-hour nap and drooled on a floor, so explain to me how that's exhausting."

"Mentally exhausting," I snap. "This is mentally exhausting. If you'd just met me that first morning, all of this could have been avoided."

"Why? Are you not having fun?" He smirks.

"No. I'm not. How is this fun? Parading around the city with you has not been my ideal day."

"And here I thought you were having a good time, lass."

"How did you get that impression?"

He shrugs and then quickly glances at my chest. "Your nipples have been hard all day."

I am going to murder him.

Murder. Him.

This is not how I pictured my night going. I envisioned snuggling up with Louise on my bed and watching *Outlander* while eating my favorite Thai food from the place two blocks away. I envisioned wearing one of my night shirts, fuzzy socks, and tying my hair up and out of my face. A little lavender oil on my wrists, and the familiar comfort of a fluffy feline tucked next to me. The perfect night.

Instead, I have the frightful sound of club music blasting me in the head. I'm still wearing a pair of tight jeans, my hair is constantly falling over my face, and instead of a fuzzy feline, I'm sitting between two sets of couples doing their best to score some action tonight, their eager bodies constantly bumping against me. *So gross.*

I lean forward and look at the brunette with long wavy hair, plump lips, and really shiny legs that Roark has chosen for the night. She must have put oil on them, after she left half her shirt at home. I don't quite see the appeal, but then again, I'm a country girl who never thought having to show half my breast is the way to win a man's affection.

Despite how I feel about the girl, I should probably still warn her.

Leaning more forward, I scoot around Roark's body and tap her on the knee. When she glances at me, giving me one of the nastiest looks I've received all day, I curtly wave at her. "Hey, hi. I'm Sutton," I shout over the music and point to Roark. "I thought I'd warn you. During our activities today, we stopped by the doctor to check to see how his venereal disease is doing. Results back soon." I hold up my crossed fingers to her.

When she gives Roark a full-on once-over and then stands, I know my job here is done. We didn't go to the doctor today, but if he wants to make my life hell, I can easily be a cock blocker.

Once she's gone, Roark expels a long breath and then leans against the couch. He glances in my direction and says one word. One word that satisfies me, knowing I won this round.

"Cute."

He shakes his head and finishes off his drink, sets it on the table in front of us, then stands. Before he can get far, I pull on his shirt. "Hey, where are you going?"

"Outside to get some fresh air."

"I'm going too." I stand and stumble over the people next to me. Roark rights me and takes off, looking far more annoyed than necessary.

He's fast, so I panic as I make my way through throngs of people, neglecting my jacket and scarf. I move past two bouncers, who know me by now, and follow Roark out a back door that he props open with a piece of wood.

Once outside, the chill of the air hits me first, and then I hear the flick of a lighter. Leaning against the wall, head bent over, Roark lights a cigarette then rests his head against the brick once it's lit, blowing out a long puff of smoke.

Smoking has never been attractive to me, but for some reason, in this moment with Roark under a dim street light, his Adam's apple poking out, one leg kicked up against the wall, there's something very hot about the entire picture.

Not bothering to look at me, he holds out the cigarette and says, "Want a puff?"

"No. I don't smoke."

"Good. Don't ever start."

I fold my arms over my chest and move back and forth, my long-sleeved shirt doing nothing to block the cold from getting to my bones. Please let him be a really quick smoker.

He lulls his head to the side and looks me up and down, shaking his head. "You know you can go back in there. I'm not going to ditch you, not in a nightclub. I have better morals than that."

And for some reason, I believe him.

"The break from the music is nice."

Still staring me down, he sighs and pushes off the wall to take off his jacket that he wisely remembered. He tosses it to me, and thank God for quick reflexes, I snatch it before it hits the ground.

"Put it on so you don't freeze to death."

The wool of his jacket is so warm. "But what about you?"

"You need it more. Don't make this a big deal; put the goddamn thing on."

Well, when he puts it like that . . .

I throw the jacket over my shoulders and slip my arms through the holes, immediately getting sucked into his scent framing me in a big hug. Oh boy, this is dangerous. No wonder shiny legs was all over him. His scent alone will attract a gaggle of women, but throw in his good looks and accent and he's the man you can't help but be drawn to. Even if he annoys you. And I still can't get lunch out of my mind. My dad clearly respects Roark, and once he spouted off his *credentials* and I realized he wasn't just a professional drinker, I felt more confused. My dad is not someone to support fools, and if he has sponsored Roark, that means he believes in him. And that's what boggles my mind. Roark McCool is such a contradiction, and I don't know how to process him.

I swallow hard and try to focus on anything but his cologne.

"So," I clear my throat, "this is what you call fresh air?"

He lets out a puff of smoke. "The freshest."

"You know that's not good for you."

"Thanks, Pollyanna."

Yeah, I deserve that one. I'm nervous. Nervous for many reasons, the biggest one being how attracted I am to him. It's crazy—really freaking crazy—because even though he's been rude and surly, I keep feeling pulled toward him from the smallest of gestures, like him giving me his jacket, or his slight smirk when I get angry.

I should walk away now and consider my phone a lost cause, but for the life of me, I can't. And then instead, I step forward.

He glances at me, those green eyes cutting past the thick color of his short beard. "What?"

"Nothing."

"You're looking at me weird."

Crap. "Am I?"

"Yeah, stop it."

"Sorry." I look away and toe the ground, trying to come up with something to say. "Uh, how old are you?"

"Older than you."

"Obviously, but how much? Like forty?"

"What? Fuck you." He chuckles, thankfully. "I'm thirty-two."

"That was my second guess." I smirk.

He takes another drag from his dwindling cigarette. "Smartarse."

Silence stretches between us so I ask, "Don't you want to know how old I am?"

"Only young people say shit like that, as if they need to prove they're seasoned, not as young as they seem."

Ignoring him, I say, "I'm twenty-four."

Lazily his eyes drag up my body and settle on my face. "Yeah, it shows."

"What's that supposed to mean?"

Flicking his cigarette on the ground, he stands tall and sticks his hands in his pockets while assessing me. "You're eager, ready for work, and too bubbly to have really experienced the hardships of life just yet. Unharmed, innocent, and fresh from the educational womb, you have a lot to learn about real life."

He pushes past me, his little lecture not bothering me since it's coming from a pessimistic man. Hot man, but very pessimistic.

"What?" he asks, looking at my hand pressed against his arm. Large flakes of snow start to fall from the sky, lighting up the area around us.

With my best smile, I point at his discarded cigarette and say, "Are you going to pick that up? It's littering if you don't."

Exasperated, he picks up the cigarette butt while muttering, "Unbelievable."

I have no idea what time it is, as it seems like time stands still in this dark abyss of a nightclub. I do know I've had three sliders, probably twenty shrimp—if I'm honest—some mac and cheese balls, and at least four little macaroons that tasted like heaven on my tongue. I've drunk water the whole time, being that girl, and on occasion my toe has tapped to some songs I've thought were a little catchy.

Roark has been sitting next to me, an arm draped over the back of the couch, the other gripping a tumbler of whiskey he's barely touched since we've been back inside.

His client is here. They spoke for what seemed like ten seconds, shook hands, and then the giant basketball player was on his way. He's now in a dark corner with a girl on his lap and she's doing all sorts of gyrating.

Let's just say this has been an eye-opening night for me.

I glance at Roark, whose eyes are looking at nothing really in particular. "Soo . . ." I drag out. "Are you ready to go?"

I'm expecting a witty retort, something to put me in my place like he's done all day, but instead, he stands from the couch and leaves his partially finished drink on the coffee table.

"Yeah, let's go."

Thank God.

I quickly put my jacket on, wrap my scarf around my neck, and then pull my winter hat from my purse and secure it on my head. When I turn to Roark for him to lead the way, his brow is pinched, taking me in.

"You act like we live in Alaska."

"It's cold and snowing; at least last time we saw the outside it was snowing. I like to stay warm."

Rolling his eyes, he waves to a few people and heads toward the front of the club. I try to keep up with his long, purposeful strides, but I keep getting knocked around, rubbed up against, and pushed in different directions.

"Christ." I hear Roark's Irish lilt right before his hand clasps around mine and pulls me behind him.

Warm and large, his hand wraps around mine, securing tightly, sending a wave of warmth straight up my arm.

I've held hands before, so this isn't new, but what is new is the way his fingers hold on to my hand so tightly, or the rough texture of his skin as if he doesn't sit behind a phone for his day job.

I'm so consumed by the feeling of our palms pressed together that I don't even notice the guy blocking my way until he slams into me, sending me backward. If it wasn't for Roark hanging on to me, I would have easily face-planted onto the sticky, alcohol-covered floor.

"Hey, dipshit," Roark booms, still holding on to my hand while gripping the guy's shirt and getting in his face. "Watch where you're going."

I've seen that look in Roark's eyes before. He had it right before he pummeled the guy in the hot dog shop. I need to diffuse this before it gets any worse. Especially if my dad is Roark's sponsor. He would be so upset if Roark got into more trouble.

Stepping in, I place my hand against Roark's chest and step between the two men. Roark's chest vibrates as he takes a step closer.

"Stop," I sternly say, pulling his attention away from the guy. When his eyes land on me, I say, "Don't start anything. It's not worth it."

His jaw works back and forth, and I can see his temper start to ease. I hold my breath, waiting for his next move, hoping I diffused the situation. The speed in which this man becomes angry astonishes me. It's like an immediate switch. Scary really. I feel his heart beating so quickly against my hand, he's shaking. I've never seen this sort of . . . raw anger at such close range. And it was only me who was bumped, not him. He takes a quick, shallow breath and turns away, heading toward the front of the bar, still holding my hand, and I smile to myself. *What is he thinking right now?*

But that smile quickly falters when we step outside to what feels like an all-out blizzard. At least half a foot of snow has already fallen. All the sidewalks are covered, the streets are clear, and there doesn't seem to be a soul in sight.

"Was it supposed to snow this hard?" I ask, pulling my hood over my head.

"No idea. Don't pay attention." Without another thought, he turns to the right and starts walking, his hand no longer holding mine.

"Hey, wait," I call out. "Where are you going?"

"Home."

"To get the phone?"

"Sure," he calls out, his head turned down and hiding from the fast-falling snow.

"Sure?" I jog through the thick, cold snow to catch up to him. "What do you mean, sure?"

"I think you have bigger things to figure out."

"What do you mean?"

He picks up his pace and crosses the street, barely looking both ways, but then again, he doesn't need to because the streets are clear. No wonder he hasn't hailed a taxi.

"It's two in the morning, it's snowing, and you live in Brooklyn. How the hell do you plan on getting back home?"

Oh.

Crap.

He takes a right down a posh-looking street and then jogs up to the entryway of a nice-looking building. A doorman opens the door while giving Roark a quick nod. "Cold one, Mr. McCool."

"Freezing my balls off," he calls out. "Stay warm, Harris."

Stomping his feet on the ground to knock off some of the snow, he goes to the bank of elevators and presses the up button as I take in the opulence of the marble floors and crisp black walls with gold light fixtures. Very old-school New York, very cool.

The elevator dings, and just like the rest of the day, I follow Roark and watch as he puts a key card into the elevator and presses the P button, which I'm assuming stands for penthouse. If I didn't know already that he makes a lot of money, I know now.

We're silent on the ride up, my mind whirling. Two in the morning? I'm never out this late, especially by myself. *How on earth am I supposed to get home?* I could use the subway, but this late at night? That freaks me out. Even walking around with Roark scares me, and we only walked a short distance.

The elevator doors open straight into Roark's apartment, his very sparse apartment. There are no decorations, no frills. Furniture and that's it.

Hmm, I don't know why I thought there'd be more to his place.

Roark takes off his jacket and tosses it on the couch before heading to the kitchen. His built frame pushes against the fridge as he peers into it. He snags a water bottle and holds one out to me. "Want some water?"

"I'm good," I say nervously. This oddly feels a lot like that awkward moment you have with a guy right before you start to have sex. You know, the one where he takes you up to his place to make small talk, but within five minutes you're tearing clothes off? I hope Roark doesn't have that impression of me. He's going to be sadly mistaken if he does.

Water bottle in hand, he leans against the counter and takes down half the bottle in one swig. It's weird that I'm impressed.

"So, about that phone." I rock on my heels, looking around.

"Yeah, it's on my nightstand, charging." At least he had the decency to charge it.

"Can you possibly get it for me?"

"I can."

He doesn't move.

"Okay. Like now?"

"What are you going to do? Head back to Brooklyn?"

I adjust my purse on my shoulder. "Uh, I haven't really thought that far ahead."

"Figures." He finishes his drink and tosses the bottle in the sink. "Guest room is off to the right. Everything you need is in the attached bathroom."

"What? You think I'm staying here?"

He shrugs and passes through the living room. "Your choice."

He walks down a narrow hallway, and I'm tempted to follow him again but think better of it, knowing he's getting my phone, but when he doesn't return after a good ten minutes, I wonder if I should have followed him.

Why does he have to make things so difficult?

Unsure, but also desperate to have a small piece of me back, I walk down the hallway and call out his name. When he doesn't answer, I move even farther to a partially open door.

His bedroom.

If I open this door and he's passed out on the bed, snoring, I'm going to kick him right in the ass.

But when I press forward, his bed is empty and instead, I find him walking around in a low-slung towel, wet hair, and droplets of water cascading down his perfectly defined chest.

Oh my.

He glances in my direction. "Took you long enough." He grabs my phone from the nightstand and tosses it at me, then heads back into the bathroom where I hear him brushing his teeth.

I stand there. Unsure.

Do I attempt to go home? I'm not traveling the streets by myself, especially at this hour. But staying at Roark's screams madness. Although, madness describes my day perfectly. The only thing that's making me even consider staying is that he's my dad's agent, and if Roark ever tried anything, Dad would hear about it and wouldn't be happy.

"Are you still standing there?" Roark asks, hand poised at the knot of his towel.

"What?" My gaze snaps up. "Well," I fidget under his stare, nervous as to what to say, "we, uh . . . we didn't have a proper goodbye."

Out of all the things to say . . .

"If you're looking for someone to tuck you in or bid you farewell with a goodnight kiss, you've come to the wrong place." Turning away, he whips his towel off and slips into bed.

It's the second time I've seen his butt today and it still has the same effect on me, setting a ball of fire off in my stomach, warming up all my veins.

I chew on my lip, and he must notice because he sighs and says, "What?"

"You wouldn't, uh, want to escort me to Brooklyn, would you?"

"Not even if you offered to suck my cock before we left. I'm naked, in bed, and about to go to sleep. You can either leave or you can go to the guest room. Either way, tell me now so I can set the security system."

Oddly, that's the reaction I expected from him. I guess I don't have a choice in the matter. I'm not going out on the streets in this blizzard by myself, which means one thing: I'll be shacking up with Roark McCool for the night.

Pointing my finger at him, I say, "No funny business, you hear me? I'll be locking my door and I sleep very lightly, so any movement in my room and I'll hear it. I will report you if you try anything."

"Christ," he mutters, dragging his hands over his face. "Trust me, lass. You don't have to worry about me coming anywhere near *you*. Now get out of here. I'm tired." *Yup. Hearing you loud and clear.*

I chew on the side of my mouth. "You know, you could be a little nicer. After all, we did spend the day together."

"Not by my choosing." He fluffs his pillow. *Not really by my choice either, Mr. A-Hole.*

I fiddle with my fingers. "Do you always sleep naked?"

Lifting up from the bed, he points at the door. "Go. Now."

"Okay, yeah. Sure. Night, night."

Night, night? Come on, Sutton. Try better to *not* look like a fool.

When I look back over my shoulder, all I can see is the slight shake of his head. Figures. I've humiliated myself enough today, why not end the entire day with a simple night, night?

Just perfect.

CHAPTER SEVEN

Dear Sebastian,
  Who the fuck says night, night?
 Who at the age of twenty-fucking-four says night, night to a grown-ass man?
 Sutton Grace, that's who.
 Christ. What a goddamn day. I couldn't shake her off me to save my life, and do you know what the really messed up in the goddamn head thing is? I liked it.
 Yeah, I liked having her around. I liked her shock, her innocence, the way she grumbled whenever I did something she didn't approve of. I liked every fucking second of it, and if that isn't a red flag I don't know what is.
 So, I set out to get rid of her. I thought the nightclub would be her final straw, but instead she sat back on the couch, ate like a queen at her palace, and cutely tapped her foot to the music.
 Tapped her goddamn foot.
 What did I do with that? What every other idiotic man would do. I brought her back to my place and told her to sleep in the guest room. Mind you, the room is entirely too far away for me to even notice, but it's like I can feel her breathing the same air. I know she's there, and that's why I'm up at three in the morning, writing to you like some agonized teen. Hell . . .
 This entire time I thought I was writing to a talking crab, kind of cool,

but not going to work for me. Sorry, Sebastian.
Roark

ROARK

Light sleeper... bullshit.

Fully dressed for the day and drinking a hot cup of coffee, I stare at Sutton, whose mouth is half open, drooling all over my goose-down pillow, ass high in the air, and arms strangely flanked at her side. I've never seen anything like it.

Honestly, it looks like she's an ostrich with her head stuck in the ground. I don't know what to make of it.

There is really only one thing I can do at this point...

To maintain my reputation, I might have taken a few pictures for emergency use later. Can't pass up an opportunity like this.

I pocket my phone and walk closer to the bed, unsure how to wake her up. I could shout, scaring the shit out of her, or I could turn on a blaring alarm right next to her ear, guaranteeing a straight piss to my Egyptian cotton sheets. I could poke her with a broom—if I knew where one was. Smack her in the ass like she's a newborn baby. Gently rock her back and forth until her eyelids flutter open or soothingly rub her back. Maybe let the sun shine through the curtains.

Nah, I'm not that nice.

Instead, I pick up a pillow from the ground and toss it at her. Hair scattered all over her face, she lifts up and looks around, trying to gain her bearings. Brushing her hair out of her face with her hand, she makes eye contact with me and yelps, startling backward on the bed.

I sip my coffee casually. "Morning."

She pats down her body, clearly checking for clothes and then sighs in audible relief. "We didn't have sex."

"Thank fuck, right?" I press my hand to my chest. "What a

relief. I can't afford to get pregnant right now."

She narrows her eyes. "Don't be a jerk."

"It's my nature, lass. It's what I do." I nod at her. "Now get your arse out of my bed; I have to get to work, and I'm betting you do too."

Her eyes widen. "Oh my God, what time is it?"

I flick my eyes down to my watch and then take another sip of my coffee. "Quarter past nine."

"What?" Frantically she springs out of bed and starts running around the room gathering things. "Why didn't you wake me up?"

"Do I look like your goddamn alarm clock? Not my responsibility."

"I can't believe I slept in." Slipping on her shoes but fumbling terribly, I hold back the smile I'm sure would grant me a kick straight to the crotch. "What kind of trickery do you have in that bed?"

Amused, I ask, "What are you talking about?"

"You know exactly what I'm talking about. It's like you had a sleeping potion in it or something."

"It's called money, Sutton. It buys you sleep."

She glances at me. "Not true, some of the richest people have insomnia."

"Then they're not doing it right."

Although, I barely got any sleep last night, because good old ostrich-ass-in-the-air was in the other room, fucking with my head. But I won't mention that to her.

Finishing with her last shoe, she stands, grabs her purse, and starts walking out the door when I clear my throat and nod toward the nightstand when she looks at me. "Forgetting something?"

She spots the phone and groans. "This contraption. I wouldn't be here if it wasn't for this damn thing."

Clearly not in the best mood—I don't think she's a morning person—she stomps through my penthouse but stutter steps when she sees the kitchen island. Turning back around, she gives me a quizzical look.

"Did you make breakfast for me?"

"Don't flatter yourself. I ordered some shit from the place across the street. Feel free to take something to go."

Yeah, I might have gotten something specifically for her.

"There's huevos rancheros in there." I point to the top to-go box. "You know, since you're from Texas."

"That's my favorite." She reaches for the box and gives me a grateful look, which quickly turns into a snarl. "Oh no, you don't. Don't try to be nice to me now. That ship has sailed. Niceties were thrown out the window the minute you took my phone hostage and missed our first scheduled meeting."

"Not trying to be nice." I leave my empty cup on the counter. My housekeeper will get it later. "Just don't want you bitching to your dad about what a bad host I was."

I walk toward the elevator and she follows, food to go in hand along with a cup of coffee I might have gotten her as well.

"Oh, we won't be telling my dad about this. He doesn't need to know."

I press the down button on the elevator. "I don't lie to my clients."

"This isn't lying; this is just not talking about it. That's all."

"Eh." I shrug. "I would rather tell him." The elevator opens and I walk in, tossing my jacket over my shoulders. She follows in quickly, a little huff in her step.

"Why do you have to be so difficult?"

"Because it drives you crazy." I toss a grin in her direction that she practically spits back with her eyes.

"Seriously, don't tell my dad."

"Too late, I already sent him a text this morning."

Eyes even wider than before, she says, "No, you didn't. What did he say? Did you really tell him?"

"Told me he couldn't have picked a better guy to court his daughter. Said he always thought we would be great together. Oh, by the way, he thinks we're dating."

I'm pretty sure fire shoots out of her ears when she screeches, "What? Why would he think that?"

"According to the Old Testament, if you sleep in my house, that means we're dating."

"The Old Testament? Are you drunk?"

"I wish I was."

The elevator doors open and I start walking away when she catches up to me and pins me with her hand to my chest. For being such a little thing, she sure packs a big punch.

"Does he really think we're dating?"

I grin. "Nah. I didn't tell him anything, but seeing your reaction was so worth it." I give her a pat on the arm, feeling rather chipper now and say, "Have a good day, Sutton."

And with that, I take off out of my apartment building and flag down a taxi, leaving a very irritable Sutton Grace behind me. For the first time in my life, I'm leaving my apartment with a smile on my face—because that little spitfire is so goddamn fun to tease.

∽

Sutton: *We need to get together.*

Roark: *It's been two hours. You really can't be away from me for that long? #clinger*

Sutton: *I'm not a clinger! We have to get together to talk about your community service.*

Roark: *Nah, I'm good.*

Sutton: *I don't think you have a choice in the matter.*

Roark: *Aren't you a fucking treat.*

Sutton: *Oh, I'm sorry, am I interrupting your massage? Or your multiple visits to the post office?*

Roark: *You're interrupting a good cigarette. Now my mouth tastes bitter.*

Sutton: *Maybe you should stop smoking. There's an idea.*

Roark: *You get your phone back and now you're sassy? How does that work?*

Sutton: *Just trying to find an effective way to communicate with you.*

Roark: *Effective would be with your shirt off, because then I would pay attention.*

Sutton: *Don't be a pig.*

Roark: *You know, you don't hear people call each other pigs very often anymore. I kind of like it.*

Sutton: *You're not supposed to like it.*

Roark: *It's a shame you can't control my emotions.*

Sutton: *We are getting off topic. We need to meet.*

Roark: *Hmm . . . do you really foresee that happening?*

Sutton: *Please don't be difficult.*

Roark: *Where's the fun in that?*

"This is why you ditch your friends who get hitched to a relationship," I grumble, slouching in my chair.

"He's five minutes late," Rath says.

"And I want a goddamn drink. How come I can't order one until he gets here?"

"You're acting like a child."

Maybe, but I need something. Christ, I've had meeting after meeting since I got my phone back—a huge reason why I wasn't bothered about trading with Sutton—and I'm exhausted. Everyone needs something, everyone wants more money, and everyone is looking for the next big endorsement. I don't know how many times today I said good things come to those who wait. Even thinking it makes me want to throw up in my mouth, because it's a bullshit saying. Whoever came up with that saying probably never got anything good in their life because they sat on the sidelines and waited instead of taking action.

Taking action for my clients is my job, and I'm doing shit behind the scenes they don't need to worry about. Therefore, I tell them they need to be patient.

Athletes are never patient.

When do I get a shoe deal?

When am I going to be on *The Tonight Show*?

When am I going to have a multi-million-dollar, multi-year deal?

You know when? When you pull your head out of your goddamn ass and score a few touchdowns.

I might have shouted that at a client today. It was the end of the day, and I was already irritated. Thankfully the dude was cool, laughed, and agreed with me. He hit the gym after that.

But I could really use a drink right now to wash the day behind me, and Rath is being a turd-nugget, not letting me order until our best friend, Bram, gets here.

"Ah, there they are," Bram says, hands clasped together, staring at us. "My boys."

Jesus Christ.

He floats—yes, fucking floats—over to us, a huge smile on his face, love beams pouring out of his eyes as if Cupid is right behind him, permanently striking him in the ass.

Rath is scooped into a hug—a full embrace—and then set back in his chair. From over Rath's head, Bram points at me and wiggles his finger. "Come here, you handsome Irish bastard."

I hold up my hand. "I'm good."

"Nope." He shakes his head. "You don't get to pass up Bram snuggles." Before I can move, he swoops to his knees and buries his head in my chest . . . and nuzzles.

"What the fook are ya doin'?" I ask, my accent strong with my anger as I try to push him away.

His nose runs along the lapel of my suit coat. "You smell like heaven."

"Get out of here." I palm his face and push him away.

With a laugh, he retreats to his seat, unbuttons his jacket, and sits down. Hands on the table, he looks between us and then says, "I'm in love."

Christ.

"We know," Rath and I say at the same time, irritation heavy in our voices.

Bram has been dating Rath's sister for a few months now, so it's no surprise he's like this—a bubbly idiot with a relentless smile. Hell, he's been in love with the girl for years. It took him a really, really long time to admit it—not admit it, but make a move. He was Ross Geller to an extreme.

He adjusts his collar as he says, "You don't have to be rude about it. I'm just sharing. Isn't that what this is all about? Sharing?"

"Yeah, sharing things we don't know already," Rath says, flagging down our waitress. Thank God.

When she arrives, I talk above the guys and quickly say, "Jameson, neat."

"Stella, please," Rath says.

When she turns to Bram, he rubs his stomach and says, "You know, a nice warm milk would be delightful right now."

What the actual fuck?

"No." I step in, waving him off. "He'll have a tequila mule. Thanks."

A little confused and probably slightly disturbed, she takes off as Bram complains. "Hey, I really wanted a warm milk."

"You're not drinking that shit around me. Not happening. And also, you're a grown-arse man, so nut up and drink some beer."

"Sheesh." Bram unfolds his napkin and sets it on his lap. "What's up your ass?"

"Nothing." I push my hand through my thick hair.

"It's a girl," Rath says, causing Bram to practically jump out of his seat and do a kickball chain right in front of us.

"A girl?" he gushes. "Not Roark McCool, permanent bachelor. My fucking heart can't take it."

You know when people say payback's a bitch? This is my payback. I might not have been the best of friends when Bram was going through lady problems with Julia. Yeah, I helped him, but I was a dick about it most of the time.

I can feel him rearing back and letting me have it now, especially with that evil glint in his eyes.

But to be fair, this isn't the same thing, not even close. I'm not in love with the girl, nor do I want to date her. Yeah, she's gorgeous and has amazing tits, but it doesn't mean I'll make a move.

Okay . . . and yeah, she's fun to drive crazy, but that's not the same thing as what Bram has with Julia or the struggle he went through.

"It's not what Rath is making it out to be."

"He held her phone hostage for days and she slept over last night."

"What?" Bram's eyes nearly fall out of their sockets. "A reoccurring interaction? What's this nonsense? Roark McCool doesn't have reoccurring interactions with women."

Christ.

Thankfully the waitress brings our drinks at that moment so I have a second to compose myself and not lash out, bringing unwanted questioning from my friends.

"You already slept with her?" Bram asks, sipping his drink then puckering his lips. Being in a relationship has really softened the bastard. Once the most popular guy on campus, he now spends his Friday nights curled up with his girl. I can't remember the last time he went out with us. It's been a really long time.

"I didn't sleep with her."

"You didn't?" Rath asks, surprised. "When you said she stayed the night, I thought you had sex with her."

"How come you know about this girl and I don't?" Bram complains. "Dude, you know I'm the romantic. Rath over here has a brick for a heart, you need to discuss these things with me."

"I don't have a brick for a heart," Rath says.

"No, you're just hung up on your ex," I say with a smirk.

He shifts in his chair but doesn't say anything. His silence is all I need. Now to get Bram to shut up. I turn toward him, and he folds his arms across his chest in challenge, as if to say *you have nothing on me*. And it's true, I don't. I used to when he was pining after Julia, but now it's like he's an open book for everyone.

"So . . . who is the girl?"

For fuck's sake. Might as well get it over with.

"I'm going to preface this with I'm not interested in her, so before your little heart starts beating wildly for a potential coupling, it's not going to happen."

In a snarky tone, Bram replies, "Never say never."

He's so fucking annoying.

"We ran into each other at Gray's Papaya right before I got in that fight. I dropped my phone and so did she. They were mixed up and Rath grabbed the wrong one. Naturally curious, I looked through her phone, which wasn't locked, and started going through all her crap."

Bram elbows Rath and says, "I would have done the same. I love snooping."

"And I might have taken my time delivering the phone back." I shrug. "I don't know, it gave my asshole personality something to do. That was until I found out she's the daughter of Foster Green."

"What? Seriously?" Bram asks. "What are the odds?"

I pull on the back of my neck. "Tell me about it. She then followed me around all day yesterday until two in the morning when I finally took her back to my place to give her the phone back. At that point it was too late, the streets were covered with snow, and she was too nervous to travel back to Brooklyn. She slept in the guest bedroom. That's it. End of story."

"Besides having to work with her now," Rath adds, finding his voice again.

Bram claps his hands in amusement. "What a twist; I didn't see that coming." He takes a sip of his drink and says, "Let me guess, you have to work for her dad's foundation to fulfill your community service?"

I scratch the side of my jaw. "Something like that."

"Fucking perfect. You two are going to fall in love."

"We're not going to fall in love. Not only is she my client's daughter, she's only twenty-four."

"So?" Bram shrugs. "Eight years isn't that big a deal when you think about it. And Julia is younger than I am."

"Julia is only two years younger than you," I point out, kind of agreeing that age doesn't matter all too much. She just seems younger to me because I work with her dad. *And she's so naïve and prim . . . and fucking adorable.* No. Scratch that. Client's daughter . . .

"Two years, eight years." He weighs his hands. "Same thing." He's so delusional. "Tell me this, do you find her attractive?"

"I'd be blind if I didn't. But she's not my type. Way too innocent. She has that whole *good girl* vibe going with the big eyes and the inability to swear. I would feel like I was robbing her of her innocence if I attempted to do anything with her."

"You've thought about it," Rath says with a smile.

"Not in the way you're thinking. It's not something I'm interested in."

"You say that now. . ." Bram drags out, "but just you wait. You're going to be begging to go on a date with her. I can see it in your eyes."

I don't know what the hell he's seeing, but there is nothing there, nothing at all.

∽

Sutton: *I gave you a day to gather yourself. Now can you please act like an adult and tell me when we can meet?*

Sutton: *Avoiding me is not a choice you're going to want to make.*

Sutton: *I'm not afraid to get my dad involved. Don't make me play that card.*

Sutton: *Okay, you're tempting me. I have an email typed out to him, ready to send, ratting you out.*

Sutton: *I just put his name in the address bar.*

Sutton: *I'm about to press send.*

Roark: *Jesus, six texts in an hour. I have a goddamn job, you know.*

Sutton: *Oh hi. How's your day?*

Roark: *What do you want?*

Sutton: You know what I want.
Roark: You don't have to ask, lass. Come and take it.
Sutton: Are you talking about your penis?
Roark: Heavens no. That would be unprofessional.
Sutton: Ah, I see what you did there with the sarcasm.
Roark: See, asterisk not needed.
Sutton: Look at this fun banter. Don't you want to do this in person and talk about the camp?
Roark: No.
Sutton: We have to meet up.
Roark: The only thing I HAVE to do is take a leak. Talk to you later.
Sutton: You can . . . "take a leak" and talk to me at the same time.
Sutton: Hello?
Sutton: How long does it take you to pee?
Sutton: Does your pee ever burn.
Sutton: ~~~ sign of an STD.
Roark: You're so goddamn annoying.

~

Sutton: Did you smoke today? Remember when you told me you were going to quit?
Roark: What? I never said that to you.
Sutton: Ah ha! Got you to answer on the first text.
Roark: Unbelievable. Didn't anyone ever tell you lying is a sin?
Sutton: You lie to me constantly.
Roark: Never claimed to be a saint.
Sutton: Neither have I.
Roark: You're not kidding anyone, Sutton. You're a good girl.
Sutton: Not true. I do things.
Roark: Someone who is a badass doesn't say they "do things"
Sutton: Oh yeah, well . . . I used to steal Tic Tacs while in line at the grocery store.
Roark: How old were you?
Sutton: Irrelevant.

Roark: *Were you seven?*
Sutton: *No . . .*
Roark: *Yeah, okay. Night, Sutton.*

∼

Sutton: *Rise and shine. Are you ready for our meeting today at nine? I'm bringing scones.*
Roark: *We don't have a meeting.*
Sutton: *We could.*
Roark: *I'm busy.*
Sutton: *You're not! I know you're not. Please, for the love of freaking Jesus, meet up with me.*
Roark: *Why do you need me so badly? Just give me a job.*
Sutton: *Your job is co-organizer.*
Roark: *The fuck it is.*
Sutton: *Don't you read your emails? Whitney said the only way she's going to approve your hours is if you help me organize. We're in this together.*
Roark: *She did not say that.*
Sutton: *Yes, she did. Check your emails.*
Sutton: *Did you check them?*
Sutton: *Hello?*
Roark: *I'm going to have a conversation with your father about this.*
Sutton: *Don't even bother. I already tried talking to him. He's set on this decision.*
Roark: *Then just do it all by yourself and slap my name on it.*
Sutton: *I wish I could, it would be a hell of a lot easier, but it's too much work and I need your help with celebrities.*
Roark: *Christ.*
Sutton: *So . . . nine? Scones?*
Roark: *No.*
Sutton: *Roark! PLEASE!!*
Sutton: *Hello?*
Sutton: *Don't ignore me!*

CHAPTER EIGHT

D*ear Ralph,*
*   Ralph, Ralphy? Ralph-sef?*
Yeah, not feeling it.

Did you hear the news? Word on the street is Foster Green is an imaginative and evil asshole. I love the guy for many reasons, millions of them sitting in my loaded bank account, but ever since he decided to be my sponsor, it's like he somehow detached my balls, stuck them in his little fanny pack, and is wearing them around his waist, keeping them in close quarters, making it impossible for me to get around his little game.

Co-organizer? Do I look like a goddamn planner? I don't do shit like that. I hire people . . .

Whoa, hold up a second.

An idea just sparked in my head. Yes, a very brilliant one. An incredibly brilliant idea.

Maybe this diary thing isn't so bad, after all.

Don't get excited, that was a lie. I'd rather poke my balls with a freshly sharpened pencil than sit here and write to you.

Roark

~

SUTTON

Sutton: *Did you know I make the best butter cookies out there?*
Roark: *You're just going to text me random things now?*
Sutton: *You're refusing to answer my phone calls.*
Roark: *You can stop those by the way. I'm never going to pick up. Stop wasting your time. Work efficiently.*
Sutton: *I highly doubt you're the one to be giving out advice on work ethic.*
Roark: *I don't know. My bank account thinks otherwise.*
Sutton: *You're so full of yourself.*
Roark: *And yet you keep texting me.*
Sutton: *When are we meeting?*
Roark: *Tomorrow, noon, at Makers on Broadway.*
Sutton: *What? Are you serious?*
Roark: *Yes, don't be late.*
Sutton: *You better not be kidding me.*
Roark: *I would never.*
Sutton: *Yeah, right.*

~

Clutching my folder close to my chest, I shift from side to side, looking around for Roark. I'm early so I don't need to panic yet, but he does have a track record for not showing up, and his instant change of heart was a little startling. I almost didn't believe him, so when I called the restaurant to see if he made reservations and he did, I was shocked to say the least.

"Miss Green, your table is ready. This way."

"Thank you." I glance back at the door one more time before heading toward the back of the restaurant. She sits me next to a window, offering me a street view. At least I can keep an eye out for Roark if he walks this way.

After getting situated, I pick up the menu but all the words kind of float together, making it impossible to concentrate. To be honest, I'm a little nervous about seeing Roark again. Not because of what we have to talk about, but because of the way my body reacts to him whenever he's around. I get all hot and bothered, my face flushes, and for some reason all I can picture is his ass when he talks to me.

I might also think about it when he texts.

I blame him.

Butt cheeks should be sacred, not something you show a stranger willy-nilly, and do you know why? Because when you have nice, tight butt cheeks, it's all the other person can think about. And is that fair? No.

Now you can see my apprehension of seeing Roark.

Butt cheeks.

Firm, tight butt—

"Miss Green?"

Startled, I nervously laugh and look up to find a young lady with brown hair standing over me, a welcoming smile on her face and a laptop bag clutched to her side.

"Yes?"

She holds out her hand proudly and says, "I'm Siri, like the lady on the phone."

"Uh . . . hi." I shake her hand, because I don't want to be rude.

"It's so nice to meet you." She sets her bag down and removes her jacket before taking a seat across from me. "Can you believe this weather? They have no idea what to do with all the snow, but of course the city never sleeps, right?" She picks up the menu and gasps. "Oh, I love a good wedge salad."

Am I missing something?

Who is this Siri, and why does she know me?

And why is she acting like I've been expecting her this whole time?

"Can I get you something to drink?"

Siri looks up at the waitress and nods. "Unsweetened iced tea please, and can I get the wedge salad? I'm famished." She hands off the menu and smiles at me.

"And for you, miss?"

I blink a few times, utterly bewildered. What is happening right now?

"Uh, I'll have the same," I answer, perplexed.

Once the waitress leaves, Siri starts up again. "Do you have a love affair with wedge salads too? I'll tell you, it's an absolute problem for me. Whenever I see one, I always get it because I can't help myself. It's the bacon. I really think it's the bacon. What about you?"

Smiling psychotically—I can feel it—I nod and gently place my hands on the table, trying to be as nice as possible. "I'm sorry"—I swallow hard—"but do we know each other?"

She chuckles. "No, but I do come on a little strong, so I can see how you would get that impression."

Still confused, I glance around the restaurant for Roark, wondering if he's standing at a distance, watching me, as if this was some weird joke he's playing on me, but when I don't see any sign of him, I turn back to Siri who's sitting there . . . staring at me.

"You're very pretty." She covers her mouth, almost embarrassed. "I don't mean to be weird, but I'm a little outspoken." You think? "But you are very pretty. Your eyes are gorgeous. Such long eyelashes. Are they real?"

Okay, is this some weird setup? Am I on a date and don't even know it?

"I'm sorry." I try to be as polite as possible. "But I'm a little confused. I'm supposed to be meeting Roark McCool for lunch—"

"Oh my gosh, of course he didn't tell you. That's so Roark." *That's so Roark?* As if they are *really* familiar with each other. Who is this Siri, really? "I'm his assistant. He put me on this project. He wants me to head up everything with you. I'm super excited. I was doing research all morning, and I have so many wonderful ideas. Starting with moving the entire camp to the city. We'd be able to have so many more celebrities at our disposal, and the media coverage would be explosive. We could really turn this into a promotional piece."

I hold my hand up, my politeness slipping. "Excuse me, but the plans are set for the ranch in Texas. We don't want media attention, because that's not what this is about. Roark is supposed to find and liaise with the select athletes chosen. I'm sorry if this is rude, but I'm afraid your involvement on this project is not needed, Siri."

"He said you would say that." She smiles, but it's not so charming this time. "I'm going to level with you, Sutton. Roark is a busy guy. He doesn't have time in his day to talk about menial things like kids' camps."

"Menial?" My voice rises. "Let me tell you this, Siri. I spent an entire day with the man, following his every move, and if he has time to go to random post offices and have two-hour massages, the least he can do is have the decency to show up to this required business meeting." I toss my napkin on the table, now devoid of all my southern charm. "And I'll have you know, what my father does for those kids is anything but *menial*. I suggest you research a little harder next time."

With that, I grab my things and storm out of the restaurant with one though on my mind, giving Roark a big southern tongue-whipping.

～

Sutton: *I have lost all respect for you.*
    Roark: *Didn't even know you had a little left.*
Sutton: *Why didn't you come to the meeting?*
Roark: *Didn't Siri explain?*
Sutton: *Excuse my language, but Siri is a bitch. She was very rude and unpleasant.*
Roark: *Funny, I heard the same thing about you.*
Sutton: *She called my dad's camp menial. I don't know about you, but that is both condescending and insulting to me. I don't take kindly to people disparaging my dad and the years of hard work he's put into helping others. He takes more pride in that than the stats he's racked up and the awards he's*

won over the years. So for your assistant, sent on YOUR behalf to represent YOUR thoughts, to belittle his legacy like that is unacceptable, Roark. I know you have no respect for me. Whatever. But this has certainly taught me how little YOU respect my dad. And in my eyes, that's even worse. Clearly, all you care about is the money you've made from him. It's disgusting. You disgust me.

Roark: *Hell, Sutton. I'm sorry.*
Roark: *Sutton?*
Roark: *Hey, you there?*
Roark: *Fuck.*

~

After a long bath, a large hot chocolate with a cup of marshmallows, and half a package of Oreos, I've finally calmed myself down and can act like a rational adult.

At least that's what I told myself when I was in my apartment, but now that I'm pacing the lobby of Roark's apartment building, waiting for him to get off his nightclub shift, I'm thinking rational adult is nowhere to be found and crazy person is present.

I thought I said my peace through text, but when I saw his texts after, the heavy regret in his words, I had to see if he meant it, if he really was sorry. *But he's out partying, so there is my answer. Surely . . .*

Maybe a little crazy, maybe a little desperate, but that's where I'm at, because that's where he's put me. I'm not sorry for what I said to him, because it was all true, and it still angers me. But if he's sorry . . .

"Can I get you a water bottle, Miss Green?" Harris asks.

"I'm good, Harris." I look at my phone. One fifteen. "How long does Mr. McCool usually stay out?"

"Depends on the night. I wish I could be more exact."

"That's okay." I take a seat on one of the stiff couches in the entryway. "Does he stay out late every night?"

"Almost every night, but at least once a week he stays in." He winks. "But you didn't hear that from me."

The door blows open and Harris rushes over to prop it open for a very wobbly and glassy-eyed Roark. Oh great, he's drunk. I should have known. This was a stupid idea. Why did I bother?

"Mr. McCool, good evening."

"Hey Harris." He pats him on the shoulder and makes his way into the entryway. He gives me a brief glance before continuing toward the elevators. He's about to press the up button again when he slowly turns back around and looks at me, head tilted. "Sutton?" He studies me for a few beats before something crosses over his features. Before I can address him, his eyes narrow and he strides toward me, taking my hand in his, pulling me toward the elevators.

"What are you doing?"

He presses the up button and the elevator immediately opens. He pulls me in, inserts his card, and pushes the P button. He then turns on me and laces his fingers with mine, an intimate hold I wasn't prepared for, and in that second as we climb up the multiple floors in his apartment building, his warmth spreading through me, I feel the icy façade I erected start to melt away.

I want to be mad, I want to yell and scream at him, make him feel as bad as I felt earlier, but with one glance at the regretful look in his face, I realize he was sincere in his texts. Not just sincere, but heartfelt and that cools the heated anger that was billowing inside of me while I was waiting downstairs.

I know it shouldn't . . . but it does.

There is something about this man that scarily pulls on my heartstrings in ways I've never experienced before. He runs hot and cold, confusing me and flipping my opinion of him from good to bad in seconds. He's exhilarating with his smart mouth and quick wit, but there is also a softer side of him I could bet my life he doesn't show to many people.

And I know I can honestly say I'm one of the few people who is privileged to see past the bad boy persona.

The doors part and he pulls me into his apartment, eyes fixed on me, the heat in his pupils sending off a serious warning alarm.

It didn't go unnoticed that he came home alone, or that when he saw me, there was the smallest of smiles that graced his handsome lips and now he's desperately holding onto my hand, willing me to stay with him.

And with all the unfamiliar feelings swirling inside me, I know I should let go of his hand and walk away, but my brain can't seem to move my feet, no matter how much it screams and yells at them. I want to stay, I want to see where this electricity that's sparking between us goes. I want to know what that soft, sincere look will bring me.

"Hey," he says, pushing a piece of my hair behind my ear. My face turns to him for the briefest of moments.

Oh God, this isn't good. I did *not* come here for intimacy, nor did I come here for a booty call—not sure if that's what he wants, but from the look in his eyes, I feel nervous about his next move.

"Roark."

He cups my face, his thumb passing over my cheek, my stomach somersaulting from the touch. "I'm sorry," he finally says, his voice raspier than normal, but the intention in his words is so genuine, so sincere. It's confusing . . . and tempting.

Swallowing hard, I look up at him. "Do you really mean that?"

He nods. "I do. I really fucking do." His thumb strokes my cheek again as his eyes search mine. I barely know this man, but there is this pull I feel toward him, an ache starting to form in the pit of my stomach, an ache only for him. An ache I want relieved. He nods behind me toward the hallway breaking the spell and says, "Go."

Wait. What?

"Go?" My excitement drops.

He nods again, as if he's trying to convince himself and takes a step back, sticking his hands in his pockets. "Guest bedroom. Now."

Is he serious? He wants me to go to the guest bedroom? After all of that, the look, the apology, the light touches. He just wants me to leave?

If I truly think about it, I don't want to stay here. *But then, I don't want to leave either.*

Mustering up a little bit of backbone, I say, "I'm not staying here again."

He levels me with those searing green eyes. "It's almost two. Are you really going to make your way back to Brooklyn now?"

I hate that he's right. "I can get a hotel room."

"Don't be stupid, Sutton." He nods again. "Go. Sleep."

"But I wanted to talk to you."

"Not now. Not like this." He takes a step back while running his hand through his hair. "Go, Sutton."

I don't want to talk with him like this either, however I don't want this abrupt end to our evening. But it looks like I don't have a choice.

Sighing heavily, I turn away and walk toward the guest room, wishing he wasn't drunk, wishing we could hash this all out.

Right before I touch the handle, I hear him say he's sorry one last time.

Ugh, why can't he not be drunk? He seems so open, so vulnerable, as if he dropped the sarcastic and witty wall he likes to hide behind, making him that much easier to communicate with.

But then again, maybe he's in that state because he's drunk.

I spend the next few minutes getting ready for bed, picking up a T-shirt he left on the dresser, which makes me wonder if he was expecting me, if he knows me well enough that a text wouldn't have been sufficient. *But when did he put it here? Why would he think to?*

The shirt smells like him, and I shamelessly take in a deep breath as I slip it over my naked body. I brush my teeth, wash my face, and then head to bed where I plug my phone into a charger. That's when I see a text from him.

Roark: *You look pretty tonight.*

I squeeze my eyes shut and hold my phone close to my chest. Oh Roark . . .

Sutton: *You're drunk.*
Roark: *I know.*
Sutton: *Why, Roark?*
Roark: *I didn't like how I treated you. I had to wash away the day.*
Sutton: *You could have just messaged me, called, come to my office.*
Roark: *I could have.*
Sutton: *But you didn't.*
Roark: *I'm an asshole, Sutton. The sooner you realize that, the better.*
Sutton: *You have moments when you're not.*
Roark: *Don't hold onto them, because they're few and far between.*
Sutton: *They are, but when you have those moments, they make a big impact.*
Roark: *Like when?*
Sutton: *A few minutes ago, when you said I looked pretty.*
Roark: *Stay away, Sutton. Stay far, far away.*

But what if I don't want to . . .

CHAPTER NINE

Deal Sal,
 I've always been a fan of alcohol. Have been since taking my first sip at the ripe old age of thirteen. It's been a friend, a confidant, a protector against emotions, and a good fucking time. Never once have I been mad at alcohol, nor have I ever said anything terrible about it, even when I've been kicked in the crotch and buckled over the next day from too much imbibing.

But last night, Sal, last night alcohol betrayed me.

Some might have thought I was too drunk to remember anything about last night, but I've never been that kind of drunk. I've been the lucky inebriated asshole who remembers every idiotic thing he's said and done, including saying stupid shit to a girl he has no right saying anything to.

You guessed it, I might have said some things to Sutton unwillingly. You know, things like 'you look pretty'—which I know every girl wants to hear —but not every guy wants to say out loud especially when he doesn't want to give the girl false hope.

I blame alcohol. I blame it for everything. For being a dick to her most of the time when she doesn't deserve it—even though most of my dickish moves happened sober. I blame it for holding her hand in the elevator, for entwining our fingers, for taking a moment to breathe her in, something I would have never done sober. And I blame it for the wicked thoughts I had about her last night, especially the one where my head was buried between her legs. And I blame alcohol for having to jack off in the shower this morning so I am somewhat presentable when I go to wake the ostrich.

Christ.

Thanks, Sal. You know, I might consider keeping the name. We'll see.

Roark

ROARK

Just open the goddamn door. It's your apartment, you own that doorknob, so put your hand on it and twist.

I reach out but don't grab it.

Hell, what if she's naked or something? I'm barely making it through my morning remembering those big, bold eyes of hers and the way she smelled like a fresh meadow even though it was so late.

The hand not holding my coffee drags over my face while my mind debates. She was upset last time when I didn't wake her up, even though technically it's not my responsibility. Still . . .

I sigh and reach for the handle again, slowly opening it. *Please don't let her be naked. Please don't let her be naked.*

Although . . . a little nip slip wouldn't kill me.

No! It would. It would destroy me.

Don't be naked.

I creak the door open and peer in.

What the hell?

I push the door all the way forward and find the bed completely made up and empty. The bathroom light is off, and it looks like no one has even been here.

What the fuck? Did she go home last night?

She better not have.

I pull my phone from my pocket and walk toward the kitchen, where I set down my coffee to type out a text to Sutton.

Roark: *Did you go home last night?*

I wait for a response, wondering if she possibly woke up early and traveled home to her place, but when I don't hear back from her after ten minutes, I start to panic. So many things could have happened to her if she went home last night, and I don't think I would forgive myself if she met with trouble.

Pacing, I consider my next move. A phone call. That's simple.

I dial her number and wait.

And wait.

"Hi, you've reached Sutton. Sorry I missed your call, but if you give me a little bit of time, I'll be sure to get back to you. Have a great day."

Fuck.

I hang up.

Her voice sounds so chipper, so sweet with the cutest hint of a Texas drawl.

Why didn't she answer?

I tap the counter, my fingers drumming over the hard surface as I decide what to do. Maybe another text.

Yes, a text. Maybe she's in a meeting and couldn't answer. A text she can discreetly answer.

Roark: *Hey, can you just let me know you're okay?*

Simple. If she had any decency at all, she'd text me back. Given her addictive southern charm, she'd never let a text go unanswered, especially one that clearly shows concern. Hell, should I have used asterisks to show concern?

I bite my lip and stare at the text. Maybe.

Fuck, okay . . .

Roark: *Just a quick text. *concerned**

I've been playing it cool. I'm managing the panic that's currently floating in my chest, but that text, yup, that made me look desperate.

Very desperate.

But you know, I'm desperate to make sure she's okay, because she's my client's daughter, one of my closest clients, and I would feel like utter shit if something happened to her on my watch. Not that she is mine to watch over, but she was here last night, and if she was upset, really that upset and she left, that's on me. I don't want to disappoint my clients. Ever.

That's why I'm doing this. Trying to reach out. For my client.

Not because I'm starting to feel something for her . . .

∼

Half an hour later with no response. I'm going to kill her if she's not already dead.

Remember when I said I was panicking? That was nothing compared to what I'm feeling right now. I'm in full-blown heart attack mode as I make my way to her office at her dad's foundation. I have no idea where she lives or I would have gone there, and I sure as shit wasn't about to ask her dad. The office was the next best thing.

When the elevators part, I storm to reception and ask, "Is Sutton Green here?" Startled, the woman who's worked behind the desk for years now, the same woman whose name I can never remember, greets me with a smile.

"Mr. McCool, how nice to see you—"

I grip the desk and lean over it, trying not to look as crazy as I feel. "Is Sutton Green here?"

The poor lady swallows hard and nods while pointing. "Down the hall, third door on the right."

And just like that, the lid of my head pops off and a ball of fire furies out of me as I spin on my heel and stomp toward the third door on the right.

It's going to happen. I'm going to kill her.

Right here, in her dad's business, I am going to murder his one and only child.

Not even bothering to knock, I whip the door open, causing Sutton to jump drastically in her chair and spill tea all over her desk.

Hand to her chest, breathing hard, she glances up at me in utter shock. "Roark, what the hell are you doing?"

With my foot, I slam the door closed, then I lean over her desk, hands gripping the wood, my eyes narrowed. "Why the fuck haven't you answered your phone?"

"What?" She genuinely looks confused.

"I sent you multiple texts and called. Are you trying to punish me? Is that your game, Sutton?" I'm positively seething and there's no chance I can pull it back, not when there are too many unwanted and fucking confusing emotions flowing through me right now.

"I . . . no." Scattered, she reaches for her purse and digs around while sopping up the tea with some napkins. "I don't have my phone on me. It's . . . here it is."

Fuck.

I reach for it. "Give me that." She doesn't need to see my texts. She sure as hell doesn't need to see my asterisk usage.

She pulls away quicker than expected, scooting her chair away and hitting the wall behind her. She clutches the phone to her chest and says, "No. This is my phone."

"It was mine for a while." *There is maturity and logic buried deeply within my demand.* "Now give it." I hold out my hand.

Head thoughtfully tilted to the side, she says, "What don't you want me to see or hear?"

"Nothing, just give it to me. I need to check . . . uh . . . for poison. There was rat poison all over my apartment last night, and I want to make sure it didn't get in your phone."

"You're such a liar." She looks down at the screen and her eyes soften. "Aw, you used asterisks."

"Christ," I mutter, turning away, hand in hair.

"And you called."

"Well, you're not dead, so I'm leaving."

"Wait." She races out of her chair and rounds her desk where she pulls on my hand to keep me in place. A wave of lavender hits me all at once as she tugs on me, forcing me to look at her. "Roark, you were concerned."

She's not going to let this go. I can see it in her eyes. Sighing, I say, "Yeah, okay. I was concerned. I expected you to be in the guest room, so when you weren't there, I thought that maybe you tried to go home, and when you weren't answering your phone, I thought the worst." And Harris wasn't on shift, understandably, so I couldn't even fucking ask him when she left.

Her fingers lace with mine, and I know I should pull away. I know I need to discourage the intimate hold, but for the life of me, I can't. Not when I have this weird sensation to make sure she truly is okay.

"I set an alarm this time, figuring you wouldn't be up for a while given your state last night, and I went back to my place to get ready for work."

I nod. "Yup, makes sense."

Her hand reaches up and fidgets with the lapel of my jacket. Christ, she's way too damn close. "Thank you for checking on me. It makes me think you actually do have a heart."

"A small one, but it's there . . . on occasion." Knowing I owe her an apology, I suck up my pride and try to keep my hands to myself, even though my fingers are itching to push her hair behind her ear.

Eight years younger.

Client's daughter.

Sweet and innocent.

Not the kind of girl for you.

No. I'm not the kind of man for her.

Subtle reminders as to why I need to keep my distance.

"Hey, I, uh"—I pull on the back of my neck, I'm not good at this apology thing—"I'm sorry about yesterday, and how everything went down with Siri. I had a long conversation with her, and there'll be an apology made from her as well."

"I don't care about Siri. I mean, I kind of do." She glances at the ground. "I care about how you treat the work I value. You act like it's a joke when it means a lot to me. I'm not here to chase you around. If you really don't want to help, I can do it all myself, but I ask that you give me the phone numbers for the celebrities who can assist at the camp. I'm not going to force you to do anything you don't want to do."

When the hell did I gain a conscious?

"I'm sorry, Sutton. I wasn't . . . in sending Siri, it wasn't to undermine you or your job. And I certainly didn't think about how it would look regarding your dad either. I'd never disrespect him, Sutton. Please believe that. I'm kind of an arsehole and don't recognize when I'm hurting someone."

"I can't believe you're actually apologizing," she teases as I pull away, needing some distance.

"Yeah, well don't get used to it. I'm feeling bloated this morning, off my game, so you got lucky."

She chuckles and takes a step back to sit on her desk. "So, are you going to help me?"

Why does she have to look so goddamn beautiful in this tiny-as-shit office? It's doing things to me, especially when those ridiculously long eyelashes of hers flutter, pulling back like a curtain to reveal giant pools of blue.

Christ.

When have I ever referred to eyes as *pools of blue*? Not until now, that's for damn sure.

Avoiding her question, because spending more one-on-one time with this woman is terrifying me, I glance around the four walls of her office. No windows, no walking room, and she barely has a functioning light.

"What the hell is this? Did it used to be a . . . a janitor's closet?"

"Yeah. It's the lemony smell that clued you in, isn't it?"

"This is where they stick you? The daughter of the founder? What kind of treatment is that?" Furious, I turn toward the door about to tell Whitney to find Sutton a better place to work when once again, Sutton pulls on my hand.

"Don't."

"You can't work in this space. The fumes alone are horrible."

"They're renovating. It's temporary and not a big deal. I don't want special treatment just because Foster Green is my dad."

"Well, you sure as hell should get special treatment."

She shakes her head. "You, more than anyone, have proven to me I don't deserve respect for being my dad's daughter, Roark. So, no. I also don't deserve special treatment, but thank you for your concern. Now . . . the camp, please?"

Fuck. She's not wrong.

You, more than anyone, have proven to me I don't deserve respect.

I'm such a dick. Keeping her phone, making her follow after me to asinine appointments, telling her she had to stay in the guest room when I should have made sure she got home safely . . . sending Siri to meet with her yesterday . . . And she's not even saying those words in anger. Like I deserve. It's as though she's . . . resigned. And she has a fucking master's degree. *I am such a fuck-up, and she's a much better person than I am.* "Yeah," I sigh, annoyed. Annoyed at myself, not her. There is no more avoiding it.

"And you promise you'll show up to the meetings we agree upon?"

Staring at the floor, I nod. But possibly because that's not good enough for her, she lifts my chin with her delicate fingers and forces me to look her in the eyes. In that moment, I realize this is how it's going to be between us: a demand for honesty, respect, and time. All qualities I've never been able to give to one single human. I've always faltered in at least one category, but the way her eyes fix on me, a startling awareness strikes me: I want to try for her.

"Look at me and tell me yes, that you will dedicate your time to helping me."

Licking my lips, I study her for a beat before I say, "I'll show up."

A beautiful smile plays over her lips as she drops her hands and goes back to her desk, trying to act professionally, but she's terrible at hiding her joy. She flips open her planner and asks, "When?"

I push my hand through my hair. "I don't care. Tonight?" Did I just say that?

Shocked, she shyly smiles. "Tonight works. How about eight?"

"Yeah, that's fine."

"Don't you need to look at your schedule?"

I take a step toward the door. "I'll move things around if there's a conflict." I pause and then say, "Do you want to meet at my place? I can have my chef make something, and we can work."

"Sure, if you're okay with that."

I open her office door. "It'll be easier that way," I answer, even though I know damn well it won't be easier, because the temptation to see what those plump lips can do will be a huge distraction. "Eight. See you then."

I take off before I can hear her response, wondering what I just agreed to.

~

Tumbler in hand, I lean against one of the many windows in my apartment, counting down the seconds until Sutton arrives. Harris has already informed me of her arrival, so now I'm waiting for the elevator to ding.

To say I barely got anything done today would be an understatement. After I left Sutton's office, I went to mine and tried like hell to focus on some contracts that needed another look-over but couldn't concentrate to save my life. All I could think about was how in a matter of twenty-four hours, my life feels as though it's been flipped upside down. I've shown far too much concern for another human being, and it's freaking me the fuck out. I barely show concern for Rath and Bram, so why should I care so much about Sutton?

I'm going to blame it on her dad and the connection we have. *Again.* I can admit that I wish all my clients were like Foster Green. What Sutton said about Gaining Goals was so true. He's genuinely philanthropically minded, and I probably have no clue how much he gives away to charities, but I'm guessing it's a shit load. He *never* publicizes that, and I honestly respect the hell out of the man. And his daughter, who could be a spoiled, rich society brat, who accepts humbly that her fucking desk is in a lemon-smelling closet, is cut from the same cloth. Genuinely selfless. *I'm such a prick in comparison, yet she persisted to chase me to help her.* Fuck, she was willing to do everything herself for the charity, only asking for phone numbers from me. Nice one, asshole. But the anticipation I feel about her arrival stems from my respect for her dad. That has to be it. Nothing else.

I finish off my drink and hop a few times while shaking out my arms. *Come on, you son of a bitch, act like a dick. Act like a dick.* I tap my cheeks a few times, crack my neck from side to side, and think mean thoughts. I can do this.

Forget the sensitive bastard that showed up this morning. You're back to your normal self. If anything, Sutton expects *him* and I can't let her down, not anymore.

The elevator dings and the doors slide open.

I got this.

Sutton takes a step into the room, beaming with a sweet and excited smile, wearing leggings past her belly button and a loose-fitting, off-the-shoulder crop-top sweater that reveals a patch of her stomach as she moves. Jacket in hand, she makes herself at home, resting it along the back of a chair and then making her way into the living room after she takes off her boots.

"Gosh, it's cold out tonight." She removes her hat and swishes her head back and forth, fluffing her long blonde hair.

Fuck.

Fucking hell.

This is not good.

Nope.

She has to go home. That sweater, what the hell was she thinking? Her breasts are shaped like perfect round globes against the fabric, and the black lace of her bra strap is revealed by the wide scoop of the neckline. Getting work done with her wearing that is going to be next to impossible.

And then she turns around.

Christ. I drag my hand over my face.

Her high-waisted leggings mold to her delicious little ass and extend up the small of her back, leaving nothing to my imagination. And not a goddamn panty line in sight. Just perfect.

"What did you say was for dinner again?" she asks, digging in her purse.

You. You're for dinner.

"Uh, no clue. It's in the oven."

She pops her head up, notebook in hand, completely oblivious to how hard she's making me in what I'm sure she considers a "comfy" outfit. To me, she might as well be wearing lingerie. "It smells amazing. Is it ready? I'm starving."

"Yeah, just warming."

"Perfect," she answers with cheer. "Shall we sit at the table to eat and work?"

"We can eat first then work."

"Great. Want me to set the table?"

"Nah." I get my legs to start working and make my way to the kitchen, where I pull out the casserole in the oven and then grab plates and silverware for both of us. "Looks like he made shepherd's pie."

"Oh, isn't that a traditional Irish dish?" She bounces next to me. When the hell did she get there?

"Yeah. Have you had it before?"

"No." As if she lives here, she moves around the kitchen, grabbing a water from the fridge and then holds up a bottle to me. "Would you like one?"

"I have a drink—"

"No booze while we're working." She points her finger at me. Sternly. "I need you coherent."

I divvy up some portions and take the plates and silverware to the table where I set them down. "Sorry to disappoint, but I started drinking before you got here."

With a saunter in her step, she tosses a water bottle at me and flips her hair over her shoulder. "Well then, sober up, we have a lot of things to get through tonight."

When she says shit like that, it makes me want to reach for the bottle even more. Enduring a long night with her in *that* outfit, smelling so incredible, it's going to be pure torture trying to keep my hands to myself.

She takes a seat across from me, folds the napkin I grabbed from one of the drawers over her lap, and holds up her water bottle to me. I reluctantly hold up mine. "To a wonderful partnership."

"You're fucking cheesy." I clink my water bottle with hers, the colliding plastic making a less-than satisfactory sound.

"No, I'm excited. We're going to bring this camp to the next level. I can feel it."

Really? Because all I can feel is my raging boner against the zipper of my jeans.

"Did you mutter something?" she asks, fork halfway to her mouth.

"No."

I've made some really bad decisions in the past week, but inviting Sutton here for dinner before we work has to be the worst idea of them all. Despite the scent of potatoes and beef, I can smell the faint fragrance of lavender, a smell I've come to connect with her now. The way her mouth wraps around her fork . . . hell, I keep envisioning my cock as the utensil feeding her shepherd's pie rather than her fork, and it's fucking with my messed-up brain.

Silence stretches between us as we both make a dent in our dinner. Mine is intentional silence, but Sutton's isn't. She's way too consumed by the taste of her dinner and making little appreciative sounds that she hasn't spoken a word.

"So, what part of Ireland did you live in?"

Small talk, no fucking thank you.

"We can just eat in silence." I stuff a large forkful into my mouth and chew, looking away from her.

"You know, we're going to be working with each other a lot, so it might be nice to know a few fun facts about one another. Don't you think?"

"No."

Chew. Swallow. Chug water.

"How about you tell me three things about you, and I'll do the same. How does that sound?"

"No."

Her fork clanks on the plate, finally pulling my attention away from the very entertaining and vastly interesting wood grain of my hardwood floors. "Do not shut down on me, Roark."

"I'm not shutting down. I'm choosing not to share."

"Why?"

I shrug and then take another bite.

"Roark McCool, tell me three facts about yourself."

I lift a brow from her attempt to be strict. "Do ya really think that's going to work?"

"Yes, I do."

I give her a brief smile before turning back toward my dinner. "It didn't."

She groans, and it sounds sexier than what I think she intended. Either that or my libido is shot through the roof right now and anything she does is going to be sexy—even if she plucked a piece of hair from her head and started flossing beef out of her teeth with it.

"Fine, I'll tell you three things about me."

"Not necessary."

"I got my first period in sixth grade—"

"What?" I cringe. "Why is that a fact you tell people?"

Startling herself, eyes wide, she says, "Honestly, I wasn't expecting to say that. I don't know why I did. But now you know."

"I didn't need to know."

"Consider it a fun fact." She shrugs. "I've only had sex with two guys." She slaps her hand over her mouth, looking absolutely mortified. A fit of pure rage starts to climb up my spine as I think about the two possible guys who had sex with her. "Oh God, I really don't know why I said that. I'm nervous and when I'm nervous, I say the first thing that comes to mind."

Controlling myself, I nod, not wanting to dive into the whole sex thing, because there are too many questions rolling around in my head. Way too many things I want answered like: did they make her come on their tongues? Did they worship her perfect breasts for hours on end? Did they appreciate the little moans I know flow past her lips when she's turned on . . .

"That was so unprofessional of me. Here I am, scolding you for being unprofessional and then the first meeting we have I'm telling you about my period and my sex life, well, lack thereof. It's been a while since I've been with a penis. Or a good penis. Not that you need to know that. You don't." She bites her bottom lip. "It was small, the last one, really, really small, and I know it's not about the size, but I feel like it barely went inside me—"

"Stop."

She nods. "Okay."

We both turn back to our food, my mind whirling with her oversharing.

Small penis.

Been a while.

Lack of sex life.

Fucking hell, my arms are itching to swipe this table clean, toss her up on it, and show her exactly the man I am: greedy with an appetite.

"What are you thinking?" She presses her hand against her forehead. "I'm so embarrassed right now. I can't sit here in silence." Clearly. "Just tell me what you're thinking."

I chew on my dinner and grind out, "You don't want to know."

"Yes, I do. Anything to get my mind off this embarrassment."

I cut a sharp look in her direction and say, "You. Don't. Want. To. Know."

"Oh," she shies away. "Okay."

More silence.

If she's wearing underwear, what kind is it? Thong? G-string?

Lace to match her bra? What does her ass feel like? Firm? Our conversation about anal play jumps to the forefront of my mind. God, she's never done it before. Would she like it? Even if it was just a little bit or probing, would she like it?

"Your jaw is clenched really tight. Are you okay?"

No, I'm not fucking okay. I'm hard as a rock with no promise of release for at least a few hours.

"Fine."

"You don't seem fine. There is a vein in your forehead that's starting to look scary. Are you tense? Do I make you tense?" She leans forward, her sweater dropping so I get the perfect view of her tits encased in her black lace bra.

Son of a bitch.

I push away from the table, startling her, and head straight for the bar where I hide behind the counter and pour myself two fingers of whiskey.

"Hey, what did I say about drinking?"

"I need some."

"Really? You can't wait that—"

"Sutton, just shut the fuck up for two goddamn seconds. Okay?" I grip the back of my neck, pulling on it hard, trying to ease the heavy flow of blood heading straight to my cock.

This has never happened to me. I've been horny many times, and I've wanted plenty of women, but nothing like right now. Nothing so intense that I feel like I'm going to burst out of my own skin with need. And I don't know if it's because she's off limits, or if it's the innocence dancing around her, but with every word that drips from her lips and every flick of her smooth little fingers, I want her more and more.

"Don't be mean, Roark. Please."

She goes to stand, but I point my finger at her sternly. "Do not get out of that chair."

"Why are you being a jerk right now?"

"Because . . ." I yell, losing all sense of control. It's the sweater.

That goddamn perfectly appealing sweater that shapes every sexy piece of her chest.

"Because why?"

"Because, Sutton, I've never wanted to fuck someone as bad as I want to fuck you," I shout. "You wanted a fact about me, well there you go. I think you're fine as fuck, and if I'm moody with you it's because I want you."

Her mouth drops open and her eyes widen, complete and utter shock crosses her face. "You want to have sex with me?"

"I want to fuck you."

"Oh."

She looks away and goes to say something but doesn't.

"It's not going to happen," I add, seeing how her mind is already starting to race. "So get that out of your head."

"It's not?" She shakes her head, as if realizing what she just asked. "I mean, it's not. We're colleagues."

"And you're eight years younger than I am and my client's daughter and frankly, I think you'd be a clinger."

Her eyes narrow as she puffs out her chest. "I would *not* be a clinger. I'm not a virgin."

"Yeah, got that from one of your fun factoids." There is a good fifteen feet between us, and I want to keep it that way so I stay behind the bar. "But from the sounds of your uninspired and lackluster descriptions, you've never experienced good fucking."

"I know about sex," she says.

"But have you ever come?"

"Yes."

"With a man?"

She looks to the side. *Bingo*.

"That's what I thought. After I fucked you, I'm one hundred percent sure you'd be a clinger."

"You're awfully full of yourself." She folds her arms over her ample chest, propping her boobs up, enticing me. "How do you even know you could get me off?"

I give her a once-over. "Trust me. I know."

Clearly irritated with my confidence, she turns back to her food, huffing in the process and stabbing the meat with her fork. I inwardly cringe, hoping she's not envisioning me in her brutal attack on the shepherd's pie.

This might sound a little dickish, but I believe in what I said. She would be a clinger . . . or she would fall in love. Fuck. No. Where Sutton is involved, there is no casual. She's not the kind of girl who can have a one-night stand and then move on with life. She's way too sweet with her heart on her sleeve. No way, not going there, no matter how much her ass in those leggings begs for it.

Wanting to cut the growing tension since we still have to work together, I clear my throat. "So, you only told me two facts, what's the last one?"

She glances up in my direction, anger laced in her pupils. Good, let her be angry. Anger is so much better than happy to see me.

Mulling it over, she takes a few seconds before she answers, but when she does, it packs one hell of a punch. "My third fact? Easy . . . my bra size is 34D."

Sharply, she smiles at me and then turns back to her food.

Touché.

Yup, she's a 34D. I'm confirming it for the twentieth time tonight. Every time she bends over to write something in her notepad on the coffee table, I look down her sweater.

It's a great view that's kept me hard the entire time we've been talking about the camp. I can't tell you anything about what we've been planning, as my mind has been anywhere but on helping children. Instead, it's been on the way she licks her lips every few minutes, or the way she poises her pen at her mouth when she thinks, or how she lights up when she gets an idea.

And . . . her tits.

I've been obsessed with the things ever since I ran into her.

Now that I know a little more about them, I want to become well-acquainted best friends. I've never been best friends with breasts before, but I'm open to the idea.

"Are you paying attention?" she snaps at me, pulling my gaze away from her chest.

"What? Yup." I scratch the side of my jaw. "You were talking about equipment."

"I was talking about dietary restrictions."

"Same thing." I shrug.

"It's not the same thing." She sighs in exasperation. "Roark, I need you to focus."

I lean back on the couch. "There is no focusing when you're wearing that sweater. It's billowing all over the place. Why did you wear that?"

She glances at her sweater and actually seems shocked I have a problem with it. "It's comfortable."

"It's a goddamn scarf." I lift from my seat on the couch and go to my bedroom where I pull out a long-sleeved T-shirt and take it to her. I toss it on her lap and say, "Change into that. We'll get more done."

"I'm not going to change my shirt because you're horny and frustrated by my *tits,* as you so elegantly called them."

I'm not going to deny her assessment of me so I just shrug and say, "Fine, good luck."

I drape my arm over the back of the couch and get comfortable. I won't blatantly stare at her chest, but I know I'm going to grab another peek in about a minute, because the need to look at them has become like clockwork for my eyes tonight.

She starts rattling off about something and, as expected, she bends forward giving me a great view of the swell of her breasts. I sigh in happiness. There they are again.

"Are you seriously looking down my shirt again, after I called you horny?"

"It's what horny men do, they look down shirts, especially after you reveal bra sizes. I'm just verifying."

She groans and huffs and in seconds pulls her sweater up and over her head. My mouth falls open as I watch the black lace bra barely contain her tits. They jiggle around with her movements, almost revealing nipple, and as she struggles to unfold my shirt, I beg for her bra to bust open right then and there. But there's no use. God hates me, and before I can truly commit the sight in front of me to memory, she's pulling my shirt over her head. The sleeves are entirely too long so she starts to fold them up, and the shoulders hang off her in a cute way.

Damn it.

That was supposed to help.

Once she's done fixing the sleeves, she folds her hands on her lap and looks me square in the eyes. "I'm asking for an hour. Can you focus for that long?"

Shifting in my seat, I sit up and clasp my hands together. "Yeah."

She shakes her head and sarcastically says, "Wow, you brave, brave man."

I'll give it to her. She has her dad's wit, which is a problem. Because I really like her dad.

An hour turned into two, making it midnight by the time we finished. Without any alcohol in my system, thanks to the water bottles Sutton kept throwing in my direction and making me drink, I'm completely sober and tired as shit.

I don't think I've felt this level of exhaustion in a really long time, probably because my job at night is to stop myself from feeling anything. Apparently, I've been doing a good job.

After packing her bag, Sutton heads toward the elevator until I stop her. "Where are you going?"

"Home." She glances at the shirt and says, "Oh . . . sorry." She sets her things on the ground and, once again, takes her shirt off in front of me, affording me the best view of the night, then puts that damn sweater back on. "Here." She holds out the shirt.

"I don't care about the damn shirt, you're not going home."

She exhales. "I can't spend the night every time it's late, Roark. I need to grow up at some point."

I take her hand and pull her toward the guest room. "It's not about growing up." I slip my fingers through hers, reveling in the sensation for a moment and maneuver her into the doorway of the guest bedroom. "It's about being safe."

"Plenty of single women walk around the city at night."

"Yeah, well, I'm not taking my chances."

What I wouldn't give to fucking reach out and press my hand to her cheek, feel how soft her skin is, to see if she falls into my touch.

Sheepishly she smiles, our hands still tangled together as she pats her bag. "I brought clothes just in case we went late."

I bite my bottom lip, my control starting to slip as I watch how cute her coyness is. She's trouble, big fucking trouble, and I need to stay as far away as possible. I take a step back, but her hand holds on tight to mine.

When I look at our connection, her voice pulls me back to her eyes. "Thank you for tonight, Roark. Even if we started off a little rocky, we got a lot done."

"Yeah, sure."

She takes a step forward and I swear to Christ Himself, my heart unexpectedly flips in my chest. Leaning forward on her toes, she presses a sweet but chaste kiss across my cheek then pulls away.

Smiling up at me, a lock of her blonde hair falling over one eye, she says, "Have a good night." And then she retreats into her room, shutting the door softly.

Raking my hand through my hair, I press my lips firmly together and force myself to walk away even as her lavender scent sticks to me. I'm going to need a neutral zone next time we get together. Having dinner at my place is no longer an option. Not when everything about her tempts me. *I lied when I said I'm not into her the other day to Bram and Rath—obvious, I know.*

Reluctantly, I make it to my room, get ready for bed, strip down, and slip under my covers, my cock still rock hard from the entire night. Nah, it's from not having sex for . . . fucking weeks. *How the fuck did that happen?* It's all her fault, and there is only one way to fix this problem. I glide my hand down to the base of my pulsing erection and squeeze tightly.

"Fuck," I groan, my eyes squeezing shut. I've waited all goddamn night for this.

My hand moves up my cock only to drop back down as my phone beeps next to me on the nightstand. I pause, my head lulling to the side to see if it's Sutton. When her name pops up on the screen, I consider ignoring it, but then again, what if she needs something? Damn it.

I reach over and pick up the phone.

Sutton: *Are you . . . touching yourself right now?*

Christ. Of all people, I did not expect Sutton to ask *that*. I groan, and one-handedly type out a response as my hand goes back to my erection.

Roark: *What do you think?*

She responds right away. Is she . . . is she touching herself as well? Was tonight as torturous to her as it was to me? Probably not, because I wasn't the one bouncing around in a peek-a-boo sweater.

Sutton: *I think you are.*
Roark: *You know me well.*
Sutton: *Are you thinking about me?*
Roark: *Bold question.*
Sutton: *I'm feeling a little bold tonight.*

I hope to God not too bold, because if she comes into my room, there will be no stopping myself.

Roark: *Yeah, I'm thinking about you.*

I pull on my cock, a long exhale escaping me as I watch the dots bounce on the screen, waiting her reply.

Sutton: *Am I naked?*
She is now . . .
Roark: *Yeah.*
Sutton: *What do you see?*

Is she for real right now? What happened to the sweet and innocent girl? I never would have expected something like this to come from Sutton, never in a million years.

Roark: *Are you digging for compliments?*
Sutton: *I want to know what you see when you think about me.*
Roark: *This is dangerous, Sutton.*
Sutton: *Just tell me.*

Hell. I release my cock and use two hands to type, making it faster.

Roark: *You're naked on my bed, your porcelain skin a brilliant contrast against my black comforter. Your hair is fanned out, lips parted, nipples hard as pebbles, legs spread, and your pussy's wet and ready for me. You're writhing beneath me as I drive my cock deep inside of you. And in the distance, I can hear your soft cries of pleasure as I make you come over and over again.*

I toss my phone to the side and grip my cock tighter, the picture I painted so vivid in my mind that I forget about texting and focus on the pleasure ripping through my body. Chest rapidly moving up and down, my teeth grinding together, I feel my blood pooling at the base of my cock, my orgasm seconds away . . . when there is a knock at my door.

I still, wondering if I imagined the sound. "Roark?"

"Sutton," I breathe out heavily. "Go back to your goddamn room."

The door creaks open and in seconds I'm flying out of bed, nabbing a discarded shirt from the ground to cover my junk as she peers around the door, wearing *only* the shirt I let her borrow. Her eyes widen when she sees me, dropping right to my crotch and then back up. Thank God I have the shirt covering me up or else she'd be getting quite the show.

"Leave, Sutton."

She takes another step forward, my resolve seconds from snapping as she reaches out for my hand. I let her take it because I'm a fool. She pulls me closer, and the only thing blocking her view of my hard-on is a black T-shirt. Her fingers dance up my arm to my shoulder. I squeeze my eyes shut as she lightly explores my chest, her nails scraping along my skin and over my nipple.

I suck in a sharp breath and quickly pin her against the wall, her wandering hand above her head as I stare at her.

"What are you doing?"

"Exploring," she answers unabashedly. "You said you were thinking about me. Why not have the real thing?"

My cock jumps at the thought. I could easily take her right now. Toss her on the bed, spread her legs, and have my wicked way with her. Even though my body is humming for that to happen, my head is telling me no.

"You know I can't have the real thing." Unlocking her hand from the wall, I cup her cheek and slowly rub my thumb across her skin. *So soft.* "I can't."

Her hopeful eyes dim. "Why not?"

"You know why not."

"But you want me?" I nod, unable to voice my need. "Okay then." She lets out a sigh. "That's always nice to hear." With a sad smile, she walks to the door, and I feel like a giant asshole.

"I'm sorry, Sutton."

"I know, me too."

CHAPTER TEN

Dear Winston,
    Saw the evil wench today. She told me I still have a lot of inner rage. More like pent-up frustration. It's like someone has put a cork up my pee-hole and told me I'm not allowed to come. Maybe an overreaction since I've jacked-off twice a day, every day this week. But when I'm around Sutton, which is a lot, it feels like I'm blocked up, and the pressure keeps building and building until I get fucking mad.

And for some unknown reason, I can't seem to find my way to any nightclubs. They don't interest me. Instead, I stay at home, tumbler in hand, watching some irrelevant show on TV while I text Sutton.

I'm not a texter. I've never been a texter, but good Christ, when I see her name pop up on my phone, I get . . . fuck, I get giddy.

What's that shit about?

I shouldn't be that excited to receive a text, especially since what we talk about isn't even of importance. There are a few texts here and there about the camp, but the majority of our texts are her talking about something positive, and me being a dick about it.

Anyway, when the therapist—can't remember her name to save my life, but who cares—asked me if there were any new developments in my life, I almost said, "There's this girl." But thank fuck, I caught myself. That would have been opening a can of worms I wasn't ready for. So, you're the one who gets to hear about it.

There ya go, Winny.

Roark

ROARK

"There's my man," Foster says, walking up to me with an open hand. I clasp it just before he pulls me into a hug. "How's it going?"

"Ya know." I chuckle, trying to hide the panic in my eyes. Has Sutton talked to him? Has she told him anything about us? Not that there is an *us*, but has she said anything? You know, something incriminating like *I saw your agent's ass*, or *your agent told me he wants to fuck me*, or *your agent can't stop staring at my tits when we're working.*

Why didn't I check with her beforehand?

Because then it would seem like we're hiding something and believe me, we're not hiding anything. If we were hiding something, my dick would know about it.

We both take a seat at the table I was trying to work at while waiting for Foster but didn't get much done besides one pass through a contract.

I point to the glass on the table and say, "Already ordered your steak, and it should be ready shortly."

He picks up his iced tea and takes a sip. "You're full service, aren't you?"

"Only for the divas," I say, garnering a chuckle from Foster.

"I can be more of a diva if you want."

"Nah, that's okay."

Leaning back in his chair, he says, "So how's therapy?"

Great, it's going to be one of *those* meetings.

"Fantastic," I answer with a smile and a tip of my water glass. Yeah, water, and not because Sutton thinks I shouldn't drink during business but because Foster would probably lecture me, and I'm not in the mood for a lecture right now. Or ever, really. *And why do I care that both Greens are lecturing me about drinking . . . Fuck.*

He considers my answer and then says, "That sounds an awful lot like sarcasm."

Nailed it; nothing gets past him. If it was written in a text by Sutton, my answer would've been put in asterisks.

"Some people are meant for therapy, some aren't. I'm not a touchy-feely guy, so sitting through that hour of madness feels like pure torture to me."

"Being open and expressive of your feelings is not a bad thing, you know. Doesn't make you any less of a man."

"I noticed that the day you bawled in front of the press when you said this next year would be your last. You could barely get two words out of your mouth."

He smirks. "I'm an emotional man and hey, it landed me that sponsorship with Kleenex." He knowingly points his finger at me.

"True, can't forget that golden opportunity."

"It's more amusing than anything. Fans love it."

I sip my water, hating that it doesn't burn as it makes its way down my throat. "You know, I did hear the new requirement fans are looking for in a quarterback is ultra-sensitive and cries on camera."

"It's why the Steel have kept me on for so long; they love a guy who can please the fans."

We both chuckle and I begin to level with him, knowing fully well he's going to grow serious in the next minute, so might as well cut him to the chase. "I write in the diary every day."

"You do? I thought you would have enjoyed the therapy sessions over the diary."

I shake my head. "The diary is personal. I keep that to myself. The therapy sessions feel like I'm forcibly cutting myself raw for the therapist to judge. I hate that. Hate every second of it actually."

"That makes sense. You've always been a private man."

"If you ask, I'll tell you, but I'm not about to hand out information like it's a cookie at Christmas."

"I can respect that." He lets out a long breath. "As long as you're making progress, that's all I care about. You're like a son to me, Roark, a son who makes me a lot of money." We laugh. "I want to make sure you're okay."

You're like a son to me.

Except I know that in Foster's mind, it's a positive thing. Unlike my pa who considers me a fuckwit and wants nothing to do with me.

"I appreciate that, Foster."

He looks around and puts both hands on the armrests of his chair. "Not to spoil the intimacy of this conversation, but is there a bathroom nearby?"

I point behind us. "Down the hall on the right."

"Thanks." He takes off, and I pull my phone from my pocket to keep myself busy. And then I smile.

Sutton: *Did you email Brock, Freddie, and Carmichael?*
Roark: *Always working.*
Sutton: *Someone has to. So did you?*
Roark: *Who says I'm not working right now?*
Sutton: *Are you?*
Roark: *At a lunch meeting.*
Sutton: *And you're texting me . . .*
Roark: *Cut the sass, he's in the bathroom. I multitask.*
Sutton: *A modern man you are. So did you email them?*
Roark: *If I didn't?*
Sutton: *Roark! I asked you nicely.*
Roark: *And I asked you for a picture of your tits, and I didn't get that.*
Sutton: *You could have had my *tits* a week ago.*
Roark: *I liked it better when you weren't so sassy.*
Sutton: *Lies. Now please email them!*
Roark: *Already did, lass.*
Sutton: *Why, why do you torture me?*

Roark: *Because it's easy.*

"Look at that smile on your face," Foster says, coming up from behind and startling the ever-living crap out of me.

"Christ." I chuckle. "Didn't know the prostate was working that well on ya, old man. Fast pee-er."

"I might have some salt in my hair, but everything is still fully functioning." He points at my phone. "I know that smile. It's the smile of a man who's smitten. Who's the girl?"

And an actual bead of sweat forms on my back and rolls down my spine in the span of a second.

First of all, I'm not fucking smitten, never have been, and never will be. Second, there is no way in hell I'm telling Foster I'm texting his daughter, so I come up with a lie.

"No girl. Just something one of my friends sent me. Idiot shit."

"Ah." He nods. "Seemed like you were really into that text."

I shrug, unable to respond. *Was I into the text?* I mean, maybe, I don't really remember anything over the last few minutes. Sutton wrote the word tits. So, naturally, I'm thinking of hers. Surprised I can form words...

Trying to move on, I say, "Sutton has a real hold on the camp. She's organized. Kind of whipped my arse into shape."

Agreeing with a nod, he sips his water. "She's very good at what she does and part of the reason she's so good is because she truly cares. She always has. She's the reason I still have the foundation, because she pushed me to keep bringing joy to others even during the tough times."

"I can see how that's a huge factor."

"Have you discussed when you're going to Texas?"

"Uh, what?" I ask, lending my ear closer, trying to see if I heard him right.

"Texas. You have to be there for the camp."

"Oh yeah, I knew that. Probably just the day before and then leave after it's over."

Foster's brow creases. "You're only going down for five days? Does Sutton know that?"

"I have no clue. We haven't talked about it."

The waitress brings our food, interrupting whatever Foster was going to say. Both our steaks look well prepared, as well as the accompanying salads I ordered for both of us. Once she leaves, Foster turns back to me as he starts to cut up his steak. "We'll need you down there for at least two weeks."

"What?" I say, practically choking on my own saliva. "Two weeks? Why?"

"There's camp prep, camp, and post-camp. We need you for all the days. It's hands-on, and helping out with that will give you the last of the community service hours you need."

"Two weeks? I don't know, Foster. I have clients—"

"Who will understand that you need to work remotely. Not all of them live in New York, so they're used to not having you at their beck and call. We have Internet and phone on the ranch, so you'll still be able to work. We're going to need those hands of yours to get everything ready."

Why do I picture Foster greeting me at his doorstep with a lasso in hand and cowboy boots on loan for me?

"I'll have to check my schedule," I say, trying to avoid two weeks in Texas.

"I have a feeling it'll be clear," Foster says with conviction.

Hell. Someone is going to get a call.

"You finally decided to call me back," I say, lying on my bed, completely naked and watching an animal documentary about polar bears on Netflix. Noting the *absence* of whiskey. "Took you long enough."

Sutton chuckles softly. "Long day at the office. I figured whatever you had to tell me wasn't that important or you would have texted me."

"I could have been dying."

"Well, next time, if you're dying, let me know your last wishes so I won't feel bad about not calling you."

"Harsh but fair."

Her sweet laugh echoes through the phone. "What do you want, Roark?"

"Did your dad happen to tell you we had dinner tonight?"

She pauses and then says, "No. Oh God, did you tell him I tried to have sex with you?"

"I'm a dick, Sutton, but not that big of a dick." I actually haven't told anyone, besides my giddy diary.

"Oh, thank God." She exhales. "That would have been so embarrassing. If you did, I would have told him you were the one who showed me your ass first."

"You keep bringing that up. Is the image of my arse engrained in your brain?"

"It is," she answers honestly. "It was a nice ass."

"Was? Is it not a nice arse anymore?"

"Eh, it's all right now."

"Liar." I chuckle.

"Enough about your butt. Tell me what you talked to my dad about."

I prop my hand behind my head. "Your dad told me something today that I think you've neglected to inform me of."

"Oh no, did he tell you about Texas?"

"Bingo," I answer, playfulness in my voice. "When were you going to tell me about that?"

"I was working you up to it. You don't seem like someone who can kick it out in the countryside of Texas."

"Yeah, not so much. I prefer the city."

"Fresh air won't kill you."

"You know the kind of fresh air I enjoy," I counter.

An irritated groan falls from her lips. "You're not smoking still, are you? That's so bad for you, Roark."

"Do you know what's bad for me? You."

"Me?" she asks, and hell I wish I could see her face. I love the expression she makes when I shock her.

"Yeah, you."

"How am I bad for you?"

I press my fingers into my scalp, giving my head a little massage as I speak. "You're trying to eliminate all my vices. It's not good for me, and it's ruining my image."

"Oh," she answers softly. "You don't have to smoke and drink to maintain your image, you know."

"And how else do you expect people to think I'm a bad boy without a whiskey in one hand and a cigarette in the other?"

"You don't need accessories to be a bad boy, Roark, it's all about the attitude."

"Attitude isn't everything, lass. I prefer my accessories, as you put it."

"Your accessories are going to lead you to an early death."

"Might as well live life now then," I counter. "Send me a picture of your tits, so I can start living life right now."

"You're relentless. Not that I don't trust you, but I would never send a picture of my bare breasts to anyone especially since I'm Foster Green's daughter. If that ends up in the wrong hands I could ruin everything my dad built."

"I'll be very careful with it."

"No. Never going to happen, but if you want to see them in real life, I can make that happen."

"No." I copy her answer, even though my cock is hardening from the thought.

"Your loss. Anyway, back to Texas."

Dick hard, I hold back the irritated groan bubbling up in my throat. "Two weeks in Texas is not going to happen."

"It is. Sorry, but we need you for two weeks, plus my dad is going to want to give you the full ranch experience."

Twisting my lips to the side, trying to envision myself in a country atmosphere, I ask, "What exactly is the full ranch experience?"

"You know . . ." She mutters something I can't quite understand.

"Can you repeat that?"

She mutters again and all I can make out is horse.

"Uh, what about a horse?"

She yawns loudly. "I'm tired. I really should get to bed. Unless there's anything else you need. I'm going to get going."

"Yeah, I want to know about this horse," I press, wild thoughts forming in my head.

"So, nothing else? Okay. Well, thanks for emailing the guys. Let me know what they say when you find out. Night, Roark."

"Wait—" But she hangs up before I can get another word in. *Vixen.*

Damn it. Her avoidance makes me nervous. I'm not much of a horse man. I've never ridden one, and I don't plan on straddling the back of one at any point in time.

Not even to see a great pair of tits.

~

"What about this one? How do my eyes look while holding it near my face?"

"What do your eyes have to do with a diamond?" I ask Bram, who dragged me along for ring shopping. "Your eyes are going to be bloodshot from crying anyway."

"I'm not going to cry." Before I can counter his statement, he laughs and shakes his head. "Who am I kidding? I'm going to be a bawling mess. Do you think she's going to say yes?"

"Don't ask stupid questions." I pick up a ruby ring and hold it out to him. "If you're looking for something to match your eyes on that day, this one will be perfect."

Bram eyes the ring and then glances at me. "This is an important day for me. Can you not be a sarcastic asshole for a second?"

I set the ring down. "If you wanted someone to help, you should have asked Rath. He is Julia's brother, after all."

"And that's why I couldn't ask him. I wanted to be able to find this on my own."

"Then why the fuck are you asking for my opinion if you want to do this on your own?"

"For confirmation," he answers, holding up a ring to the light.

"Still not doing it on your own."

Frustrated, he lowers the ring and gives me a once-over. "Why are you being a bastard right now? Have you not gotten any ass lately? Whenever you get like this, impossible to be around, it's because you're hard up. Is that the problem?"

God, yes.

"No."

"Is it?" And then he pauses, a slow grin playing at his lips. "Oh hell, is it that girl?"

I push off the glass counter and start walking toward the door. I'm not getting into this with Bram because he's going to make it a huge deal when it's not, and I don't feel like standing around while his happy heart lights up with excitement.

"Send me a pic when you find the ring."

"Hold up." Bram quickly stands and gets in front of me, hand to chest. "You're not leaving. You can't leave. I need help."

"You don't need help. You know Julia better than anyone. You're the only one who could pick out the perfect ring."

"I know, but now I want to hear about your girl problems."

"I don't have girl problems. You're about to have girl problems if you don't move the fuck out of my way."

Not even the slightest bit scared, Bram says, "What's her name again? Sally?"

"Move."

"Wait, no, it isn't Sally. It's Sara, right?"

"Bram . . ."

Snapping his fingers, he says, "No, it's Sassafras. That's right."

"Sutton, you *fucking* moron."

And I know it was exactly what he was looking for, but Christ, I didn't want him thinking her name was Sassafras.

"Ah, yes, good old Sutton. How is she?"

"She's a lot better than how you're about to be."

Out of the blue, Bram taps my cheek and then the other, but a little harder. I move away just as he gets in one more swat.

"What the hell are you doing?"

"Waking you up to your feelings. Is that black soul coming alive?" He reaches for me again but I shove his hand away.

My fist clenches at my side. *He's your best friend; do not punch him. You've made it over ten years without ever shoving your fist down his throat. Now is not the time.*

"Don't fucking touch me again or you're not going to like what happens."

Bram rolls his eyes. "Dude, wake up and see how you're reacting. You clearly like the girl. Why are you torturing everyone with your surly attitude?"

"Because torturing people is what I do best," I answer and sidestep him so I can reach the door. "Get the six-carat bezel set halo ring, you know she'll love it."

"It's over three hundred thousand dollars."

I glance over my shoulder. "Good thing you're a rich motherfucker."

The door closes behind me and the bright sun hits me first, a rarity in New York City. Usually it's blocked by all the tall buildings. I shield my eyes and flag down a taxi. The boys think I'm crazy for taking public transportation, but I'd rather not have a guy wait around for me in a car when I can easily flag someone down and be on the move. I'll use a driver on occasion, but everyday life is me in a taxi.

I sink low into the seat after giving him my cross-streets and look out the window as Bram's words bounce around in my head.

Is your black soul coming alive?

I normally wouldn't give Bram's mush much thought, but I don't know if my black soul wants to be resurrected. Yet it sure as hell has found a small heartbeat.

I've woken up at six the past few days, worked out, and eaten a non-liquid breakfast—and I'm just as shocked as you are.

Look what a decent night sleep will bring you—responsibility. But I don't think I like it. I don't like being *that* guy. You know, the one who reads the paper in the morning after a perfect execution of his morning routine. They're boring. I like the unpredictability of waking up at some weird hour and trying to squeeze in everything I have to do before taking meetings.

I'll admit, I have been able to work through some contracts early in the morning and maybe type up some winning emails that have brought in a shit-ton of money for my clients and me.

But still, I don't even recognize myself when I look in the mirror. There aren't heavy bags under my eyes, nor are my eyes bloodshot. I don't have a decent smoker's cough in the morning, and instead of Baileys as a "creamer" in my coffee, I drink it black, with a splash of sugar, because why the hell not?

What is happening to me? Next thing I know I'll be wearing a tie and waving to people on the street as I pass them, newspaper tucked under my arm with a sunny disposition on my face.

I don't like it.

But I also kind of do.

Fuck.

Sitting in my office, I look at the skyline and consider all the sorry motherfuckers like me who have a morning routine. They're dignified, well-established men, each with a good head on his shoulders. I catch my reflection in the window . . . is that me?

I really did lose my bad-boy accessories. Now I'm just a—Christ, I'm like Rath, a ruthless businessman.

Ah, hell.

I press my hand to my forehead, a small smile peeking past my lips. Who would have thought I'd ever be like Rath? At least I still have my sarcasm, thank fuck for that.

My phone buzzes next to me.

An international number pops up, which can only mean one thing: it's my shitty mother. By now, you'd think I'd ignore the phone call and not pick up, but if I did that, she'd keep calling and calling and calling; it's her way of getting what she wants.

Grinding my teeth together, I take a deep breath and answer. "Hello?"

"Aye, there's me boy," she answers, her voice sloshed, her words slurring. Apple doesn't fall far from the tree in my family.

"Hey Ma, what's up?" I try to keep the annoyed tone out of my voice, preparing myself for the reason she's calling, the only reason she's calling. This phone call comes about once a month, and if I'm really *lucky*, twice.

Looks like we're going for round two this month.

"Roark, when are you going to come back home? When are you going to stop abandoning your family?"

Oh wow, she's going to jump right into it this go-around.

I drag my hand over my face. "How much do you want?"

"Don't you talk to me like that, using that annoyed tone. I'm not the one who left me family with nothing but a few potatoes in the field that your father can't even harvest himself because of his disability."

His "disability", as she incorrectly puts it, is alcoholism.

"If you were here, we wouldn't be famished, poor, and dealing with a leaky roof. You abandoned your family."

Same story every time.

Same guilt trip.

Same hatred in her voice . . . for her own son.

"You left your roots for a high-rise."

"I know, Ma. You remind me every goddamn month."

"Don't you dare use God's name in vain, like that. I taught ya better." She taught me nothing besides how to take down a Guinness bomb without throwing up after. "At least I thought I did, but it seems like I didn't make a lasting impression." The tears start to form, and I let out a long sigh. "What did I do to deserve this treatment from you? You never come home, you don't love us. Your father is sick and needs you, Roark."

He only *wants* my checkbook. He *needs* to support his bad habits.

"I have a meeting, Ma. I have to go."

A loud sob escapes her. "You've always been ungrateful for everything I've given ya. At this point it would be easier if you were dead. At least I could mourn the loss of my oldest son and move on, rather than being taunted constantly, knowing you're in America, living a posh life while your family can barely afford food for the table. Before you lived in that high-rise, you lived in this stone house."

I count to three, but it still doesn't work. My skin itches, my anger starts to boil, as my mom presses every one of my buttons, and a dark cloud starts to move in over my head.

Teeth grinding together, there is a grit to my voice when I speak. "I'm sorry I'm such a disappointment to you, Ma."

"I just wish ya showed more care for us, for the people who've always been there for ya."

"Right. And?" I ask, wanting this to be over.

"Can you send us some money?"

Squeezing my eyes shut, I shake my head, knowing exactly what my night is going to entail.

CHAPTER ELEVEN

D*ear I Don't Give a Fuck,*
 All they ever want from me is money.
They don't care about how I earned that money, how I'm faring, or the name I've made for myself. All they care about is the green in my pockets and how quickly I can get it wired to them.
I dread the monthly phone call. I know it's coming, and I dread it.
It's a sharp reminder that even though it may seem like I have family, I really am alone in this world.
Bram says I have a black soul, well there's a goddamn reason for it.
Bottoms up.
Roark

∼

SUTTON

B*ang. Bang. Bang.*
 I shoot up from my bed, scaring the crap out of Louise, who runs in midair and flees under the bed. Blanket clutched to my chest, heart pounding, I look toward the door. Was that a knock on my door? Or a neighbor's?

What time is it?

Pitch-black, I light up my phone to see a bunch of unanswered text messages and the time. Three o'clock.

Bang. Scratch. Scratch.

I turn my head toward the door. That's definitely coming from mine. Heart rate picking up even more, I weigh my options. No one I know would be up this late, so it might be a drunk neighbor who has gotten lost in our little brownstone building. That has happened before. Instead of getting up to answer the door—I'm not the girl who gets killed off first in a horror movie—I bring my knees to my chest and open my text messages, all from Roark.

Oh no. My eyes are slightly blurry from my abrupt wake up, but I can still make them out.

Roark: *Hi.*

Roark: *What are ya doin?*

Roark: *Sleeping? Of course you're sleeping. Like an ostrich, right?*

What is he talking about?

Roark: *Kind of wish you were sleeping in my apartment. I like when you sleep there.*

Roark: *Are you wearing my shirt?*

I glance down and bite on my bottom lip. Yeah, I am and I haven't washed it, because I like the way it smells . . . like him.

Roark: *If you were wearing my shirt, I would slip my hand up your thigh to see what kind of underwear you're wearing.*

Roark: *It's a thong, right?*

Roark: *Fuck, I want to see you in a thong so damn bad. On my lap, I want you on my lap.*

My face heats up just as there is another scratch on my door and then . . . a voice.

Heart pounding against my chest, I set down my phone and walk to my door as quietly as I can, tiptoeing against the hardwood floors. I press my hands against the wooden door and peek through the peephole and hold my breath. That's when I see Roark, leaning, his head lightly knocking against the door.

How on earth does he know where I live?

And why is he here?

"Sutton," he whispers, just as another scratch hits the door. "Open up."

"Roark?" I ask through the door, causing him to rear. He sways back and forth then lifts his hand as a welcome.

He's completely wasted.

Oh, Roark. I sigh and unlock my door, opening it just wide enough to fit my body in the entrance. Despite his obvious state of inebriation, my body can't help but react to him. I take him in—black jeans, black shoes, black long-sleeved shirt, no jacket, and his hair perfectly styled on the top of his head. He looks absolutely delicious with his shirt clinging to his muscles and his jeans riding low on his hips. Dark and broody with a hint of sensitivity under that searing gaze, he's all trouble, and I want to be a part of it.

He takes a step forward and puts a hand against the doorjamb of my apartment, his eyes scanning my bare legs and braless chest. "Hey," he says softly. "Did I wake you?"

I chuckle. "Yeah. It's three in the morning."

"Is it?" he asks, and I get a whiff of the whiskey on his breath.

I nod and fold my arms across my chest while leaning against the wall. "It is and you have me wondering how you know where I live."

He smiles wickedly at me, and the mischief in his expression tempts and teases me. "I have my ways." Hands in his pockets, he rocks on his heels and nods toward my apartment. "Can I come in?"

"You're drunk."

"I know."

"This isn't a booty call."

His brow frowns. "You'd never be a booty call to me, Sutton."

God, it melts my heart when he says things like that. I should tell him to go home, but my body reacts differently as I step aside and let him in. When he starts to pass me, he reaches out and takes my hand in his, clutching tightly as he walks through the threshold of my apartment. It's nothing compared to his. It's two rooms—living space and bathroom—but it's perfect for me. All I need.

I flip the nightstand light on, providing some light to the space as Roark looks around. He doesn't say anything, just observes. What's he thinking? Is he even thinking about anything? He's a pretty lucid drunk, even when he's wobbly in the legs.

Finally, he turns toward me and asks, "Can I use your bathroom and toothbrush?"

"Bathroom, yes, toothbrush, no. I have a spare under the sink though. Toothpaste is in the medicine cabinet."

"Thanks, lass." He glances around and asks, "Uh, is there a bathroom?"

I chuckle and point behind him. "The only door on the right over there."

Nodding, he releases my hand and takes off. Unsure what to do, I get back in bed. He came all the way to Brooklyn when most likely he was drinking close to his apartment. If he's not here for a booty call, why is he here? And what caused him to get so drunk?

I glance at my shirt, the way my nipples are puckered against the fabric, something that happens whenever he's around. My body begs for him, and there is nothing I can do to stop it. Picking my phone back up, I finish reading the texts he sent, hoping for a clue why he's here.

Roark: *Have I told you I want to fuck you? I think I have.*

I re-read the text above the last, reminding myself of how he wants me to sit on his lap. Well, if this isn't a booty call, I don't know what it is. From the texts he sent, it seems like there's only one thing on his mind.

I turn back to the texts.

Roark: *I don't want to be at this nightclub anymore. I want to see you. Are you sleeping or are you ignoring me?*

Roark: *Why is Brooklyn so far away?*

Roark: *I need to hire a car service so I can transport you safely.*

That makes my heart swell. Even drunk, he can be thoughtful. Thoughtful but confusing. He doesn't want to start anything with me, and yet, he wants to protect me, he's constantly texting, and he's here in the dark of night, apparently not for a booty call.

I don't think I could be more confused.

The bathroom door opens, and Roark steps out into my tiny studio apartment wearing nothing but a pair of black briefs. The light from the bathroom lights up every contour of his chest and his chiseled arms. Reaching back, he flips the light off and then struts toward me. Swallowing hard, my skin prickling with need, I watch him close the distance between us. When he reaches me, I hold my breath, wondering where this is going.

He nods at the mattress. "Scoot over, lass." He must see uncertainty in my eyes because he says, "We're just sleeping, now scoot over."

Okay with that, I turn the light off on my nightstand then move over on the bed. He slips in right behind me. Unsure of what to do, I sit up and awkwardly watch him get comfortable. Once he's settled, lying flat, one hand propped behind his head, his gaze lulls to the side. "Are ya going to lie down, Sutton?"

"Do you want me to lie down?"

"I sure as hell don't want you hovering over me while I sleep." He tugs on my hand. "Come here."

He turns on his side and guides me down onto the bed so we're facing each other, both our hands tucked under a pillow. Lazily, he smiles at me and pushes a strand of hair behind my ear. "Thanks for answering your door."

"Why are you here, Roark?"

He shrugs and swipes his thumb across my cheek, our bodies only a foot away from touching. "I didn't want to go home, and none of the girls at the nightclub interested me."

That makes me pull away. "Were you with any of them?" That would make me sick, if he had girls hanging all over him then comes to my place. I might be desperate for his touch, but I'm not that desperate. I have my standards, and being second fiddle to other women isn't one of them.

"How could I be?" he asks. "Not when you're the only goddamn thing I think about."

Smiling, I lean back into his touch, melting at his answer. "You think about me, but you won't be with me."

He shakes his head. "Nah, I don't deserve you, Sutton. You're the type of girl you take home to meet your parents, and I'm not the guy who takes women home."

And just like that, he shatters the ounce of hope brewing inside me. He could be that guy. I can see it in him, in the little acts of thoughtfulness he shows, the sincerity in his eyes whenever he sees me, but for some reason, he refuses to accept it.

"Then why are you here?" I ask quietly, unable to look him in the eyes.

"Because I needed you." His hand moves down my body to my hip where it rests. "Rough day, Sutton. I needed you."

The rhythm of my heart skips a beat. "Do you . . . do you want to talk about it?"

He shakes his head and yawns. "No, I just want you in my arms." He nods behind me. "Turn the other way."

"Are you going to spoon me?" I ask, teasing him.

"Yeah, I'm going to spoon you so fucking hard, now turn over." His answer sets off a wave of butterflies in my stomach.

Unable to hide my smile, I flip to my other side only to be pulled into Roark's warm chest by his impressively strong arm. He situates our pillows and buries his head in my hair, his arm wrapped around my waist, our bodies pressed closely together.

I can't breathe, being this close to him, having him holding me protectively. It feels like too much.

"Fuck, you smell good," he says, nuzzling my hair, then down my neck. A wave of goosebumps spreads over my skin. "Lavender," he mumbles. His hand that's wrapped around my waist slips to my thigh where he maneuvers it under my shirt. I still as his hand glides back up my body, past my hip bone, to my stomach where it settles.

Breath held captive in my lungs, I'm still unsure what to do as his hand spans across my stomach and his nose runs against my ear. "Are you okay if I touch your skin?"

A dull throb pulses between my legs, my nipples pucker tightly against my shirt, and I have this intense urge to rub my legs together, to somehow give into the heavy feeling settling in my core.

"Yes," I breathe out heavily.

Thankfully he's too tired to notice the desperation in my voice or the need thrumming through my body. His thumb is so close to my breast, just a few more inches and he'd be touching it. I'm tempted to scoot down, and I think about it for a second before I stop myself. I don't want an accidental boob graze, not from Roark. I want his intention to be to want to touch me, to feel every last inch of me.

"Thank you, Sutton," he whispers.

"For what?"

His lips graze my ear, setting every nerve in my body on fire, pulsing, throbbing. So needy. I shift against him, moving my ass against his crotch, and he groans and nibbles on my ear.

I need him to do that again. I reach behind me and tangle my fingers through his hair, encouraging him. His breath filters through my ear before his teeth tug on my lobe.

Yes.

I move my rear against his crotch again, and this time I'm welcomed by his hard erection.

His hand grips tighter on my stomach, his thumb stroking my skin. I lightly moan as he moves his mouth down my neck. He doesn't kiss, he doesn't nibble, but it's almost like he's feeling the contour of my neck with his lips.

It causes a feather-like sensation to roll down my arms and across my stomach. He's barely doing anything—just a graze of his lips and a swipe of his thumb—and I'm already wet, ready, desperate for him to give me more.

Unable to control my movements anymore, I turn in his grasp

so my back is on the mattress. His hand rotates over my stomach, his thumb almost directly between my breasts.

"Sutton, turn back around."

Feeling bold, I say, "Touch me, Roark. I want to feel you all over my body."

"Christ," he groans, the tip of his thumb grazing my breast. "Sutton, stop moving."

Chest heaving now, the juncture between my thighs needy for this touch, I spread my legs, dropping one open and place my hand on top of his.

"What are you doing?" he asks.

Instead of answering, I glide his hand down my stomach and just when I start to move past my belly button he stops. I groan in frustration. "Roark, please."

"No," he whispers in my ear. "Not now, not like this." His tongue peeks out and licks across my ear. I take the opportunity to slip his hand past the hem of my boy shorts.

He sucks in a sharp breath, his fingers dancing dangerously where I want them. "Touch me," I whisper. "I'm so wet, Roark."

"Fuck," he sighs, his breath picking up now. "Fuck, Sutton."

His fingers glide along my pubic bone, teasing me. "Just one finger, that's all I need. I'm about to combust, Roark. Just give me something."

I can hear him swallow hard before he speaks. "I can't. I'm drunk, Sutton."

"I don't care."

"I do," he says, removing his hand and putting it back on my stomach.

I groan out of pure frustration and flip to my side, turning away from him. Why does he have to make this so complicated? It's just sex. It's not like I'm asking him to make a baby with me. I just want some pleasure. No, that's not all I want. I want Roark to be the one pleasuring me. Making me feel desired, turned on . . . sexy. I know I'm not, but boy do I need that right now. His touch. His caress. His body over mine.

"Don't be salty, lass," he says close to my ear, his thumb drawing light circles on my stomach.

I don't say anything. Instead, I bury one hand under my head and shut my eyes. The throbbing in my body grows more persistent, reminding me there will be no relief for me anytime soon.

Turned down twice by this man. Will he ever say yes? Will he ever give in? I'm beginning to think he's not going to. If he would hop on the opportunity to bed me, tonight would be the night, but even drunk, he has the stupid sense to leave me alone.

"Sutton, you know I want to."

"Your words mean nothing to me right now, Roark."

"Ooo," he coos. "Sharp declaration."

"Don't be playful. I'm mad at you."

"Ah, come on," he says. It's a whisper, and it feels like a caress. *But not the sort of caress I need.* "Just enjoy the cuddle, lass. This doesn't happen . . . ever. Consider that a victory tonight." His lips press a sweet kiss against my cheek as he snuggles in closer, his erection fitting against my ass, his chest covering my back like a weighted blanket, and the secure hold of his arm wrapped around my waist offers me a sense of security I don't think I've ever had. And by the sounds of it, he probably hasn't either.

Even though I'm completely turned on to the point of pain, I consider what he is offering me. It might not be sex, but in some ways, it's greater. It's a piece of intimacy he doesn't share with others. For that, I need to be grateful. The other part of this will come—I'll make sure of it—because if there is something I've realized tonight it's that Roark is starting to make his way into my heart. Slowly, but he's carving a path.

∽

"Ah, fookin' A," I hear next to me on a painful moan, scaring the crap out of me. I jump at least a few inches in the air and turn around to find Roark, holding his crotch, eyes shut in pain.

Last night comes flashing back to me: Roark's text, his late-night visit—or rather early morning. The touching. The non-touching. The blue-balls I suffered last night.

His confessions.

The way he held me.

His sweet kisses along my ear and neck.

"Ya got me in the nads, Sutton." He takes a deep breath. "That's one way to take care of morning wood."

My sympathy finally kicks in as I press my hand to his arm. "I'm so sorry. I must have forgotten you were here. Did my knee connect with you in the wrong way?"

"Ya could say that." Letting out a long breath of air, his green eyes pop open and his breathing seems to steady. "Damn, woman. If you wanted to wake me up, just give me a shake."

I chuckle. "I'm sorry. I truly didn't mean to knee your junk."

"Are ya sure you weren't getting back at me for disturbing your sleep last night?"

"No, you're the resentful one, remember?" I sit up in bed. Immediately his eyes fall to my chest where I know he's taking in my hard nipples. It's a given. I'm almost used to it by now.

Once he gets a good eyeful, his eyes travel back up my body. "You smell good, like flowers."

I wasn't expecting that. I press my hand against the sheets and say, "I spray lavender oil on my bed, helps me sleep."

"It smells like you, gives me a goddamn hard-on."

"I feel like everything does that to you."

He reaches out and pulls me back down on the bed, his hand snaking around my waist. "Not everything, lass." He strokes a strand of hair out of my face before sighing and turning around, leaving me breathless.

He tosses the sheets to the side and struts toward the bathroom, his back muscles flexing with every step he takes. I'm so focused on his backside, I'm almost caught staring when he stops and spins around to face me.

Scratching the side of his head, he looks around and asks, "Is there a second floor to this apartment?"

"There is a second floor, but it doesn't belong to me. What you see, is what you get. This is it."

Eyes wide, he asks, "This is your entire apartment? My bedroom is bigger than this." He takes in the kitchen. "You don't even have a real fridge. That's something I had in college. What about an oven?"

Amused, I sit up in bed again. "I have a toaster oven that works perfectly fine."

"Where's your kitchen sink?"

"In the bathroom."

He scoffs. "And how much do you pay?"

"Enough to make you question my sanity." I gesture to the side. "But look at the pretty fireplace and the light that streams through the floor-to-ceiling windows in the front and the cute little alcove. It's perfect."

"You don't have a sofa."

"Why do I need a sofa when I have a bed?" I ask, wiggling my eyebrows.

"You need a sofa for fucking."

"What's a bed for then?"

"So much more," he says with a smile before heading into the bathroom.

Sighing like a love-struck teen, I flop back onto bed and drape my arm over my eyes. God, what I wouldn't give right now to have Roark come out of the bathroom completely naked and push me up against the mattress, only to spread my thighs and finally give me what I've been wanting for weeks now.

To prevent getting hot from the thought and having a repeat of last night, I concentrate on the old ceiling and the intricate carvings that have been painted over too many times to count. It's one of the reasons I loved this apartment so much—so much history packed within four small walls. And even if the fireplace doesn't work, and I don't have a true working kitchen, and there is a draft that seeps from the old windows, I love it here.

The bathroom door opens and I turn my head to the side to see Roark dressed in his pants but that's it, and they're not even zipped.

I keep my tongue from flopping out the side of my mouth as he approaches, his hair a mess, a sleepy look in his eyes, and a lazy smile on his face. It's scary how, with every step he takes, my heartbeat races faster, my nerves skyrocket, and my desire for him grows.

"You're one of those people."

"Huh?" I ask, hoping I wasn't staring too much.

He sits down next to me on the bed and presses his hand on my thigh, looking down at me. "This is going to sound really cheesy—"

"I like cheesy." I smile up at him.

"I figured, but you wake up looking gorgeous." His hand glides up my thigh, and my breath hitches when he reaches my hip bone. "You know I wanted to go so much further with you last night, right?"

"I could feel that you did." I glance at his crotch and he chuckles.

"Okay, I don't want you thinking otherwise since I didn't take it any further."

"Yeah." My teeth roll over my bottom lip. "You're a tease."

"Not on purpose. You're just a temptress. You know where I stand."

"Unfortunately." I sigh, my hope cracking once again. "Can I ask you a question?"

"I don't know, am I going to need coffee for it?" He rakes his hand through his unruly hair.

"Maybe."

Standing from the bed, he walks to my "kitchen" and pulls on the back of his neck while he examines it. His bicep bulges, a boulder in the center of it as the little muscles above his ass tighten. I want to know what they feel like under my touch, how they ripple—

"Where are your other mugs?" he calls out, plugging in my tiny Keurig.

"I only have the one."

He pauses what he's doing and looks over his shoulder. "You only have one mug?" I nod. "Why?"

"It's just me. Why would I need more?"

He picks up the plain white mug with a Gaining Goals logo on it. "You could have picked something with a little more personality." He continues to make coffee as I talk.

"As if you have mugs with personality. I'm sure I would find a bunch of black mugs in your cupboard."

"Yeah, but I'm not the guy with the personality that screams fun mugs."

"And what kind of personality do I have?"

The coffee finishes and he looks around the little shelves for sugar, which he spots quickly and drops a little spoonful in the cup before stirring. There's something about Roark finding his way around my kitchen with ease that's so comforting and sexy.

Walking toward me, he answers, "Bubbly, cute, sweet." He looks up. "You need those type of mugs. Pink ones with polka-dots. Something like that."

"Pink with polka-dots?" I chuckle. "I'll keep that in mind."

He motions for me to scoot over on the bed, so I do, and he doesn't take long to slip under the sheets with me and put his arm around my shoulder, pulling me in close. He hands me the mug and says, "We can share."

Share.

This all seems so domestic, like there is something brewing between us rather than simply sexual tension. I could've guessed that last night when he showed up at my apartment drunk and wanting to cuddle. Needing to hold me, touch me. There really is something brewing, I just want to know what.

I take the mug and give it a blow before looking up at him, a smile playing at my lips. "I usually add milk too."

"You couldn't have said that while I was up?" He takes the mug from me and goes to the kitchen.

"I didn't know we were sharing."

He splashes some milk in the coffee and gives it another quick stir. "What kind of dick would I be if I made myself coffee and not you? Now if you had more than one mug, there wouldn't have been any confusion."

"Aren't you clever?" I ask just as he gets back into position, but this time, he keeps the mug for himself.

Arm around my shoulders, he pulls me into his side, his fresh scent warming my toes. "Okay, what was your question? Coffee in hand, I'm ready."

Second-guessing myself, I say, "Umm, never mind."

"No way." He shakes his head. "I made coffee in the tiniest kitchen I've ever seen, so you're asking me that question."

Chuckling, I rest my head against his shoulder, feeling incredibly nervous, but also curious about his answer. "So, what's going on between us?"

He's silent for a second, and my breath hangs on his every word. Finally, "Hell if I know." He scratches the side of his jaw. "I know I can't have you, but I can't seem to stay away either."

"That makes no sense. You touch me like we're together. You speak to me like there's more than friendship, but when it comes to anything physical, you shy away."

"I don't shy away. I stop myself and for good reason."

"Why?" I ask frustrated.

"You know why, Sutton."

"So you're allowed to basically turn me on whenever you're around and then take off, leaving me yearning for your touch?" I push off his chest and turn to look him in the eyes, which are focused on the wall across from us.

Quietly, he says, "It's not easy for me, Sutton. Don't think this is something I enjoy. Okay?" He rubs his jaw. "Listen, I'm sorry I came over last night and confused things. I blurred the lines, and I shouldn't have done that."

Now he's pulling away. I knew I should have kept my mouth shut.

"It was having a rough go of it last night, and I just . . . fuck." He sighs and throws both legs over the side of the bed, ready to retreat, but I grab his shoulders before he can.

"Don't go, Roark. Talk to me. Why was it a rough night?"

"You won't understand."

As if he slapped me, I rear back, insulted. "I might not be tortured like you, Roark, but I pride myself on being empathetic."

The hurt in my voice must register because he sets the coffee down and turns around, regret on his face. "I didn't mean to insult you."

"Well, you did."

Sighing, he leans back against the headboard of my bed and tugs on my hand until I'm straddling his lap. His hands go to my thighs, softly rubbing them up and down. It's moments like this that absolutely confuse me. When did we get to this point? This intimate part of our relationship where I feel like we could tackle anything together, where I want to hear about all his troubles and smooth the crease between his brow with my soft encouragement.

Where was that turning point?

This is why I'm confused, because right now, this is what I want with him, and he gives it to me in small doses but doesn't fully commit.

Be patient, I remind myself.

"I'm sorry, Sutton. I didn't mean to insult you. You just have this perfect relationship with your dad, and that's not the case with my family."

Leaning forward, I press my hand against his chest. "Is that why you were upset yesterday?"

His hands climb up to my waist and he pulls me closer so our chests are almost touching. He glides his hands to my butt where he holds on tightly and rests his head against the headboard so his

Adam's apple pops. I'm tempted to lean forward and taste his neck, to run my tongue along the column then to his lips where I would desperately devour him.

"Yeah." His grip on me goes tighter. "My parents are . . . hell, they're awful." I really can't believe he's opening up to me. I sit back and listen, my hand slowly rubbing against his thick chest. "I grew up in a small town outside of Killarney. The best earning job is farming, and that's not what I wanted with my life. I did a foreign exchange program at Yale, liked it so much I stayed and studied there. I knew America was where I wanted to be, where I was going to make the most of myself. My parents didn't take too kindly to that. Still don't. They didn't care much for me growing up, always relied on me as a second pair of hands rather than treating me like a child, so when they found out I was earning money, they started calling every month, laying on the guilt trip that I owe it to my family to provide for them."

My brow pulls together. "They call you for money?"

"Like clockwork. And I give it to them every time."

"What for?"

One of his hands leaves the grip on my backside so he can pull on his hair in frustration. "Easier that way. I listen to the emotional abuse my mom spins at me, ask her how much, and then wire it."

"Roark," I sigh, pressing my hand to his cheek. "Family should never use you like that."

"I know." The sad look in his eyes, the frustration in his muscles, it almost breaks me to see him like this. "It's another reason I can't have you. The minute they find out I'm dating the daughter of Foster Green, the demands would be endless."

And it feels like the real reason starts to surface. He's not only protecting me from the self-destructive habits he seems to have, but from his family as well.

Knowing that makes me more determined to be in his life. A friend. His confidante. Someone who doesn't take from him but gives back.

Not wanting to offer empty suggestions, I try to soothe his soul by shifting my hand through his hair. "I'm sorry, Roark, but I will tell you this. You'll never see me want you for anything except the man who lives inside of you."

His eyes flick toward mine, the green so beautifully mossy this morning, even after a heavy night of drinking. His hand slides up my back, dragging the shirt with him as he slowly dances his fingers over my skin. "You're special, Sutton."

"And don't you think it's time you have something special in your life?"

Head tilted, he studies me. "I want something special, that's for damn sure." His jaw works side to side as he thinks, his eyes searching mine. Finally, he says, "I have this event I have to go to next week, would you want to go?"

My pulse skips a beat as a smile pulls on my lips. "Like, as a date?"

"Sort of . . . like a business partner."

And once again hope falls. Frustrated, I slide off his lap and groan as I flop to the side of the bed. Staring up at the ceiling, I feel the bed shift as he hovers above me, his hair falling forward. Before he can get a word in, I say, "You frustrate me."

"You're not the first person to tell me that."

Sitting back, he stands from the bed and picks up our shared mug. He takes a long gulp and hands it to me as I sit up as well. As Roark retreats to the bathroom, I sit there, contemplating my life and how beyond irritating it is. Of course, I grow feelings for the most stubborn man in New York City.

Shoes on, pants zipped, Roark walks back into the room while pulling his long-sleeved shirt over his head. My eyes trained now, they go straight to his naked torso and reluctantly watch him cover it. I was so close and now feel so far.

Adjusting his shirt, he walks back toward me and stops at the foot of the bed. Last night's cologne clings to his clothes, wrapping me in warmth. Slowly, he reaches out and cups my cheek, lowering his head to mine, our foreheads connecting. He takes a deep breath and says, "Thank you for last night and for this morning. It meant a lot to me, Sutton." Lifting his head, he presses a sweet kiss to my forehead, lighting me up inside, then he steps away, sticking his hands in his pockets as if to stop himself from touching me again.

"Think about the event. I'll talk to you later. Have a good day, lass."

With a parting wave, he lets himself out. Once the door is shut, I let out a disappointed sigh and lie back on my bed. What in the world happened in the last twenty-four hours? *How did I become the person he came to when troubled?* I feel like I was given a tiny entry into his world, but then just as swiftly pushed away. It's so confusing. *He* is so confusing.

I have no will to really do anything. Roark confounds me, and there's really no one I can talk to about this. I'm not heartbroken, but . . . concerned. Do I want to be the friend he turns to when none of the girls at the club *do it for him*? Gah. It's a dull, gray day, making it perfect weather for me to have a lazy day, curled up in my bed watching movies. I've gone with a romantic comedy binge starting with *How to Lose a Guy in Ten Days*—that Kate Hudson is such a sassy character—then I moved on to *When Harry Met Sally*—where Billy Crystal sings Surrey with the Fringe on top, my favorite—and now I'm almost done with *Crazy Rich Asians*. God, the part where the girl walks down the aisle and it feels like time stands still as the water flows makes me cry every time.

Louise is curled on top of my lap, replacing the need for a weighted blanket. Who needs one when I have a sixteen-pound cat that does the trick?

Her purr vibrates against my hand with every stroke I make across her body, and as the movie plays, I can't help but allow my mind to drift to last night. The intimacy I shared with Roark, the need I felt vibrating from him, but the iron-clad restraint he had—even when drunk—stopped him from taking that next step.

Unless he really doesn't want to. I've seen the women he's attracted to, and although he said he can't stop thinking about me, I certainly don't fit that mold. My dad is his client. It's a hurdle, but I wouldn't think a deal breaker. Dad thinks very highly of Roark, otherwise he never would have teamed us together for the camp. Our age? Such a non-issue. His family? I have no idea how much they ask for, nor why, but if Roark has been *giving* to them for all these years, why would he think dating me would make any difference? He's allowed them to exploit him for years.

I guess the real question is, why is this a problem for me at all? *Do I want something more with him?* His reasons don't seem insurmountable to me, so maybe I need to accept that there are self-erected barriers only he can remove should *he* wish to. Yes, I want to be intimate with him, because I've never known this sort of physical attraction in my life. He is right. I've never had an orgasm during sex with a guy. But something tells me it's not just the lack of sex that frustrates me.

I want more from Roark McCool than hot sex. I want him, body and soul. Patience has never been my strong suit, and he's testing my ability to sit back and let things play out. I keep reminding myself, every time I get frustrated, to take deep breaths and think about what patience could bring me. If I move too fast I might scare him away, and that's the last thing I want. *I also want his friendship... strangely.*

Knock. Knock.

Louise stills on my lap and I carefully move her to the side, toss my blanket off my legs, and pad to the door to look through the peephole. My heart stutters in my chest when I see Roark standing on the other side of the door.

Excited, I unlock everything and open up. A smirk crosses his face as he gives me a quick once-over. I'm wearing purple thermal leggings and a matching top with my hair piled in a bun on the top of my head, and I'm not wearing an ounce of makeup. And from the way he's looking at me, I'm guessing he likes it . . . a lot.

Leaning against the doorframe, hand on the door, I ask, "What are you doing here?"

He takes a step forward, hands behind his back. His cologne is the first thing to grab hold of my heart, next is the devastating smile that crosses his face as he brings a bag from around his back between us. "I got you something."

"You got me something?" God, he makes me smile so hard.

"Yeah." He nods at my apartment. "Can I come in?"

I step to the side, allowing him to breeze on in. Dressed in dark jeans, tan boots, and a black jacket, he spins around and hands me the gift as I shut the door.

I take it—it's kind of heavy—and say, "Want to take your coat off?"

He sticks his hands in his pockets and shakes his head. "I'm not staying, just dropping that off."

I hide my disappointment as I walk over to my bed and cross my legs, letting the present rest in my lap. Still in the middle of the room, Roark keeps his distance but watches intently as I start to pull the tissue paper from the bag. "Did you wrap this yourself?"

"Would it impress you if I said I did?"

"Maybe."

He smiles wickedly. "I paid someone to do it."

That makes me laugh out loud. Of course he did. Shaking my head, I pull out a round object and start unwrapping it, unveiling a pink mug . . . with white polka-dots. I can't seem to shake the smile that is permanently on my lips.

"You got me a cute mug."

"Two." He holds up his fingers.

I reach into the bag and pull out another. This one is not pink with polka-dots, instead, it is a cat head with little ears and whiskers.

"Oh my God, this is so cute."

Looking shy, he shrugs and says, "When I saw it, I thought you needed it since you have a cat and all."

"I love it." I hold on to it tightly. "Thank you, Roark."

"No problem." He heads to the door. "Just promise you'll get rid of that boring mug and use these from now on."

"Promise."

He reaches for the door knob, and I quickly pop out of bed, setting the mugs down and going to him. "Hold on, wait a second." I step between him and the door, blocking his exit. "Are you going to let me thank you properly?"

"What does properly entail?"

"A hug."

"Just a hug?"

"Do you want more?" I ask, pressing him.

"You know I want more." The veins in his neck tense. "But a hug will do." Before I can respond, he pulls me in by the hand and wraps his arms around me, his chin resting on my head.

"Thank you," I whisper. "That was really thoughtful. I don't think I've ever received something so thoughtful from a guy."

"Then you're not hanging out with the right people." He gently presses a kiss to the top of my head and pulls away. He must expect me to move to the side. But when I don't, he playfully tugs on the hem of my shirt. "Are you going to let me out?"

"What are you doing for the rest of the day?"

"I have some things I have to take care of."

His hand remains on my shirt, his fingers playing with the fabric. "You have things to take care of here too." Good Lord, did that just come out of my mouth? My cheeks blush from my boldness, but it must do the trick because Roark groans and closes the space between us, pushing me against the door.

The hand playing with my shirt now slides to my bare skin, his thumb rubbing over my exposed hip bone. His other hand falls to the door, next to my head, bracing him. His forehead connects with mine and his nose rubs against mine for a few heartbeats.

My breath stills in my lungs as white-hot temptation courses through me. *Be patient, let him make the move.*

"Why are you so goddamn perfect?"

"I'm far from perfect, Roark."

His gaze connects with mine. "You're perfect in my eyes."

His searing yet beautiful eyes bore a hole straight to my heart, seizing the breath from my lungs and halting the blood pumping in my veins.

Please just kiss me.

Every muscle, every bone in my body vibrates with need for this man. Just one taste, that's all I want, one little taste to let me know what it's like to have his lips on mine.

His hand moves up my side as his breath starts to pick up. I can feel it, him wavering, his wall cracking and crumbling. I can sense his indecision. I can feel his need for me in the firm grasp he has on my body. He wants this, just as much as I do.

Unable to take the standstill anymore, I hook my fingers through his belt loops and bring him in closer. He sucks in a breath as I move one of my hands to his jacket and unzip it, only to slip my hand under the tan sweater he has draped over his body. *Who is this vixen, and what has she done with sweet and demure Sutton?*

Almost as if he's in pain, his eyes squeeze shut. "Sutton."

My nose nuzzles against his, our breath mixing together, our lips inches apart. "Kiss me, Roark."

"Sutton," he repeats, this time more strained.

"Please, Roark. Just kiss me." My hand travels over his rippled abs that contract and flinch under my touch.

His grip on my side grows tighter, his hand spanning over my ribs. "Do you know what I want?" he asks, his nose running down the side of my head to my collarbone. "I want to peel these clothes off you, slowly, then take you to your bed and spread your legs wide." My breath catches in my chest. "I would kiss every last inch of your legs until I reach your pussy that would be so goddamn wet and ready for me, but I wouldn't kiss you there. Instead, I would kiss you from your stomach to your tits, where I would worship them." His lips glide over my skin but never move, almost just a hover of a touch. "Sucking, pinching, nipping. I would taste every inch of them until your hands were pulling on my hair, your moans begging for release, your body writhing underneath mine."

A low gasp escapes me, because I'm unable to hide how much I want everything he described. Every kiss. Every touch. Every taste. I want it all. *Need it all.*

"Then I would lower to your legs and do the whole thing all over again until you come from my kisses alone. I would watch you fall apart underneath me and then . . . I would leave."

"What?" I ask, as if he just performed that entire seduction on me and said he was leaving. "Why?"

"Because," he murmurs against my skin before pulling away and looking me in the eyes. He pinches my chin with his forefinger and thumb. "You deserve more than me, Sutton."

He pushes off the door, grabs my hand, and helps move me to the side. Shocked and stunned, and also ridiculously turned on, I'm unable to protest as he opens the door and walks halfway out of my apartment. "I'll see you later, Sutton."

And then he departs, leaving me angrier and more pissed off than I was this morning.

Who does that?

∽

Roark: *I can feel your anger from here.*

Sutton: *Wow, you're pretty attuned to my feelings then.*

Roark: *I didn't have to get very far to know how you might be seething.*

Sutton: *Seething is not a good enough word.*

Roark: *Why so angry?*

Sutton: *Hmm, I don't know, maybe because you keep turning me on and then leave me hanging with no release.*

Roark: *Did you . . . do anything to take care of it?*

Sutton: *Yeah, and it felt good, having my hand between my thighs, working out the frustration you put there.*
Roark: *Fuck.*
Sutton: *Your loss, Roark. Every time you leave my apartment, or leave me hanging like that, just know that means it's my hand getting to do the work, not yours.*

I don't know what's come over me. Maybe because it's eleven at night and Roark is texting me. Maybe it's because I've been physically wound up twice today with no release from the man I want more than anything, but I'm feeling bold and I'm not even sorry about it.

My phone buzzes in my hand, Roark's name on the screen. I'm tempted to let it go to voicemail, but knowing him, he would call again, so I answer.

"What?" I lie flat on my bed, my finger twisting a lock of my hair. "Unless this is about camp, I don't want to talk right now."

"It is about camp."

My heart falls. I don't want him calling me about the stupid camp—I don't mean stupid, it's not stupid. I'm frustrated. Sexually frustrated and wound up like a tight ball.

Trying to hide how irritated I am, I say, "What's up?"

"I booked my flight for Texas for the day after that event I have to go to."

"Okay . . ." I drawl out.

"That's it."

"That's all you called me for, to tell me you booked a flight when you could have easily taken a private jet down?"

"You know how I am about personal transportation. I don't mind riding with the masses."

I rub one of my eyes, trying to comprehend this man. "Okay, well good to know. Thanks for calling me at eleven at night to tell me that. Unless you have anything else to tell me, I'm going to go."

He's silent for a second, and I'm about to hang up when he finally says, "Did you think about the event?"

"Yeah, that's going to be a no for me," I answer more bitterly than I would have liked.

"Sutton," he sighs. "Please go with me."

Okay, I need to take a step back for a second.

Why am I angry?

Because he won't have sex with me.

Should I be angry at that?

Well, not really, since technically he doesn't owe me anything. We're not dating, and we really are only colleagues. It's not like he's technically done anything wrong. Are the lines blurred? Yeah, big time, but if this case was brought to a judge does Sutton Green have the right to be mad at Roark McCool? Not really, no.

Resigned, I say, "Who is the event for?"

"Jericho Stanton."

"The basketball player?"

"Yeah, it's a fundraiser for the local YMCAs here in the city. He raises a lot of money; it's a high-end event. He said my donation isn't good enough this year. He wants me there . . . with a date."

That puts a smile on my face. "Do your clients always try to shape your life? My dad, Jericho, anyone else?"

He chuckles, the deep vibration rumbling my own body, as if we're both sitting on my bed and my head is resting on his shoulder. "Yeah, they all have a hand in trying to make me better. I think they worry about me flying off the deep end and hurting their careers."

"Valid concern."

"Won't happen. I know when things start to get bad I pull away from my, as you like to call them, accessories."

"Do you have to pull away a lot?"

"Nah, I'm pretty good. There are only a few times where I've had to assess what I'm doing." He lets out a sigh. "That's beside the point. Do you think you can make it?"

"What's the dress code?"

"Short red dress, lots of cleavage." And that response right there is why I'm so confused, why I feel like I'm going to combust in seconds from my stomach constantly being rolled into a tight, tight ball.

Unable to commit, I say, "I don't know, let me think about it." Before he can respond, I add, "I have to go. Have a good night, Roark."

I hang up and toss my phone to the side, unsure of what to do. Nibbling on my bottom lip, I consider my options. I can either let him continue to flirt with me, tease me, make me feel electric inside only to tamp it down with a wet towel. Or, I can be the one to set the off-limits boundary, to let him know we are purely working together, and that's it. *After all, that's all he's offering.* If he wants to talk to me, it needs to be professional—not that he really knows what professional is.

The thought of shutting down his intimate touches just about slices my heart up, but then again, today was a hard day. I'm not sure how many more of these kinds of days I can take.

I think it might be time to draw a line in the sand.

CHAPTER TWELVE

Dear Travis,
    Not sure I like Travis for you; feels like I'm talking to a two-year-old rather than a listening warrior. I think Travis is a quick no for me.

I made over two million dollars today. With one signature, secured it in the old bank account. Normally I would be elated, but for some reason, it just feels like another day. Ever since I left Sutton's apartment on Sunday—her tiny fucking apartment—I've felt off. Like I left something behind, but for the life of me I can't figure out what it is. This is what I do. It's what I'm fucking good at. Two million in the bank. Should be at the club . . . but that's not where I want to be.

I leave for Texas soon. I'm dreading it and not because I'm not great with kids, or because the whole cowboy ranch thing isn't really a shining beacon of my personality, but because I know I'll be seeing Sutton day in and day out. I don't think I can face such constant temptation. I barely made it through last week and I only saw her a couple of times.

And the tension between us is increasing at an unhealthy rate. I know I should have stayed away the other night, that I should have just gone home rather than to her apartment, but when I thought I was giving my address to the taxi driver, it was Sutton's.

I should stay away, but I can't.

I need to stop thinking about her, but I can't.

I know I'm frustrating her, but I can't seem to stop.

Hell . . . when did this diary become all about one girl?

Probably the moment I saw her at Gray's Papaya. I should have known then she was going to destroy me.

Roark

ROARK

I have no idea why I'm in my office today. I could have done all my work somewhere else, like in my apartment, or at one of those coffee houses all the hipsters like to hang out in, but instead I decided to come to my office. My boring, plain office that has zero personality or warmth. Not that my apartment is any better, but at least it has my bed. And for two nights, it had Sutton.

Leg crossed over my knee, I look at the city below me, the water tanks on top of the buildings, the gray clouds that never seem to disappear in the winter, and the offices across from mine with people milling about, performing tasks I'm sure they hate.

Three contracts are on top of my desk, my email is full of requests, and my phone vibrates on my desk every five minutes.

Fucking Mondays.

I drag my hand over my face.

The intercom comes to life on my desk. "Mr. McCool, Miss Green is here to see you."

Well, fuck, I think my Monday just got a whole lot better. I press the red button and say, "Send her back."

I glance around my office, considering straightening it up but decide better of it. Instead, I strike a casual pose and wait for her to come through my door.

It doesn't take long and hell, my breath catches in my chest when she walks through, a smile on her face and a thank you to my assistant on her lips.

Wearing a pink wool coat and tight black pants with high heels, she struts into my office with confidence, her slightly curled hair blowing back with her strides. She's highlighted those devastating eyes with black mascara and her lips, glossy and so goddamn sexy.

I swallow hard, knowing damn well it's going to be hard to keep my hands to myself, especially when her lavender scent starts to take over my office. Shit, that's going to stay awhile and most likely drive me crazy with need later.

"Hey," I say as she takes a seat across from me. My assistant shuts the door, leaving me alone with Sutton, just the way I like it.

She folds her hands on her lap and lifts her chin. Christ, I think I'm about to hear something I don't want to hear.

"Why don't you take off your jacket?"

I can see her considering not to, but given how warm it is in my office, she unbuttons her jacket. Like it's an erotic strip show, I watch her fingers work the buttons out of their holes, parting her jacket ever so slightly until she shrugs the entire thing off, revealing a white silk blouse with black lace bra underneath. *Warrior clothes. My girl means business.*

Okay, maybe she should have kept the jacket on.

Knowing I tend to stare at her breasts, I lean back in my chair, arm propped up, and cover my mouth with my hand as I force myself to look her in the eyes. It's painful, but I'm doing it.

"To what do I owe the pleasure of your presence, Miss Green?"

I expect her to ask me when I became so proper, but instead, she gets right down to business. "I came to talk to you about our working relationship."

Yup, I was right. I don't think I'm going to like the reason she's here.

"What about it?"

"It needs to stay that way, a working relationship."

I nod. "I couldn't agree more."

"Which means we need to stay professional."

"I love being professional," I say, as my eyes glance at her tits.

Her nostrils flair. "Do you know what acting professionally entails, Mr. McCool?"

"Mr. McCool?" A smile spreads across my face. "Hell, I like the way that sounds coming off your tongue, but can you do me a favor? Whisper it next time."

"Roark, I'm being serious."

"I can tell, from the stick that seems to be shoved up your arse. If you want me to respond, be real."

I don't want this fake—prim and proper—Sutton to tell me what she wants. No, I want the tenacious, canny, and unrestrained beauty I've gotten to know over the last few weeks. I want *that* girl to confront me.

"You want me to be real?" Her eyes start to well up. Shit, I didn't expect her to get emotional. "Fine." She takes a deep breath and says, "I can't do this touching, flirting thing anymore with you. We either date, or we're colleagues. None of this in-between stuff." Her chest puffs out. "I know what I'm worth, Roark, and I deserve more than being strung along, waiting for the next treat you decide to toss my way. If you want to touch me, feel my skin, cuddle into my back, smell the lavender in my hair, then I need a commitment from you; I want all of you too. If that's not something you can do, then the texts stop, the touching stops, the flirting stops, and the staring at my breasts stops. If you can't give me that, then we resume work, finish up this camp, and go our separate ways."

Fuck.

I know she's right, we can't continue this charade—this sexy repartee—without progress or someone getting hurt, but am I really willing to give up the chance to feel her skin against mine? Am I willing to throw away the late-night conversations and the sweet, playful texts from her? *They've grounded me. Soothed me. Can I lose that?*

No. I don't think I can.

Not really.

But can I give her what she wants? Dating? Commitment?

Fuck, I don't think so.

I must have been thinking far too long because she stands from her chair and throws her jacket back on. "I'm going to take your silence as your answer that you can't commit." She flips her hair out from her collar, letting it fall gracefully over her shoulders and walks toward my office door. "I'll see you in Texas, Roark."

"Wait," I finally say, ungluing myself from my chair and making my way to her. I take her hand in mine and slowly nudge her against the wall, unsure what my next move is. I watch as her chest rises and falls a little more rapidly, how her lips part, and her eyes search mine, looking for answers I don't have.

"What, Roark?" she asks, her body stiff, her hand loose in mine rather than holding it tightly like she has in the past. *I can't lose her. Can't.*

"I . . ." I swallow hard. "I don't want you to go."

"But can you give me what I want?"

"Does it have to be so black and white?"

"Yes," she answers with conviction. "This isn't fair to me, to give me little pieces but not the full thing. If we're going to be intimate, I want all of you, not glimpses." She looks at her hands and murmurs, "It hurts me."

Feeling her slip away second by second, I let out a deep breath. "You know I can't let you go."

"You're going to have to," she says, side-stepping away from me.

I grab her wrist before she makes a full retreat. "I don't know what you want me to say, Sutton. I don't do relationships."

"You have said I deserve more, so why don't you try to be the more? Why don't you want more . . . with me?" *Fuck. She shouldn't be questioning that. Ever.*

"Because I know I can't."

"Can't . . . or won't?"

"Is there really a difference."

She pulls her wrist away from me. "There is to me. One shows your weakness, the other shows your indifference. I can handle weakness in a man, but indifference, that's something I don't bother with." She looks at me tentatively then shakes her head. "You're indifferent. I'll see you in Texas, Roark."

With one final tug, she exits my office, leaving me in a state of uncomfortable and unexpected panic. I know I can't give her what she wants—at least I don't think I can—but I can't have her slip away.

I push my hand angrily through my hair and turn toward the windows of my office, away from Sutton's retreating back.

"Fuck," I mutter, my body vibrating with frustration, my mouth going dry, my veins begging for relief. Apart from the fucking phone call from my ma, I haven't *needed* this for weeks, felt this unexplained uneasiness within me. How can watching her walk away stir this . . . unease? This restlessness?

Because she's the one who gave you the reason to not indulge.

I walk to the mini fridge and grab a few small bottles of whiskey, uncapping them in one twist. I take a long swig, toss the empty bottle and then take down the other. I *can't* have her, so I need help easing the pain that's starting to erupt all over my skin.

***

Roark: *Can I come over?*
Sutton: *It's one in the morning. I don't work this late.*
Roark: *It's not about work.*
Sutton: *Then no.*
Roark: *Let me come over. I want to snuggle into you, hold you.*
Sutton: *Are you going to give me what I want?*
Roark: *You know the answer to that.*
Sutton: *Then you know mine. Good night, Roark.*

***

Roark: *Tomorrow is the fundraiser. I have a stylist on hold for you at Bloomingdales.*
Sutton: *Tell them not to waste their time. I'm not going.*
Roark: *Come as a business associate.*
Sutton: *Because that's all I am to you?*

Roark: *I can't do more.*
Roark: *Please, Sutton. Come.*
Sutton: *I'm sorry, Roark. I'm not like you. It will be too confusing.*
Roark: *Please...*

∼

Roark: *I keep turning around thinking I'm going to see you.*
Sutton: *You're not.*
Roark: *Are you really not here?*
Sutton: *Yes, I'm really not there.*
Roark: *Fuck.*
Sutton: *What did you expect, Roark?*
Roark: *Maybe that you would set aside your wants for one goddamn night and be there for me. After all, aren't we at least friends?*
Sutton: *We are colleagues. We work together. After camp, we're done.*
Roark: *Bullshit. You can't just stop talking to me.*
Sutton: *I can and I will. I hope they raise a lot of money tonight. Don't miss your flight tomorrow. Our schedule is jam-packed, and we need you ready to work.*
Roark: *Please come.*
Roark: *Suttttton. Where r u?*
Roark: *I want 2 c u.*
Roark: *Fuckkkk I swear I keep seeing u at this party.*
Roark: *Are u sleepin?*
Roark: *Can I come over?*
Roark: *Lass...*

∼

She told me not to come over. She said she wanted nothing to do with me. She wants so much more than what I can give her and yet, here I am, standing outside her door, desperate, wound up with need, and about to do the one thing she told me not to do: take something I don't deserve.

I raise my fist but then stop myself and rest my forehead on the wood.

I drank way too much tonight. Hell, I drank way too much the last few days. Ever since she left my office with that pain in her eyes, I haven't been able to get my head on straight. Am I really so scared of intimacy that I turned her away?

Yeah, I am.

I have no fucking clue what love is; I was never taught the emotion. I have no idea how to feel it or how to give it. Sutton is a girl you love. She's . . . God, she's so fucking perfect.

The long blonde hair that falls past her shoulders, those smoldering yet innocent eyes, and her sweet southern accent that rolls off her tongue. She's addicting, and I need a piece of her.

Before I can stop myself, I knock on the door, loudly.

It's past two in the morning. It's way too late, or maybe early, whatever way you want to look at it, but this can't wait. I need to see her, need to look into her eyes, need to hold her hand. Something, anything, I just need her to open this door. *To let me in even though it's unwise.*

"Sutton, open up." I knock again, worrying that even though I know she can hear me—I'm being plenty loud enough—she might not open out of principle. I give the door another knock, just as the locks start to unlatch, sending a wave of calm through me.

The door opens, and she stands in front of me, wearing one of the two shirts of mine she still has, her hair a tangled mess, and her eyes barely open.

Fuck, she's gorgeous.

"Roark, please don't do this to me."

"You stopped texting," I say, stepping into the apartment and shutting the door behind me.

"It was late."

I move forward but she takes a step backward, so I take another step forward and we do the same "dance" until she's pressed against the opposite wall, me closing in.

"I wanted you at the event tonight."

"Sometimes we don't get what we want, Roark."

I reach out and take her hand in mine, my eyes cast down. "You were punishing me."

I hear her sigh and look up in time to see her shaking her head. She moves into me and rests her hand on my chest, her fingers playing with the lapel of my suit jacket. "I wasn't punishing you, Roark. I'm trying to keep my heart safe. I feel a lot for you, and I can't keep playing this tug of war."

"I'm sorry." I glide my hand up her arm, past her collarbone, to her cheek where I slightly cup it. She leans into my touch and my heart skips a beat. My body hums, my mind's a pile of mush, all clarity gone.

I want her, so goddamn bad.

I can't go another moment without knowing what she tastes like, without learning the feeling of her lips passing over mine.

I'm desperate to hear what she sounds like when I'm working my hands over her body.

"Fuck . . . Sutton." Chest heavy, my pulse pounding, I lean in.

Eyes wide, her hand gripping tighter to my suit jacket, her body hums, her breasts rising and falling, waiting for my next move.

The air becomes stagnant as the city sleeps around us, not a single sound echoes through the plaster walls, making my pulse thunder in my ears.

Don't do it.

I bite the side of my cheek, unable to listen to the rational part of my brain. The demand for her is too strong, and it's why I feel myself pulling her toward her bed.

"Wh-what are you doing?" she asks, and when her legs hit the mattress, she's forced to sit. A small gasp pops out of her, but when I kneel on the bed and guide her back until she's lying down, her eyes soften. "Roark . . ."

My hand falls to her leg where I pass my fingers lightly over her thigh, up to her hipbone, dragging her shirt with it. It's then that I notice she's not wearing any underwear. My shaky hand pauses as I stare at her.

And like a broken branch in the woods, my will snaps, echoing through my head with such a mighty force I blow full steam ahead.

Removing my hand, I stand up, her worried eyes searching mine until I remove my suit jacket, and roll up my sleeves. A satisfied smile crosses over her lips as I position myself between her legs and offer my hand. When she takes it, I pull her to a sitting position and reach for the hem of the shirt, pulling it up and over her head.

She's completely naked. It's the first time I'm seeing her bare-chested, and fuck me. Round and plump breasts with dusky pointed nipples. A little more than a handful, and I'm about to get lost in them. *No wonder I've been obsessed.*

I drag my hand over my mouth, taking her in before lowering her onto the bed. "Gorgeous," I mutter. Where do I start? I've thought about this moment countless times in the shower, in bed, in my office while on a conference call, and now that it's happening, I'm freezing up.

Maybe it's because I shouldn't be doing this—indulging in a small taste, a brief touch, anything to soothe this burning ache inside me. *I'm being fucking selfish, but I can't not be. She's a goddess. My anchor.*

I lift her leg and start kissing her, letting my scruff mark up her silky white skin, branding her momentarily as mine. Her hands grip the comforter beneath her as I make my way closer to her upper thigh.

I lower myself onto the bed and scoot her up higher so I can utilize the bed as support while I explore her body. In a better position, I lower my mouth to her thigh, my head right next to her pussy. I press little kisses along her skin, lightly flicking my tongue, causing her to jolt in surprise and then moan as she relaxes.

I work my mouth up and down her leg, never getting too close to the juncture between her legs. I'm not ready for that yet, not even close. I'm going to savor her, savor this moment.

Moving back up, I drag my tongue over her hipbone, where I make small circles for a minute before gliding up over her stomach.

I glance at her face—her eyes are shut and her lips are parted—then notice her breasts rising and falling rapidly.

"Are you wet for me, Sutton?"

Her head lulls to the side. "So wet," she whispers. I'm tempted to reach down and feel for myself, but not yet, I need to acquaint myself with her breasts first.

"Your tits, fuck, they're so hot. Ever since I saw you in just your bra, it's like they've been torturing me in my dreams." I glide my hand up to one and give it a squeeze. *Shit.* I take a deep breath as my cock strains against the zipper of my pants. "I've wanted these so bad. I've thought about sucking on them, playing with your cute little nipples, and then fucking them with my cock."

"Roark," she says breathlessly, her eyes flying open as I lower my mouth to one of her nipples while massaging her other breast. "Oh, Roark," she moans as her fingers weave through my hair.

So goddamn erotic, hearing my name come out of her mouth like that, as if I'm the key to her happiness.

I pull and suck, and flick my tongue over her nipple, loving the way she moans beneath me, her hips moving up and down, seeking any kind of release. It's hot as fuck.

I move to her other breast, giving it the same treatment, as one of my hands falls between us. From the sounds she's making to the needy push of her hips against mine, she's extremely turned on, but I need to know how wet she is, how ready she is.

When she senses what I'm doing, the beautiful girl spreads her legs even wider, letting me know I can do whatever the hell I want, and I plan on it.

My hand wanders past her belly button, straight to her pussy. I hover for a second before lightly running my index finger along her slit.

"So fucking wet," I mutter against her breast. Christ, so turned on, so willing. It causes me to lose my control. I slip my finger inside her, tight and perfect, and then slip out. I add another finger, and she cries out in pleasure as my thumb rubs against her clit.

"Roark, oh my God." Her hands go to my shoulders and I consider how experienced she is. It's as if no one has ever touched her like this.

"What do you want?" I ask, rolling my tongue over her nipple.

"I want you." Her hands grip my shoulders even tighter when I press down on her clit. "I . . . want . . . you."

Unable to process what that really means, I release her nipple and move my mouth down her body until I'm positioned in front of her pussy. I release my hand, causing her to cry out, only to replace it with my mouth.

"Yes," she says, her torso lifting off the bed. I press my hand to her chest, lowering her back down, helping her to relax as my tongue goes to work.

I knew she was going to be sweet, I knew being with her was going to be a new experience for me, but never in a million years would I have guessed she'd taste this damn good or sound this damn amazing.

Her little body convulses under my tongue, writhing up and down, her head lulls side to side as her teeth mark her bottom lip. Her fingers cling desperately to the sheets, and I watch in fascination as I bring her to a full-blown orgasm in seconds. With zero shame, she yells my name, her body aching for more. I hold her still and flick my tongue over her clit again and again as she continues to spasm, until she says she can't take it anymore and flings her arm over her eyes.

"Oh my God," she mutters, her hips thrusting up one last time before she finally settles. I press a few kisses to the side of her legs before lifting up and pulling her under the covers. I kick my shoes off and fall in behind her, my cock hard as stone, nuzzled against her naked body.

It takes her a few minutes, but then she moves her head to the side and tries to look at me from over her shoulder. I make it hard as my grip around her waist tightens, and I try to bury my head in her hair, her seductive, lavender-scented hair.

"Roark."

"Hmm," I answer, sleep starting to consume me.

"What about you?"

"What about me?" I kiss her ear as my hand drifts to her breast where I palm it, as if it's my own personal snuggle pillow.

"You're really hard."

"I know."

"Let me take care of it." She starts to move but I stop her.

"No. Just lie here with me. Let me hold you."

"Roark, that's not fair." She starts to move her body along my shaft but I stop her.

"Just sleep with me, Sutton. Please." On a heavy sigh, she acquiesces and allows me to pull her in even closer. "Thank you," I whisper in her ear.

It's the last thing I remember before I wake up . . . and bolt.

CHAPTER THIRTEEN

Dear Sir,
    This entry doesn't even deserve a name.

I fucked up, royally. I know I did, and I didn't need to be confronted about it.

It's seven in the morning and instead of lying in Sutton's lavender haven, snuggled next to her, I bolted the minute she turned on her shower.

Did I leave a note?

Nope.

Didn't even shoot her a text. Just left.

I panicked, because I woke up this morning feeling . . . fuck, feeling like I was on top of the world. Even after a heavy night of drinking, nothing could have brought me down, except the knowledge that one person did that to me—brought me to the pinnacle of happiness. And that made me panic.

Sutton makes me happy. I've never said that about another person, which is terrifying as well. But I can't deny what I feel whenever she's around. The only problem? I know I can't treat that feeling the way she wants me to. She wants a man, deserves a man, who's going to be there for her, take care of her, emotionally and physically. I can't deliver in that way.

This morning was a prime example of that.

And I can't give you an explanation as to why I left, other than, I *panicked. Now I have to take a flight to Texas and spend two weeks on a goddamn ranch with her.*

The flight attendant is going to be very busy bringing me drinks today.
Roark

∽

SUTTON

"Aren't you in Texas?"

"Yes," I answer, holding back the tears threatening to fall.

"Then what's the emergency?"

I lean my head against my childhood headboard and scrunch down into my covers, my heart heavy in my chest. I look to the side, my nose burning from the emotions bubbling up inside me.

After I got out of the shower and saw that Roark had left, without even a note, I stood in the middle of my apartment, shocked.

Then anger took over, and I was tempted to text him, to give him a piece of my mind, but knowing Roark, he'd probably sweet talk his way back into my good graces. He's sharp on text, and I couldn't do that to myself. So I turned my phone off, finished packing for Texas, and headed to the airport.

I held it together for the six hours of travel until I got to the ranch, went to my room, and collapsed on my bed. That's when embarrassment followed by anger hit me.

How dare he? After I told him I couldn't do this back and forth tango. He still messed with my head . . . messed with a small piece of my heart.

"Roark came over last night."

"Oh yummy. Did you do anything exciting? Did you touch his penis?"

"No, but he did go down on me." I remember the euphoric

feeling he delivered. "I've never felt anything like it before, Maddie. I came so hard I didn't think it was going to stop."

"Well . . . that just made me horny."

"Maddie, I'm trying to be serious here."

"So am I, tell me more."

"He left when I was in the shower."

Silence.

"Wait, what? He left? Did he leave a note?"

"No." He didn't leave anything except his scent and a reason for my humiliation. I wipe a stray tear away. "A few days ago I told him I couldn't do this ambiguous thing anymore. He could date me, or we had to go back to being colleagues only."

"Wow, Sutton. I'm totally impressed. What did he say to that?"

"Not much. I guess that's my fault. I didn't get a steady answer from him. He came over last night, and I was going to turn him away, but when I saw the look in his eyes, I believed he wanted more. And then, things escalated and before I knew it I was naked and he was between my legs."

"That's so hot."

"Maddie," I groan. "Please."

"Okay, yeah, sorry. Best friend duties. Uh . . . well, I'm sorry he's a dick, but at least you got an orgasm out of it."

There she is, always looking at the positive side of things.

"Yeah, the best orgasm of my life." I sigh. It was beyond anything I've ever felt before.

"He seems like a guy who delivers life-changing orgasms. His eyes alone promise it. Let's think about this rationally. You're not in love with him, right?"

"No. I mean I have feelings for him."

"Feelings are okay. This is fixable. When does he get to Texas?"

"Later this afternoon. He's staying in the room across from mine."

"Gah, that won't be awkward."

"Tell me about it." I can thank my dad for that setup, although he's clueless as to what's going on. "I'm dreading seeing him, Maddie."

I bite the inside of my cheek, trying to will myself to stay strong. *Don't cry.*

"Why? This is the perfect opportunity for revenge."

Revenge? "What are you talking about?" I ask, sitting up in my bed. "How could I possibly get revenge and for what?"

"For messing with your head. Granted from what you told me, Roark seems like a complicated man with a dark past, so he's bound to do something to screw up his chance with you. I think it's in his bad-boy blood. It's not an excuse, but I think it's a fact."

"Yeah, even though I want to think he's the biggest dick in the world, I agree with that. He's a little broken and doesn't really have a working moral compass. It's as if he's floating, trying to make the best decisions he can with what he's been given."

"Hold up," Maddie says with a stern voice. "He's broken, yes, but we're not feeling sorry for him, not after he wronged you. He needs to learn his lesson. It's the only way he can grow up and be the guy you're looking for."

"And how do you propose I do that?"

"Revenge."

I roll my eyes and stand from my bed, feeling a little better. I begin to unpack my suitcase. Even though I have a lot of clothes here, I brought a few additional comfortable items with me.

"You said that already. Elaborate."

There's a sinister tone to her voice when she talks, and I can't help but smile over my diabolical friend.

"He arrives later today, he's sleeping in the room across from you, and that tells me one thing: you have the opportunity to make his life a living hell. Flaunt it, Sutton. Show him what he's missing out on and when he tries to hold your hand or get intimate, be strong and move away. After having a piece of you last night, he's bound to be hungry for more."

"How do you know that? He left me." *Why he bothered to come over still angers me.*

"Yeah, but the guy is infatuated with you. There's no doubt in my mind he's thinking about every second he had with you last night and trying to drink away the memory because he wants more. For men like Roark, when they set their eye on someone, pursue them, and then finally have a taste, they can't walk away. Trust me, he still very much wants you, but he doesn't know how to handle his feelings."

"You don't know that for sure."

"I don't," she relents. "But I also know a man doesn't go to girl's place in the middle of the night to hold her if there are no feelings involved. He likes you, Sutton, and being the idiot he is, he doesn't know what to do with that."

Huh, she has a point.

"So instead of giving him an ultimatum, I should show him what he's missing out on?"

"Exactly," she says, and if I could see her face, I know there'd be an excited glint in her eyes. "He knows New York City Sutton, but he's never seen Country Girl Sutton. Wear those short shorts and white crop tops. Toss some hay, ride a horse, show him how your hips can perfectly rock up and down on that powerful steed . . ."

I snort, just thinking about it. "That's so mean."

"But perfectly deserved. Set up the torture chamber, Sutton. It's time to make this fool realize what he *could* have had."

Feeling lighter, and now with a smile on my face, I think about all the ways I'm going to make Roark sweat. He thinks he's here for a charitable camp, but little does he know I'm about to shake up his entire world.

"Thank you, Maddie. I love you so much."

"Back at you, girl. Now *if* you think he's worth the effort, snag the guy and bring him back here so I can give him the *best friend* warning."

"I'm on it."

From a distance, I spot a black town car making its way up the long, freshly paved driveway of Green Ranch. Showtime.

Standing next to me is my dad, wearing his signature Levi's—that he's paid to endorse of course, thank you, Roark—and a short-sleeved grey T-shirt. His sturdy black Stetson sits on top of his head while his black matching boots dig into the porch. He's in his element, more than when he's on the football field. He's a Texas man through and through, so whenever he gets back to the ranch, it takes no time for him to look and feel part of the place again.

Not wanting to look too slutty in front of my dad and wanting to ease Roark into this side of my life, I put on a pair of jeans, my worn boots, and a very tight-fitting white T-shirt. And to top it all off, I put on my white Stetson. I remember getting my first real hat. I was six. Dad said I would always be a white-hat girl, and he's kept it that way. As he puts it, my white halo must grace my head when on the ranch.

Little does he know, there are devil horns peeking out through my halo.

The town car nears—my dad ordered it for Roark—and I steel myself. I'm in control. He's the one who left, the one who should be feeling weird. Not me.

Mission Tempt Roark is in full motion as the car comes to a stop. I hold my breath as we step forward. The door to the car opens, and my dad and I stop in our pursuit as Roark falls out the back, small bottles tumbling to the concrete with him as he clutches the biggest bottle of Jameson I've ever seen.

Oh, Roark.

I glance at my dad, who has a very disappointed look on his face. He places his hand on my shoulder, silently telling me to stay where I am as he makes his way toward the drunk man in our driveway.

Roark looks up, pushing his black Ray-Bans off his eyes, and gives my dad a crooked smile. "Fosterrrr," he draws out, "I made it."

He struggles to get up, but when he does, he leans against the car and holds his bottle of whiskey like a baby. For once, Roark's signature hot combination of skinny jeans and a snug-fitting Henley look out of place, as if he was plucked straight from a nightclub in New York City and transplanted here. *Which he probably was.* His beard is thicker, untrimmed, and from where his glasses have lifted up, I can see dark circles under his eyes, heavy and bold.

Looks like Maddie was right. He's hurting worse than I am, which is good to know. *Or he simply resorted to what he likes best.*

"Have you been drinking all day?" my dad asks, his voice booming.

Not even caring, Roark nods. "Yup." He holds up his hand. "But don't worry"—he sways to the side—"I didn't get into one fight."

Stepping forward, my dad's powerful shoulders flex as he reaches out and snatches the bottle of alcohol from Roark. "You can't have this here."

Roark leans backward. "The kids aren't here, yet. Consider it a welcoming gift."

"I don't mean on the ranch. I mean in this county."

Roark's brow pinches tougher. "What?"

Roark is in for a very rude awakening. I'm almost giddy as I try to hide my smile.

"It's a dry county. There are very few in Texas, but the ranch falls within one of those county's lines, which means no alcohol."

Roark's eyes widen. "No alcohol?"

"No." My dad holds out his hand and says, "And no smoking either. Hand them over."

"What? No smoking here either?" Roark looks around, the bright sun causing him to pull his sunglasses back up. "What kind of straight-laced county is this?"

"The no smoking is my rule. Now hand them over."

Reaching into his back pocket, Roark pulls out a packet of

cigarettes and places them in my dad's hand. What is Roark going to do without his "accessories"?

Maybe actually clean up a little.

Nodding toward the car, my dad says, "Grab your luggage. Sutton will show you to your room while I dispose of this crap. You are to take a shower, sober up, and get ready for some hard work. We need an extra pair of hands to get the chores done before dinner."

"Chores?"

My dad nods. "Did you think this was a vacation? Far from it." He leans forward and gets into Roark's face. "You just entered hell, and you're about to get yourself cleaned up, whether you like it or not. You're a good guy, Roark. It's about time you start reaching your full potential."

Muttering something under his breath, Roark takes his suitcase from the driver and starts walking toward the house, and that's when his eyes focus on me for the first time. His step stutters and his eyes rake me up and down from under his sunglasses, his lips parting open ever so slightly. Just the sort of reaction I was looking for.

Putting on a cheery smile, I say, "This way, Roark."

I spin on my boots and give him a good sway as I make my way in the house. I hold the door open for him and guide him up the stairs. I glance back a few times and find him struggling to keep a straight line as his eyes are fixed directly on my butt.

Maddie was so freaking right.

This is going to be fun.

When we reach his room, I open the door and gesture inside. "This is where you'll be staying." I point to the door across from his, and even though he's staring at my breasts, I keep talking. "My room is right across from yours. We're sharing the bathroom right there. Make sure you knock before coming in."

"Knock, sure, got it."

He leans against the wall, looking absolutely exhausted. Did he get any sleep last night? From the looks of it, he didn't.

"I suggest you take a shower like Dad said and get some coffee in you. It's going to be a long afternoon if you don't. Everything you need is on your bed. Welcome to the ranch."

I start to walk away when he grabs my arm to stop me.

Just to drive him crazy, I whip my head around and smile brightly at him. "Yes, is there something else?"

"Sutton," he grumbles. "I'm . . . I'm."

I reach up and pat him on the cheek. "Don't sweat it, Roark. Let me know if you need anything."

I pull away and walk down the stairs, leaving him with a confused look on his face and an untapped desire in his eyes.

∽

Do not snort!

You're only going to make it worse.

Oh man, it's so hard not to though. I've never seen a man struggle so hard in my life. Barely sober, looking wrecked, Roark lifts another hay bale over and attempts to chuck it onto the truck bed, missing once again.

"Motherfucker," he yells, kicking it and then wiping his brow with his forearm.

The heat from the sun is relentless today, especially for a guy who's not used to it, and thanks to my dad's demands, the ranch hands are not letting up on him.

"Come on, lad," one of the guys says. "Are those pretty muscles or do they actually work?"

I'm sure they work, there is no doubt in my mind, but Roark's barely regained his coordination and is struggling.

Sweat is dripping down every part of his shirt, there is dirt caked on his face, and his jeans are an ashy brown rather than crisp black from the amount of times he's stumbled his way through chores. There is only one thing left, feeding the horses, but he's obviously done for the day.

"Fuck you," Roark mutters as he reaches for the hay bale again.

I walk past him, a bale in my grasp, and chuck it into the truck, using just the right swing to get it up and over the hatch. Roark watches me.

I point to his bale. "Want me to do that for you?"

His eyes narrow. "No. I got it."

"You sure? Seems like you're struggling a little."

"I'm not struggling. I'm just, fuck." He wipes his forehead again. "I think I'm actually hungover, for one of the first times in my life."

I pat his shoulder as if we're pals, rather than two people who find one another attractive but can't quite figure out how to make it work between them. "That's what happens when you drink: hangovers follow."

I haven't had a hard day on the ranch in a long time because of school and trying to make my career happen, but today felt good. I know, weird right, to be happy about doing physical labor, but it's what I grew up with. During football season, I would go back and forth to New York to visit with Dad, but my true home was Texas, and Dad was very adamant about me carrying my weight around the ranch.

If he heard I wasn't doing my chores, he'd fly from New York to lecture me, only to fly back for practice the next day. I learned quickly he hated that, and the tongue lashing I got would be proof of it, so I made sure I pulled my weight.

And I learned to appreciate it. Maybe not right away, because what teenager wants to be shoveling horse crap on the weekend? But over time, I understood why Dad was strict with me. He wanted me to realize the benefit of hard work, both academic and physical. I confidently believe I earned my position with Gaining Goals, and I'm proud of myself.

Letting the water run down my sore muscles for a few more

seconds, I breathe in the steam billowing below and let out a long breath. What a day.

What a wonderfully long and rewarding day.

I switch off the shower, dry off, and then wrap the towel around my body, stuffing the end between my breasts to keep the towel in place. I brush out my long, wet hair, moisturize my face, and put a touch of lavender behind my ears and on my wrists.

Satisfied, I open the bathroom door and walk down the hallway toward my room where I see Roark leaning against his door, his eyes shut, a towel dangling from his hand. When he hears me approach, he stands up and looks in my direction. Immediately his eyes start to rake over my body, and from the burning look Roark has on his face, I'm very happy I decided to leave my clothes in my room.

"Shower is all yours."

He scratches his beard, eyes still trained on me. "Thanks."

I pause in front of him, letting him take a longer look while the lavender scent I know drives him crazy floats between us. "Do you need help turning the shower on? I can show you how it works."

"I, uh . . . I think I can handle it."

I press my hand against his chest, innocently batting my lashes up at him. "Are you sure?"

His eyes fall to my hand then back up to me. "Yeah."

I pat his chest and walk over to my door. Looking over my shoulder, I say, "Well, I'm just across the way. You know where to find me."

I begin to walk into my room when Roark says, "Hold on."

Hand still on the door, I turn toward him. "Yeah?"

"Can we talk?"

"I don't think that's necessary." I smile brightly. "We don't really have anything to talk about."

"Bullshit," he growls. I'm taking it he doesn't like how nice and sweet I'm being. My dad was right, you catch more flies with honey.

Fully turning toward him, I reach out and wipe a piece of mud off his brow. He tries to lean into my touch, but I pull away before he can make too much contact. "Listen, there's nothing really to be said. We're good. Don't worry about it." My towel starts to come undone, so I grip the knot, but making sure to hold it low.

His gaze drifts down to the abundance of cleavage I'm displaying. He rakes his hand over his mouth and squeezes his eyes shut.

"It's been a long and painful day, Sutton. Don't tempt me."

"What are you talking about? I'm not tempting you."

"You're not?" His brow shoots up. "You've been sweet to me all day after I left your apartment without saying a word, and you're strutting around this house like a goddamn temptress with your tight white shirts and towel dances."

"Towel dances?" My nose curls. "I highly doubt standing here in the hallway and talking to you like an adult is considered a towel dance."

"You know what I mean," he answers exasperated. "You're punishing me."

I pat his chest and give him the sweetest smile I can muster. "And why would I do that, Roark? We're friends . . . just friends. You made that quite clear this morning. I'm good with that. Now if you'll excuse me, there are some homemade beans on the stove I want to make sure I'm first in line for. Hurry up and shower; Dad doesn't like it when people are late for dinner."

Satisfied, I walk into my room and shut the door, a huge smile plastered across my face. This really is going to be so much fun.

CHAPTER FOURTEEN

D*ear Satan,*
 Yeah, Satan, because I'm really hoping somehow this godforsaken diary makes it into his hands.

I'm living in hell. Pure, torturous hell.

What kind of county decides to ban alcohol? I'll tell you, the kind that was bathed and clothed by the devil himself. There is no other explanation.

Fuck. Really that's the only way to describe how I'm feeling right now. Just . . . fuck.

It's bad enough my vices have been stripped from me, leaving me feeling raw and exposed, but having to sleep in a room across from Sutton's and share a bathroom with her, that's goddamn torture.

After she got out of the shower and strutted toward me in that white towel, my tongue nearly fell out of my mouth. Freshly wet and sexy with her low-slung towel, I got hard in seconds. And this whole nice act she's pulling with me? I don't trust it. There is no way she's cool with what I did. I know her, and she wears her emotions on her sleeve, so I don't believe for a second she's fine.

Which makes this situation even more irritating because I wish she'd get angry at me, yell, scream, do something, but instead she's strutting around like nothing happened.

And I swear to Christ, your enemy, that she's hotter in the country. I don't know if it's the fresh air, or being back at her childhood home, but she has this intoxicating *air about her*. It's different and really fucking hot.

It's why I spent a good ten minutes jacking off in the shower to her lavender scent that was mixed with the steam of the shower. It was as if Sutton was wrapped around me.

Yeah, I'm fucking losing it, Satan. Please, for the love of God, end my misery and take me to your dungeon. Do weird shit to me, I don't care, but just take me away from this purgatory. I won't last another thirteen days.

Roark

~

ROARK

"Isn't she wonderful to watch?" Foster asks, standing next to me as we both lean on the split-rail fence of the round pen.

After two hours of shoveling shit and chasing chickens—don't even ask—I now have the pleasure of watching Sutton exercise the horses with Josh.

Who's Josh? Oh, the horse trainer Sutton seems to be very chummy with. Every time he grants her a compliment, she gives him a blistering beautiful smile under her perfectly white hat. Josh is about to get his neck wrung by yours truly if he shouts she looks good one more time.

Because she does look good, damn good.

Foster is watching like a proud father, his steed galloping along the ring, his daughter expertly trained and encouraging the horse with soothing tones.

Josh is standing in the middle of the pen, offering occasional guidance, a stupid black hat on his head, and a plaid shirt that looks doofy on him.

And I'm over here, a pathetic motherfucker, eyes fixated on two things: the way Sutton's tits bounce up and down in her black T-shirt, and the way her hips rock up and down on the horse.

Cock fully erect, I lean against the fence, practically drooling.

Who knew exercising a horse could be so hot? I swear to Satan himself, every time she glances my way, she knows exactly what she's doing to me. Tormenting with her hips, puffing her chest out, that laugh, that smile. It's like a goddamn dagger to my stomach, twisting and turning it.

"She's very astute," I answer, not knowing what else to say to Foster that won't get me into trouble. Because I'm pretty sure saying something like "I'm hoping your daughter's tits spill out of that shirt at some point" isn't really appropriate.

We spent the morning working around the ranch, setting up some things for the camp, such as the cabins and the obstacles, and now, after lunch, we're getting ready to go on a long ride with the horses. It's supposed to be beautiful along the "range" but all I can think about is how I'm going to have to mount one of those beasts and not look like a fool in front of Sutton while doing it.

Foster's large hand grabs my shoulder and gives it a little shake. "You look nervous. No need to worry about the ride. It's going to be fun."

Nervous, yeah. Hard-up, most definitely. Desperate for a drink and a smoke, one hundred percent.

"Never ridden a horse. Not really nervous, but I don't want to look like a dick, ya know?"

Foster laughs. "Yeah, we have that pride we have to hold on to."

"Always." I expected Foster to rip me a new asshole for how I arrived yesterday, but he didn't. And I feel so pathetic and shamed regardless.

"Don't worry, I'm setting you up with my calmest, sweetest mare. Her name is Grammy, and she'll take good care of you."

"Grammy, huh? What color is she?"

"Black."

I nod in appreciation. "Just like my soul. We'll get along nicely."

"All done?" Foster calls out.

"Yup," Sutton answers, bringing the horse to a stop. She tosses her hair over her shoulder and to my horror, I watch as Josh reaches out and grabs her by the waist, bringing her down to the ground. I stand taller, the hairs on the back of my neck at full attention. They stand for a few seconds, talking as his hands stay on her hips. The grip I have on the fence turns lethal as I count the seconds they stand there.

What the hell are they saying?

Do they have history?

Is that why Sutton is so calm with me, because she knew she'd see this guy all along?

Tossing her head back, she laughs and then pats Josh on the chest, and I nearly blow through the fence like a tornado and charge toward Josh, ready to buckle his knees with a piece of the fence.

Finally, they part and carefree Sutton walks toward us, hands stuffed in her back pockets, a huge smile on her face. "That was so much fun. I can't remember the last time I did that. Lady is such a smooth horse. Josh has been doing a great job with her."

Fucking Josh.

"Josh has been a great attribute to the ranch, taking excellent care of the horses while I'm gone. He's great," Foster answers and then claps his hands. "Are we ready to go on a ride along the range?"

"Can't wait." Sutton gives me a glance. "Are you going to go back to the house?"

"No. I'm going with you."

A small smile peeks past her lips. "Have you ridden a horse before?"

"No, but I feel confident in the quick bond I'll develop with Grammy."

"You put him with Grammy?" Sutton gives her dad a look. What's that look for? What do they know that I don't?

"She's very tame."

"She also is very ornery," Sutton counters.

"He'll be fine, right, Roark?" Foster asks with a grin.

I don't like the word ornery, but it's not like I'm about to put up a fight about it either, so I hold steady with my confidence.

"What are we talking about?" Josh asks, playfully bumping into Sutton who grants him with another one of her beautiful smiles.

I'm going to fucking snap if she does that again.

"We're going for a ride on the range, want to join us?" Sutton asks.

"Doesn't he have shit to do?" I ask, the words slipping from my mouth before I can stop them. Everyone turns toward me, and I have an *oh shit* moment, so I quickly try to recover. "I mean, do you have shit to scoop before you go? I can help."

"That would be awesome," Josh answers, the jolly fucker that he is. "You can scoop up the pen and I'll saddle up the horses with Foster. How does that sound?"

Sounds like I just gave myself shit duty.

"Yeah, sure," I mumble, walking away to the wheelbarrow and shovel as everyone else heads to the tackle barn.

How did this become my life? Not long ago I was in the city, having a good time at nightclubs, hanging with my boys, getting my job done with my expected expertise. All that was thrown out when this undersized bombshell appeared in my life, overturning my contentment for habitual debauchery with her smile and mettle. One taste of her mouth and I was driving my tongue up and down said beauty's clit. Now I'm shoveling horse shit into a rusty old wheelbarrow while Sutton is getting all buddy-buddy with Josh, the horse whisperer.

Where did I go wrong?

I know the exact moment I went wrong, though. When I left Sutton's bed like a fucking spineless gobshite. That was the turning point for me, the worst decision I've made in a very long time, because instead of hanging out on a beautiful farm with Sutton under my arm, smiling up at me, I get to watch her sway her hips all over this godforsaken place while every man who works here watches.

I roll the wheelbarrow over to the first pile and start scooping a load of horse droppings into it.

Fucking ridiculous.

I continue moving the wheelbarrow around until I scoop up the last of it. That's when I turn to find Sutton sitting on the fence, hands braced at her side, watching me. "You're good at that."

"Great." I roll my eyes and put the wheelbarrow back with the shovel. "Something to add to my list of accomplishments. Can shovel horse shit."

"You never know when it'll come in handy." When I reach her, she hops down from the fence and dusts off her butt. Sure, she can hop down from the fence all by herself, but she needs Josh's help when she's getting off the horse. "Grammy's all ready. Want to mount her?"

There's someone else I'd rather be mounting.

"Sure." I dust my hands off on my jeans and ignore the fact that they are once again covered in dust.

"Didn't my dad tell you black doesn't do well out here? We should get you fitted in some cowboy gear."

"I'd rather drop dead."

"You don't think you can pull off cowboy boots?"

"I can pull them off, easily. I just don't want to."

She shakes her head while giving me a once-over. "I don't know. I don't think you can pull them off, but then again, not everyone can look as good as Josh in a pair."

She knows exactly what she's doing.

She tries to walk away, but I snag her wrist before she can get too far and pull her back. Growing serious, I lift her chin and look her square in the eyes. "Tempt me all you want. Flaunt your cute little ass in those jeans, wear the lowest-cut shirt while riding a horse, I don't give a fuck—well I do, but do it all you want. But I swear to God, Sutton, do not throw another man in my face. Don't play those fucking games."

She studies me. "I'm not throwing him in your face."

"Bullshit. Why else would you talk about him like that and let him touch you all over? You're trying to make me jealous."

"You made your choice about me when you left my apartment

yesterday morning. *This* is my home. There is no point *throwing* another man in your face, Roark. You left."

"Don't fuck with me, Sutton." *She's right. She's so fucking right. I don't deserve to feel jealous.* But, unfortunately, I can't hide that I'm so pissed.

She rolls her eyes, clearly not taking me seriously. "And what are you going to do? Ignore me? Leave me alone? Never talk to me again? You're pretty much already doing that, so what's the difference?"

"Don't fuck with me," I repeat. "Or else you're not going to like what happens."

"Try me, Roark. I can handle pretty much anything you throw my way at this point."

My jaw moves back and forth as I chew on that information. Honestly, what would I do? I'm just tossing empty threats her way, unsure how to handle the entire situation. *And she knows that.*

Am I jealous? Fuck yeah. I don't want anyone even looking at Sutton, let alone touching her. And yeah, I have no claim to her whatsoever but that still doesn't mean I want to see other guys throw their dicks in her direction.

I take a step back and drag my hand over my face, irritated with myself, irritated with the entire situation. "Let's just get the horses and get this over with."

"If you're going to act sour, you might as well not go."

"I'm sure that's exactly what you want, for me not to go so you can hang out with Josh some more." *When did I become so petulant?*

"Why does it matter?" she counters. "It's not like I belong to you."

"You sure as fuck do," I say before I can stop myself. Anger seeps from my pores as my hands twitch at my side, the realization that I want her more than anything hitting me square in the chest. I close the distance between us and talk through my teeth. "The moment ya came on my tongue was the moment ya became mine. Don't fook with me."

Not even flinching, she says, "In order for me to be yours, I have to want it too and honestly, Roark, I'm over it."

"If you were over it, you wouldn't be flaunting your tits every chance you get."

She gives me a once-over. "Who said it was for you?"

"I swear to Christ, Sutton." But before I can toss her another empty threat, she walks away.

Fuck.

∽

Grammy is a temperamental bitch.

You know what else? Riding a horse isn't great on the old balls.

My sack is numb.

My back is tight from not wanting to startle Grammy.

And I can't feel my goddamn thighs.

How do people find this enjoyable? Yeah, sure the scenery is nice and all, but nice enough to endure this torture? No fucking way.

And then there's Josh and Sutton having a little laugh fest up ahead, sharing jokes, and riding in sync while I'm back here with Grammy trying to make sure she doesn't kick me off again.

Yeah . . . again.

When I first mounted the crotchety wench, she wanted nothing to do with me and bucked me off. Thankfully I'm agile and landed on my feet. It was an impressive landing, and if I had been drunk there is no doubt in my mind I would have thrown my arms up in the air like a gymnast, waiting for my scores. Instead, I gave the old lass a pat on the arse and mounted her again, holding on tight, silently pleading with the mammal to work with me.

And since then, she has.

"What do you think?" Foster asks, maneuvering his horse next to mine like a pro. It's odd, seeing him in this element, where he looks like an oversized quarterback on a horse. I'm so used to seeing him in a suit or football gear but seeing him like this—a cowboy hat on his head, chaps on his legs, reins in his hands—seems so strange but also natural. *This is home to him.*

"You have a great property, Foster."

"Thank you. I love it here." He looks toward his property as we make our way to the barn. *He seems content.* "This last season will be hard, saying goodbye to the many people who've played a huge part in my career, but there is promise of a new beginning at the end." He gestures toward the barn. "Peace . . . and lots and lots of baths."

I chuckle as Grammy slows down. "Are you thinking about settling down?" Foster gives me a look and I roll my eyes. "Come on, who are you kidding? I know you have a thing going on with Whitney."

His eyes narrow and he slows down his horse as well. "Quiet down," he whispers, his eyes flashing to Sutton, who's in a deep conversation with Josh.

Fucking Josh.

"She can't hear you and even if she could, she's twenty-four. I'm sure she'd like to see you with someone so you're not alone for the rest of your life."

He tugs on his hat and keeps his voice down so I can barely hear him. "I would love to settle down, put a ring on Whitney's finger, but there's a lot stopping me. She's six years younger than I am, for one."

I hide my cringe. "Age difference doesn't really mean anything these days."

"She also works with me."

Christ. "You know, office romances are in right now."

"And what about Sutton?"

I wave him off. "She probably has her own things she's dealing with. Just from getting to know her through this camp project, I'd say she'd be cool with it."

"I don't know."

I shrug. "Fine, be a lonely bastard for all I care. Just show up for your obligations so I get paid."

He chuckles and then grows serious. "And what about you?"

"What about me?" I ask, knowing exactly what he's talking about but wanting to stall the conversation.

"When are you going to settle?" I notice he doesn't say settling down, but again, I want to ignore that jibe. He's not being cruel.

The sun starts to descend behind the horizon, casting the sky in an orange bliss, the clouds bordered in purple. I can see why Foster loves it out here. Calm and peaceful, away from it all. It reminds me of Killarney a bit, yet it's not as lush. I could possibly see myself relaxing in a place like this one day, minus all the horse shit.

"Settling down isn't for me. Fast-paced life, that's me."

"It's not, and I didn't say settling down. I said *settle*." He stops his horse, so I pull on Grammy's reins, and thankfully she listens. "In order to settle down, you need to find what it is that brings you calm. It's in you, and for a week or so, I saw it. And now it's gone. You like to think fast-paced is the life you need, but you're covering up for the life you really want."

"Oh yeah?" I chuckle. "And what life do I really want?"

"The one you never had as a kid."

Hell, I'll give it to Foster, he sure knows how to identify someone's weak spot. He should be my therapist, because in one sentence he virtually wrapped up my entire life in a nutshell.

"Yeah, well, not everyone can have the white picket fence."

"You can, you just choose not to."

I glance at Sutton, who dismounts her horse minus Josh this time. Damn right. "It's easier that way."

"To not let yourself feel?" Foster presses.

"Exactly. The minute you allow yourself to feel is the minute it gets thrown back in your face. I prefer to be numb, which has been pretty damn hard to do since I got here. Thanks for that."

He doesn't answer right away, but instead stares at the sunset, looking regal as fuck on his steed. "I've worked with a lot of young boys who've had that attitude. I've seen some grow into men who find their way through the murk of this world, and I've seen some not make it." Foster turns to me. "You're not a boy, but you're not a man either, Roark. You're somewhere between. A man takes his life into his hands and makes the most of it. You're a damn fine agent, and I'm grateful for you, but you're also riding a thin line of losing everything you've ever worked for. Don't be a fuck-up, be a man." Looking me dead in the eyes, he says, "There comes a time in a man's life when he has to decide whether he's going to take action and make something of himself, or if he's going to sit idly and never reach his full potential." He clasps my shoulder. My mouth is dry, and my stomach is flipping in knots. "You have a lot to give, allow yourself to hand it out. You'd be surprised by how happiness can change your entire outlook on life."

Smiling crookedly at me, he gives me one more pat before taking off toward the barn. I should dislike what he said to me, but instead I'm caught by his words.

". . . you're also riding a thin line of losing everything you've ever worked for. Don't be a fuck-up, be a man."

Be a man.

Don't be a fuck-up.

That's a fucking blow to hear, yet, somehow it resonates with me unexpectedly. My mind is whirling with possibilities.

Don't be a fuck-up.

Be a man.

Two days later Foster's words are still bouncing around in my head.

I know we've worked together for a while, but he was able to pick me apart in seconds. There are reasons I don't want to allow myself to truly feel beyond lust. Lust is easy. Safe. Never leads to disappointment, either in me or the other person. Love is conditional. Limited. *"You've always been ungrateful for everything I've given you. At this point it would be easier if you were dead. At least I could mourn the loss of my oldest son and move on."* Move on. My own ma would prefer I was dead. *What does that say about love?* The people who are supposed to love me unconditionally only give a shit about the green I have in the bank. Wish I was dead. *What does that say about me?*

Fuck, I need a drink. I need something to rid this blooming feeling of inadequacy inside of me. Drinking makes it easy to quickly forget. It's why I live on a whiskey diet, so I don't lie awake at night, thinking of all the things I could have but am too goddamn scared to attempt to have.

Like Sutton.

I want her, but not only physically. I want her brain, her heart, her soul. I want to know what it's like to stay up all night and talk to her about nothing. I want to know what it's like to comfort her when she's upset. I want to feel her tears on my fingers, knowing I'm the only person in the world who can console her. I want to know what it feels like to be completely addicted to someone to the point that when we part in the morning, I miss her ten seconds later. I want all of that, the good, the bad, and the ugly that comes with being in love.

And I think, no . . . I know Sutton can be that girl.

But what if, fuck, what if she dives into a relationship and realizes, just like my parents, that I'm worthless? *That's* not a chance I can take. I'm already on the verge of falling off the face of the earth any second, I don't need the extra push. Because if Sutton loved me and I eventually lost her love . . . *I can't.*

Sighing, my forehead pressed against the wood molding of the wall, I grip the doorknob and prepare myself for another day of brutal chores, more camp setup, and watching Sutton be her beautiful self.

I swing the door open just as Sutton opens hers as well. I pause mid-stride when I take her in. Decked out in the tiniest cut-off shorts I've ever seen, her trusty boots and . . . oh fuck no.

"What is that?" I ask, pointing at her chest.

She glances down and then back at me. "My shirt."

My brow soars. "You call that a shirt? It's cut off. I can see your entire midriff." I bend a little. "Are you wearing a bra?"

She points down the hall. "I left it in the bathroom. I was going to get it."

Perky and perfect, her breasts tempt me once again and even if she was wearing a bra, I'd be able to see it. There's no way she's wearing that shirt outside with all the ranch hands swarming the property.

Nope, not going to happen.

Before she can make her way to the bathroom, I push her through her bedroom door and shut it behind me. For a second, I observe her modest childhood bedroom: tan walls, floral bedspread, a poster of a horse above her bed. It's fucking cute.

"What do you think you're doing?" she asks, hands on her hips, her shirt riding high.

"You're not going out there like that. I can see your nipples."

She rolls her eyes. "I'm going to wear a bra. And honestly, this is none of your business, Roark."

I pull on my hair and turn away, frustrated with this entire situation. She's driving me completely nuts, and I don't know what to do about it. She's right, it isn't any of my business how she dresses, and even though I want her to wear a turtleneck and slacks, I know I can't ask her to do that.

"Fuck," I mutter. Hand still in my hair, I say, "If you're going to wear that, please stay away from me."

There is a softness in her voice as she presses her hand to my back. "Is everything okay, Roark?"

I shake my head, my body tingling from how close she is. "No. I'm struggling, Sutton."

She comes up to my side and tries to look me in the eyes but I don't turn my head. "You can talk to me, you know."

"I can't."

"Roark—"

I pin her against the wall next to her door in one swift movement, catching her off guard. Her eyes are a little wild, her chest rises and falls against mine as she asks, "Wh-what are you doing?"

"I don't know," I answer, my hands pinned at her waist, itching to move up. When I take an inch, her breath catches in her chest, so I move my hand up even higher until the underside of her breast is rubbing against my finger.

"Roark," she breathes out. Heavily.

I lean forward and press my mouth to her ear and nip at her lobe. Her head lulls to the side and even though she's been nothing but a giant temptress the last few days, I feel the need she has for me in the way her hands fall to my shoulders and then up my neck to weave through my hair.

I move in closer, pressing my hips against hers while I cup her breast at the same time.

"You're driving me crazy, Sutton." My lips work up and down her neck. "You think this is easy for me? Being here, my room across from yours, watching you talk to other guys? It's killing me."

"Then do something about it."

"What do you want me to do?" I ask while lowering my head to her breast, lifting her shirt up and sucking her nipple into my mouth.

"Yes," she says on a sigh. "That feels so good, Roark." Her encouragement spurs me on and breaks something inside me. I lift her up by the waist and carry her to the bed where I lay her down gently. I press my hips against hers, letting her know how much she affects me.

I bring her shirt up and over her head, exposing her breasts. She's so beautiful it's almost painful. I lower my mouth back to them as I rock my hips into her, my erection finding small relief in the friction. But I want more.

She must read my mind, because her hand reaches between us and falls under the hemline of my jeans where her fingers pass over my bulge.

I lift up, head lowered, and hiss out a long breath, giving her more access. My muscles tighten, my eyes fall shut, and her little hand curls around my cock, my briefs the only barrier.

"Fuck," I mutter. "Sutton . . . I." Her hand slides inside my briefs, and I swear I'm seconds from coming from her touch alone.

I glance up to see her mouth parted, her eyes wild as she says, "You're so big, Roark."

And that's my undoing. That innocent look, the surprise but joy that crosses her face, it breaks my resolve.

I reach down and undo her shorts, yanking them off in a smooth movement, then push my jeans down, leaving my briefs on. Like a teenage boy, I press my erection along her spread legs and seek the comfort of her warmth. My erection peeks past the waistband of my briefs as I glide it up and down her thong-clad center.

"Oh. My. God," she moans and I shush her, bringing my mouth to her neck again, my hips rocking against hers in long strokes and then quick short ones, my body really unsure of what it wants.

No clothes would be better, but I can't do that to her, not when I'm unsure of the feelings bristling inside me, but fuck, I just want some relief.

"I've never wanted something more in my life," I say, surprising myself, but . . . it's the truth. "You drive me crazy with need, Sutton. The last few days have been hell for me."

"But don't you know? You can have me, Roark."

I grind my hips harder, my legs starting to tingle, my balls beginning to tighten.

"That's what I'm worried about. You shouldn't be so willing where I'm concerned. I'm not right for you."

She spreads her legs even wider and links her hands behind my neck. "Why won't you let me be the judge of that?"

I grind our hips together as I lift my head to look down at her. Lips wet and ready, eyes focused on me. Kissing her would bring this need to a whole new level. I know the moment my lips meet hers, there will be no returning. I won't be able to stop.

Is that something I want to put her through, offer her a man who's unsure if he can ever return what she gives him?

I don't know if I can do that to her.

So instead of lowering my head, I keep my eyes locked on her as I drive my hips over hers, rocking us both to a peak.

She bites on her bottom lip, her neck straining, her orgasm floating, ready to fall over. Christ, I'm right there with her, my heart pounding in my head, my body thrumming with pleasure.

Knock, knock.

"Sutton, are you in there?" Foster's voice calls out, stilling my hips in an instant.

Holy fuck.

I quickly stand, my erection painfully hard as I back away and look around her room. I spot her closet and quickly flee while pulling my pants up.

A small moan pops out of her during my retreat, and it echoes through my head as I lean my body against the closed closet door, unable to catch my breath.

Strained, Sutton says, "Yeah . . . just had . . . a clothing mishap. Be right down." Clothing mishap, yeah, I would say missing half your shirt is a clothing mishap.

"Oh okay, just checking. Have you seen Roark?"

"Uh no . . . did you check the horse pen? He's really good at taking care of all the excrement."

Foster laughs as I frown. Real fucking funny. "Good point, I'll go check. Hurry up, we have a lot to do before the kids arrive tomorrow."

"Yup, be right down." The strong footsteps of Foster's boots echo down the hallway as he retreats. We must have been so far gone to not even notice their approach earlier.

On a heavy sigh, I lean my head against the closet door as it opens. Back tense, cock hard as stone and stuffed in my jeans, I turn to find Sutton wearing nothing but a thong. Come on, this really isn't fucking fair, especially with another day of hard labor ahead of me.

I reach out to her and bring her into a hug where my hands fall to her bare ass. I kiss the top of her head and say, "I'm sorry."

"Sorry for what?"

"For letting that get out of hand, for being a dick to you, for believing you belong to me when you don't."

She lifts up and looks me in the eyes. "But that's where you're wrong, Roark. No matter how much you try to push me away, it doesn't change how I feel about you." She bites her bottom lip and grips the front of my shirt. "I've tried to act like you don't matter to me, that I can move past this crazy affection I have for you, but it's impossible. With one look in my direction, you have me melting at your feet. And there's nothing I can do about this feeling. So, when you come into my room and press your lips all over my body, I will always give in, because it's what I crave." And that makes me one lucky bastard—something I don't deserve.

"You shouldn't," I say on a whisper.

"I know, believe me I know, but I can't resist you. No matter how hard I try, I can't." Her hand reaches up and strokes my cheek, her eyes filling with unshed tears. "Please don't pull away from me. I so wish you could see the value in us being together."

Sadly, she lowers her hand and moves past me where she pulls on a pair of jeans and a regular shirt. When she departs the closet, I call out, "Bra, Sutton."

She gives me a sad smile. "Still in the bathroom." And then she takes off.

I lean against her shelves, an overwhelming sense of Sutton surrounding me as I try to uncomplicate my head.

I so wish you could see the value in us being together.

I can see it, hell, I can feel it, almost as if she's been slowly etching it into my bones over the last few weeks. Weakened and tired, I head out of her room and down the stairs where I watch Sutton give her dad a hug before they walk out of the house together.

What I wouldn't give to be the man she gives those hugs to,

the man she looks up to with that smile, or the man who protects her from the rest of the world.

"*No matter how much you try to push me away, it doesn't change how I feel about you . . . I've tried to act like you don't matter to me, that I can move past this crazy affection I have for you, but it's impossible.*" But how do I become the man who deserves her? How do I become *her* man?

And then I hear Foster's thoughts, which combine to further cement these thoughts.

A man takes his life into his hands and makes the most of it.

Foster was right, I'm not *that* man—*yet*—but maybe it's time I find out how to start acting like him.

CHAPTER FIFTEEN

Dear Jasper,
 Jasper is the name of a pig I talked to the other day as I fed him what looked like sewer slop. He had kind eyes, so I thought I'd try the name out here. Not sure if it works, just reminds me of the old hog.

 I honestly don't know what to say right now. If my therapist was here, she'd ask me annoying questions like how do you feel? What's on your mind? Any hurdles you've had to face lately?

 Well . . . since she's not here—not that I would want to talk to her—but since she's across the country, probably diddling around on her doodle pad, I'll write the answers here.

 How do you feel? Like absolute piss.

 What's on my mind? Sutton. Day in and day out it's been Sutton.

 Any hurdles you've had to face lately? Only a few, you know, nicotine cravings, the need for one shot of whiskey. Release, sweet fucking release.

 And then there's the biggest hurdle of them all . . . emotions. I'm dealing with a bunch of emotions I've never felt before. Things like . . . jealousy, emptiness, yearning.

 I can see myself letting my walls down and lending out my hand to Sutton. I can feel my guard crumbling and needing something other than alcohol to console me.

 I want to hold Sutton's hand.

I want to kiss Sutton whenever I damn well please.

I want to tell her shit, like my fears and my triumphs.

I want to share meals with her. She gets my spuds, I take her Brussels sprouts. Shit like that.

I want her to wear my shirt at night, and I want to wake up with my arm around her in the morning.

Jesus Christ . . . I think I want a relationship.

Roark

∽

SUTTON

"How do you feel about everything?" Dad asks, taking a seat next to me by the fire.

Showered and in comfortable loungewear, I lean back in my camp chair and stare at the crackling flames. It was a long day, prepping all the cabins, organizing registration, making sure the gift bags were all correct with the right sizes. But we did it, and we're more than ready for the festivities to start tomorrow. My job is done, and now I get to sit back and let the rest of the staff take over.

I close my blanket over my shoulders. "I feel really good. I don't think we could be more prepared."

"I couldn't agree more." My dad gives my leg a pat and looks over at me, the creases near his eyes crinkled with a smile. "I'm proud of you, Sutton Grace. You've become a very beautiful and hard-working woman."

"Thanks, Dad," I say awkwardly, not really sure how to react. "I'm glad Whitney gave me the opportunity to take over. Is she going to come down here?"

He nods and leans back in his chair, crossing his leg over his knee. "She's at a hotel, due to arrive tomorrow morning before the campers."

"Oh good. It would be weird if she didn't show up." I wince.

"Do you think she's going to criticize my work?"

He shakes his head. "She's not that kind of boss, but she will run over everything, double-checking to make sure we covered all our bases. I wouldn't expect anything less."

"Me neither." I look toward the clear sky, stars sparkling brighter than I've ever seen. "Are you going to be sad when you retire next year?"

"I'll miss the game and the people, but I think it's time. I've been suiting up for almost two decades now. I think it's time this old man takes a break."

"Think you're going to coach the local high school team?" I smile at him. "You know they're just waiting for you to offer your help."

He lifts his hat and then runs his hand through his hair. He's the only one yet to take a shower, offering the chance to everyone else first. "I think I'll take my first year off and then I'll probably trickle in and help. I don't think I can stay away from the sport for that long." He gives me a nudge. "Which reminds me, when are you going to give me grandkids? I'm retiring; I'm ready to be a grandpa now." He chuckles softly.

"Uh, not for a while. Kind of need to have a guy in my life first, plus I want to establish my career. You're going to be waiting a while. Sorry."

He snaps his fingers in disappointment. "Are there any prospects out there?"

Only one who hides behind a shield of armor so impenetrable that I'm certain I'll become an old woman before I can get past it.

I shrug, not really wanting to talk about Roark with my dad, or relationships for that matter. It's too sensitive a topic, especially since the man I truly want is about fifty feet away in the house.

"That's all you're going to give me? A shrug? Throw your old man a bone, is there someone in the city you're talking to?"

Should have known he'd be persistent.

Maybe if I keep things vague, I can get this weight off my

shoulders, and then maybe gather some advice because if anything, my dad is really good at helping guide me, always has been.

"Well, there is this guy."

Rubbing his hands together, he leans forward. "Now we're talking, tell me all about him."

Yeah, that won't be happening.

"We met a few weeks ago and at first I really didn't like him, but over texts and some few chance encounters, I've developed feelings for him."

"Does he share the same kind of affection?" I nod, knowing fully well Roark does. "If he likes you, why do you have that look on your face?"

I roll my teeth over my bottom lip, trying to put into words what I know about Roark without defining him to my dad.

"He won't give in to his feelings, at least not for the most part. I don't want to get into too many details, you know, since you're my dad and all—"

"All I ask is that you use protection. Do I need to have that conversation again?"

"God, no." I hold up my hand. "Please, Dad, don't."

"Okay, but make sure you're following everything I taught you."

"I am." My face flames, and I know it has nothing to do with the fire in front of me, but rather the burning embarrassment of this conversation.

"Good girl." He motions with his hand. "Continue. You said he won't give in to his feelings?"

"Yeah, he had a pretty bad childhood and it's affecting him now. I think he's scared he might hurt me, but what he doesn't realize is he's already hurting me by not truly being with me." I sigh and slouch in my chair, pulling my legs into my chest. "All I want is to date him, Dad. I want to be able to go out on dates and hug him when I see him. I want to be affectionate and help him through his bad days, but every time I try, he tells me he's not good enough for me and no matter what I say, he won't change his mind."

Smiling to himself, he says, "That's how your mom was. Didn't think she was good enough to be with me, when in fact, she was the reason I was so damn happy all the time. As you know, you came along earlier than planned"—he chuckled—"and she thought she was destroying my chances at a career. Little did she know, she bolstered them. Yes, I had added responsibilities, but having you, both of you, helped drive me to do my very best. I was the lucky one." He turns toward me and says, "The easy thing would be to give up and move on, but it's the fight that makes the end result worth it. Don't give up on what you want, Sutton Grace, even if you get hurt. If he has feelings for you—like he should—don't give up trying."

Standing, he stretches his hands over his head and lets out a long yawn. "I'm going to call it a night. Think you can douse the fire yourself?"

"As if you have to ask."

"Well, now that you're a city girl and all, thought I might have to remind you."

He presses a kiss against my head as I say, "You can never take the country out of the girl, Dad."

"True." He takes a step toward the house and then says over his shoulder, "We have a week left here, then you can get back to the city to that man of yours. Maybe send him a few texts while you're here, letting him know you're thinking about him. It's a nice gesture." *Is he saying that from experience?* "Good night, Sutton Grace. See you in the morning."

"See you in the morning, Dad."

Once he's out of sight, I turn my attention back to the fire, staring at the dancing flames and thinking about what my dad said. He thinks the easy thing would be to give up, and that almost seems more torturous than not trying, because I don't think getting over Roark would be very easy.

But even with giving in earlier today, he still pushed me away, still apologized for being intimate. *And again, he didn't kiss me on the lips. Why? Are stolen—apologized-for—moments worth that?*

No. I don't want that.

I want him to never apologize for touching me, but to want to touch me more. I want him to have confidence that I truly, madly want him and not just his body, but his soul.

And even though a small part of me believes it can happen, there's a big part of me that believes no matter what I say, no matter how many times I attempt to show him how much I care, he'll never change his mind, and I'll be constantly fighting a losing battle.

The realization of nothing ever happening between us hits me harder than I expected, and tears start to well up in my eyes. I wish he could see the man I see; this overwhelmingly caring dickhead, yet loyal man. I wish he could rid himself of his self-loathing and understand how happy he makes me, even when he's teasing me, which is most of the time. The glint in his eyes and the tone in his voice reveals there's a deeper connection between us.

Staring at the fire, I let the tears fall, allowing myself to have this moment. I can't hold it in any longer; it's too consuming, too overpowering.

Leaning forward, I rest my arms on my bent knees and then lay my chin on my arms, giving in to the sorrow, the pain, the helplessness I feel when it comes to Roark. If only he would give us a chance, if only—

"Out here by yourself, lass?"

Startled, I wipe my eyes quickly and whip around to see Roark standing to the side, staring at me. How on earth did I not hear him approaching? There is a pinch in his brow as he kneels to my level, his fresh soapy scent hitting me first, then his minty breath.

"Are you crying?"

"No." I wipe at my eyes again, even though that's clearly giving it away.

His mouth quirks to the side. "Your eyes beg to differ. What's going on?"

"Nothing. Just the smoke getting to me."

He turns toward the fire in front of us, noticing the smoke blowing in the opposite direction. Damn wind. "Yeah, okay." From behind him, he snags a chair and pulls it up right next to me and takes a seat, facing me completely. "Talk to me. Are you nervous about tomorrow?"

"No." I shake my head. "I'm really confident about tomorrow."

"Okay, so why are you upset?"

I press my cheek to my arms and look at him, giving him a sad smile. "Just us, that's all."

"Us?" His brow lifts, and he scoots a little closer. "What about us?"

I let out a long sigh. "My dad asked if there were any guys in my life and I told him—"

"You didn't tell him about me, did you?" Sheer panic crosses his face as he looks back at the house, as if my dad is about to run out on the porch, wielding a shotgun.

"No, I wouldn't do that, but I did casually talk about this guy I liked and told him what I was going through."

He frowns. "What are you going through?"

"The ups and downs of wanting to be with you but getting nowhere." I gaze at the fire, unable to look him in the eyes. "I like you, Roark, a lot, but I don't know how much more I have in me to fight for what I want. I'm emotionally spent, but every time you're around me, I can't help but hope and wish, and pray that maybe this will be the time you give in, that this will be the time you ask me out on a date, that this will be the time you finally kiss me." I shrug my shoulders, pressing my chin against my arms. "A girl can wish."

Tension fills the air as silence hits both of us. If only I was like Mel Gibson in *What Women Want* and could read his thoughts, then this whole tango would be so much easier. Instead, I have to sit here awkwardly and wait for him to say something, something that's most likely going to hurt me in the long run.

Finally, "I talked with your dad too."

"What?" I smile, unable to hold back the humor in the idea of us both talking to my dad about each other but never revealing who we're really talking about. "When did you talk to him?"

"The other day, while horseback riding. He asked me if I planned on settling at any point. Gave me an entire lecture on being a man." Roark rubs his hand over his scruff. "It was the most honest conversation I think I've ever had. He made me think about a lot of things and the future I want to have, the life I want to lead." He chuckles to himself. "Hell, in that moment, he was more of a dad to me than my father has ever been."

That warms my heart.

"He's a good man. I'm glad you could confide in him. He likes you, Roark, and only wants the best for you."

"Yeah, I know." He glances at the ground. "He uh, he made me think about what's going on between us, kind of blew up my mind."

"What did he say?"

Roark folds his hands together. "Nothing you need to know, but one thing did stick out." He nods, as if he can hear my dad saying it now. "Be a man." His eyes meet mine, and I'm surprised to see such intensity as he stares at me. I haven't seen this expression before. "I want to be the man you deserve, Sutton, but I'm not sure how to go about it." He scratches the back of his neck, looking nervous. "I don't know anything about relationships or how to care for someone. All I know is this feeling I have for you, this mind-numbing, soul-shattering feeling coursing through my body, isn't going to go away, so I can either continue to try to fight it, or I can ask you for help."

"Help?" I ask, surprised as my heart stutters in my chest.

He nods and unfolds my arms, taking one of my hands in his. "I want this, I want us, but I have no idea what I'm doing. I'll need your guidance and understanding and a promise that if I fuck up, which I know I will, you'll be patient. This is all new for me."

"Roark"—I press my free hand against this cheek and rub my thumb over his scruff—"we're human, so we're bound to screw up at some point."

"But I've never truly received love before."

"Well, there's always room to learn." I drag my thumb over his bottom lip, my body itching to be close to his. "Does this mean you want to take me out on a date?"

A beautiful smile pulls at the edges of his mouth. "Yeah, I think it does."

My happiness matches his as we both smile at each other. "And you're not going to cock-block me anymore?"

He nips at my thumb, causing me to laugh and pull away. "Fuck no. I don't think my dick can take any more torture."

"And does this mean you're going to quit smoking?"

His brow pinches together. "Quit smokin'? I didn't know that was in the plan."

"It is if you want in my pants."

"Hell." He drags his hand over his face. "You're going to take away all my accessories, aren't ya? Make me a preppy boy."

I shake my head. "No, I want you just the way you are, asshole tendencies and all."

"Then why are you taking away my cigarettes?"

"Because I want you to be able to fuck me without losing your breath." I smile brightly at the shocked look on his face. Heck, I might be a little shocked myself.

"Worried about my stamina, lass?"

Casually, I shrug. "I don't know, you sounded a little winded when you were dry-humping me."

"Winded?" he asks, sitting back. "You thought I was winded?" I shrug again. "I wasn't fucking winded, I was desperate. Do you have any idea how hard it's been for me to hold back? To not take you against a wall every time I saw you? I've had to control myself for weeks now, so if I was breathing hard while rubbing my thick cock along your pussy, it's not because I was winded," he says, his words lighting up my entire body. "It's because I desperately wanted you."

Is it hot out here, or is it just me?

I bite my bottom lip, and his eyes fall to my mouth.

I wet my lips, and he does the same.

I shift in my seat, and he sits on the edge of his.

"Are you going to kiss me, Roark?"

"I don't know," he says, placing his hand at the back of my neck and pulling me closer before weaving his fingers through my hair. "Do you want me to?"

"You know I do. I've been waiting forever to know what it feels like to have your lips on mine."

"If that's the case . . ." He nods for me to come closer and then pats his lap. "Come here, Sutton."

Excitement beats through my veins as I unfold from my chair and move toward him, taking the blanket with me. I drape it over my shoulders and straddle his lap, my knees falling to either side of his body. He grips the blanket and pulls it tighter around me before moving his hands to my face where he gently strokes my cheeks.

"You're so goddamn beautiful. I don't know why I've been denying myself for so long."

"Oh, you know, because you're older than I am, because my dad is your client, stupid crap like that."

He chuckles. "Ah, so we're taking the mature route, I see."

"Just letting you know how stupid you've been."

"I guess that's something I can count on when it comes to us."

Us. That makes me smile as I settle more onto his lap.

"I like hearing you say that. *Us*. It feels so right."

"It does." He presses his forehead against mine. "Christ, Sutton. I'm nervous."

"Nervous?" My hands slide up his thick chest. "Why?"

"Because I really don't want to screw this up." *Oh God, I could love this man.* I finally feel as though I'm seeing all of him. He's more . . . raw, less masked. How can he have so little faith in himself? It has to do with his horrible family. If only they knew the damage they've inflicted. It makes me so angry.

My hand rubs over his heart. "You won't." I nudge his head

with mine and say, "Now kiss me under the stars. Give us a moment to remember for a long time."

His lips part, his hand cups my jaw, tilting it back slightly right before his lips press against mine. I sigh into the connection and explore. He's sweet at first, gliding his mouth over mine, learning his way around, and then the intensity starts to grow as he grips me tighter.

His mouth parts and so does mine, but he doesn't explore with his tongue yet. He softly open-mouth kisses me, keeping my head steady as he tilts his head side to side, not missing an inch of my mouth.

I shift on his lap and he groans into my mouth, swiping his tongue across my lips, enticing me, looking for more, so I match his swipe with one of my own. The minute our tongues clash, they tangle together, and our grip on each other grows stronger, our need intensifying.

This is so much more than I ever expected. I knew he'd be a good kisser, simply from the way he made me come on his tongue. But the contrast between soft and hard in his kisses, the way he takes charge, the taste of him in my mouth, it's more than I thought possible. With each kiss, he's ruining me for every other man out there... not that I want to ever kiss another man after this.

Mouths connected, he glides his hands down my body to my hips where he holds tightly. I slowly start to rock back and forth on top of him.

He stills me and breaks our kiss. "Not here, Sutton."

"Not here, what?"

Pushing my hair behind my ear, he looks at me sweetly. "We're not about to dry-hump in front of a fire where your dad could easily see us. We shouldn't be doing this . . . here."

My brow rises in question, shocked by the goody-two-shoes vibes he's giving me. "You're telling me you don't want to get caught? This coming from the guy who rarely gives two shits about anything?"

He chuckles and grips me tighter, and that devilish smile slices through me. "If it was anyone else, I would be laying them out on the dirt right now, but it's different with you."

For some reason, that doesn't settle well with me. "Is there not enough passion between us for you to sweep me off my feet?"

"The complete opposite," he answers. "I would get way too lost to be able to stop if your dad came out here . . . or that douche Josh."

I chuckle and play with the collar of his shirt, the fire lighting up the lines in his brow. "You really don't like him, do you?"

"Not even a little. He's been checking you out way too much, and he's been really fucking handsy. I was insulted for you."

"Josh is a nice—"

"Josh is a douche, end of story."

"Is that how this is going to be? You're going to be a jealous fool?"

He nods . . . unapologetically. "And you have the right to be jealous too. You know, Miss Angelica was flirting with me the other day, trying to get me to eat her biscuit."

I roll my eyes. "Miss Angelica is seventy-five years old, and she was trying to get you to eat her biscuits, plural. Don't be a pervert."

"I don't know, there was a certain glint in her eye that told me, if I followed her back to the kitchen, she'd show me her cupboard, if you know what I mean."

"You're stupid." I chuckle.

He laughs too and moves his hands up my bare back. "And yet you still want to be with me."

"Yeah, I must be crazy." I playfully grip his cheeks and plant a kiss on his lips. When I go to pull away, he keeps me in place and once again, his mouth locks with mine. I sigh into his hold and let him take over.

∼

Blanket laid out across the meadow, the fire put out, I lie next to Roark and stare at the sky, enjoying the stars glittering above us as he keeps me warm with his arm wrapped around me. I dance my hand over his chest and snuggle in close, still a little shocked that he's here, next to me, after the back and forth we've been through.

"Do you ever see yourself moving back here?" he asks, his voice rumbling over me.

"Maybe one day, but right now I'm focused on my career."

"You could really do that anywhere, so if you had to choose a place to live, where would it be?"

I press my lips together and give it some thought. "You know, I don't think I'm really cut out for New York City. I love the atmosphere, but a lot of time I feel out of place."

"You're a country girl. You look like you're in your element out here. The smile on your face when exercising your horses nearly brought me to my knees."

"Are you trying to get me to move back here?"

"Hell no, but I can see you doing it at some point and I don't blame you. It's gorgeous here. I can see why your dad is excited about retirement. Life seems to slow down in the country."

"It's why he loves it so much, because he feels like he has time to sit back and breathe in the fresh air. I'm excited for him to have a break from the tough schedule he's been keeping."

"He'll wear retirement well."

Lifting up on my elbow, I meet Roark's eyes. "This is going to sound stupid but thank you for taking care of him for the last few years, making sure he gets good deals that represent his brand and foundation."

"You don't have to thank me, Sutton. It's my job."

"A job you do well."

His brow quirks up. "Is that so? I thought I was the most unprofessional person you know."

"You are, but shockingly you're still able to do your job. I don't get it, but it works for you."

"I got lucky," he answers, tugging on a strand of hair and then wrapping it around his finger. "When I first got to the States and was attending classes at Yale, I was slightly wild with the partying."

"You? No way. I don't believe that for a second," I say, sarcasm dripping from my lips.

He squeezes my side, a smile on his handsome lips. "I was excited to be free from my parents, so I drank and partied a lot. That's how I ended up in the same fraternity as my two best friends, Bram and Rath. From then on, I saw opportunities, schmoozed with the right people, and it wasn't long before I gained credibility amongst friends—*despite* my partying. For some fucking reason, they trusted me with their careers, which was how I became their manager. I have no idea how to explain the way I got into this business besides pure Irish luck, but I take the job seriously, even if at times it doesn't seem like I do."

"It shows. Are all your clients happy?"

"Eh, not all of them. I've lost a few, but I think it's because our personalities haven't meshed. I really can't work with the pompous, uptight athletes. Too needy, and I don't deal with that crap."

"You don't want to deal with people who are needy, and yet you're the neediest man I've ever met."

"What? I'm not fucking needy."

"You came to my apartment one night because you needed to hold me."

"That was different." His voice turns soft. "It was a bad fucking night for me, and you were the only person I knew who would take that pain away."

And now I feel like a jerk for joking about it.

"I'm sorry, I didn't—"

He quiets me with a finger to my mouth. "Don't apologize. Just know you helped me that night." He plays with my hair, and I love how affectionate he is when his personality seems the exact opposite. "Whenever you're around, I feel at ease."

"Are you flattering me, Roark?"

"Telling the truth." Sitting up, he lowers me to my back where he hovers above me. "What am I going to do about tomorrow?"

"What do you mean?"

"There are going to be all these teenage boys at the ranch, and I don't want them thinking they can stare at my girl however they want."

I roll my eyes. "Don't be ridiculous. They're going to be staring at my dad the entire time. Believe me, I'm chopped liver whenever my dad is around."

"You don't plan on wearing that crop top, do you?" He lifts a questioning brow.

I chuckle softly. "No, that was only to drive you crazy. I actually waited in my room for you to open your door so I could run into you in the hallway."

His eyes narrow. "You fucking tease. I knew it. I knew you were driving me crazy on purpose. And Josh?"

I shrug. "He's just a nice guy, and it helped that you were crazy jealous around him."

He drags his hand over his face and then shakes it. "Do you realize you almost gave me a coronary these last few days?"

"If you weren't so stubborn, maybe I wouldn't have had to drive you crazy."

"I don't believe that for a second. I still think you would have tortured me."

"True." I laugh. "I would have."

"Strangely, it's one of the reasons I'm drawn to you. You give me shit."

"Only when you deserve it." He laughs. Leaning down, he presses a soft kiss against my lips, his hand tangling in my hair. When he pulls away, he says, "Will you take that white top back to New York? I want to see you shower in it."

"Is that so?"

He nods. "Yeah, I totally jacked off in the shower thinking about you in that, all wet and sexy."

"You masturbated in the shower?"

The laugh that drags out of him is sexy and entirely too much trouble. "I've had my hand on my cock every goddamn day I've been here, sometimes twice a day."

My eyes widen. "Are you serious?"

"Don't be so naïve, Sutton. Do you really think I could be this close to you and not be affected? If I wanted to be able to walk straight, I had to do something about it."

"You should have asked for help."

He shakes his head. "There is no way I can get close to you like that here, not with your dad in the same house. I almost lost it this morning. I can't have another incident like that. We shouldn't even be out here right now."

"He can't see us."

"Doesn't matter, it's too close for comfort. There won't be any fucking until we're back in the city."

Well, that doesn't sit well with me, and he must notice because he places a kiss on my lips and then connects our foreheads. "Don't worry, when we're back in the city, I'll make sure I make up for all these lost days."

"Promise?"

"Promise." He lowers his head and presses one more kiss across my lips before rising to his feet. He pulls up his low-hanging jeans and then takes my hand in his to help me from the ground. Together we shake the blanket out and then fold it up. We walk toward the ranch hand in hand, and it feels sublime. Such a small thing, but finally being able to hold his hand feels so right.

We reach the wooden stairs and Roark turns toward me. His thumb drags over my lip before he bends down and kisses me softly. It's intimate and everything I've ever wanted from him. I feel all my muscles turn to mush.

When he pulls away, my body aches for more. "Good night, Sutton. I'll see you in the morning. Tomorrow is your big day."

"Couldn't have done it without everyone's help and your epic shit-shoveling skills."

"Smart-arse." He kisses me one last time and heads toward the front door. For the first time, I don't mind watching him walk away. With his narrow hips, broad back, and sexy swagger, it's absolutely not a hardship. Never in a million years would I have believed I'd want a guy like Roark—arrogant, cocky, rude—but once I peeled back his first layer, I found a kind, caring, and sweet man. A man I can't wait to learn more about. *A man who wants to be with me. A man who wants us to be an us.*

CHAPTER SIXTEEN

D*ear Gerald,*
I'm going to preface this by saying in the past I've stated I don't want to treat this diary as a place to gush like a teenage girl in puberty, but . . .

HOLY FUCK can Sutton kiss.

I knew those lips were going to do damage to my tough exterior, but I didn't think they'd knock down every wall I ever erected. With one tiny press of her mouth against mine, everything crumbled around me, leaving me exposed, vulnerable, and begging like a desperate lust-struck boy.

It's the way she carefully cups my cheek and then slowly moves her hands through my hair. It's the lightness in her kiss even though her tongue is demanding. Light and then hard, light and then hard. Fuck, if she can about throw me over the edge with only her kisses, what else can she do with that sinful mouth of hers? I bet some really wicked things.

And knowing that she's in the next room over, yeah, I didn't get one ounce of sleep last night and it's why I'm up before the sun this morning.

Up before the sun . . . that's a term they use here on the ranch. I think they're branding me, and for some reason I'm okay with it. An Irish cowboy, not sure how popular that is, but I think I could pull it off, as long as I can wear my own non-cowboy boots and a beanie. Then I'm good.

The rebel cowboy, I can go along with that.

Roark

ROARK

Fuck, I'm sore.

All the pent-up tension from not being able to touch Sutton, the withdrawal from cigarettes, and the countless hours I've spent doing manual labor around the ranch, is coming to a head this morning as I move around my room getting ready for the day.

After I took a shower, I watched the sun rise from my bedroom window, hands propped behind me on the bed, wishing Sutton was next to me enjoying the view, but knowing the way she sleeps—ostrich position and all—I'm guessing she wasn't up early enough.

Campers are supposed to arrive between ten and noon today. I'm to help with registration and guide anyone who needs help finding their way around. I also get to wear a neon-green shirt and hat, so . . . that's fun.

Jeans on, I reach for my shirt as a light knock sounds against the door. "Come in," I say, only to see a freshly showered Sutton slip past the door.

A smile gracing her lips, she tiptoes toward me and presses her hands against my chest, then slips them up to my neck where she brings me down for a kiss. I drop the lime-green monstrosity and cup her generous ass in my hands, pulling her in even closer.

Wearing her tight-fitting jeans and a camp shirt, she looks natural but breathtaking. She doesn't need all the frills like makeup and curled hair. Fresh from the shower, cheeks a little pink, wet hair, she's stunning.

Slowly she pulls away but not before pecking a few quick kisses.

On a sigh, she takes a step back. "I should have waited to kiss you until after we were back in the city." Her hands glide down to mine where they lace together. "Because now that I've had a taste, it's going to be torture not being able to have more."

Tell me about it.

"We can always meet up in the barn for a roll in the hay."

"Have you ever done that?" she asks, a crinkle in her nose, but a knowing glint in her eye.

A little shocked I ask, "Uh, I'm the one who should be asking have *you* ever done that country girl?"

"Not really, but I have been topless in the hay before, and it doesn't feel good."

"Please tell me you were having a topless party with your girlfriends and you weren't with a guy."

She chuckles. "Think what you want." She looks behind her and sighs. "I should get downstairs and help out." She eyes the shirt on the bed. "You're going to look so good in that. I gave you one size smaller so it's all tight and clingy to your muscles."

"Did you really?"

She nods. "Even if we weren't together by today, I guaranteed myself a nice view to make it through the next few days."

"And then were your plans to torture me with that shirt in the hallway again?"

"Maybe." She bites her bottom lip.

"You know"—I push her hair over her shoulder—"you look all innocent and sweet but on the inside, you're sinful."

"Don't be giving away my secret." My phone rings on the nightstand, and she takes that moment to part. "I'll see you downstairs."

I walk over to my phone, but watch her ass sway as she walks away. God, I can't wait to get her naked again.

"Hello?" I answer the phone, not even looking at the caller ID.

"Mr. McCool, it's Darcy." I glance at the time, noting it's nine in the morning in the office. What would Darcy be calling me for?

"Hey Darcy, what's going on?"

"I'm sorry to bother you but something came up with Xavier

Memphis's contract, and we need you in the office. He's freaking out."

Fuck, Xavier plays baseball for the New York Bobcats, and we're in the midst of figuring out an extension on his contract. Very high-profile, one we can't afford to mess up—well, can't afford for him to lose out on the contract.

"What's going on?"

"Something about the jersey royalties not being approved. I'm getting calls from both Xavier and The Bobcats. He's been to the office two times already this morning, demanding to see you."

"Shit." I push my hand through my hair. "Okay, let me figure out what to do. I'll give you a call. Tell them you've been in touch with me, and I'll get back to them shortly."

"Okay. Thank you, Mr. McCool."

I hang up and reach for a black shirt out of my suitcase. Looks like I'm going to have to wear the neon-green shirt for Sutton another day.

∽

Roark: *Landed and in the car. Thanks for the plane.*

Foster: *Anytime.*

Roark: *And about the community service, I'll make it up. I promise.*

Foster: *I have no doubt you will. Get Xavier straightened out. We don't want him crying in the dugout again.*

Roark: *He's never going to live that down. I'm sorry again.*

Foster: *You're good. Thank you for all the help leading up to camp. And hey, try to stay away from the cigarettes.*

Roark: *Don't plan on buying a pack. Good luck.*

I set my phone down and look out the window as Foster's driver takes me directly to my office for damage control. The last thing I wanted to do this morning was hop on a private plane and make my way back to the city, especially since I didn't get a chance to say bye to Sutton because she was busy with camp prep.

I've never really had a conscience before, but ever since Sutton walked into my life, it's been rearing its ugly head, letting itself be known, and right now I feel all kinds of guilty for having to leave her, especially when I was set up to help.

Scratching the scruff on my jaw, I contemplate texting her. She has to know from Foster I'm not there, but should I let her know myself?

Probably. Sounds like something a responsible guy would do.

I pick up my phone from the seat and type out a text, feeling weird having to check in with another person.

Roark: *Just landed in NY. I'm assuming your dad told you I had an emergency that took me away from camp. I'm sorry, lass.*

I press send and rest my phone on my lap as I stare at the cityscape, wondering when this became my life, where I hang on a girl's every word, desperate to not fuck up.

Bram and Rath would probably keel over and die if they saw me right now, or at least could listen to my internal dialogue. I've always been the confirmed bachelor, the one who's never been expected to settle down, the crazy single guy at everyone else's weddings.

And by no means am I settling down, but a relationship, this is a first.

I consider texting them, letting them know I've gotten a little soft, but I receive a text from Sutton before I can pull up my friends' names.

Hopefully her quick response doesn't mean she's mad at me.

Sutton: *Don't ever talk to me again.*

Uh . . . okay, not the exact response I was expecting.

A light sheen of sweat breaks out over my forehead as I try to think of a response.

Sutton: *Just kidding. I wish I could have seen your face when you read that. I bet it was pure panic. Am I right?*

Fucking smart-ass. She's been hanging around me too much.

Roark: *Where is the sweet girl I first saw at Gray's Papaya?*
Sutton: *She's been corrupted by an Irishman.*
Roark: *Apparently. Christ, you had me sweating.*

Sutton: *I know I should feel bad, but I don't. Not after all you put me through when we first met. Sometimes payback is delayed, but still gratifying.*
Roark: *I'll remember that.*
Sutton: *Don't you dare think about torturing me.*
Roark: *Wouldn't dream of it.*
Sutton: *Liar.*
Roark: *I'm really sorry I had to leave.*
Sutton: *I know. You're staying in the city?*
Roark: *Yeah, I need to see these contract negotiations through.*
Sutton: *How inconvenient. Who am I going to kiss now?*
Roark: *If you say Josh, I'm going to spank you.*
Sutton: *Ooh, spank me, huh?*
Roark: *It's official, you're corrupted.*
Sutton: *I'm about to give you a run for your money.*
Roark: *I sure as hell hope so.*

~

"Why do you keep looking at your watch?" Rath asks, sipping from his tumbler of whiskey. "And why the hell aren't you drinking?"

After hours of negotiations with The Bobcats and their front office, we were able to settle on a royalty number that was satisfactory with both parties, but I'm keeping my eyes on them. They've been known to do some shady shit, and I wouldn't put it past them to make a change when the contracts are drawn up.

I took Xavier out to dinner to calm his nerves and tried to reinforce that everything was going to be okay. He's borderline needy, but after a hectic day like today, I don't mind putting in the extra effort.

After we parted ways and he went back home to celebrate with his wife, I answered the five missed texts from Rath, who was looking to go out tonight. Since I didn't have anything else going on, I hit him up and we parked our asses at a small Irish pub off Fifth.

"Not feeling like having a drink," I answer, knowing the answer isn't going to fly with Rath.

He sits up and looks me in the eyes. "You don't feel like having a drink?" He gives me a once-over and then grows serious. "Dude, are you sick? Like do you have some kind of terminal illness?"

"No." I roll my eyes. "I just don't want one, okay?" I glance at my watch again, counting down the minutes until I know Sutton will be in her room alone.

"There's something going on. In all the years I've known you, not once have you ever turned down a drink. What's up? Did something happen to you that I don't know about?"

"No. I'm just not drinking, so drop it."

"Can't." Rath shakes his head, lips firmly planted together. "Sorry, but—" He pauses and his eyes light up. Oh Christ. Sometimes I truly hate how fucking smart the man is. Didn't take him a minute to figure it out. "You like Foster Green's daughter, don't you?"

Seriously, nothing gets past this man.

I'm not even going to try to deny it, so instead, I lean against the bar and fold my hands together. "Yeah, I do."

"And she's a good girl, right?"

"Yeah."

"Holy shit," Rath says in awe. "I can't believe you found a girl who can tame you."

"She's not taming me," I say, already sick of this conversation. "I'm just trying to make a difference, you know? Applying myself."

"You apply yourself fine, but you're taming and toning down." He holds up his glass to me. "Good for you. I'm glad to see you're not living the life of live fast and die hard. I'd like to have my friend around for a while."

"If I haven't died yet, I don't think I ever will."

Chuckling, Rath nods. "It's scary how true that is, but seriously, you like her?"

"Yeah. We're . . . dating."

"Seriously?" The humor in Rath's voice dissipates as he asks, "When did this happen?"

"Yesterday." I chuckle. "Kind of new."

"Just a little. What happened?"

I shift on my bar stool, my knees growing tight from the bent position. "I don't know, man." I rub my jaw. "I couldn't get her out of my head. I tried, man, did I try hard, but with every attempt, my want for her only grew stronger. Even though it's terrifying and I've never done this before, I knew there was no chance in hell I could walk away. There is something special about her I can't pinpoint that makes me so goddamn needy whenever she's around."

A knowing smile crosses his face. "You really like her, don't you?"

"I do. I really, really like her." I blow out a long breath. "Fuck, listen to me being a dickhead in lust."

"Just hearing you say the word lust makes me want to dry-heave." He takes a swig of his drink and then sets it on the bar. "What's happening to us? First Bram, now you. What happened to being bachelors?"

"Aren't you seeing that Farrah girl?"

"Nah." He waves me off. "She was just a good time, nothing serious there."

"Still holding out for whom we shall not talk about?" I wiggle my eyebrows at him.

"When I say don't talk about her, I mean, as a whole, don't even mention that we don't talk about her. Fuck, man."

"Shit, you're so touchy." I poke his shoulder. "Loosen up."

"When did this become about me? We were talking about your love life and the fact that you're balls deep in a woman who's one of your clients' daughter. What are you going to do about that?"

"Nothing." I shrug as my phone vibrates. "I'll see where this goes. No use in making a big deal out of it while we're figuring things out." *Part of me feels okay about Foster though. He's the one man* who's shown faith in me as a person. But, we'll see. I pull out my phone and see that it's a text from Sutton. "Looks like I have to go." I pat Rath on the back. "I'll see you later."

"Wait, you're just going to leave me here?"

"Yup."

I take off without a second glance, flag down a taxi, and give the guy my cross streets before pulling out my phone to read her text.

Sutton: *I'm so tired.*

Roark: *Rough day at the office?*

Sutton: *Busy. We were down a person because he had to go coddle a grown-ass man.*

Roark: *Your dad really did fill you in.*

Sutton: *He showed me the video of Xavier crying in the dugout. I watched it three times and couldn't stop laughing. And the world thought Kim Kardashian had an ugly cry face. They have no idea.*

Roark: *We tried to spin it as him being ultra-sensitive but couldn't quite make it work.*

Sutton: *He sobbed over a pop-fly and then yelled into a towel.*

Roark: *Well aware. It's been the one flaw in my career, unable to make better use of the situation. At least I could have gotten him a tissue sponsorship like your dad, but he wouldn't glorify his emotions.*

Sutton: *It's the most ridiculous thing I've ever seen.*

Roark: *Changing the subject, how was camp?*

Sutton: *It was great. You should have heard the cheers when my dad greeted them. I love seeing the looks on the children's faces, the awe, the admiration. It's so wonderful to see how the kids look up to him.*

Roark: *I'm sorry I missed it.*

Sutton: *Where are you?*

Roark: *Driving home. Went out with Rath. I didn't have anything to drink.*

Sutton: *You don't have to report to me, Roark.*

Roark: *I know, but I wanted you to know anyway. I wanted to be present when we talked tonight.*

Sutton: *Are you planning on calling me?*

Roark: *Just waiting until I get back to my apartment. Give me a few.*

⁓

Roark: *FaceTime?*
Sutton: *I don't have headphones, and I don't want my dad to hear.*

I dial her number, and she answers on the first ring. "Forgot your headphones? Doesn't seem like a very Sutton-like thing to do," I tease as I slide into my bed and prop one of my hands under my head.

"It's not, but then again, that morning this guy kind of broke my heart, so I was off my game."

"Oh, okay, blaming me for your forgetfulness. I see how this is going to go."

"And I see that you're not taking responsibility."

I smile, loving how she feels comfortable enough to spar with me. "You know I feel like shit about that morning."

"I know," she sighs. "Can I ask you something?"

"Anything."

"If you didn't leave that morning, what do you think you would have done?"

Staring at the ceiling, I think about it. "I don't know. Fleeing seems like the only thing I know to do. I don't think I was ready at that moment to start something up with you. I probably would've said something really shitty and destroyed your spirit. Walking out was probably the best idea."

"I wish you hadn't."

"Yeah, I know." I sigh, hating that I can't be the well-balanced person she deserves. "I won't do it again, if that helps."

"I know you won't. What are you doing the rest of the week, finishing up on the contract negotiations?"

"Yeah, maybe buying some new sheets."

"New sheets? That's weird." She chuckles. "Why?"

"I assume you're going to want to stay the night when you get back to the city."

"You don't have to get new sheets for me," she says.

With a smile, I say, "I do if I don't want your gnarly toenails cutting up my nice ones."

"What?" she asks. "I don't have gnarly toenails."

"I'll put a label on them. These sheets only used when Sutton is over. I've marked up the guest sheets already from the brutal beating you've put them through."

"I have not messed up your sheets."

"Am I going to have to send you empirical evidence?"

"Yes," she says, challenging me.

Pulling up Safari on my phone, I quickly search torn-up sheets, save a picture of tattered white ones, and send it to her in a text message.

"Evidence is on the way."

She waits, and I know the minute the text comes in because she scoffs loudly. "Those are not your sheets."

"I know it's hard to tell from the massacre they've been through, but I can guarantee you, they used to be on my guest bed."

"Are you trying to win me over? Because it's not working."

"Win you over? Pfft," I playfully say. "Lass, I already got ya hooked. I'm trying to train you now."

"Train me?" I swear to God, if she was here I'd be watching her eyeballs pop out of their sockets. "There'll be no training me. I'm the one who trains you."

"Why? I'm perfect already."

"Not full of yourself at all."

I chuckle. "Got to be a little full of yourself if you're going to make it places."

"Is that right?"

"Yup. Look at all the great athletes out there, like your dad. He doesn't sit back and let everyone think he's average. Even the most humble puff their chest from time to time. You have to. Try puffing your chest, Sutton."

"If I puff my chest, you'd end up staring at my boobs."

She couldn't be more accurate. "And there's a problem with that because?"

"Because I have eyes."

"Aye, ya do. Pretty ones at that."

She's silent for a second and then says, "When your accent gets heavy like that, it's really hot."

"Yeah, your pussy getting wet?"

"Roark! Oh my God, don't say that. What is wrong with you?"

A full-on belly laugh escapes me. Holding my stomach, I let the laughter fill the phone as I hear a small chuckle come from the other end. "Ya don't like me talking about your wet pussy?"

"I mean . . . not like that."

"And there's the innocent girl I've been missing. For a second there, I thought she ran away and was replaced by a sex-crazed vixen."

"I would hardly call me a sex-crazed vixen. Way to exaggerate."

"Don't you know, Sutton, that's the way of the Irish? If we're not over-exaggerating then we're not telling a story correctly."

"Now you have me questioning every story you've ever told me."

"Never question an Irishman and his stories; it's bad luck." I shift in bed and put the phone on speaker so I can turn on my side and still talk to her.

"Is it really?"

"Nah, that was an exaggeration."

She lets out a long sigh. "You're exhausting."

"Just wait until I get you naked. I'll show you how exhausting I am."

"What if we're not compatible sexually? Man, what a letdown that would be."

Brow pinched, I ask, "What do you mean? Of course we'll be compatible."

"I mean, we might not. My friend Stacey was dating this guy a year ago, and she swore he was the one. They were the cutest couple I ever saw. He was super hot, had this whole alpha male thing going on: huge pecs, biceps for days, the most handsome—"

"Move on."

She chuckles and clears her throat. "Really attractive. Anyway, they held off for a month and a half before having sex, but the tension between them was ridiculous. Back and forth repartee, touching, kissing, but never fully engaging in the act. Whenever I was in the same room as them, I thought the air was going to implode from how tense it was being around them. The looks they gave each other . . . I have no idea why they waited so long, but it was torture for everyone around them. And then finally, after a tension-filled game night, they went back to Stacy's apartment and banged like bunnies. At least, that's what we thought happened. Stacy called the next day, told me she finally had sex with Harrison and broke up with him that morning. When I asked her why, she said it was everything she could have asked for when it came to sex: giant penis, great attention to her body, marked her up in all the right spots. The attraction was there, the pace was there, the grunting, the moaning, but when it came down to it, neither one of them could orgasm. It was like they were edging for hours, unable to find release. They wound up getting themselves off before going to bed. In the morning, they worked out they couldn't sexually mingle, so they broke it off."

What the hell is she talking about?

"So, you're telling me, everything was great, they both were sexually attracted to each other and were doing all the right things but couldn't get off?"

"Exactly. Isn't that sad? What if that's us?"

"It won't be. I know how to make you come already. Remember?"

"But it was with your tongue. Your penis is entirely different. Stacy said Harrison had a huge penis, so compared to you, you could be even worse."

"Wait." I sit up in bed. "Are you saying you don't think I have a huge penis?"

"Just giving you a little wiggle room for disappointment."

I blink a few times, even though she can't see me. I have no idea what's going on right now but I don't like it. She thinks we might not be sexually compatible, that I might not have a big enough penis for her. Who is this girl and what has she done with Sutton Green?

"I . . ." Hell, I don't even know how to respond and before I can, she starts laughing. And if I wasn't so disturbed, I might chuckle along with the infectious sound, but instead, I wait for her to stop.

"Oh, Roark . . . that's how you exaggerate a story." Motherfucker. I bite on my bottom lip, trying not to smile. "Got to go, early morning. I'll talk to you later."

And she hangs up before I can say bye. She bested me. Fuck did she best me, and I liked every goddamn second of it. Well, except when I thought she doubted my penis . . .

∽

Roark: *So . . . about last night.*

Sutton: *What about it? Good morning, by the way.*

Roark: *Morning, lass. When you were talking about being compatible, you were joking, right?*

Sutton: *Do you prefer that I was joking?*

Roark: *I prefer for you to stop yanking my dick.*

Sutton: *Oh, so you don't want me to give you a hand job?* ****WINCES**** *That might be a sign of not being sexually compatible.*

Roark: *Sutton.*

Sutton: *Yes?*

Roark: *I'm being fucking serious.*

Sutton: *Are you having stage fright? Maybe try role-play when you're home by yourself. You might not be so nervous when it first happens.*

Roark: *I'm not fucking nervous.*

Sutton: Sounds like you're nervous.
Roark: How can you tell? I didn't use your coveted asterisk.
Sutton: It's because I can read your texts well. It's okay, big daddy, you can perform all the orgasms.
Roark: Your sarcastic encouragement is not appreciated.
Sutton: Poor baby. Come to my bosom. *Holds arms out*
Roark: I want my innocent, sweet girl back.
Sutton: I think she was left behind in New York.

~

Roark: Can I ask you something?
Sutton: If it's about the size of your penis . . . no.
Roark: I'll send you a dick pic.
Sutton: Spare me. No girl in their right mind wants a close-up of a guy's dick.
Roark: How do you know? You've never seen mine, and you might really like it.
Sutton: It's a stick of flesh. I'm good.
Roark: You make my penis sound so lackluster.
Sutton: Women don't idolize the male genitals like men do.
Roark: Cleary you haven't seen a good penis before. I'll change that for you.
Sutton: Don't hold your breath.

~

Sutton: Two more days and I get to see your face.
Roark: I'm flying to China for a week to meet up with a clothing brand.
Sutton: What? Are you serious?
Roark: No, just wanted to sense your disappointment.
Sutton: You jerk. I was really upset.
Roark: Good, just means you're excited to see me.
Sutton: You know I am.

Roark: *I don't know, not with all this lack of sexual compatibility talk.*

Sutton: *Stop. You know I want to see you.*

Roark: *I want to see you too.*

Sutton: *When you say things like that, it makes my entire body heat up.*

Roark: *Yeah?*

Sutton: *Yeah. Can I ask you something?*

Roark: *Always.*

Sutton: *This is really stupid, so feel free to tell me no.*

Roark: *Spit it out, lass.*

Sutton: *Will you pick me up from the airport?*

Roark: *Already planned on it.*

CHAPTER SEVENTEEN

Dear Tommy,
 This is going to be quick because I have three meetings to tackle before I go to pick up Sutton from the airport.

You heard that right, I'm picking a girl up from the airport.

Out of sheer will, too.

I know what you're thinking, you're trying to impress her with your attentiveness.

Not even close, smart ass. I truly want to see her, and I don't think I can wait for her to make her way through the city by herself. I want to see her as soon as I can.

And what does that make me?

A lust-struck man.

I blame it on the lack of alcohol in my system . . . that or those big blues eyes I can't seem to knock out of my head.

Fuck, I can't wait to see my girl.

Roark

∽

SUTTON

What a long freaking week, but so rewarding. Yesterday, I watched all the kids personally thank my dad for the opportunity to attend his camp. Cards and letters were placed in his hand as he took countless pics with each child, making their year. I watched in admiration as he took the time this past week to learn every kid's name, something special about them, as well as their strengths and weaknesses on and off the field. I've never been prouder nor loved my dad more than I have this week.

I told him that when he dropped me off at the airport. He wouldn't let me fly home on a commercial flight, of course—taking a private jet is always weird, but at least I get to fly back with Whitney.

"You must be exhausted," Whitney says, one leg crossed over the other, wearing a crisp all-white suit, looking as beautiful as ever.

"I am. It was a long two weeks but well worth it."

"You impressed me, Sutton. Seeing you care so much for every camper. You stepped up whenever we needed an extra set of hands, even if it was the dirty work. Someone else in your position might not have done the same thing, and that shows me you have great character, just like your dad."

"Learned from the best. Just because there might be more money in my bank account than someone else's, doesn't mean I'm better than they are. Dad instilled that in me."

"He's a smart man," Whitney says with a soft smile while looking out the window. "We have a few short months to hammer out the details of your dad's final season, so are you up to jumping back into work on Monday?"

"Am I not going into the office tomorrow?"

She shakes her head. "Take tomorrow off, have a nice little three-day weekend, and then come back refreshed to start moving on all the details of your dad's retirement. Your input is going to be vital."

"That means a lot, thank you."

She winks at me. "You earned it."

Staring out the window again, I watch at how poised she stays, always so confident and fair. It's why I like Whitney so much. She might expect a lot from me and demand that I work hard, but if anything, she's fair, and I appreciate that more, especially since I'm the boss's daughter. She never gives me special treatment, and I couldn't be happier about that.

The rest of the flight we make casual small talk, but eventually we both end up shutting our eyes until we land, the small plane coming to a stop on the tarmac next to a hangar. I gather my bags and follow Whitney out of the plane and down the steps, where I see Roark, arms crossed, leaning against a black town car.

Crap.

The minute Whitney spots him, she stutters for a second and then turns to me. Wincing, I give her a small smile and hope and pray she understands. She looks back at Roark, who unfolds his arms and sticks his hands in his pockets, his stance widening slightly. He looks so good, and all I want to do is drop everything in my hands and run to him, but with Whitney's mind churning, I hold back.

When we're handed our bags, Whitney stops me and asks, "Is this something I need to be worried about?"

I have no idea what that means, so I shrug.

She gives Roark another once-over before turning back to me. "He's here for you, is he not?"

I swallow hard, feeling like I got caught by my dad. "He is." I tell the truth because I can't seem to convince myself to lie to the woman, not when she's been so wonderful to me for so many years.

"Is he being kind to you?"

"Yes," I answer, my throat tightening up. "Very."

She nods and presses her hand to my arm before saying, "Be careful. I like Roark, but he has a dark side to him, and I'd hate to see you get hurt."

"I know," I answer, my mouth going dry. "But I can't stay away."

Whitney chuckles under her breath. "I understand that feeling more than you know."

Chewing on the side of my cheek, I say, "Please don't say anything to my dad. Let me tell him when the time is right."

Patting my hand, Whitney says, "I don't know anything." She glances at Roark one last time. "Careful with that Irish accent, it's lethal."

I laugh. "Tell me about it. Thank you, Whitney. I appreciate your sensitivity."

"Anytime." She gives me a brief smile before walking in the opposite direction to another waiting vehicle.

Before moving toward Roark, I give Whitney a second to get in her car so I can have more of a private moment with the man I've been pining after.

As Whitney's car disappears, I make my way to Roark, who hasn't moved a muscle since sticking his hands in his pockets. A few feet from me, he smiles softly and reaches his hand out. I take it immediately and let him pull me into his strong body. His grip falls to my hip as I loop my hands around his neck, my suitcase abandoned behind me.

"Hi," I say shyly.

"Hey lass." With his free hand, he strokes my cheek while staring into my eyes. "I didn't think Whitney would be on the plane."

"Me neither."

Worry in his mossy eyes, he asks, "Everything okay?"

I nod. "She said she wouldn't say anything and I should be careful of your Irish accent. Said it could be lethal."

"Yeah?" He smiles. "I think she's a smart woman. It is lethal."

"I know." Standing on my toes, I thread my fingers through his hair and push up toward him. "Kiss me," I whisper, so close to his lips.

Smiling, he closes the rest of the space between us and presses a sweet kiss to my lips, melting me in his arms. Even though it's only been a week, it feels like it's been forever since I've seen him, since I've been able to taste his mouth on mine, and now that we're together again, I want nothing more than to spend the next three days lounging in his apartment—or mine—naked and doing nothing but exploring one another.

I like the idea so much that when he pulls away, I say, "What are you doing over the next three days?"

He smiles and runs his hand up my back. "You."

Giddy, I pull him to the car before grabbing my suitcase and say, "My place or yours?"

He taps his chin and says, "Tuna can or luxury suite? Hmm . . ."

"My place is not a tuna can."

"I can make it from your bed to the bathroom in four steps."

"Your legs are long."

"Your apartment is tiny," he counters. "We're going to my place, end of story. Plus, we need to try out those new sheets. They were put on the bed today." He helps me into the car and presses a kiss to my forehead before pulling me into his side and holding on to me, not once letting me go as we make our way through the city to his apartment. Excitement and anticipation bubbles inside me.

"Are you sure you didn't want to stop at your place to pick up any of your things?" Roark asks as we make our way up the elevator to his apartment.

"Anything I need is in my bag, plus I don't plan on wearing many of my clothes."

He raises his brows. "Are you planning a sex-a-thon in that pretty head of yours?"

"Maybe." I bite on my bottom lip. "Isn't that what you were planning?"

The elevator doors part, and he rolls my bag behind us as we make our way into his apartment. "You don't even want to know what I've been planning."

Once in the living room, he turns toward me, sweeping me off my feet into his arms . . . as someone pops up from the couch and scares the crap out of both of us.

"I fucked up everything," he shouts, arms flying out to the side.

"Jesus, Bram," Roark says, gripping me tightly. "What the hell are you doing here?"

A blond-haired man in torn red sweatpants and a soft, cashmere sweater approaches, looking a little crazy, despite his incredibly handsome face and piercing blue-green eyes.

He pulls on his hair that looks like it's been through a wrestling match with his hand. "I messed it up, man, everything. All my hard work went straight down the shitter." He glances my way and plasters a kind smile on his face, as if he isn't about to jump off a cliff. "Bram Scott, you must be Sutton."

Roark sets me down. I take Bram's hand in mine and say, "Nice to meet you."

He shakes my hand and then turns back to Roark, panic in his eyes. "What the fuck do I do?"

Annoyed, Roark answers, "Well since I have no clue what the fook you're talking about, I don't know."

"The proposal, I messed up the proposal."

Ooo . . . if he's talking about a marriage proposal—from the sight of him, I'm going to guess that's what it is—that can't be good.

Taking a step back, I say, "You know, I think I'll give you guys some time to yourselves." Roark's grip on me tightens.

"You're not going anywhere. Bram can leave."

"I need your help," Bram pleads, and I actually feel really bad for him.

"Go see Rath. He's her brother, after all. What better person to help you than her brother?"

"I did, but he's with a girl."

Roark gestures to me. "What the fuck do you think I'm doing right now?"

Giving me a soft smile of acknowledgement, he says, "But you're still fully dressed, so in my head, it's fair game."

Chuckling, I say, "He has a good point."

Roark shoots a look in my direction. "Don't agree with him."

"You know, I like you, Sutton," Bram says. "I think she should stay. She might have good input."

"Of course, she's staying, but you're leaving." Roark reaches for Bram but he sidesteps out of his reach.

Holding up his hands, he says, "Don't get handsy with me."

"Christ, Bram, will you just fooking leave?"

"No. I need help."

Tense and irritated, Roark says, "Here's some help, tell her you're a dumb-arse and then hand her the ring. Solved." He points to the elevator. "Now get out of here."

Poor Bram.

Resting my hand on Roark's arm, I gently say, "Why don't we order some food, sit down with Bram, help him, and then we can have a nice evening?"

"Yes, that's a great plan." Bram walks over toward the kitchen, pulling his phone from his pocket. "And because I'm a nice guy, dinner is on me."

"You're fucking right it's on you," Roark says, exasperated, before taking my suitcase to his room.

He is so not happy. Oddly, it makes me giggle. I like angry Roark, because it only leads to good things for me.

"So, are you going to keep stuffing your face or are you going to tell us why the hell you're in my apartment right now?" Roark asks, sitting back on the couch, his arm draped behind me.

Mid-bite of Thai noodles, Bram sets his bowl down and dabs a napkin across his face. "Looks like my welcome has expired."

"Your welcome expired the minute I got home, so get on with it already."

Brows pinching together, he says, "You know, I'm in dire need of a best friend right now, it would be nice if you weren't a dick for a second."

I rest my hand on Roark's thigh and try to soothe the anger that's building inside him. His gaze snaps to my hand and I realize maybe my placement wasn't the best, maybe a little too high. I retract my hand, and before he can yell at Bram again, I lean over and whisper into Roark's ear.

"I know you want nothing more than to be alone with me right now, but if you show a little compassion to your best friend, I'll put on that little shirt for you tonight."

Eyebrows raised, a smirk on his face, he says, "Is that a promise?" I nod and like the desperate man he is, he brings his attention to Bram. "All right, spill."

Bram eyes me, a thankful look on his face. "Whatever you whispered to him, I appreciate it."

I smile and link my hand with Roark's, resting my head on his shoulder, enjoying the comfort of being close to him. Did I want to fall into bed the minute we arrived here? Yes. But seeing one of Roark's best friends is good as well. Seeing him relate to a friend, not a client, and not someone he's trying to bed, gives me more insight into who he is as a man. *Bram trusts him. Trusts* in *him.* That speaks volumes.

"I had everything planned out, dinner, wine, her favorite cheesecake from a bakery downtown. It was all set up and perfect. She came home from work, I was dressed like a goddamn GQ model, apron around my waist. What woman doesn't want to come home to that?"

"Sounds like a nice image to walk home to," I say, trying to ease the worry etched all over Bram's face.

"It was and everything was going great. The ring was in my pocket, we were eating my dinner, talking about our days, and when the time came . . . I choked."

"Were you scared?"

He shakes his head. "No, I physically choked, on a Brussels sprout."

"Oh God, are you okay?" I ask.

He shakes his head, his hand rubbing his forehead. "I mean, obviously I'm still alive, but in the midst of Julia giving me the Heimlich and freaking out, I"—he pauses, twisting his hands together—"I might have peed my pants a little."

"What?" Roark lifts off the couch and busts out in laughter, clearly not worried about making his friend feel better. "You fucking pissed yourself?" Bram's face doesn't move as Roark slaps his knee and continues to laugh. I try to hold it together, but Roark's laughter is too infectious. I cover my mouth, not wanting to be rude. "She squeezed the piss out of you."

Okay, I snort.

Sitting there, lips pursed, Bram waits until Roark calms himself, wiping the tears from under his eyes. "Oh shite, that's great. You pissed yourself during your proposal. You really fucked it up."

"That wasn't even the bad part."

"Wait? There's more?" Now truly invested in the story, Roark sits up, hand on my thigh. Poor, poor Bram. "What happened next?"

"After she dislodged the Brussels sprout—thanks for the concern by the way—I stood there, unable to move because I had pee in my pants. She asked if I was okay and instead of answering her, I waddled to our bedroom."

"Fucking waddled. Oh, that's great. You know what? I'm glad you stayed, this is one of the best stories I've ever heard."

"What did I say about not being a dick?"

Another wipe under his eyes. "Sorry. Continue . . . *please* continue."

Exhaling, nostrils flaring, Bram says, "I went to the closet to change for obvious reasons. It wasn't a lot of pee, but just enough to warrant a new pair of boxers and therefore jeans too, just to be safe. When I was bare-assed, bent over, nut sac on full display, looking for another pair of jeans, Julia walked up and gathered my pants, asking if everything was okay."

"Oh no, did she feel the ring?"

He slowly nods. "Yup. There I was, limp dick and sore throat, watching my girlfriend juggle my pee pants and the ring I bought her." Roark lets out another bout of laughter but Bram talks over it this time, only engaging with me now. "When she asked what it was, I freaked, grabbed the closest pair of pants I had and fled to Rath's place." In despair, Bram rubs his thighs up and down. "I don't know what to do. I don't know why I ran, maybe because I was so nervous she was going to say no after she squeezed pee out of me, I have no clue, but now it's going to be awkward. She knows I was going to propose, so do I act like I wasn't going to or do I suck up my pride and ask if she wants to marry the guy who chokes and pees his pants?"

Still chuckling, Roark says, "That's a great question. I mean, if I were you I'd be in a bar right now, trying to forget the entire night. And then when I went home and she asked about it, I'd pass out on her tits and call it a night."

"Roark." I slap his arm. "That's awful advice." He shrugs as if he doesn't care. I turn to Bram. "Don't listen to him. Alcohol doesn't solve problems."

"It sure hides them," Roark interjects and leans back on the couch, pulling me with him, but I shrug him off.

"First of all, if I were Julia right now, I'd be worried and want to know if you're okay. Do you have your phone with you?"

Bram shakes his head. "I was in such a hurry, I didn't bother grabbing it. She's probably tried calling a few times by now."

"Of course, because she loves you, and she's worried. Your best bet is to go home, show her that you're okay, and then suck up your pride. Tell her you had these big plans for making the moment perfect, but sometimes being perfect isn't what life is all about." Scooting a little closer, I continue, "I would touch her sweetly and then bend down on one knee, tell her how much she means to you, how grateful you are that she's in your life, for life-saving moments as well—it's always good to add some humor—and then ask her if she'll spend the rest of her life by your side. No doubt in my mind that she'll say yes."

"Even after everything that went down tonight? You don't think she's running for the hills trying to get as far away from me as possible?"

I shake my head, attempting to put Bram at ease. "I don't think so. I think she'll be grateful that you're okay and excited that the man she loves is proposing."

Bram's eyes start to light up, his chest starts to puff out, as his shoulders straighten. "I think you're right. Okay"—he stands and claps his hands together loudly—"I'm going to do this. I'm going to propose to my girlfriend." Bram holds out his hand for a high five that I give a quick snap. "You're a lifesaver, Sutton. Thank you so much."

"Not a problem." I stand as well. "I'll walk you out. Let me get my suitcase."

"Wait, what?" Roark says, standing as well. I quickly retrieve my suitcase, the wheels echoing down the hall. "Where are you going?"

I slip on my jacket and drape my purse over my shoulder. "I'm going home. I think it's best we call it an evening."

"Uh . . . what happened to your promise?" Roark asks as Bram watches with humor over the exchange.

"You lost that privilege when you gave your friend crappy advice. It wouldn't have hurt you to try."

"Yeah, it wouldn't have hurt you to try," Bram adds with a confident head nod.

Roark points his finger at Bram. "You stay out of this."

Slinking away, Bram heads toward the elevator and presses the down button. I follow closely behind. The doors slide open and I step in after Bram. Roark blocks the door and looks me in the eyes. "Are you really leaving right now?"

"Yes. I am." I push his chest out of the elevator doorway and let the doors close on a very fuming Roark.

When the elevator starts to descend, Bram says, "That's not going to go over well."

"Not so much," I answer, a smile pulling at my lips.

"Why did you do it?"

"He's sexiest when he's angry."

Bram chuckles. "You're evil, woman, but I like you."

"Thank you. He'll be at my place within the hour."

Bram leans against the elevator wall, studying me. "Oh, he will and you're going to have one hell of a time explaining yourself."

"No explanation needed for what I have planned."

Bram lifts a brow. "Are you going to make good on that promise you made him?"

"It was never my intention to break it." I give him a big smile that causes him to roar with laughter.

"Shit, Roark is in way over his head with you."

∽

Roark: *What the fuck was that?*
Sutton: *Are you yelling at me through text?*
Roark: *Yeah, I fucking am. Why did you leave?*
Sutton: *I don't respond well to yelling. Once you tone it down, I'll speak with you.*
Roark: *Sutton, I swear to Christ.*
Sutton: *That's not toning it down.*
Roark: **Takes deep breath* What the fuck was that? *Said while holding a butterfly**
Sutton: *I just snorted.*
Roark: *Where are you?*
Sutton: *I told you, I went home.*
Roark: *Why?*
Sutton: *Felt like you needed a second.*
Roark: *Well, I've taken a second, now open your door.*

Sutton: *Are you outside?*
Roark: *Yes, so open your goddamn door right now.*

Swallowing hard, but filled with excitement, I adjust my top, fluff my hair, and prepare myself as I open the door to find Roark, hand on the wall, looking down at his phone, his hair a mess. He's fuming. I think I woke up a beast. *And I am so not sorry.*

CHAPTER EIGHTEEN

D*ear Ralph,*
Bram pissed himself while proposing. Holy shit, that's the best thing I've heard all year. Well, that's not entirely true, the best thing I heard all year was Sutton's moans while I flicked her with my tongue.

Still though, the poor bastard. I do feel a little bad for him. He loves Julia so damn much, and I know all he wants to do is marry the girl. It's why after he left I sent him some encouraging texts. Why didn't I say those things in front of Sutton? Because I was pissed and irritated.

I'm still pissed and irritated but now for an entirely different reason.

Sutton left.

She left as if it was no problem at all, and the only reason I'm not panicking and having a complete mental breakdown over it is because of the smallest of smirks I saw playing on her lips when the elevator doors closed. She's playing cat and mouse, her idea of foreplay.

My idea of torture.

But if it's angry sex she wants, she's about to get it.

Wish me luck, Ralph. This is going to be a night I remember for a long time.

Roark

ROARK

Fuming and turned on, I wait for Sutton to open the door to her apartment. The balls on this fucking woman—to walk out of my apartment, taking my friend's side.

It set me into a fit of rage but also made me smile. Sutton Grace, *my Sutton Grace*, not only got along with Bram but showed compassion and kindness in his time of need. I never doubted he'd like her—because she's incredible—but Bram is one of the only guys I've truly leaned on, and she swooped in and took him under her wing, helping him with his problem. It made me want her even more, and then she ran away.

I'm so not fucking happy.

The door to her apartment unlocks, and I press my hand against the doorway, trying to tamp down my anger. The door peeks open and I don't see anything, just the inside of her apartment. When I go to say something, she opens the door wider, but stays behind the wood, out of view.

I charge in and she shuts the door quickly.

That's when I see her.

Standing across from me, in nothing but a black thong and that cut-off white shirt . . . wet, so every inch of the fabric is plastered to her fantastic tits.

Speechless, I stare as she struts toward me and places her hand on my chest. Immediately I palm her ass and bring her in close, her shirt making mine wet as well.

Her hands move up my neck to my hair when she says, "What took you so long to get here? I've been waiting."

I squeeze her ass, loving how much of her there is to grab. "Why are you playing games, Sutton?"

"It's okay for you to play games, but not me?"

"When did I play games?" I ask, lowering my mouth to her neck where I start nipping along the column.

"When we first met, with my cell phone."

"That doesn't count. We weren't together then."

"You still tortured me." She moves her hands down my back to my jeans where she slips her hands under my shirt and starts pulling it up and over my head. I assist her and toss the fabric on the ground, bringing my lips back to her neck.

"Still different. Now that we're dating, we don't fuck around with each other."

"Are you lecturing me?" she asks, her nipples poking my chest with her heavy breaths.

Loving her scent, I run my nose along her ear, down to her collarbone as my hands travel up her back. She smells so damn good, and her soft skin is unlike anything I've felt. It's as if it's never been touched before. I can see myself getting lost in her body very easily.

"Yeah, I am." I lift up and look her in the eyes. "Don't fuck with my head, Sutton. It's already messed up as it is."

Her eyes soften as she reaches up and presses her fingers along my scruff. "I wanted to get you over here and surprise you." She pushes me backward until I sit on her bed. I quickly kick off my shoes before she sits on my lap. I circle her with my arms, my hands landing on her backside where I slip them under her thong.

She rests her arms on my shoulders, tilts her head to the side so her long blonde hair falls with her, and she starts to move her hips. I groan and waste no time making her lips mine. Soft and willing, her lips match my needy kisses, our tongues clashing in the middle. Her hands work their way into my hair, and my hands start to slide her thong down her legs. She lifts up, and I help guide the fabric off her body with help from each leg. I toss it with my shirt and quickly reach between her legs where I press a finger into her wetness.

She moans into my mouth as my finger finds her clit, and I start rubbing it as her hips very slowly work back and forth over my finger.

It's so fucking hot that my cock jumps against the zipper of my jeans.

I straighten out my finger and let her ride it, her kisses intensifying, her grip growing stronger. So wet, she glides up and down as I add another finger and slip inside her.

"Yes," she groans, now moving up and down. Her head falls back and I take advantage of her exposed neck and see-through shirt. From her neck, to her chest, to her nipples. I drag one into my mouth and squeeze her other breast with my hand that slipped under her shirt. She continues to ride my fingers, her tight channel closing in around me, and all I can envision is my dick getting the same treatment.

Desperate to find out what it feels like to be inside her, I flip her onto the bed so her back hits the mattress, and pull a pack of condoms from my back pocket. I toss them on the bed and reach for her shirt, dragging it over her head, exposing her completely. Not even a little shy, she lies there, naked, and fuckin' gorgeous as she stares up at me. She spreads her legs, and I watch in slow motion as her hand travels down her stomach to her nub, and she starts to massage it with two fingers.

Her hips rotate and her nipples pucker as she bites her bottom lip.

Holy Fuck.

She nods at my pants and says, "Lose them, Roark."

Eyes on hers, I reach down and undo my pants, dragging them down my hips along with my briefs. I kick them to the side along with my socks and stand tall as my cock juts out at her. Not even trying to be coy, her gaze immediately falls to my dick, and her mouth drops open. Best reaction ever.

She glances at me and her cheeks blush—the hottest fucking thing I've ever seen. There she is, the girl I first met, purity brimming from her eyes. I grip my cock and tug on it, staring at her while she continues to rub herself out, her legs falling open even more.

"You're so fookin' beautiful, Sutton." I snag a condom from the box on the bed, tear it open, and roll it over my more-than-ready erection right before leaning forward and hovering above her. "Are you sure you want this, that you want me?"

"More than anything, Roark."

I stroke her cheek, and the moment slows, becoming more intimate. "I've never felt like this about another person. It's different, and it's fucking terrifying."

"If it helps, I'm feeling the same thing." Her thumbs pass over my lip. "I've developed feelings for you, and I'm afraid they run deeper than I expected." Her eyes turn glassy with moisture. "I like you a lot, Roark."

Fuck.

I press a kiss against each of her eyes and then her nose, trying to soothe the worry etching her brow. I nudge my nose over hers and smile. "I like you a lot too." I lower my hips, my cock pressing against her entrance. "I don't know where you came from, but I don't want to let you go." *And that's the God's honest truth. I can't imagine my life without this woman.*

She reaches down and wraps her small hand around my length right before she guides me inside. Her mouth falls open, she inhales, and then moves her hips until I'm fully inserted.

Fucking hell, she feels so good.

My muscles clench.

So damn good.

"I'm not fucking around, Sutton, you're mine now. Do you understand that?"

She nods and brings my mouth to hers. Before kissing me, she says, "The possession is mutual. You're mine."

I pause, my hips stilling as I connect my eyes with hers. "I . . . fuck," I breathe out, my heart swelling in my dark, empty chest. "You don't know what that does to me, hearing you say that."

"It's true." She shifts her hips, and I grind my teeth together.

"Lass, I need to move."

"What are you waiting for?"

This girl, she's killing me. I drop my lips onto hers and pepper her with open-mouthed kisses as I slowly start to ease my hips in and out of her. I slip one of my hands into her hair and grip her breast with the other, lightly kneading her nipple. Her chest rises, her moans fill me up, and her sweet pussy lights up every nerve in my body.

So good.

So tight.

So perfect.

"God," I groan, releasing her mouth for a second, needing to catch my breath.

I push into her harder, picking up my pace.

"Yes," she chants, her neck straining, her fingers digging into my back. "Oh Roark, oh my God, Roark."

The way she says my name, the breathless whisper she uses, it pulses through my veins like oxygen, sending my body into a frenzy. I connect our foreheads, my hands bracing on either side of her head, my chest straining above her. Fuck, my orgasm starts to build at the tips of my toes and climbs up my legs, inch by glorious inch.

"Fuck," I breathe out heavily as my balls start to tighten.

Sutton's grip tightens, her pussy clenches around me, and her head tilts back as she cries out in ecstasy. "Roark, yes. Oh my God."

I pump harder, faster, using her orgasm to set off mine as she pulses around my cock. Like a fire hitting dry grass, the heat in my body ignites in a flash, my stomach drops, and pleasure erupts deep inside me as I still and come inside Sutton.

"Christ," I mutter, slowly working my hips in and out until we both open our eyes and stare into each other's souls. And then I sense something I've *never* felt before.

An understanding passing between us.

This is real.

This is more than I expected. Than she expected.

This could easily be forever.

In Sutton's tiny apartment, I rest my head on her fluffy pillow. She's curled into my side, and I stroke her hair, feeling consumed with a vast array of emotions.

The first being I want to protect her. I never want anything bad to happen to her, and given she lives here in Brooklyn, it scares me knowing I can't be here all the time. I make a promise to myself to hire a driving service for her. On days I can't be with her, I want to know she's safe. Might be ridiculous, but given the way we met, I think it's worth it.

Second, I want to talk to her. Hell, I want to talk to her about everything, and I'm not a talker, despite my Irish heritage. I'd rather drink a pint of Guinness than sit down and have a chitchat. But I have this need building inside me as we lie here, her soft sleeping sounds filling the night, to wake her up and talk about my childhood, tell her my favorite Irish dish—even if it's lame—tell her all about the small town I grew up in. I want her to know every little piece about me, and that's never happened before.

Then there's the passion coursing through me. If I hadn't worn her out twice already, I'd be waking her up right now to have her again. Relationships and emotions have never been my thing, ever, but with Sutton, I want it all. I want emotions involved when we're having sex. I want her to tell me she likes me . . . a lot, when I'm deep inside of her. I want her to shiver when my lips caress her, telling her how she makes me feel. Sex is different with Sutton in the best possible way, and I want more of it . . . all of it.

And that godforsaken scent of lavender. It's around her all the time, and it's driving me crazy. Now when I get a whiff of the smell, even when she's not around, I get hard. It's getting out of hand, and yet, lying here with her, I take in deep breaths, trying to get as much of her scent inside me as possible.

Who am I right now?

I'm not that guy.

But even though I'm not, there is no way I'm turning back, not when I somehow got lucky and was able to secure Sutton as my girl.

She's different, she's challenging, she's sweet, and she's also spicy when she wants to be. She makes me want to be better, she proves to me that I can be better, and she believes in me.

She fucking believes in me. And I had no fucking idea how much I've needed that.

I press a soft kiss to the top of her head and grip her tighter. Now that I'm committed, giving this relationship thing a go, there is no way I'm fucking it up, and if I do, I'll be ready to grovel.

~

"Put some clothes on," Sutton says, standing by her bathroom, one hand on her hip while the other brushes her wet hair.

"Why?"

"Because we're going out. It's past noon, and we haven't eaten anything."

I smile wickedly at her. "I don't know about you, but I'm pretty full from eating your pussy twice already today."

Her face falls as her cheeks blush a furious shade of red. "Can you not say it like that? You make it so vulgar."

"I make it sound so hot." I pat the side of the bed and rub the comforter. "Now get back over here, I'm hungry again."

She rolls her eyes and disappears into the bathroom. "We need actual food or I'm going to start getting hangry."

"I told you we can order in."

"We need fresh air," she counters, popping out of the bathroom in that terrycloth robe I've been dying to pull apart.

"My form of fresh air isn't allowed anymore, so I'm good here."

"Roark," she breathes out heavily. "Please, let's go out to lunch —it's on me—and then we can come back here and you can do whatever you want to me."

I scoff. "You're not buying anything, not when I'm around."

"Don't be that guy."

"What guy?" I ask, brow furrowed, still rubbing the bed, trying to entice her.

"The alpha guy who demands he pays for everything. I make a paycheck, and I can afford things too."

"How much do you make?"

Hand on hip, she asks, "Why does it matter?"

"Because, I probably make your salary in a day, that's why." It's so not true. Some days I probably make her annual salary in an hour, but I'm not telling her that. I pat the bed again. "Now come sit down; I'll call for food."

"That was a very pompous thing to say." The playful look in her eyes fades, and I inwardly groan, knowing my chances of getting her back into bed just plummeted.

I fling the covers back and reach for my jeans. "It's the truth. If anything, I'm always going to tell you the truth."

"Just because it's the truth doesn't mean it isn't rude."

I punch my legs through my jeans then stand, tucking my semi-hard dick past the zipper. Her eyes watch me the entire time, gazing at my cock, her chest rising and falling a little faster. Okay, maybe my chances didn't entirely evaporate.

"Never said it wasn't rude, just said it was the truth." I walk toward the bathroom and when I pass her, I tug on her robe, loosening the straps so the sides fall open, then continue to the bathroom where I stare in the mirror and adjust my hair.

I glance to the side and check out her partially exposed stomach and cleavage.

"You're being an ass," she points out, not fixing the robe.

I adjust my hair a few seconds more before stepping out of the bathroom, then I tip her chin up and whisper, "I'm sorry for being an arse . . . but it's true."

She swats my chest causing me to laugh. "You are infuriating."

"Yeah, I know, lass. Now are ya going to get dressed or are ya going like that? I need to know so I understand how I'm going to approach every guy on the street."

Lips pursed, eyes narrowed, she stares me down and drops her robe to the ground, exposing her beautiful body.

I shake my head at her. "Not a smart move, lass."

She folds her arms in front of her chest. "If you try to act like a barbarian and toss me on that bed, you're going to be in big trouble."

I take a step toward her and she holds up her hand. "Roark, I'm being serious. Don't even think about it."

Another step.

"Roark."

I close the last few inches and scoop her up over my shoulder. "Roark," she screeches and then laughs when I press a kiss to her ass and take her the two steps to the bed. I toss her onto the mattress and watch as her hair fans out and her tits bounce with her fall.

Fucking perfect.

I shuck my jeans in seconds and then hover above her, but before I can do anything, she pushes up and slams me onto the mattress so my head is at the headboard. Shit, I didn't see that coming, but I like it.

"Nice move, lass."

She doesn't respond, instead, she sits on my stomach, hands to my chest. "Do you really think we're about to have sex right now?"

"My dick does." She reaches behind her, finds my already erect cock and rolls her eyes.

"You're thirty-two, shouldn't you be less . . . sexually potent?"

"Are you calling me old?"

She shrugs with a smile. "You're not a spring chicken."

Eyes wide, I answer, "I'm not some fucking geezer with a cane."

Her smile grows. "Might as well be since you're in your thirties."

"Are you looking for me to spank you? Is that what you're asking for? I can arrange it."

"Is that an older-man thing, likes to punish the girl he's with?

I'm just so young, I have no idea," she says in an innocent yet obnoxiously sarcastic voice.

I run my tongue over my teeth, contemplating what I should do. I should "punish" her, but before I can make a move, she spins around and faces her back toward me and in one fell swoop, bends forward, taking my cock in her hands.

"Ah, fuck." I breathe out slowly, my hands instinctively going to her ass. "Sutton."

She grips the base of my cock tightly and the lowers her mouth to my cock where she lightly licks the tip. A hiss escapes my lips, so she does it again, but this time she swirls her tongue around the head and pumps my length.

Holy shit, that feels amazing. I rest my head against the pillow and try to relax my body into the mattress as she works her tongue around my cock. With each swirl, each pass of her tongue, I feel myself sinking further and further into bliss.

She doesn't have to work hard to make me writhe in ecstasy.

I peek my eyes open and that's when I see it, her ass in the air, her pussy so fucking wet that I feel a bolt of pleasure shoot up my cock. She's turned on from taking me in her mouth.

I need to do something about that.

Hands on her ass, I pull her to my face and swipe my tongue across her pussy. Her mouth stills and then a long moan falls past her lips as I make another swipe. Taking a few seconds, she gathers herself as I continue to work the small bundle of nerves.

Tightening her grip again, she begins to move her mouth up and down my length, her tongue swirling, her moans vibrating my cock in the best way possible, so I return the favor. I hum against her clit and she bucks her hips back, her throaty groans like a bolt of lightning straight through my veins.

My entire body breaks out in a sweat, my balls begin to tighten, and my toes start to curl as my impending orgasm rests at the base of my cock.

Fuck.

I can't go without her.

Holding off as best as I can, my entire body thrumming with an impending release, I work my tongue over her clit, swiping, flicking, pressing hard and then pulling away lightly. In seconds, her hips are rotating against my mouth and she cries out, her sounds muffled as she pumps my cock up and down with her hand.

My focus narrows, the sounds of the street outside drown away as pleasure rips through my body. My muscles still, my chest strains, my thighs clamp up, and I expel a loud groan as I come, gripping her ass tight.

It takes me a few moments to catch my breath, but when I do, I twist Sutton around and pull her up on my chest where I kiss her forehead. And I had no fucking idea how much I've needed that. *Could she be more perfect?*

After a few quiet moments, she says, "I've never done anything like that before."

"It was hot as fuck."

She peeks up at me. "It was." The sweet smile that crosses her face reminds me, though she might be open and willing to try new things, she's still an innocent girl underneath. "Want to order some food?"

I chuckle. "I fucked the sense back into you."

She kisses my chest and laughs herself. "I hate to admit it, but you did."

"What were you like as a kid?" Sutton asks while licking some cheese sauce off her finger. We ended up ordering cheesesteaks, and what I thought was going to be a simple meal has turned into an erotic show of Sutton fitting the hoagie in her mouth and licking every single finger. It hasn't been easy controlling myself.

Clearing my throat, I take a sip of my Coke—just plain Coke, nothing in it, boring shit. "A troublemaker. A stook—you'd say a punk—who knew how to get under everyone's skin. I terrorized people in town, at least when I was younger. When I turned ten, I was put to work."

"What do you mean put to work?"

I wipe my fingers off and sit back against the headboard. I chose to wear my pants while Sutton is wearing my shirt. "At the pub, I washed dishes for four dollars an hour every day after school. And then when I was done, I'd do homework in the corner until my dad was shit-faced, and that's when I'd drag his sorry arse back home."

"How many hours did you work?" Sutton's voice is concerned, and it does something to my heart, tripping it up.

"Depended on the day, but on average about five hours a night."

"Did you get the money?"

"Nah." I shake my head. "Paid my dad's tab with it."

She presses her hand to her chest, probably not quite believing what she's hearing. "From the age of ten, you worked so your dad could drink?"

"Pretty much. As he put it, I was doing my part for the family."

"That's horrible, Roark."

I shrug. "It was all I knew, but it was the main reason I wanted to leave. When my English teacher told me about the exchange program at Yale with scholarship opportunities, I applied. I never thought I'd get in, but when I did, I knew it was my way out. When I was studying at Yale, and partying"—she rolls her eyes—"I was also studying to get my green card."

Her brows shoot up in surprise. "You have your green card?"

"I do."

She snaps her fingers in disappointment. "Darn, there goes my chance to have a green card marriage checked off my bucket list."

"Sorry to disappoint."

She winks. "I'll forgive you." Then she grows serious. "I'm impressed, Roark, that you're self-made and have been able to build a business around you without any help."

"Impressed, huh?" I pull her in closer. "That wasn't your first opinion about me."

"Because you got in a fight with a guy over ketchup."

"Ah, I can't help what happens when I have alcohol running through my veins, which it hasn't been now for a fucking long time might I add."

She smiles sheepishly. Fuck, I want to kiss her. "You can drink, Roark. You just couldn't drink at the ranch."

"I'm aware of what I can do. I'm a grown-arse man, and if I want to skip the alcohol, I will."

She leans forward and runs her finger down my chest. "And smoking?"

I pull on the back of my neck. "Yeah, that's been a bitch, and I'm doing that for you. Or else, after what we did half an hour ago, I'd be smoking a cigarette for sure."

"Isn't my kind of fresh air better?"

"No."

She chuckles. "It's good you quit."

"I wouldn't say quit, more like currently suffering."

"Poor baby, can I help you with your cravings?" Her finger swipes over my nipple.

I raise a brow in question. "What kind of help are we talking?"

"The sexual kind," she answers cutely before taking her shirt off.

Who am I to deny the girl what she wants? I move our food out of the way and push her against the mattress. Her hair spans across the comforter, framing her like a goddamn angel. I move my hands up her sides and lean above her.

"You're addicting, you know that?"

"The best kind of addiction, right?"

I nod and bring my mouth to her neck where I mumble, "The only kind of addiction I want."

CHAPTER NINETEEN

Dear Branson,
 Branson . . . hmm, sounds like I'm a manager, calling for Branson, the fuck-up of the company, to get into my office so I can rip him a new one.

Don't worry, Branny. That's not going to happen.

Just stopping in to let you know I spoke with the evil witch with the stick up her ass, told her I was speaking with you consistently, and then I might have mentioned Sutton.

I know, I know. What the hell was I thinking? It just slipped. She called me out on smiling, which I've been doing like a goddamn fool day in and day out, and apparently I can't seem to tamp it down while in therapy.

Of course, her mouth twitched, and I knew she was hiding a knowing smile, it was evident from the annoying glint in her happy smile. As if she was giddy that I have a girl in my life. It was the first time I ever saw a shred of personality peek through her tough-as-nails veneer.

And do you know what that glint in her eyes made me do? It made me tell her that Sutton is the daughter of one of my clients. I know Bran-man, I'm cringing too.

The glint in her eye quickly disappeared and was replaced with a judgmental sneer, erasing any humanity from her face.

You know how therapists aren't supposed to throw down their opinion? They're just supposed to sit back and listen, asking stupid questions? She apparently forgot that, because she told me dating Sutton didn't seem like a good idea, despite the dancing floating hearts around my head whenever I talk about her.

You can imagine my shock when she told me to consider making a change where Sutton was concerned. I wanted to tell her I would consider making a change all right, and it would be firing her stuck-up ass. Of course, the court system wouldn't care for that, so instead, I stood from the couch, buttoned my suit jacket, and told her she had a poppy seed in her teeth and walked out the door.

She didn't.

But I saw she had an everything bagel and decided to make her sweat it out.

I don't need her judging me, not when I already know what I'm doing is not entirely kosher. And yeah, I'm going to have to tell Foster, man to man, that I'm dating his daughter, but when the time is right.

I have it all planned out. Don't worry.

Roark

~

SUTTON

"Please don't embarrass me."

"What could I possibly do that would embarrass you?" Maddie asks as she pushes her chestnut hair behind her ear. "I have some decorum, you know."

"I know, I'm just . . . nervous."

"Meeting the best friend is a tough one, I know, especially after the last time I saw him. Don't worry, I won't do anything to embarrass you."

The door to the small coffee house opens, letting in a breeze, followed by a bundled-up Roark wearing his signature beanie, black pants, and black jacket. His scruff is expertly trimmed, and there's a light, rosy hue to his cheeks from the chilly morning. He's so handsome it makes me want to sigh like a teenage girl.

He gives the place a quick once-over then spots us. A crooked smile on his face, he makes eye contact with me and approaches.

Maddie takes that moment to look up from her phone and spot him. "Well there he is, in the flesh, the best sex Sutton has ever had."

Roark pauses when he gets to the table and raises a brow in my direction.

Honestly, Maddie?

Chuckling, he leans down and hooks my chin with his finger and places a sweet kiss on my lips before whispering, "Best, huh? I like that."

Blushing, I press another quick kiss to his lips and pull away as he takes a seat next to me, scooting his chair close so he can drape his arm behind me.

After he's settled, he reaches across the small table and holds out his hand. "Maddie, it's nice to properly meet you."

She glances at me then turns to Roark. "Yes, nice to properly meet you." What was that glance for? I don't like that look in her eyes. "Can you say fuck me?"

Oh Maddie . . .

Confused, brow pinched together, he humors my friend and says, "Fook me."

"Did you hear that?" Maddie claps and does a horrible impersonation. "Fook me. God, that's hot. No wonder he's the best you've ever had."

"Maddie," I reprimand under my breath. "Be cool."

"Is that all ya talk about? Fookin'?" Roark asks, his accent growing heavier, which I'm sure he's doing on purpose.

"We talk about other things where you're concerned, but it usually starts with that."

"Oh yeah?" He twirls a piece of my hair around his finger. "Give me specifics."

"Not necessary," I say while shaking my head.

Apparently Maddie has a different idea, though. "She tells me everything from positions to girth."

"Girth?" Roark leans back to look at me as I blush terribly.

"Yeah, girth, and I must say, congrats." Maddie takes a sip of her drink and then continues. "Also, thank you for giving my girl her first sixty-nine experience. She would not stop talking about it."

"Maddie, for the love of God, stop." I press my hand to my forehead, utterly humiliated.

Leaning into me, Roark presses his lips against my ear and says, "Don't be embarrassed, it's hot that you talk about it." A shiver runs down my arm as he pulls away and addresses Maddie. "How long have you known Sutton?"

Thank God he changed the subject.

"Since freshman year in college. Pretty little Sutton here was lost at NYU, and she asked for some help. I had no clue where I was going but needed a friend, so I pretended to find the admissions building. Luckily we stumbled across it. After that, we went to the cafeteria, talked over bowls of cereal, and our friendship was solidified." Maddie glances in my direction. "Best friends for life."

"Not sure after this," I mutter, crossing my arms over my chest. Sensing my irritation, Roark moves his hand behind my neck and gently massages the tension out of it with his expert fingers. I will say this, even though he's not experienced in relationships, he sure knows how to do everything right.

"Lighten up." Maddie nudges my leg under the table. "You knew what was going to happen when you asked me to meet your boyfriend."

"You said you'd be cool," I mutter from the side of my lip.

She shrugs and takes a sip of her water. "I think we all knew that was a lie."

Roark chuckles next to me, the vibration of his laughter easing the tension in my shoulders. "I like her, lass," he says softly. "Just wait until you meet Rath and Bram—when he's not in a panic from peeing his pants."

"Peeing his pants?" Maddie asks, resting her chin on her propped-up hand. "Do tell why your friend pees his pants."

"He was choking on a Brussels sprout, got the Heimlich, and then peed. It was a production. He doesn't just pee his pants. He's a very nice guy," I say, hoping Maddie doesn't think Roark hangs out with guys with wonky prostates.

"That sounds horrifying." She looks to the side before turning her attention back to us. "Is this Bram taken?"

Oh Maddie.

"Recently engaged," Roark answers, drawing a gleeful surprise from me.

"He asked?"

Roark nods. "He took your advice, asked when he got home, and of course Julia said yes. They're in Barbados right now celebrating. They'll be back on Friday."

Maddie snaps her finger in disappointment. "Why are all the good ones always taken?"

"The only thing you know about Bram is him eating Brussels sprouts and peeing his pants. You call that good?" Roark asks, a little perplexed.

"If a man can admit to peeing his pants, I want to know him. Shows he's not too full of himself. I like that." Maddie gives Roark a once-over. "Ever pee yourself, Roark?"

He shrugs. "Probably. I've been drunk enough. I did really like peeing in Bram's laundry basket back in college."

Maddie chuckles as I turn in my seat, a little horrified. "You peed in laundry baskets?"

His wicked smile cuts through me. "When you're that blasted, anything round and white resembles a toilet. Don't worry, lass, I did his laundry for him the next morning."

"That's considerate," Maddie says, pointing her finger at Roark. "Very considerate. You got a good one."

Even though this is probably one of the most ridiculous conversations I've ever had, I don't think I could agree with Maddie more. I did find a good one—despite the peeing in laundry baskets thing. Roark is the type of man I know will always protect me, who will always strive to make me happy as I do the same. We've each met our match, and I can see my future with this man at my side. I sincerely hope he's feeling the same exact way.

As Maddie and Roark converse about college, I glance at him and take in the small crinkle near his eyes as he smiles and laughs, the way he so easily meshes with my best friend. It makes it that much easier to know I'm with the right guy. From our initial interaction, I never would have thought this is the man I want to be with, but slowly, with his witty comebacks and sweet and unlikely gestures, he's won me over . . . completely.

And now, I can't stop thinking about him. I hate not being at his side or lounging in one of our beds, talking about anything and nothing while we cuddle, skin on skin. Behind the reckless, bad-boy exterior and the asshole comments, he truly is a loveable and addicting man, one I don't plan on letting go . . . ever.

"So, I met Maddie." Roark places a giant walnut and fudge brownie on the table and takes the seat opposite me at his dining table. "When are we going to tell your dad?"

I knew that was coming.

It's not the first time he's mentioned telling my dad about us, and I think it's because he respects my dad greatly, and holding something back like this from him is wreaking havoc in Roark's mind. But I feel nervous. I know my dad likes Roark and respects him, but my dad has always been protective, and given Roark's history, I'm not sure he's the type of guy my dad would've picked for me.

But Roark is so much more than his past record. He's protective, he's sweet, and he cares about me more than I think anyone, including my dad if that's possible, ever has. He will do anything for me and strives to put a smile on my face every day. Those are attributes I want to focus on when talking to my dad about Roark, and I think if I take that approach, he might very well approve.

I need to find the right time.

It's all about timing with my dad; I've learned that the hard way. I can still remember the time in high school I told him I was going on a date with Luke Jameson. I told him five minutes before Luke showed up. Needless to say, my father, at six foot three, was pretty intimidating to poor Luke, and also needless to say, the date didn't happen. And I was never asked out after that all through high school . . .

Or the time I told him I was thinking about going to school out of state, that I no longer wanted to live in Texas, but wanted to explore New York where he spent many years playing football. He wasn't too happy about that either, because he wanted me to be safe in my pocket of comfort in Texas. Yes, I was book smart and not world savvy, but I wanted to change that. It's almost laughable that it was Maddie who first got me to stay out past nine after all my protests about being mature enough to take on city living. He has always wanted to be the one to protect me, to veto anything he thought would adversely change me.

So with Roark, I need to tread carefully. I know he cares for the man, I just need to make sure he's in a good position to learn about our new relationship.

I scoop up a bite of brownie with the fork Roark brought over and start to chew as I stare at the dessert. "I think we still have some time before we tell him."

"Is that so?" Roark asks, leaning back in his chair, his large arm draping over the chair next to him. Shirtless, his chest muscles contract as he shifts, his eyes trained on me as his unruly hair falls over his forehead. "You think we have some time still? What exactly does that mean?"

He's not angry, not even a little upset, just inquisitive. It almost makes me more nervous. "I think we should spend more time getting to know each other before we tell my dad."

"Thinking about changing your mind, lass?"

"What? No. Of course not." I take a deep breath. "I like where we are right now, and I don't want to lose that." I bite my bottom lip and say my biggest fear out loud. "What if he doesn't approve, Roark? What then? I'm not ready to lose you."

"If he doesn't approve are you going to break up with me?" he asks, shifting forward now and clasping his hands together under the table.

"No," I shake my head. "It would make things exponentially harder if he doesn't approve, and I don't want to deal with hard right now. I like how things are between us. Can't we keep it that way for a little while longer?"

Understanding washes over him as he visibly relents. "Yeah, we can."

"Thank you." I stand from my seat and round the table where I straddle his lap and loop my arms around his neck. Wearing nothing but his T-shirt and a pair of underwear, I settle easily on his thighs and press a warm kiss across his lips that he easily reciprocates.

Hands on my thighs, he takes a deep breath and leans back to look at me. A serious expression passes over his eyes before he says, "You're not ashamed of me, are you, Sutton?"

He can't be serious.

"Oh my gosh, no." How could he think that? I cup his cheeks. "Roark, if you think that, I clearly haven't been doing my job to reassure you how much you mean to me."

He rubs my thighs up and down, the warmth of his hands spreading all over my skin. "I'm sorry I asked; it was stupid."

"It wasn't, and if you asked, it's because I put something in your head to doubt me, to doubt us." I force him to look at me, those seldom serious eyes penetrating straight through my heart. "Please don't doubt us, Roark. When I say I'm the happiest I've ever been because I'm with you, I mean it. I know you want to tell my dad, get it over with, but give me a little more time, okay?"

He nods. "I'll give you all the time you want, as long as you're mine."

"I'm all yours." I shift on his lap, hooking my feet around his legs.

"You better be." He brings my mouth to his and leisurely explores my lips with his, occasionally swiping his tongue across them, sending a bolt of arousal straight through my center. When he pulls away, he drags out my lip for a second with his teeth, teasing me. "If we're not telling your dad right away, I think it's time you meet the boys . . . properly."

"The boys?"

He nods. "Bram and Rath."

Oh . . . THE boys. This should be very interesting.

Very interesting and fun.

"What happens if I find Rath more attractive than you? Aren't you nervous about that?"

"No."

Roark flanks my side, his hand securely fastened around mine as we walk to the restaurant Rath and Bram chose to meet me. Only a few more blocks at Roark's powerwalking speed.

"How can you be so sure? Isn't he incredibly intelligent, ruthless, and rich?"

"Taking notes when I talk to ya, lass?"

"Maybe." I chuckle. "But seriously, you're not worried at all?"

"No." He stops in front of the restaurant, grabs the door, and turns toward me, his eyes intent on connecting with mine. "I'm not worried, because after what I did to you this morning and the way you cried out my name in worship, trust me, I'm feeling pretty damn secure right now. Plus, I'm sexier than Rath." He winks and then guides me into the restaurant as my face heats from the memory of this morning.

Not that I would ever be interested in anyone but Roark—it's fun to tease him, though—but clearly that's not something to tease him about, because he'll never fall for it. There's no way he ever will, especially after what he said. This morning, oh God, I've never come so hard. He handcuffed my hands with sheets to his headboard then spent what felt like half an hour running his lips up and down my body until I was so turned on I couldn't think of anything else. And when he gave me release, I moaned his name loud enough for the entire building to hear.

It was unlike anything I've ever experienced, and I don't think it's simply Roark's outstanding bedroom skills at play here. I trust him. Completely. And it allows me to surrender control to him, and holy shit, is it worth it. *Only* Roark could generate such rapture within me.

"You know, if you keep blushing like that, I'm going to skip dinner and take you back to my place to do something about those red cheeks of yours," he whispers in my ear.

I turn into him and smile, embarrassed he can see the effect he has on me.

He chuckles and wraps his arm around me, pulling me into his chest. "You're so goddamn sweet, Sutton." He places a kiss on the top of my head and gives the hostess our name.

She weaves us through the dining area to a back doorway covered by a velvet curtain. When she pulls back the heavy fabric, two men are sitting at the table, drinks in hand, smiles on their faces as they converse. They both turn in our direction, and while Bram greets me with a friendly lift of his hand, Rath gives me a more serious once-over.

Alone, the curtain draped again, Rath and Bram stand while Roark makes introductions.

"Bram, you already know Sutton."

"I sure do," he says, pulling me into a hug.

"Congratulations on your engagement. I'm so happy for you," I mutter against his broad chest that holds me captive for a few seconds too long.

"All right," Roark says, tugging me away. "Enough of that shit."

Chuckling, Bram gives me a wink and then takes a seat. "Thanks, Sutton."

When we turn toward Rath, I'm a little taken back by the intensity in his expression. A few inches taller than Roark's already towering height, Rath takes a step forward, his shoulders broad and bulky, his jaw twitching as he continues to assess me. I can see why Roark has called him ruthless. He doesn't seem to be the soft, touchy-feely type, nor does he look like he knows how to smile.

It's kind of confusing, how these three men are best friends, because their personalities seem to be so different, but maybe that's why it works.

I offer my hand as Roark introduces me. "Rath, this is Sutton."

He takes my hand and gives it a tight squeeze before letting go. "Nice to meet you, Sutton," he says in a deep, gravelly voice—one I believe you only hear when a man wakes up from a long night's rest. But looking at Rath, I'm going to bet he doesn't know what a long night's rest is.

"Nice to meet you." I swallow hard, feeling very intimidated by him. Maybe that's why Roark knew my teasing was just that, teasing. There's no way I'd be able to handle a man like Rath, his intensity alone would wear me out in an hour.

Roark pulls out my chair and removes my jacket before taking a seat, his chair sliding next to mine, like when we met with Maddie.

But unlike the casual coffee date, dinner in a velvet-curtained space seems much more intimate, but I guess I can't expect anything less from these three high-powered businessmen—businessmen who used to be raucous frat boys from what Roark has told me.

He delighted me the other night with some old college stories of his boys, the kind of stories I never would have believed if I met these two in their professional element. Bram's past infractions of walking around shirtless and taking shots off anybody in his way, I could partially believe given the way I first met him. But if I met Rath in his office, and someone told me he was once found high in a fetal position in his closet, clutching his pillow like a childhood teddy bear, talking to it, I wouldn't believe it.

From across the table, Rath eyes me cautiously while Bram rubs his hands together, getting ready for the inquisition. "Tell us the secret, Sutton."

Confused, I ask, "What secret?"

Bram brings his drink to his lips, nods at Roark, and answers, "The secret to taming the Irish rogue sitting next to you."

"Christ," Roark groans. He shifts in his chair before whispering in my ear, "You don't have to answer any of their dumb questions."

With a small smile passing over my lips, I place my hand on Roark's thigh, keeping him close just like he's keeping me close, and I say, "It's all about making him squeal like a lady in the bedroom."

Bram spits out his drink while the smallest smirk passes over Rath's face. With the napkin from his lap, Bram quickly wipes his mouth before saying, "I wasn't expecting that answer."

Roark looks at me and says, "Neither was I. I think ya got things mixed up, lass. Weren't you the one squealing this morning when my fingers had a viselike grip on your nipples?"

Immediately, my face flames. I should have known better than to test Roark, especially in front of his friends. Softly, as if to soothe me, he kisses the side of my head and chuckles. He bested me this time. Who am I kidding? He'll probably always best me, and I know it's one of the reasons I'm falling hard for this guy. He teases me with no shame, *but* his version of soft and sweet beguiles me.

"Have you pinched Roark's nipple yet?" Bram asks, heating up my face even more. "He loves that."

"How do you know?" Roark asks, his posture completely relaxed in his chair as his thumb slowly draws small circles on the back of my neck.

With a wicked smile, Bram speaks over the rim of his glass. "You asked me to tweak them for you one night in college."

"Bullshit," Roark counters, even though there's laughter in his voice. "You probably dreamt that I asked you, because you were always wanting to get handsy with me."

"It's the Irish accent, am I right, Sutton?" Bram winks and takes a sip of his drink, causing me to laugh.

The friendship Roark shares with his friends reminds me so much of my relationship with Maddie. Behind the joking is loyalty, honesty, and the willingness to go the extra mile. After all, Bram thought it completely reasonable to turn up at Roark's when he believed he'd ruined his proposal. Given what Roark has shared about his family, I'm so happy he's had these guys in his life. It looks like Rath and Bram have been the brothers he's needed, stepping in to fill the empty void his family created. And even though we've only been dating for a few weeks, I want to thank the both of them, for being so loyal and loving to this man.

Now I feel the pressure for them to like me even more.

At least I know I already have Bram's vote. It's Rath Westin's I'm worried about.

"What about you, Rath, do you like your nipples played with?"

I don't know why I asked it.

I don't know what on earth went through my brain at that moment.

But with his sultry yet contemplative eyes staring me down, the nerves fluttering in my stomach, and the need to be liked, it just came out. I can't tell from the rise of his rakish eyebrow if he's amused.

At least Bram and Roark are, because they chuckle as I awkwardly wait for Rath's answer.

Rath shifts in his seat, his eyes still trained on me, and I realize in that moment why Rath is the successful businessman Roark boasts about. In the few seconds he holds eye contact with me, I'm starting to wilt under his gaze. I wouldn't want to face this man in a boardroom. Not for a second.

Finally, he answers, a small smile pulling at his lips. "Only when Bram does it."

Bram presses his hand to his chest dramatically. "Dude, that touches me deeply."

Rath shrugs. "You have the best fingers in the city."

I chuckle while Roark shakes his head. "Way to make it creepy, you two."

Bram points at me. "She's the one who started talking about nipples."

"Me?" I point at my chest. "Roark was the one who brought up nipples, I just spoke of squealing."

"She has you there," Rath says as the waitress places a plate of nachos in the middle of the table.

Nachos.

Wasn't expecting that. Neither was I expecting all three men to dive in with such urgency as cheese drips from the chips. Call me crazy, but given where we are and the social standing of these men, I would have bet my week's salary on them ordering something like Tuna Tartare rather than a pile of nachos with cheese and jalapenos. Who knew this place even served something like this?

"Dig in, Sutton," Roark says, his mouth full of chips. "They'll be gone before you know it."

And he's right, because when I reach for my first chip, each guy reaches for their third, making a significant dent in the plate.

As I chew on the gooey cheese and crunchy tortilla chip, I chuckle, watching all three men lick their fingers and swig their drinks. I guess Roark was right: you really can't drag the frat boy out of them.

Mid-bite, Rath asks, "So we know the Irish accent is a killer for most women, but other than that, what made you want to stick around with this guy?"

I think the nipple question warmed him up, because instead of an intense stare, Rath seems more relaxed, in his element, and that puts some ease in my shoulders. *Or it could be that he's eating. Men love food.*

I glance at Roark, only a few inches away, and take in his handsome features: those eyes that can display mischief and passion, his perfectly trimmed beard that feels sensational when rubbed up against my inner thigh, his smile that frequently *still* renders me speechless . . . They're all physical attributes that would attract any woman, but it's beyond the surface that has me hooked.

"I'll be honest," I answer, keeping my eyes on Roark. "It wasn't a match at first. I actually despised the man."

"Holding her phone hostage wasn't cool, man," Bram says from across the table. *They knew about that?*

"Didn't feel like giving it back." Roark smiles at me.

"He frustrated me," I add. "Frustrated me more than anyone I'd ever met, but within that frustration, he challenged me." Roark's eyes soften. "He helped me stand up for myself, something I've never been good at. He forced me to be more assertive, another attribute I lacked. He forced me to step outside of my comfort zone and fulfill one of the resolutions I set for myself this year—live life to its fullest. I don't think there's another person on this planet who could have pushed me as much as he did. And then my appreciation for him slowly grew into something else as I started to see his softer side."

"He really is a teddy bear, isn't he?" Bram cuts in.

I lean my head against Roark's shoulder and say, "He is. He pretends to be this 'gives zero fucks' bad boy when in fact, he's a total softy to the core."

"He's a good man," Rath says, seriousness lacing his every word. "I don't trust many people, nor do I care to waste my time with people who don't have a direct positive impact on my life, and even though Roark has done some stupid shit in the past, he's loyal and would do anything for me, for us."

The tone of the room changes dramatically from Rath's admission, leaving a squirming Roark and a gushing Bram.

"Dude, do you feel the same about me?" Bram asks, making me laugh.

Rath rolls his eyes. "How many times do I have to tell you this? If it was you or Julia, my own flesh and blood, hanging off a cliff, I would lift you to safety every time."

Bram presses his lips together and lowers his head before

reaching over and gripping Rath's hand. "I love you so much, man. If I liked penis, I would marry you over your sister."

"Jesus," Roark mutters and lowers his mouth to my ear. "I neglected to tell you how creepy their bromance is."

"I'm glad you didn't," I whisper back. "I like seeing it firsthand. It's very entertaining."

"Don't let them know that." He presses a quick kiss to my lips before fully wrapping his arm around me and claiming me right in front of his friends.

It's a small gesture, but it means a lot to me.

And when I see their returning smirks, I comfortably ease into Roark's embrace.

Spread across Roark's satin sheets—the new ones he got for me—I draw lazy circles over his bare chest as we lie in the dark, our breaths finally evening out from the rigorous activity that ended ten minutes ago. All the way home in the black town car Roark insists we take now, he kept whispering naughty things in my ear, telling me everything he planned on doing the minute we reached his apartment. And he didn't lie.

He checked off *every* promise he made in the car, including sex against the window of his bedroom, followed by the current cuddle we're sharing.

His fingers dance along my scalp, twisting in my hair, as I press my naked body against his, reveling in the smell of his cologne. "So you think they liked me?"

"They think you're perfect for me."

"They told you that?" I ask, lifting up so I can look him in the eye.

He nods. "Yeah, they already knew you were perfect for me before you met them, because they could see how happy I am." His thumb strokes my cheek softly. "You make me so damn happy, Sutton."

In the moonlit room, lying on the softest sheets I've ever felt, I feel my stomach flip in a somersault before settling into place. I make him happy, this unruly, asshole of a man. I make *him* happy. I don't know how, but I'm glad I do, because I can't imagine a day without hearing his sensual voice, without feeling his tender touch, without watching his face light up whenever I walk into a room. It's addicting. He's addicting, and I wasn't lying when I said he's an addiction I never want to quit.

"You make me happy too, Roark."

"Yeah?" he asks, a shy smile moving past his lips, a shadow of doubt in his eyes.

"Yes. How could you doubt that?"

He bites on his bottom lip and looks at the ceiling for a second. "I've never been in a relationship. I've never had experience with these overwhelming feelings to keep you close to me at all times, to protect you, to make sure I see that gorgeous smile of yours every day. It's all new, and there are times I have this heavy weight building in the center of my chest, wondering if I'm doing it right, if I'm screwing anything up." He cups my cheek. "I don't want to screw anything up with you, Sutton."

"You're not going to screw this up, Roark."

"I screw everything up."

I shake my head. "That's not true, not even close. Have you ever screwed up a business contract?"

"That's different. That's business. When it comes to personal relationships, I'm a goddamn fuck-up."

"Really? Because I just had dinner with two guys who think the world of you, who've been friends with you since college. And all your clients, they've stuck around because they don't only like the money you bring in, but the relationship they have with *you*. That's how your business started, through your ability to connect with others, to read their needs and anticipate their wants. The word *relationship* doesn't only lend itself to romance, Roark. You've been in relationships with people for many years, but you haven't understood how good you are at them. In them. It's as though you've hidden behind a façade of indifference and assholery, as if you've doubted they'd actually like you. But your success, your business, proves otherwise. So, you have been in relationships, and it's what makes you so good at ours."

He drags his hand over his face and blows out a long breath. As I look into his eyes, it's pain I see there. "Then why the fuck doesn't my family love me?"

My sweet man. Their *love*? They don't know what the word means. I hate how they've damaged his incredible heart and soul. I hate how their greed and ignorance still shapes how he sees himself. But I get it. If my dad didn't love me so unconditionally, I wouldn't be who I am today.

"Roark, look at me." I tip his chin with my finger so he's forced to meet my eyes. When I have his attention, I say, "I wish I had an answer for you, an exact reason why your family treats you with anything less than unconditional love. I so desperately wish I had the answers, but I don't. All I know is what I've seen ever since meeting you. You're loving, caring, loyal, kind, and genuine, all attributes that make up an impressive man, one I want forever by my side. It hurts me that your family can't see the same guy I do. It angers me that they've not bothered to know the man you've become, the friends you've made, the lasting relationships you've solidified. That's their loss, not yours." I soothingly drag my thumb over his bottom lip before bending down and pressing a soft kiss across his lips. He wants to further it by pressing his hand to the back of my head, but I lift up, not quite finished with what I have to say.

Taking a deep breath, I continue, "I care for you, Roark, deeply." The L word is on the tip of my tongue, but I hold back, not wanting to move too fast. "And because I care for you, I'm going to be frank. The way your family treats you—manipulates you—how they so horribly make you feel bad about yourself for wanting more, that's not how a loving family acts. That's not how parents should treat their children. And I know you feel this overwhelming guilt to help them out, and that's something you're going to have to combat in time, but I want you to know, it's not okay for them to use you, to make you feel any less than you are, to guilt you into sending them money every month. That's not okay, and as long as I'm in your life, I'm going to show you every damn day how you should be treated."

His face softens, his eyes glass over as he pulls me closer, our foreheads connecting. "You've changed me in all the best ways, Sutton. I doubt I'll ever find the words to tell you how much you mean to me."

"Then show me," I say, bringing my lips to his, where he takes them softly and rolls me to my back.

Taking a moment, he studies me. His finger trails down the side of my jaw. His eyes search mine, and a wave of nerves flutter in my stomach. And then I see it in his eyes . . . love. It's right there, unmistakable. He doesn't need to say it, because in this moment, I can sense it. See it.

He loves me.

And I love him.

Without another word, Roark presses his lips against mine and for the first time since we met, we make love, slowly and sweetly. It's not hurried, and there's no need to play around and tease each other. Instead, we connect in the deepest way possible, with our hearts.

CHAPTER TWENTY

Dear Ned,
      Holy.
<u>Fucking.</u>
Shit.
I'm in love.

I know, I'm just as shocked as you are. It's taken me a few days to figure it out. After I took Sutton to meet the boys, we went back to my place and fucked hard. It was amazing, but then something happened, something changed in our relationship. Some people might call it a pivotal moment.

I feel safe around her, which caused me to open up about the one thing that weighs heavily on my chest: my family. And even though what Sutton said to me all rang true, that my family doesn't treat me the way I deserve, I know accepting that is going to take time, because there will always be the question in the back of my head, wondering why they can't love me like Foster loves Sutton.

If I were to reiterate what my pain-in-the-ass therapist told me yesterday—which pains me—living my life, searching for their love is only going to continue to frustrate me, because I can't control their feelings or actions. But I can control my life and how I treat the positive people I have in my life.

Deep, right? And normally I would have scoffed, mentally flipped her the bird, and then been on my way, but with Sutton in my life, I see what she's talking about. I have an opportunity to be happy, the chance to feel love for the first time. That means I can make a choice. Instead of wallowing about what I can't fix, I can take this opportunity to prove to myself that in fact, I am someone who deserves love. And, I can reciprocate the feeling.

Sutton is everything I never knew I wanted in my life, and it's about time I let myself feel, rather than live in a constant state of numbness.

Sorry about the gushing, lad.

Roark

ROARK

I glance at my watch one more time, the hands barely moving around the dial. I'm being impatient.

Really fucking impatient.

It's been two days since I've seen my girl because I was out of town on business, tending to one of my West Coast clients, and now that I'm back, all I want to do is wrap her up in my arms, take her back to my place, and press my lips all over her sweet body.

But someone wanted to get dinner first . . .

I guess eating is a necessity, but so is getting inside Sutton.

Leaning against the wall of the restaurant, I scan the streets of New York, incessantly searching for a wave of bright blonde hair. I find it funny, that this is where I am in my life, desperate for one glimpse of the girl who's captured my heart.

And even though it's out of the norm for me, it feels so right, like there has been this missing piece in my life and Sutton completes me

Remember how I said I can be a goddamn gentleman sometimes and use words like besotted?

Well I'm fucking besotted over Sutton.

And I'm not ashamed to admit it . . . in my head.

Growing irritated, I lift off the wall and pull on the back of my neck—the itch for a cigarette strong—and then I spot Sutton turning the corner in her bright pink wool jacket. Her hair is curled and bouncing by her shoulders and her wind-streaked cheeks are a pretty blush that matches her lip color.

Stunning . . . And then she looks up, finds me, and her face lights up. *Fuck, yes.* My girl. She races toward me, a feat given her killer heels and form-fitting pants.

The minute she reaches me, I bring her into my arms and lift her up to my mouth where I place a desperate kiss on her lips. I melt into her touch, into the way her hand grazes over my beard and the soft demands from her mouth, looking for more.

I hold on to her tightly, pulling her out of the center of the sidewalk and closer to the restaurant so we aren't blocking New Yorkers from getting to where they need to go. Two days, that was it, we've been apart for two days and it's felt like pure torture. That's how far gone I am with this girl.

Pulling away, I take a deep breath and rest my forehead against hers as my hands circle her waist. "I missed you so damn much."

"I missed you too," she replies, in that sweet southern voice. "Why did it feel like a week?"

"No idea, but how about we skip dinner and go straight to my place?"

She chuckles and tugs on my hand. "Nice try. Remember our relationship isn't just about sex. There is more to us. We have substance, and we don't have to spend every moment in bed." *Female brains are such a mystery.*

"Why the hell not? I don't remember agreeing to that theory. We can have substance in bed." I follow her into the restaurant and speak close to her ear. "How about we try it? I'll bury myself deep inside of you, and we can discuss where we want to go on vacation while your tight pussy convulses around my cock." *Ooof.*

Sutton elbows me in the stomach and speaks from the side of her mouth. "Can you please control yourself? We're in public."

I move my hand over her ass unapologetically. "This is what

you get when you force me to go to dinner after not seeing you for two days. You're tempting fire, Sutton."

Glancing up at me, a seductive look in her eyes, she says, "If you really want to play that game, I have no problem turning you on while we eat dinner. Is that what you really want, McCool? A boner with your burger?"

A smirk pulls at my lips. Damn her and her sassy mouth. "I can't think of a better way to eat my dinner."

She lifts a brow in my direction. "Oh yeah?" Carefully and very nonchalantly, she backs into me and moves her hand behind her back and cups me, as if her hand is a magnet to my cock. She gives it a light squeeze, sending my libido through the roof as I jolt backward. The small chuckle playing off her lips tells me she's completely satisfied with my reaction. "Watch it, Roark. I learned from the master on how not to play fair."

Gripping her shoulders now, I lean into her ear and say, "You're going to pay for that, lass."

Before she can respond, the hostess greets us and Sutton gives her our name.

"It will be about fifteen minutes. Would you like to have a seat at the bar while you wait?"

Sutton looks up at me and then nods. "That would be lovely."

The hostess gestures to the left. "Right through the archway. I'll come get you when your table is ready."

"Thank you." Sutton takes my hand in hers and makes her way to the bar.

"You know, fifteen minutes is a long time, maybe we should just order in."

When she faces me, I catch a giant eye-roll. "We're going to be a civilized couple and have a dinner date." She takes a seat on a bar stool and I block her in, trapping her with my large body.

The bartender sets a napkin on the counter in front of Sutton and asks, "Can I get you anything?"

Keeping my eyes on Sutton, I say, "Jameson for me and a Shirley Temple for the lady."

The bartender nods and starts tending to our drinks. "Shirley Temple?"

I give a lock of her hair a quick tug and smile. "Seemed right. And I can't remember the last time I had a drink. If I'm going to get through this meal, I'm going to need some liquid encouragement."

"You act as if it's a chore to have a meal with me."

"It's not a chore, Miss Green. It's *torture*, especially when you're dressed in those sexy tight pants and rocking high-as-shit heels."

She coyly smiles. "I might have spiced up my outfit tonight."

I rest my hand on her thigh, the other on the back of her chair. She's sitting sideways so I have a good grip on her seat. "Spiced up your outfit? You're torturing me on purpose?"

"No." She shakes her head and fingers the lapel of my suit jacket. She knows my normal casual meeting wardrobe, so I might have dressed up for her as well. Thinking my girl appreciates it too. "I just wanted to look good for my man."

"You look really fucking good." My hand slides up her thigh. "Too good, lass."

The bartender pushes our drinks toward us and I reach into my wallet to pull out a fifty, when he holds up his hand. "I'll add it to your tab, Mr. McCool."

When he retreats, Sutton brings her drink to her sexy lips and says, "Mr. McCool? Friends with the bartender?"

I shrug. "They might know me here, probably not for the best of reasons. But they do have amazing burgers, and you said that's what you were feeling. I'm surprised they don't have a table already set up for us."

She pats my cheek. "Oh, how terrible, the rich man has to wait with the commoners."

"Keep teasing me, lass, see where it gets you."

"Hopefully beneath you." She winks while sipping from her straw, the suck of her cheeks driving me crazy.

"You're going to make this as hard as possible, aren't you?"

She glances down at my crotch and smiles. "Yup. As hard as

possible is always how I like it."

I take a swig of my whiskey and swish it slowly around my mouth for a second before swallowing. "You're getting fucked hard tonight, Sutton." I move in and lower my head to her ear. "I'm going to rip those pants off you, push you over the side of my couch, spread your legs and—"

"Oh God, oh crap." Sutton pushes at my chest, shoving me back while saying, "Get away from me."

"What?" I ask, completely confused by the panic in her eyes.

"My dad," she mutters, straightening up. "He just walked into the restaurant."

Oh fuck.

"Hide."

I glance behind me. "I can't hide, Sutton."

"Well, then take your hand off my thigh."

Okay, that's a valid point. Despite not wanting to, I take a step back and put a few feet between us, a small part of me wishing Foster caught me with my hand on her thigh so we could get the announcement over with. It's not like we've been lying to Foster; we've simply kept things quiet. But over the last week or so, I've felt this need to tell him, to have his approval, and now seems like a great time to get that over with.

"Let's call him over."

"Are you insane?" Sutton asks, her eyes wide. "This is not the time nor place to tell my dad we're dating."

"He's a cool guy, Sutton. I'm sure he'll be okay with it."

"You don't know him like I do."

Ouch.

She might be right, but still, my relationship with Foster is one I respect tremendously. I think highly of the man, almost as if he was the father figure I've been searching for.

I'm about to respond, when a man bumps into me, throwing me off balance. When I turn to look at him, he smirks and sits next to Sutton, his eyes trained on her chest.

He holds his hand out to her and says, "Hey, I'm John."

Sutton glances in my direction and kindly takes the guy's hand in hers. Anger billows up inside me only for steam to blow through my ears when she smiles at him. In my head, I know she's being polite—it's in her nature—but it doesn't mean I'm not fucking pissed about it.

"Sutton, nice to—"

"She's with me, lad," I say with a stern voice, taking a step forward, but not too close in case Foster does turn in our direction.

John looks me up and down and shakes his head. "I watched her push you away, so I don't think she wants anything to do with you, *lad*."

I grind my teeth together, trying to remain as calm as possible, remembering the idiotic breathing technique my therapist spouted off at one of my sessions. What was it? *Breathe in and out for a count of ten?*

Yeah, that shit isn't working right now.

The hand that isn't holding my tumbler of whiskey clenches at my side, itching to set an example for every other guy in the restaurant.

Sutton is mine.

"She wasn't pushing me away," I grind out.

"Dude, settle down. Her hand was on your chest, she doesn't want you near her."

Anytime Sutton wants to step in here would be fucking great.

"Listen up, you thick foo—"

"Sutton?" Foster's voice questions behind me, and then he steps closer to the bar.

Sutton's eyes widen and her hand fidgets on her lap.

"Foster Green, holy shit," John says, as he stands and holds out his hand. "I can't believe you're heading into your last season. You're my idol."

Being the nice man that Foster is, he smiles at John and shakes his hand. "Thank you, but the old man has to hang up his pads at some point. Hoping to finish on a high note."

"Hopefully the front office can pull off some good drafts this year, help you out a bit on the field."

"I have confidence they'll be able to." Giving John one last smile, he excuses us, tugs on Sutton's hand, and gives me a look. I follow them to the corner of the bar, my heart beating in my throat. Why did he give me that look? Is he pissed? Does he know?

I hope he doesn't know, because I really wanted to be able to tell him myself. I think he would appreciate it coming from me.

Cautiously, I approach the father and daughter duo. He holds out his hand, and we shake. "Roark." I go to answer him, trying to find my footing amidst this awkwardness, when Foster looks over my shoulder. "I wasn't expecting to see you two here."

Sutton nervously laughs. "Small world, huh? I was getting a drink after work and ran into Roark."

Okay, guess we won't be telling the truth tonight.

I run my tongue over the front of my teeth, as a faint pang of hurt radiates in the pit of my stomach. I know she wouldn't simply up and tell her dad, but this could have been the perfect lead-in. We haven't really talked about how we're going to tell him because every time I try to bring it up, Sutton changes the subject, and now that I think about it, I wonder if there's a deep-rooted reason why.

My mind battles with my heart as I try to convince myself that the worry starting to imprint my mind is just that . . . worry. *Unfounded worry.*

"Were you two going to eat alone?" Foster asks, glancing over my shoulder again.

"Uh, I was supposed to meet Maddie," Sutton says. The lies keep spinning off her tongue. "But she cancelled. Roark got me this Shirley Temple. Wasn't that nice of him?"

"It was." Foster glances at the drink and then at mine. "How have you been, Roark? I haven't seen you in a bit."

I hold my drink down at my side, not wanting him to think I was at the bar drinking by myself. "Good." I nod awkwardly.

"That's good," Foster answers, looking distracted. "I'm sorry

Maddie cancelled on you. I was going to grab a bite to eat, we could invite John over there to join us if you like." Winking, Foster adds, "He can't be bad if he's a fan of your old man's, I guess."

How about the old man's agent? The words almost slip past my lips, but I hold them back.

"What do you think? He's a good-looking guy," Foster continues, looking a little uncomfortable at trying to play matchmaker. *He's not as fucking uncomfortable as I am right now.*

From over my shoulder, Sutton takes a look at John, for God knows what reason, and says, "Yeah, he is."

Uh . . .

What the fuck?

Is she trying to blow my gasket? Because I'm about to lose my shit if she looks at that douche one more time.

"Unless, you're still caught up on that guy we talked about? Did you meet up with him when you got back to the city?"

I hang on her answer, knowing fully well that Foster is talking about me. Sutton takes that moment to sip from her drink, avoiding all eye contact in my direction. Talk about the perfect opportunity to open up the conversation about us dating. However, she says, "Things are complicated with him."

When she quickly glances at me, my brow quirks up. Complicated, huh? Last I knew, we were anything but complicated, but I get it, we're in a public place and she's nervous.

But, fuck. I know her intention is not to treat me as her dirty little secret, but it feels like she is. *It fucking hurts.*

"Well then, should I bring that guy over here, introduce him to my beautiful daughter?"

"No." She shakes her head. "I don't think that's a good idea. Roark is here, and I don't want to make him uncomfortable."

Foster laughs and grips my shoulder. "I'm sure he wouldn't mind, he can help me scope out the guy."

Over my dead body.

Why is he pushing this? She said no, for fuck's sake.

I send death beams over to Sutton, trying to communicate

with my eyes that she needs to deter her father from his terrible idea and quickly.

"I'm really not ready, Dad," she says with more force, cluing Foster in to drop it.

"Right. Good." I've never seen Foster like this—uncomfortable. Awkward. He clears his throat. "You could get his number—"

"Dad," Sutton groans, which causes him to laugh.

He pulls Sutton into a hug and kisses the top of her head while glancing toward the door again. His eyes have been dodgy this entire time, which makes me wonder . . .

"Oh my gosh. Look, it's Whitney," Sutton says when she pulls away from Foster.

No wonder he's been one foot out of our conversation the entire time. Foster was meeting Whitney here. His distance makes so much sense now. And it looks like things are about to get interesting. "Hey Whitney, over here." Sutton waves to her.

Foster tenses next to Sutton and quickly glances in my direction as if begging for help. Even if I knew what to do, I don't think I'd help out because honestly, Sutton is an adult, and if her dad is dating someone, she should know.

And vice versa, but I'm not going to go there again.

Whitney cautiously approaches, looking stunning in a fitted red dress and black heels. Her hair is curled in waves cascading over her shoulders, and her lips match the hue of her dress. I glance over at Foster, who has a searing look of appreciation on his face.

Christ. If it isn't obvious now, the look on Foster's face bellows that he's in love.

"Hey, you guys." She avoids all eye contact with Foster—not obvious at all.

"Wow, Whitney. You look amazing," Sutton says. "That color is gorgeous on you."

"Thank you." Whitney fidgets with her clutch and tries to smile, but it looks incredibly forced.

Still oblivious, Sutton says, "What are the odds we're all here together at the same time? Kind of weird, huh?" She gives her dad a once-over. "You look like you're here for a date, and Whitney, what's the occasion? I don't think I've ever seen you so dressed up besides at a work event."

Foster and Whitney glance at each other, a worried look in their eyes.

Now if I were Sutton's boyfriend in this moment, rather than being hidden, I'd step up next to her and explain what's unfolding in front of her. Instead, I lean back on my heels and take a sip from my tumbler, watching the wheels start to spin in Sutton's head.

"You're both here, looking really nice." She twists her lips to the side, thinking. "There was nothing important on the calendar for tonight." She looks up at her dad and then to Whitney. Back to her dad. "Are you . . ." I think she's almost there; she's putting the puzzle pieces together. "Are you two seeing each other?"

Whitney bites her bottom lip and looks like she's about to throw up, while Foster stuffs his hands in his pockets and thinks over his answer.

"I didn't want you to find out like this, sweetie. I wanted to sit down and tell you, but with your new job and everything going on in your life, I didn't want to make things weird." Straightening up, he wraps his arm around Whitney's waist, who quickly melts into his side and says, "But since it's kind of obvious, Whitney and I have been dating for a while now. We're, uh . . . we're in love."

Slowly, I turn toward Sutton, a squint in my eyes as I wait for her reaction.

She blinks a few times as her mind processes, but once it does, a small tear slides down her cheek, and it takes everything in me not to reach out and wipe it away for her.

"Dad, that's . . . that's so amazing. I can't believe you didn't tell me sooner." Sutton reaches out and pulls Whitney into a hug. "Gosh, I'm so happy for you two."

And if I wasn't in love with the girl already, I would be right now. This could have gone so many ways, but instead of freaking out, she instantly accepts the new information with open arms, making her dad and Whitney both look at ease.

Sutton's not only beautiful on the outside, but she's absolutely gorgeous on the inside.

"Thank you," Whitney says, looking quite relieved. "I wasn't sure how you'd take it since I'm your boss, but I can't tell you how much it means to me that you're okay with this."

"As long as you're happy, that's all I care about." Sutton gives her dad a hug as well, one that lasts much longer than expected. She says something into his chest, but I can't quite make it out with all the background noise. This could be our moment though. Seeing he understands being in love, I'm certain he'll see the same look in my eyes for Sutton that he has for Whitney.

Awkwardly I turn to Whitney and say, "Congrats."

"Thank you." She laughs and nods. "And congrats to you as well."

Oh.

Shit.

I squeeze my eyes shut as Foster says, "Congrats?"

Christ. This is so not how things were supposed to go down.

I look at Sutton who pales immediately, panic racing through her eyes. Normally quick on my feet, I feel tongue-tied, unsure what to say, unsure what Sutton wants me to say. We must be silent for too long because Foster starts to look between the two of us. *This is it. This is where he sees my love for his daughter. We shouldn't have to spell it out either.*

"Sutton," his voice grows serious, "is there something *you* need to tell *me*?" When Foster glances in my direction, he doesn't look happy. A lesser man would wilt under his stare but instead, I hold my position and don't break eye contact.

"I, uh . . . I was going to tell you—"

"Mr. Green, your table is ready," the hostess says, breaking the tension in our little circle.

Foster rolls his teeth over his lip, looking between the two of us before nodding his head—not in a happy way—and taking

Whitney's hand in his. Without another word, he follows the hostess toward the dining room as Whitney apologetically whispers to us "sorry."

Not a single comment. Nothing.

I expected him to have something to say, but silence?

Fuck. I don't think I can take silence.

Once out of the room, Sutton presses her hand to her forehead as tears start to well up in her eyes. I'm at her side immediately, but again she pushes me away.

"That was so bad," she says, her voice shaking. "He's so mad."

"Sutton"—I take a step forward, but she takes another step back—"can we go to my place and figure this out?"

"What's there to figure out, Roark?" She gestures toward her retreating dad. "He's clearly angry."

"He's processing."

She shakes her head. "That's not processing, that's seething."

"Let's just go back to my place—"

"Hey, she clearly doesn't want to go anywhere with you." My shoulder is pulled back, flinging me around to find John, once again. *This wanker.*

Taking a calming breath, I say, "If you were smart, you'd mind your own business."

"If you were smart, you'd take a hint," John replies, side-stepping me and taking Sutton's hand in his. "Come with me."

Sutton's face says it all.

Help me.

"Drop her hand, now," I say, giving him a fair warning.

Instead, the idiot weaves Sutton through the throng of people even as she says, "That's my boyfriend."

"If he is, he's treating you like shit," I hear him say before they move out of earshot.

I want to toss the motherfucker into the wall, but I can't. It's a grand restaurant, and I can't afford to get into another fight. Even though a douche named John thinks he can play superhero. *Where the hell did this guy come from?*

So instead, I set my tumbler down on a high-top table and follow them . . . calmly. But when I round the corner to the hallway that leads to the bathrooms, all I see is red.

John has Sutton pressed up against the wall, trapping her as she tries to push him away, but he doesn't budge.

Fuck. No.

This motherfucker has messed with the wrong person. No one takes my girl from me or traps her against her will. *Fury. That's where I'm at now.*

"Get away," I hear her screech, right before I rip the guy's shoulder back and plow my fist right across his jaw.

He stumbles backward a few steps and blinks before he looks up at me and charges, bulldozing into my body and ramming me against the wall. He gets a few punches into my side before I knee him in the gut and get free of his grasp.

In the background, I hear the shrill cries of women as I charge after John, my fist connecting with his side right before his crosses my eye, sending a thrilling pain through my skull.

"Roark, stop," Sutton yells.

I can't stop. *He had his hands on my girl.* But before I can cock back my arm again, a pair of strong hands pulls me back by the collar of my shirt and pulls me through the entryway and into the streets where I'm thrust forward.

I turn to find Foster, standing boldly, hands on his hips, a look of fierce anger in his eyes. I'm still bristling with rage from what that motherfucker did to my girl. Sutton moves toward me, but before she can touch me, Foster gestures his arm to the side. "Get out of here, Roark."

I catch my balance, leaning forward as blood drips from my nose to the ground. I swipe my hand across my face and look up at the man I respect more than any other male figure in my life. "Foster, it's not like it seems."

"It seems like you haven't changed. I stuck my neck out for you and slapped my name on yours as a sponsor." He pushes his hand through his hair. "I expected more from you."

"Dad." Sutton tries to pull his arm but Foster moves forward, closing the space between us.

"When I first met you, Roark, I knew you'd bring my business and image to the next level. You lift athletes up and help portray a positive image around them and yet, here you are, still drinking, still getting in fights, hiding goddamn secrets." He takes another step closer, getting in my face. "Dating my daughter and not saying anything to me." He shakes his head. "I thought you had more respect for me than that."

"Dad, please. Don't—"

"No, Sutton. Not now," he says to her, causing her to step back with a sob.

Foster focuses his barely contained fury back on me. "You're not the man I thought you were, and you'll probably never be the man I believed you had the potential to be." He looks me up and down. "There is no way I'll let my daughter date anyone less than what she deserves. And you, Roark, you're nowhere near her level."

Retreating, he takes Sutton by the shoulder and guides her back to the restaurant. "Sutton," I call out. But it's not love I see in her tear-filled eyes when she briefly looks over her shoulder. *Is she angry too? Disappointed?* She turns and follows her father into the restaurant, leaving me alone on the streets.

Fuck.

I wipe at my nose again and then look up at the sky, wondering what the hell just happened. How did I go from teasing and joking with my girl to being kicked out of a high-end restaurant with bloody knuckles and nothing to show for it? *What the fuck?* I'm itching to punch something . . . someone. That fucker better not show his face outside.

You are nowhere near her level.

Words I never wanted to hear validated. But there they are, falling from Foster's lips. They ring truer than anything I've ever heard.

There's at least one thing I know for sure, despite everything Sutton said to me, wanting to be by my side, thinking I'm the man she wanted, she was pretty quick to retreat once her dad voiced his thoughts.

~

"What the hell are you doing here?"

I look over my shoulder to find Rath with a towel wrapped around his waist and his hair in disarray.

"Pouring myself a drink. What does it look like?"

He steps closer and switches on a light, burning my retinas with the brightness. I try to cover up my eyes as I wobble on my feet.

"What the hell happened?"

"What didn't happen?" I ask, topping my cup to the brim with whiskey. I turn around and lean against the bar counter, giving Rath my best smile over my filled glass.

"Christ." Rath looks behind him and adjusts the knot on his towel. "Guessing you're not going anywhere too soon."

"Nope," I answer, popping the P.

"And Bram wasn't available?"

"Bram is all about that love shit right now. Couldn't take it, so I came here."

"Lucky me," Rath says while blowing out a long breath. "Have a seat in the living room while I take care of something."

"Don't mind if I do," I answer, strutting toward the couch, the room spinning around me. After being tossed out of the restaurant, I went to the first bar I found and drank until I was drunk enough to grab a cab to Rath's apartment.

Why here?

Simple, I can't be at my place, not right now. Not when Sutton keeps calling and texting me. I turned my phone off, not able to take it anymore.

I read some of her texts.

She was sorry, she needs to talk to me. Please be careful, shit like that. But it means nothing to me. It can't mean anything to me.

Not after what Foster said to me.

Not after the look she gave me as she walked away.

I saw it in her eyes, almost as if she agreed with her dad.

From the hallway, Rath appears in a pair of sweatpants and holding a girl's hand as he walks her to the elevator. I hear him whisper something while pressing the down button, but can't quite make it out.

Feeling a little guilty, I wave my hand in their direction and shout out, "Sorry about the cockblock."

Rath shoots me a death glare and then presses a quick kiss on the girl's lips before sending her on her way. Once the doors are closed, he lets out a long breath and grabs himself a tumbler of whiskey as well before joining me on the couch.

"She seemed nice," I say, trying to fill in the silence.

"Yeah."

I shrug. "She had good legs."

"That she did," Rath says, leaning back and looking to the ceiling.

"But she isn't the girl we don't talk about, is she?"

"We're not here to pick apart my love life," he growls at me. "Now tell me what the fuck happened so I can go to bed."

"Where should I start?" I scratch the side of my jaw. "Foster found out about me and Sutton."

"Shit, did he punch you?" Rath asks, sitting up and facing me now.

I take a sip from my cup and hiss out the burn before saying, "Nah, that was a guy named John who was sexually assaulting Sutton in a hallway."

"The fuck?" Rath blinks a few times. "Start from the beginning."

I spend the next few minutes recollecting everything from seeing Sutton after two long-as-hell nights alone, to the douche trying to move in, to spotting Foster, to finding out about his relationship, to Whitney's slip only to follow it all up to the fight in the hallway.

"Holy shit," Rath breathes out heavily. "So Foster dragged you out of the restaurant. He couldn't have been happy."

"Yeah, you could say that." I stare straight ahead as the words he spouted at me reverberate in my head. "It's as if he took all the things I hate about myself and confirmed them." I shake my head. "You should have seen the look in his eyes. I know I'm his agent, and we have a business relationship, but I've always looked up to the man, and I've never felt so sick for disappointing someone. That's what he was, disappointed. He thought I was fighting to fight and then said . . ." I let out a long sigh. "Shit."

What the fuck is happening?

Tears start to form in the back of my eyes and I swear to Christ if they fall, I'm going to go ballistic.

Deep breaths, just like the therapist said.

"Dude, are you okay?" Rath asks, seeming worried. He should be, I'm about to have a goddamn moment.

"No, I'm not." I lean my head back and try to ease the tightness in my throat. "I'm such a fuck-up, Rath. When it comes to business, I'm unstoppable, but anything to do with my personal life I can't get right." I drag my hand over my face. "I love her, man. I love her so goddamn much."

"What did Foster say to you?"

"Just told me the truth I already knew. That I'm not good enough for Sutton."

"He said that?"

"Something like that. But to sum it up, yeah, I'm not deserving of his daughter."

"Shit . . . he's not right, you know."

I scoff at that. Okay, maybe Rath has been drinking, and I didn't know about it until just now. "He's dead accurate."

"He isn't." Rath says, shaking his head. "You are more than enough for her. From what I've observed, you balance each other out. Fuck, within minutes of meeting me, she boldly asked if I liked nipple play. That was funny as fuck, man. Green was blindsided. Given time, he'd see that you worship the ground she walks on, and show her the same loyalty and attention that you do to us, and to your clients."

I shake my head and then down a large gulp of whiskey, feeling the amber liquid settle into my stomach. "There's a reason my family wants nothing to do with me, Rath. I'm not the type of guy who gets to ride off into the sunset on a horse with the love of his life, a happily ever after right around the corner. I'm not Bram. I don't have the capacity to truly give a woman what she deserves, because I don't know how to do that."

"Just because you don't know how doesn't mean you throw in the towel. You learn, you adapt. You didn't know shit about being an agent, but you found your way to the top. This is the same thing. You have to teach yourself, and it will come to you. You have the capacity to use your heart. You do it with me and Bram."

"You're different."

"We're not. It's still a relationship, one you've held on to for over twelve years. To me, that's something to be proud of and it proves to me that you are more than capable of being in a relationship with Sutton." It reminds me of what Sutton thought. Of what I temporarily believed. *The word relationship doesn't just lend itself to romance, Roark. You've been in relationships with people for many years . . . It's as though you've hidden behind a façade of indifference and assholery . .*
.

"What the fuck ever, Rath," I answer. I'm so tired of this shit. Sutton's gone from my life now. I place my empty glass on the table and lift off the seat. I stumble down the hall, pressing my hand against the muted grey wall.

"Where are you going?"

"To bed."

"We're not done here, Roark."

"We are," I call over my shoulder. "There's nothing you can say that will change the aching realization that Sutton and I are not meant to be."

CHAPTER TWENTY-ONE

D*ear*...
    Where do I even begin?
I'm broken, in so many ways from my bloody nose to my shattered heart.

My lungs don't seem to be working like they used to, as if a heavy weight is now resting on them, making it impossible to catch a full breath of air.

And instead of drifting off into an alcohol-induced coma, I'm wide awake, staring at the ceiling of Rath's penthouse, replaying the night over and over in my head: The look on Sutton's face. Foster's cruel, yet accurate words. They keep crashing into me like a tidal wave on repeat, drowning me, suffocating me in sorrow and loss.

Loss for something I never knew I wanted, but feel desperate to have again.

She keeps trying to contact me though. I turned on my phone to see five more messages from her. She wants to see me, talk to me.

I'm tempted. Fuck do I want her.

But I know deep down, even though breathing would be so much easier with her by my side, I'm going to have to live with shallow breaths for the rest of my life.

Roark

SUTTON

"Dad, stop." I pull my arm away and try to go out the door to find Roark. Why I allowed my dad to usher me back into the restaurant is beyond me.

"Sutton Grace, do not go out that door, because you owe me an explanation. A very long one." His voice booms into my ear, silent to the people around us, but clear to me with his close proximity.

"I need to check on him."

"The more we keep our distance, the better. They have a private room for us in the back. Find your seat at the table while I handle something."

He's stern and his eyes read "don't fuck with me."

So even though I want nothing more than to run after Roark and see if he's okay, I know my dad won't tolerate me leaving this restaurant without an explanation.

But the decision isn't easy as I chew on my bottom lip and look toward the door.

"Sutton Grace, do not cross me."

Growing frustrated with my dad's attempt to turn me back into a little girl, I lean closer and say, "I'm a grown woman, Dad, so start treating me like one."

"I will when you start acting like one," he snips back and then motions to the back of the restaurant noiselessly, as all eyes are trained on us.

Knowing my dad's image is very important, I succumb to his demands and head to the room where Whitney is sitting nervously, her hands twisting in her lap, her eyes watery.

When I shut the heavy curtain, I take a seat at the table and rest my head in my hands. Whitney is immediately at my side, hand on my back.

"Sutton, I'm so sorry. I can't believe I let that slip."

"It had to come out at some point." I sigh and turn toward her.

"I should have told him a while ago." I bring my phone from my purse and start to type out a text message when Dad comes breezing through the curtain. He doesn't take a seat right away but instead paces the little space, his giant stride eating up the beautifully polished hardwood floors.

Finally, he stops and stares down at me, hands on his hips. "Care to explain what was going on? I just had to promise that man VIP tickets to the first Steel's game this season so he didn't press charges against Roark."

Why is he paying off someone who assaulted me?

"Dad, he was—"

"What the hell were you thinking, Sutton? First of all, the man is eight years older than you."

"Dad—"

He holds up his hand. "Second, he's my agent. He handles a very important part of my business, so why would you get involved with someone who's such a vital attribute to my livelihood?"

I bite back a remark, tears starting to brim in my eyes.

"And third, even though I respect his business techniques, his personal life is less than anything I would ever approve of for my daughter, and you should have known that. And tonight, sadly, proves he won't change. The man can't go a week without getting in a fight. I've known him for a long time and I've seen many black eyes on his face, so what in your right mind thinks it's a good idea to go out with him? He's a rebel, Sutton, someone who will forever be selfish when it comes to his temper." He grips the back of his neck with both hands and pulls on it, his arms bulging with tension. "Christ, what the hell were you thinking?"

What was I thinking? I was thinking and still think that there's a beautifully broken man who I fell in love with and there was nothing I could do to stop it. And nothing would make me change my opinion of the man I love.

Growing up on the ranch while my dad was in New York, playing out his football seasons year after year, I was partially raised by my grandparents, but was always told to mind my father even though he couldn't be near me. And I took that to heart, because during the off-season, he was present. He might have been an unconventional father with his work schedule, but there never was a time I crossed him because even over the phone, he would give me a tongue-lashing to remember.

But in this moment, with my dad acting so hopelessly wrong, I strap on my big girl boots and stand up to him, ready to—for the first time—put *him* in his place.

Sucking back the tears, trying my best to leave the soppy emotion out of this, I say, "What have you always told me about reacting, Dad?" He makes eye contact with me, but doesn't say anything, so I continue. "You've told me time and time again that before I react, I need to get all the facts. Well, it's time you got the facts."

Feeling calmer, I sit taller in my seat and gesture to the chair next to me. "Take a seat, Dad." I wait for a few seconds as he decides what to do. In the end, he's an honourable man and pulls out the chair. His large body swallows the wooden seat as he rests his arm on the table. His stature alone is intimidating, but his eyes say it all—they always have—he's not happy. I plan on changing that.

"Roark and I started dating a little over a month ago." His jaw ticks. "It wasn't something we were planning on. Honestly, I despised him when I first met him, but over time, something happened between us, a shift in our relationship, an appreciation for one another, the same kind of shift I'm sure you had with Whitney."

He glances over at Whitney who places her hand on my arm, encouraging me to keep going.

"I wasn't expecting to fall for him, but I did, and I'm glad I did because he truly makes me happy, Dad. He loves me, I know he does, and he cares for me, encourages me, protects me—"

"Protects you? He got in a fight . . . twice around you."

"Dad, the man *you* paid off tonight was assaulting me, had his hands on me—"

"What?" my dad booms, standing from his chair.

"Roark was protecting me," I add and stop Dad from causing another scene. "Don't worry about him for now. You need to listen to me about Roark. He's a good man. Unlike that slimeball—"

"What. Did. He. Do. To. You?"

I take a deep breath. I'm barely holding it together from what's happened to Roark, from the feel of John's hands on me . . . "It started at the bar. He kept insisting I didn't want Roark near me, which was the furthest thing from the truth. You walked into the restaurant and I asked Roark to keep his distance. John took it as I wanted nothing to do with Roark and swooped in. Roark took insults from the man, swallowed his pride as he watched me make small talk, but never took action. He was calm and reserved, when I know he wanted to claim me as his, but he couldn't." I hang my head in shame. "He couldn't because I told him not to. I wasn't ready to tell you because I didn't want the reaction you had when you found out. I wanted to preserve our relationship for as long as I could."

"You could have told me, Sutton. I would have understood."

I shake my head. "Clearly you couldn't, Dad."

"He was beating the shit out of another man; what was I supposed to think?"

"Before that, you walked away."

He drags his hand over his face in frustration. "Because . . . I was caught off guard."

"I was blindsided about you and Whitney, but I acted like an adult and was happy for your happiness. And when you left us after finding out, that's when John pulled me into that hallway and tried to take advantage of me. Roark found me and told John to step away from me. When he didn't, yes, he pulled him off me."

"He had his hands on you—"

"Yes." I'm trembling. I don't want to think about this. "Roark loves me, Dad, so imagine how *he* felt seeing that. Ask the restaurant for footage if you don't believe me. I bet it's all there. He was protecting me, Dad, and you treated him like he was a monster."

"Fuck," he mutters, pressing his hand to his palm and slowly moving it back and forth. "Why didn't you say anything?"

"I tried to, but you wouldn't let me. And I couldn't leave letting you believe anything other than the truth. He's a good man, Dad. He might be rough around the edges and has made some bad decisions in the past, but he's a good man, one you should be proud to have in my life . . . in your life."

Leaning back, he blows out a long breath of air and stares at the ceiling. "Shit. The things I said to him, Sutton. God, I'm so sorry. Why didn't he talk to me about the two of you? Before tonight, I had seen a change in him."

"He wanted to talk to you. Right from the start. And I asked him to wait. I was in the wrong, Dad, not Roark." *I was so wrong.*

My dad locks eyes with me and cocks his head to the side in question. "But you love him?"

I nod, not even having to give it thought. "I love him, Dad."

"And he treats you with respect."

"Yes."

"And you're happy?"

I smile softly. "The happiest I've ever been. He teases me, he pushes my buttons, he makes me angry, but all in a way that shows me how compatible we are. And he never asks me for anything other than my presence. He just wants to be with me, hold my hand, hold me. That's all." I pause and catch my breath. "He makes me feel special, Dad." Loved. Adored. Cherished.

Slowly he nods and places his hands on his knees. "We need to go find him."

A tear slips past my eyes as I reach over and give him a large hug. As he lowers his head to my ear he whispers, "I'm so sorry, Sutton. If you're happy, I'm happy. And you're right about Roark. I'm sorry I let my ignorance blind me."

"It's okay, Dad." I lean back and pat him on the cheek. "You can't always be perfect."

Whitney scoffs at that comment and folds her arms over her

chest, a playful smile on her lips. "He's anything but perfect, Sutton, you can trust me on that."

"Watch it." He points his finger at Whitney. "I don't need you knocking me down a peg in front of my daughter."

"Oh, you did that all on your own." She chuckles, causing me to laugh as well. Looks like my dad met his match, and I couldn't have picked a better person for him to be with. I'm shocked I didn't see it before. Talk about being professional. I never would have guessed.

"Come on." My dad rises from his chair. "Let's go find, Roark."

I roll over, the sheets tangling between my legs. The sun shines down through a slit in the curtains, and the smell of coffee permeates the room as I try to gain my bearings. My eyes flutter open, heavy from lack of sleep, adjusting to the early morning sun.

And that's when I realize where I am.

I spring forward, looking to the empty side of the bed. The pillow is untouched. I quickly swing my gaze to the bathroom and don't see any sign of life either. Gathering the robe Roark bought me at the end of the bed, the one I keep at his place, I throw it over my shoulders and sprint-walk to the living room, scanning for Roark.

Nothing.

The kitchen is similarly empty, the only "life" being the slow-dripped coffee brewing due to a pre-set timer.

Did he not come home last night? My blurry eyes read the time on the oven. Six in the morning. He never stays out that late. Where could he be?

My eyes drift to the guest room and wonder if maybe he came home, saw me in his bed, and chose to sleep in the guest room instead. Heart pounding, I walk over to the closed door, squeeze my eyes shut in hope, and open the door. A perfectly made bed and not a soul in sight.

He didn't come home.

At all.

Maybe he responded to one of my texts. I walk back to the bedroom, robe flapping at my sides, and wake up my phone, but when the screen comes to life, I see nothing. After we left the restaurant, we spent a good few hours looking for Roark, calling and texting him, but we came up short. Dad called it a night and told me to get in touch with him the minute Roark came home.

I spent the rest of the night crying on the phone to Maddie. She listened quietly, interjecting her gasps of surprise every once in a while, and when I told her I loved him and I was scared he wouldn't take me back, she reassured me, telling me there was no way he would be able to stay away. He didn't the first time.

And I'd like to believe that, but now, alone in his apartment with silence as my company . . . it makes me wonder. Could I really have lost him?

I open a text to send to Maddie when I hear the distinct bell of the elevator dinging someone's arrival. Dropping my phone, I take off down the hall just in time to see Roark make his way into the living room, head turned down, hands in his pockets. When he looks up to see me, there isn't a flinch in his reaction. Not a smile. Not a hint of surprise, almost as if last night sucked every emotion out of him.

"Roark," I breathe, feeling relieved and worried simultaneously. "Where were you last night?"

"Rath's," he answers, his voice hoarse. When he looks up, I see the bruising around his eye and nose and cringe. God, that must hurt . . . and it's there because of me.

Hands still in his pockets, he asks, "What are you doing here, Sutton?"

"Didn't you get any of my texts or calls?"

"I turned off my phone."

He speaks in a monotone while avoiding all eye contact with me, the usual playfulness in his voice gone. I'm worried.

Scared actually.

"Roark, can we please talk? Last night—"

"Last night was the slap in the face I needed." He finally glances in my direction, his weary eyes circled in bright crimson.

He moves through the living room, past me, and down the hallway to his bedroom where he starts to strip out of his suit jacket and button-up shirt.

Unsure of what he means, I follow him. "Slap in the face? What are you talking about?"

"You can't be that dense, Sutton," he answers, a dose of malice in his voice.

"You've been gone all night, leaving me worried with unanswered texts and calls, so excuse me if I want an explanation," I answer.

"Your dad called it like it is: we shouldn't be together. I knew it the minute I started having feelings for you, but I needed the reminder."

I swallow hard, trying not to react to his words but imagining myself in his shoes. He's hurt, upset, and probably a little bruised from last night's conversation. I can't take his words too heavily, not when he's probably trying to protect his heart.

Cautiously, I step into his closet, closing him off in the space, and lean against the doorway. "I understand you're upset. I can't imagine what's going through your mind after yesterday, but don't push me away when we can easily work through this. Dad knows he was wrong. He admitted it and—"

"It doesn't matter. We're not working through anything, Sutton. It's over." He pushes past me, a new shirt and a pair of jeans in hand.

"You're going to give up, just like that? After you were so desperate to see me yesterday? That's it, you're over me?"

He shucks the rest of his clothes and hops in the shower, not letting it warm up. I watch as he quickly washes his face, body, and hair. After a minute at most, he's out of the shower and wrapping a towel around his waist. When he notices I haven't moved, he lets out a long sigh.

"You know I can't just *get over you* like that, Sutton."

"Then why are you fighting your feelings? Why not make everything right instead?"

"Because," he shoots back, looking at me in the mirror, his hands gripping the bathroom counter, his chest flexing under his imposing stare. "I'm never going to be good enough for you, and I'd rather not feel like a piece of shit every time you're near me. I already hate myself as it is, so I don't need the reminder when you're around."

I'm strong, but that hurt.

Not letting my pain get the best of me, I say, "Doesn't it matter what I think? Because I do think you're good enough, you were made for—"

"Leave, Sutton. Just fucking leave."

I take a step back, shocked. His words are like a physical slap. "Roark."

Shoulders growing tense, he stares me down through the mirror, and in that moment, I don't see the man I love, nor the man I know on a deeper level. Instead, I see the mask of an angry and hurt man. "Don't make this worse than it already is. Just fucking leave, okay?" He drops his head and pushes his hand through his hair violently.

"Roark, please. I'm sorry." My voice grows tighter. "I didn't want you to leave without me, I didn't want you to have to spend the night alone. That's why I was texting. I should have stayed with you but I knew I had to smooth things over with my father, explain what happened in the restaurant. I'm so sorry, please, let's just talk about this. I don't . . ." I hold back the sob that threatens to escape. "I don't want to lose you."

Barely lifting his eyes to look me in the mirror, he speaks in a dejected tone. One word. One word that sears me right in half.

"Leave."

I don't want to leave. I want to stay here, work things out, reassure him of my love, but from the tension coiling in his back I know anything I say this morning is going to bounce straight off him, untouched and unheard.

It pains me to do this, but I take a step backward and then another, retreating to my clothes that I quickly put on before gathering my things. I peek cautiously through the bathroom door to see if he's moved and he hasn't. He stays motionless besides the tug he has on the thick brown strands of his hair.

I stand there, purse and phone in hand, shoeless, wondering if I should speak to him one more time, if I should try to bridge the gap that so quickly grew between us.

I can't muster up the words, not past the thick lump that's formed in my throat. *Oh God, please. I can't have lost him forever.*

So with a heavy heart and tear-stained cheeks, I somehow make it to the elevator, hoping and praying this isn't the last time I see him. I can't lose this man from my life. He carries my heart in his hands, and I'm aching from this gaping hole within me. *I love you, Roark. I'll always love you.* And then the first sob breaks free.

Knock. Knock.

Through bloodshot eyes, I look up from my computer to find my dad standing in the doorway. The small confines of my office shrink exponentially the minute he steps inside and shuts the door behind him.

"Hey Dad," I say, leaning back in my chair.

He takes a seat and folds his hands over his stomach, examining me before speaking. "Whitney was right. You don't look great, Sutton."

"Can't hear that enough," I say with a soft smile.

"Got a call from Roark's office."

"Is he okay?" I ask, a small slice of panic cutting through me.

"He's fine, but they said he's assigned me to one of his junior agents."

"What? Are you serious? What did you say?"

"I told them that was unacceptable and that per my contract with him, he's the only one to handle my affairs, and that I expect nothing less."

"Did you sugarcoat it?"

He shakes his head. "There is no sugarcoating in business. I scheduled a meeting with him for Thursday."

I would love to crash that meeting, but I know it won't do any good. Nothing is reaching him right now. Not the texts or the phone calls, or even the emails. And when I go to his apartment to check on him and make sure he's okay, Harris politely tells me I have to leave, even though it clearly pains him.

When Roark says it's over . . . it really is. Whitney may think I look awful on the outside, but it's nothing compared to the desolation within.

"What are you going to talk about?"

Dad rubs his jaw with his large hand and says, "That's not anything you need to worry about."

"Well, I'm worried, Dad. He won't talk to me, won't even see me." My throat starts to grow tight again, making it hard to vocalize my feelings. I take a calming breath and will my stomach to stop flipping with nerves. "I'm terrified I've truly lost him before I could fully have him."

"I think he needs time. Time to think and to feel, that's how we work. Men aren't like women who can process their feelings right away. We need to take a step back and think. Roark is a smart man, so give him time; he'll realize how important you are to him." But Dad didn't hear Roark's words or see his dejection. *I'm never going to be good enough for you, and I'd rather not feel like a piece of shit every time you're near me.* He doesn't want me.

"He's had a week. How much more time does he need?" *How long before he forgets our love and forgets me?*

Dad shrugs. "Depends. He was hurt, and the scars he's worn for years were reopened, no thanks to me. He'll need time to re-evaluate and work out truth versus falsehood."

"Why won't he let me help him? He let me in the past. He needed me in the past."

"Because, sweetie, you're what he's trying to re-evaluate. If he loves you as you say, there's no doubt in my mind he'll realize how special you are to him. With Roark, once you're in his heart, you're in. He's extremely loyal, but it's letting him accept you into his life that's going to take time."

"And if he doesn't?"

"Then he's a dumbass."

"Dad," I groan. "Not the answer I was looking for."

He leans forward and reaches for my hand, which I give him. His thumb strokes lovingly over my knuckles before saying, "If he's a smart man, which I think he is, he'll figure it out."

"I wish that were the case." I pull my hand away and push a stray lock of hair behind my ear. "One thing I learned about Roark while we were together, when he's set on something, there's not much you can do to change his mind. I think when he said it's over, he truly meant it."

"He is a man of his word," my dad confirms, ramping up the panic in my heart. "But there is one thing you don't know about the man. When he realizes he's wrong, he owns it."

"Good morn—yikes," Maddie says, when I look up at her. "Uh"—she leans forward and whispers to me as she quickly looks around the coffee house—"do you realize you look like death?"

"Oh really?" I answer sarcastically, setting my cup of coffee on the table as Maddie takes a seat with her to-go cup in hand. "I thought I looked like a dignified debutante this morning."

Maddie shakes her head. "Check the mirror again, Sutton. I love you, but you look like a Barbie doll that's been dragged across the train tracks all night."

"You're incredibly sweet."

"I'm sorry, but when have I ever *not* told you the truth?"

"I know, but at least you can finish saying good morning before insulting me."

"I'm sorry," she says sincerely. "I was caught off guard. I'm going to guess he hasn't contacted you?"

I shake my head. "Nope, and he even spoke to my dad two days ago."

"Did you talk to your dad about the conversation?"

I nod, remembering how tight-lipped he was. "He wouldn't tell me anything really. He said it was between him and Roark, and what Roark did with their discussion was up to him. Clearly he doesn't want to do anything."

"And he's still not answering you?"

"Honestly, I threw in the towel on trying to communicate with him. It started feeling desperate rather than concerned. I don't want to be that girl. If he wants me, he wants me." My stomach churns in knots as tears start to well in my eyes. "And it's clear he doesn't . . . want me."

"Oh, Sutton." Maddie scoots her chair to my side as I bury my head in my hand, hating that I'm crying in public. Maddie pulls me into a hug, her arms securing tightly around me. "I'm so sorry. I wish I could say something that would make you feel better, but I don't want to fill you with hope. Roark, from what you've told me, doesn't open up easily, nor does he permit himself to feel."

"He doesn't, and that's what I'm afraid of, that he's going to walk away, without ever letting himself figure out his feelings for me."

"Have you gone to his office?"

I shake my head as Maddie pulls away but rests her hand on mine, keeping her comfort close. "That would be too desperate, and what if he turned me away? I would be humiliated, just like I was when Harris told me Roark didn't want to see me." Tears streak down my cheeks as I barely voice what's at the forefront of my mind. "I really . . . think it's over." I suck in a deep breath, my chest rattling with sorrow. *I feel so broken and hate it. I hate this pain. This agony.*

Maddie once again pulls me into a hug and presses her hand to the back of my head. "I'm so sorry, Sutton. I know this is probably the last thing you want to hear, but love is unpredictable. Sometimes it sweeps you off your feet and carries you off into the sunset. And then there are moments where love is a learning lesson, a small chapter of experience in your long and beautiful life. Have your moment, learn from the love you had with him, and when the time is right, the ache in your chest will start to ease and the colors around you will begin to brighten again."

Even though I know she's right, that in time I'll probably get over this, I know deep down, there's no way I'll be able to truly let this love go. This was the first time I ever felt another human bury themselves within the marrow of my bones. There will always be a part of my life that reads a little duller before I met Roark McCool, and that's a realization I'm going to live with for the rest of my life.

CHAPTER TWENTY-TWO

D*ear Who Gives a Fuck,*
 I don't know why I'm still writing in this damn thing, it's not like I have anything else to really say other than . . .
 I drank until I blacked out last night.
 I smoked what feels like three cartons the night before.
 And I paid some dickhead in a bar three nights ago to beat the living shit out of me in the back alley.
 He did a shitty-ass job.
 Now I'm left with subpar black eyes, a wicked cough, and a massive hangover that has me dragging my ass even worse than before.
 For the first time since I started my company, I'm taking a sick day.
 I called my assistant, pretending to cough, saying I was going to hit up a doctor, but she and I both know the only kind of sick I really am is lovesick.
 Fuck my life.
 Roark

ROARK

It took about three shots and four swishes of mouthwash to get me here this morning, but I made it, sunglasses draped over my eyes, and a thick scruff covering up my bruised jaw.

Sitting in the back, coffee in hand, I lean into the booth and press my eyes shut, willing the pounding headache beating into my skull to settle enough so I don't toss my cookies during this meeting.

I know why he wants to meet up, and it's not to discuss business, given there's nothing pressing going on. The only reason he's here is to talk about her, and even though this is the last conversation I want to have, I know I have to take it because it's in our contract to be open and available whenever the client beckons.

Foster Green has beckoned. Therefore, I'm here.

The door to the coffee house opens, and I don't have to open my eyes to see who it is; his presence is obvious from the sound of his strong steps on the old New York City floors. He sits across from me and without looking, I slide him a cup of coffee as well as one of those chocolate croissants I know he loves, because if anything, I'm still a damn good agent.

"Went on a bender?" he asks, his voice gruff.

"If that's what you want to call it," I mutter, eyes still closed.

"I think this is the most unprofessional I've ever seen you. Are you trying to lose me as a client?"

"It would be a hell of a lot easier if that was the case." I finally lift my head, the pounding at the front of my skull incessant. "But given your stubborn personality, I know you're not about to let me out of our contract."

"Damn right, I'm not." He reaches across the table and flicks my sunglasses down, revealing my blackened eyes. He shakes his head in defeat and then leans back in the booth. "Roark, what are you—?"

"Unless your question has to do with your pending contracts, I suggest you don't ask anything. I'm not here to chitchat about my personal life." I push my sunglasses back up on my sore nose and rest my head against the booth again.

"You're better than this, Roark."

I laugh. Sardonically. "Coming from the guy who doesn't think much of me at all."

Audibly he exhales and shifts on the leather seat beneath him. "About that."

"Forget it," I say, and start to move out of my booth, not in the mood for this conversation.

"Don't move. I have something to say to you," Foster says with authority.

"Save it," I reply back, getting out of my seat. I start to walk by him when he snags my wrist tightly. "Let the fuck go, Foster, or you're not going to like what happens."

"What are you going to do? Fight me? Because that solves everything, right? Man up, sit down, and have a conversation with me."

Man up.

For some reason, it irks me whenever he uses that term, probably because I've never truly felt like a man in my own right. Just a thirty-two-year-old boy who can't get his personal life together.

"Sit," Foster reiterates.

I do what he says, because Foster has that effect on me. He digs deep inside me and pulls out this desperate boy who wants to please.

I sit at the edge of my seat, arm draped on the table as I push my hand through my hair. "Talk."

"Look at me, without your sunglasses."

I should have known this wasn't going to be easy. Facing him, I remove my sunglasses, fold them up, and set them to the side. He studies me for a few beats before the hard edges in his face go soft and his eyes turn sincere.

"I'm sorry, Roark. I was out of line the other day, assuming the worst about you when I should have thanked you."

Fuck. I was right, I don't want to listen to this.

He must sense how uncomfortable I am, because he stares me down, holding my attention. "I was blindsided, and in that mindset, I jumped to extremely wrong conclusions. The things I said to you. Shit, man, you were protecting my daughter from . . . I can't bear to think what you saw happening to her, Roark. But I also can't thank you enough for pulling that asshole away from her. Taking him out. I'm sorry—"

"Yeah, don't sweat it," I answer.

"You love her, don't you?"

Exhausted with no fight left inside me, I slowly nod. "Yeah, I do." Palm to the table, I look Foster in the eyes and say, "I love her more than my own messed-up life."

"For how long?"

I shrug. "Does it really matter?"

"It does to me."

I run my tongue over my teeth and think back through all my interactions with Sutton, the good and the bad. The moments we were teasing, the times we simply held each other, to the early interactions we had through text. Through all of that, there is one moment that sticks out to me, one moment I'll never forget.

"I had a bad fucking day. My mum called me, looking for money again. Her words penetrated the armour I usually wear when I talk to her. It was a fucking low for me, so I turned to my vices to smother the pain, but they didn't work. That's when I showed up at Sutton's apartment, drunk, and in need of something. Instead of judging me and pushing me away, she let me hold her that night and seek comfort from her warmth. I knew then, I'd never be the same." I press my forehead into my hand, coming up with my next words. "I know she's better than I am. I'm not blind to how goddamn perfect she is, and I knew getting involved with her wasn't the brightest idea I've ever had, but I couldn't stay away, no matter how hard I tried." I shake my head. "I couldn't stay away." *And now I've lost her forever and my heart has turned to stone.*

"And now?"

"And now what?" I ask, looking up at him.

"How do you feel about her now?"

"My feelings haven't changed."

"So why does she cry on the phone when I talk to her? Why aren't you with her?"

I look him up and down. "I think you know the answer to that."

"When have you ever let someone's opinion stop you from doing anything?"

"Since the person I respect the most told me I was nothing, a fuck-up," I answer, the truth flying out before I can stop it. Why do I have to be so goddamn honest? I drag my hand over my face. "I know what you said was the truth, it's what I think of myself, so even though you apologized, it doesn't erase the fact that you were right. I'm not at her level. I'm not good enough, never will be."

"I was wrong, Roark," Foster replies with sincerity. "I was really fucking wrong. At that moment, I was angry, angry that you two felt the need to keep your relationship a secret, mad that Whitney knew, mad that you were in another fight. It's not an excuse for the way I treated you, and I am completely ashamed of myself, but the words I spoke to you were purely from anger and not from the heart."

I look away. "You're one of the best people I know, Roark. You care deeply for your clients and their well-being. You are loyal through and through, hard-working, and self-made. And above all else, you have a passionate and undying love for my daughter that I've never seen in another man and for that, I'll always think of you with the highest regard." He stands from the table, lingering above me as he buttons up his jacket. "Despite what you think of yourself, you *are* more than enough for Sutton. I suggest you find a way to accept that because if you love her, and if you can believe you're the inspiring, unswerving, and trustworthy man I see, you won't let her wait any longer than she has."

He starts to walk away but I call out to him. "You think I'm a worthy man?"

Foster glances over his shoulder and says, "More than worthy, Roark. More than."

And that affirmation just about brings me to my knees.

"What are you wearing?" Bram asks, taking in my clothes as I sit at the table. "And why do you have two black eyes?"

I unbutton my suit coat and pick up the menu in front of me. "It's a suit, and you're wearing one too."

"Yeah, but you're wearing a tie with it. You don't ever wear ties. You leave the buttons at the top undone so you show off your man cleavage." He gestures at my steel-gray tie. "And you're wearing blue, whereas you always wear black. What's with the blue?" He leans back in his chair and gives me a solid once-over. "Your beard has been trimmed and your eyes aren't bloodshot."

He processes and I let him.

"You don't smell like alcohol either."

Still more processing.

"You got a haircut. You look fresh."

And one more time . . .

"Holy shit." There it is. He grips my arm. "Are you going to get her back?"

"I think so."

"You think so?" Bram turns my chair so I'm forced to fully face him. "What's the plan? What changed your mind? Are you going to propose?"

"Slow down." I glance at him. "I'm far away from proposing. I need to make sure she wants to date me again after I forced her to leave my life."

"Just flash that grin of yours, call her lass—heavy on the accent—and then stick your tongue down her throat. Simple."

"Not even you would take that advice," I deadpan.

He smiles. "Yeah, that's pretty shitty advice. Seriously though, what happened, what made you change your mind? Last I knew it was over."

"So glad news travels fast between you and Rath."

"Please, with the way you've been looking and acting, it was obvious. Did you talk with Foster?"

"I did." I pick up the water glass in front of me and take a big sip.

"When?"

"A few days ago." I set my glass down and shift in my chair to get comfortable. "It was a good conversation, one I think was much needed." Foster helped me reconsider what both Rath and Sutton said. My family has no sense of unconditional love, manipulate me, have no moral fiber, and shouldn't have any bearing on how I feel about myself. They were the fuck-ups. *They always have been.* I do know how to navigate relationships. After all, I haven't destroyed my friendships with Rath and Bram, and given the shit they've put me through over the years, that deserves a fucking medal. And he was also right. Sutton doesn't deserve to wait any longer. If she'll have me back . . .

"Have you seen Sutton?"

I shake my head. "No, and for good reason. I wasn't ready. I needed to see my therapist first."

"Miss Stick-Up-Her-Ass?"

"Yup, the evil witch herself. I asked her for advice."

"You actually sought her advice?" Bram asks, his eyes nearly popping out of his head.

"I wanted her take on my family and how I should interact with them." Turning serious, Bram leans in a little closer. He's been through it all when it comes to my family, so I'm sure he's been waiting for me to understand what I'm about to say. "I knew the phone call was coming any day and I wanted to be armed with tools to combat them, because they're the main reason I hit so many roadblocks with Sutton. When I'm with her, I don't want her to have to worry about me and whatever fucked-up shit is brewing in my head. I want us to be together with nothing between us, and my family is a huge barrier."

"Wow. I'm proud of you. What did she say?"

"She basically told me I have the right to say no, that I should say no, and anything my mum or dad might say to me in return is only to spur a reaction from me. She told me to be calm, to tell them if they want to have a relationship with me, they know where to find me, but I won't be sending any more money to them."

"And did they call?" I nod. "Did you tell them?" Bram asks, now on the edge of his seat.

"No."

He deflates. "What? Why not?"

I smile. "I had my own way of saying things."

"Oh hell," he chuckles. "What did you say?"

"She called yesterday, like I knew she would. She asked for some money for food. Said they were starving. I listened to her pleas and at the end of her rant, I told her I'm sorry for not being there, sorry she believes I'm a fuck-up who owes them something. Told her I wanted and created my own life and she should be proud of that. If she can't accept that, it's on her, not me."

"Do you believe that?"

"In time I will. And then I told her if she wanted more money, she'd have to take out a loan with interest, but in order to get the money, she has to pay me back everything I've given her first."

"Shit." He laughs. "I bet that didn't go over well."

"Not even a little. Called me some pretty shitty stuff, but I let it go in one ear and out the other. I know I'll never have a positive relationship with them, but hopefully the phone calls will stop after a while. It's a start."

"You sound good."

I play with the fork on the table, moving it up and down. "I'm not saying I'm completely better. I still got lost in a bottle last night, but at least I didn't send them any money. That's progress."

"That is progress. What's next?"

"Getting rid of these black eyes."

"And then . . . ?" Bram asks, leading me to my next topic of conversation.

"And then I see if Sutton wants me back."

"She will. Are you going to do that tonight?"

I gesture to my eyes. "What did I just tell you?"

"If I were you, I wouldn't wait too long. It's already been close to two weeks. You don't want her to build up hostility toward you. And since I'm pretty sure Sutton and her dad have a seriously close relationship, she probably knows her dad talked to you."

"Oh shit," I say as dread starts to fill the pit of my stomach. "I didn't think about that."

"Yeah. If she knows you talked to him, and you two are cool with each other, she probably thinks you don't want her anymore. Wondering why didn't show up at her doorstep immediately after talking with Foster."

Sutton and Foster are super close. She's the reason he came to see me, because she told him the truth. So she knows I met with Foster. Fuck.

The last thing I want her to think is I don't love her anymore, even after her dad spoke to me, gave me his blessing, that I still don't want her.

I glance at Bram who nods. "Yeah, you can leave. I'll order something to-go for me and Julia."

"Thanks." I stand and start to move away when Bram stops me.

"Hold up." He nods at my chest. "Lose the tie, you look like an idiot in it."

Laughing, I loosen the knot, pull the tie over my head, and toss it at Bram who looks at the label.

"Stefano Ricci. Nice. This thing is expensive."

"Consider it a thank you."

"A thank you? For what?"

With a smile, I say, "For being a constant in my life."

"Dude," he breathes out, "don't you make me fucking cry."

I roll my eyes and leave the restaurant with one thing on my mind: getting Sutton back.

CHAPTER TWENTY-THREE

Dear Yori,
  That is the name my parents were originally going to give me. Yori. What kind of name is that? Not a strong one, that's for damn sure.

Do you know what I love about New York City? It's alive all hours of the day.

Do you know what I hate about New York City?

Traffic, especially when stuck on the Brooklyn Bridge when I'm trying to get to my girl. I've been in this damn cab for over an hour, listening to the same damn ads on the TV in front of me over and over again because the touchscreen doesn't work, and I can't turn the volume off. After an hour, I'm just about convinced this could be considered psychological torture and I should turn this cab driver in to the proper authorities.

I needed a distraction, so that's why I'm typing in my notes app as my knee bounces up and down impatiently. I thought that maybe writing down my feelings might help me figure out what I'm going to say to Sutton when I see her, but frankly, I can't think of a damn thing other than: I'm sorry, please take me back, and I love you so goddamn much.

I know that should be good enough, but a part of me thinks it's not. Sutton is special. She deserves a big declaration. Then again, when has she ever been that girl? She even paid for some of our meals when we were out, even when I told her not to.

Maybe something simple is all she needs ... is all she wants.
Only one way to find out.
Roark

∼

SUTTON

"Stop staring at me, okay? I'm fine. I'm allowed to have two ice cream sandwiches if I want. I'm an adult, and I make my own decisions."

Louise stares at me, a judgmental look in her beady cat eyes. I know what she's thinking. That isn't your second ice cream sandwich; that's your third.

And maybe it is.

Maybe I like to sulk and indulge in pity food when I'm sad. There's nothing wrong with that, and since I barely ate anything during the last week, I think it's okay to replenish on ice cream sandwiches. Plus, I bought a four-pack box, which means I didn't have much room in my tiny, tiny freezer. Really, I'm doing myself a service by not wasting money and eating food I bought before it goes bad.

That's being a good person.

I take a big bite out of the sandwich and chew, staring at my computer as The Great British Baking Show plays. The only part of the show I actually like is the technical. Well, that's not true, I like it when they call things stodgy or say, "what a disappointment." The looks on the contestants' faces are priceless.

"You know, Louise, I really think we should start using the word stodgy in our everyday vernacular. We would sound so posh. What do you think?" She hops off the bed and walks over to her litter box where she starts pushing around litter. "I'm going to take that as a no."

Sighing, I lean against my headboard and set the rest of my ice cream sandwich to the side, not really in the mood anymore to eat.

I glance at my phone on the nightstand, willing it to ring or make a text alert sound, but nothing. It's been four days since my dad talked to Roark, and I've hated the absolute radio silence. And even though I don't want to conclude it's truly over, I can't help but start to believe it.

If Roark really wanted me, I thought after he'd sorted things out with Dad he'd at least send me a text. That's what we do, text each other.

But there's been nothing.

I fall deeper into my bed, pushing my computer to the side, not really interested in Paul Hollywood destroying a baker's dreams over focaccia bread.

My eyes focus on the notepad on my nightstand, and I reach out to flip it open.

My New Year's resolutions. We're still in the first quarter of the year and everything on this list feels like a joke, especially the last one.

Live life.
Try all iconic New York City food.
Go to a nightclub.
Spend a day getting lost in Central Park.
Fall in love.
Yup, that last one makes me tear up.

I can cross it off. I fell in love and I fell hard. If only that love was reciprocated. When I wrote that resolution, I thought maybe I'd find someone who'd want to spend the rest of their life with me. I never dreamed I'd end up getting my heart broken by a man with an Irish accent and soulful eyes that penetrate the heart.

Reaching out, I pick up the pink Paper Mate pen on my nightstand and put a check mark through the box that's next to fall in love, as a single tear rolls down my cheek. I then roll over on my side and look out the expansive windows of my small studio apartment just as there's a knock at my door.

Lifting up, I stare at the door, as if I have X-ray vision and can see through wood. When another knock comes, my breath catches in my throat as I run through my mind who it could be. My dad? It could definitely be him. I talked to him today, and he didn't like how sad I sounded on the phone.

It could be Maddie. She was begging me to go out with her tonight, but I told her I wasn't feeling well. She didn't buy it.

It could be Roark . . .

Who am I kidding?

I flip my covers off, walk over to the door, reach for the knob, and open it up only to find no one.

What?

I stick my head out the door and look to the right toward the front entrance, and that's when I see his retreating back, decked out in a navy-blue suit, his hair freshly trimmed.

"Roark?" I ask, my voice catching in my throat. He whips around, revealing two dark circles under his eyes and a worried expression on his face.

"Sutton. You're home."

"Yeah," I answer awkwardly, as nausea rolls around in my stomach from nerves. "Did you, uh, want something?"

He takes a step forward, his hand gripping the back of his neck. "I was hoping I could talk to you."

Don't get your hopes up, Sutton. This could be absolutely nothing.

"Sure," I say, stepping to the side and letting him in my apartment. When he passes me, I glance down at my green plaid shorts and matching top. Why don't I wear nicer things when I'm eating my feelings?

Once the door is shut, he turns around, and that's when I get a good look at his face. His nose is slightly swollen and both eyes have a disturbing shade of purple under them, cluing me in that he got into yet another fight.

When he notices me taking in his bruises, he says, "I, uh . . . did something stupid."

"Looks like it." I lean against me door and twist my hands in my shirt, unsure what I should do. My initial instinct is to throw myself at him and kiss his face until it's better. My second instinct is to walk up to him and kick him in the balls for putting me through hell over the past two weeks. I'll wait to see what he has to say before I take action.

"Can we sit down?"

"I prefer to stand, but if you want to sit, go ahead." There's no way I can sit on a bed with him right now, not when it feels like my heart is pounding in my throat.

Taking my invitation, he sits on my bed and stares at his hands for a few seconds before saying, "I'm . . ." He glances up and his eyes fixate on the notebook on my nightstand.

My stomach drops, and I see the moment he reads my last resolution because his brow creases as he looks at me. He points to the notebook and says, "What's that?"

Quickly, in a few steps, I reach out and snag the notebook, close it, and toss it on the floor off to the side. "Nothing. Nothing at all."

He stands, abandoning his spot on the bed and starts to walk toward me, as my pulse picks up to a marathon pace.

"Sutton, what was that?"

"Nothing of your concern."

"Don't lie to me."

"Lie to you?" I say, my voice growing louder. "Like you have room to talk. You want to speak the truth, why don't you start?"

"Fine," he says with finality in his voice as he closes the space between us. "I'm sorry I hurt you. I'm sorry that for a short period of time, I wasn't the man you needed. I'm sorry I made you doubt the importance of what we had with each other." He pins me against the door. "And I'm sorry it took me this long to pull my head out of my arse and realize despite everything I do wrong, you're the one right in my life." He cups my cheek as tears stream down my cheek, tears of true happiness. "I love you, Sutton, and I don't want you to ever doubt that again." These words. They're the most beautiful words in the world, and I have so needed to hear them. *He loves me. Wants me.*

I press my face into his hand and close my eyes, enjoying the feel of him again, touching me, loving me.

When I open my eyes, I say, "I love you too, Roark."

A smirk crosses his face. "So that little box you checked on your list, that was for me?"

I nod. "It was, but when I checked it, I never thought I'd be nursing a broken heart at the same time."

"I'm sorry, lass," he whispers, pulling me into his chest and wrapping his arms around me. One of his hands cradles the back of my head and he presses his lips into my hair. "I'm so goddamn sorry. I wasn't in a good place. I've barely resurrected myself from the self-imposed state of hatred I've put myself through. I planned on waiting until I felt like I was whole enough for you but realized, I really wouldn't be whole until you were back in my life again."

"You don't have to try to be perfect for me, Roark." I lift my head and look him in the eyes. "I love you because you're not perfect, because you're rough around the edges. I love you because you're the one person who makes me feel at home. When I'm in your arms, wrapped in your warmth, everything feels right, and I never want to lose that again."

"You won't." He kisses my head again, pulling me into another hug. "You're not going to lose me again, Sutton Grace."

I smile into his chest. "Is that a promise?"

"Do I need to use asterisks to emphasize it?"

"I think so." I chuckle, moving my hand up his chest to the buttons of his shirt. "Now tell me what happened to your handsome face."

"It's not important, because all that matters right now is that we're both fully clothed." He slips his hand down the front of my shirt, takes the hem, and lifts it up and over my head. When he looks down, his brow furrows. "A bra, since when did you start wearing a bra with your pajamas?"

Chuckling, I say, "Since I walk outside in them."

"Kind of lost all will to be classy, huh?"

I stroke my fingers over his rough stubble. "When you take

away the one thing I love most, yeah, I might lose a bit of class for a while."

He brings me to the bed where he lays me down gently. He shuts my computer and puts it on the nightstand then loses his jacket and shirt. I run my fingers over his strong pecs, and the short chest hair he's let grow out. Sexy.

"Don't worry, lass, I'm not going anywhere. You can stop wearing pajamas in general now."

I roll my eyes. "You're ridiculous."

"Do you know what's ridiculous? That you're not naked yet."

"Then do something about it," I say, running my finger over his nipple.

His eyes narrow and before I know it, his mouth is at my neck and his hands are gliding all over my body, stripping me down to nothing. As he presses sweet kisses up and down my neck, I feel grateful that even in the hard times, love has a way of healing open wounds. Otherwise, I wouldn't know what true love is, the beautiful and the ugly.

"Looking good, hot stuff," I whistle while leaning back on the blanket I spread on the lawn of Central Park.

"Don't miss that piece over there," Maddie heckles as we both watch Roark finish up the last of his mandated community service while checking off another resolution on my list: spend the entire day in Central Park. I just so happened to schedule it when Roark had to do trash duty in the park. Worked out perfectly, because once he finishes up these two hours, he'll be joining us.

Lifting his glance from the ground, he peers at the service coordinator and looks back at us where he flips us the middle finger. Maddie and I both chuckle, while he shakes his head and laughs as well.

"How much time does he have left?" Maddie asks, popping a grape in her mouth.

"Five minutes."

"Wow, that went by fast."

"When you have nice eye candy to stare at, time flies." I take a slice of cheese and nibble on it, still staring at Roark, mainly that perfect ass wrapped in dark jeans.

"He is quite good-looking," Maddie looks him up and down. "When did he get that tattoo?"

"He's had that since I've known him."

"Huh." She eats another grape. "I guess I've never seen him without sleeves, but then again we just survived the wintery tundra of the East Coast. Does he only have the forearm tattoo? Nothing on his ass?"

"No." I laugh. "Just the one. I remember the moment I saw it for the first time—talk about a huge turn-on. I wasn't expecting it, then all of a sudden, he had this dark ink wrapped around his right forearm. It did all sorts of things to me."

"I can imagine. It's doing all sorts of things for me now."

"Hey." I playfully swat at her. "Stop ogling my boyfriend."

"I have to ogle something." She sighs. "Think Roark wants to hook me up with someone?"

"That's really not my kind of thing," his voice booms above us. When did he get there? I swear he was just over by that tree.

He takes a seat next to me, pulls me between his legs and wraps his arms around my midriff.

"Hey," I say over my shoulder as he presses a kiss to my cheek.

"Hey you." He nuzzles the side of my ear before saying, "All that heckling got you into some serious trouble."

"Oh, I can't wait to find out what kind."

"Ahem," Maddie clears her throat. "Can you not do that while I'm right here? Also, why won't you set me up with someone?"

"Rath is single."

Roark shakes his head. "Rath is not single. Technically, he might not be with someone right now, but he's completely wrapped up in his ex. That would be doing a disservice to Maddie."

"Damn." She snaps her fingers in disappointment. "I heard he has these penetrating eyes that cut right down to your very soul."

"You said that to her?" Roark asks, pulling away to look at me.

I smile shyly. "I mean, he's hot and intimidating, kind of a lethal combination."

"And what am I?"

I snuggle into him. "A giant Irish cuddle bear."

"Christ," he mutters behind me, as I laugh.

"Seriously though, don't you have any single athletes you work with?" Maddie asks. "I like sports."

"Not going to happen."

Her eyes light up. "So, you do have some single clients. Who are they? Let's plan out a meet-cute."

"It's not really a meet-cute if you plan it," I say.

She waves her hand at me. "He doesn't need to know that. Come on, Roark." She nudges his foot. "Introduce me. I'm drama free, love a good laugh, and appreciate muscles. I make my own money, so no need to be worried about a gold digger, and I'm very bendy and open to things"—she wiggles her eyebrows—"if you know what I mean."

"Unfortunately, I do." He scratches the side of his beard, giving her idea some thought. "Still not going to happen."

"Ugh," she groans but then makes eye contact with me, an evil glint in her eye. "We'll see about that."

"I don't like the look in her eye," Roark says to me. "Should I be worried?"

"Very."

"How do your balls not hurt?" Roark asks my father as they ride side by side on their respective horses. Roark has found an attachment to Grammy, even though she still bucks him off every time he first gets on her. He's become accustomed to a proper dismount.

"They get used to it over the years."

Roark shifts. "I'm afraid I'm never going to be able to give you grandkids if you keep forcing me to take these rides along the property."

"Planning on kids already?" Dad asks as I lean in an ear, wanting to hear Roark's answer.

He glances in my direction and then back at my dad. "Yeah, I'd like six."

"Six?" I shout, startling my horse that I quickly calm down. "You want six kids?" My poor uterus.

"Why not. The more the merrier, right, Foster?"

"Six sounds like a great number."

Of course both the men would think six is a great number. They're not the one carrying them for nine months and then pushing them out.

"What about two?"

"Four," Roark counters.

"How about a ring first?" my dad cuts in.

Roark laughs and says, "All in good time, old man. How about we get through your last season first and see where I am with that girl over there. Who knows, things might change."

"What?" I ask at the same time as my father, causing Roark to roar with laughter.

"You two, swear to God, like two peas in a pod."

"Uh, what happened to *you're mine forever, Sutton*?" I ask, getting my horse to catch up to Roark.

He turns in my direction and his eyes soften as he says, "You are mine, forever. I'm glad you haven't forgotten."

We reach the barn after a good half hour walk around the property and Roark hops down first before helping me down. He insists even though I can do it myself. I think he wants to do it just because he saw Josh help me down that one time. Hand in mine, he says, "Can I take this girl away for a bit?"

"Have at it. I'm going to go see how Whitney is doing. This pregnancy has taken a toll on her. The only reason I went on the ride was because she wanted to get some sleep after throwing up all morning."

"Do you need us to pick anything up for her?" I ask, concerned for my stepmom.

"I think we're good, thank you, sweetie." Dad places a quick kiss on the top of my head and then turns toward the house with a quick jog. They married about a month ago. It was small and private, just Roark and I were invited, and then they spent two weeks in Tahiti. Dad has a couple weeks before he has to be back on the field, so he's trying to soak up as much private time with Whitney as possible.

The sun starts to set, casting an orange glow over the land, making it a beautiful night on the ranch. As Roark leads me to the fire pit, I lean in to him, loving that I can be natural with him around my dad. The last time we were on the ranch together, I had to hide my feelings not only from my dad, but from Roark as well, that was until the one fateful night by the fire pit when he finally succumbed to his feelings.

Roark takes a seat on a wide Adirondack chair around the perimeter of the already lit fire pit. He pulls me down on his lap so I'm sitting sideways. I lean in to him, cuddling closer to his side as he links our hands and entwines our fingers.

"It really is beautiful here. I don't think I was able to appreciate it last time because I was so distracted by you, and hungover for what felt like the first few days."

"You did not look good when you fell out of that car. It was hard to not run to your side."

"I'm glad you didn't," he says, his voice soft. "I had to learn to stand on my own two feet before I was able to truly take you as mine."

"And now that you have me?"

"I'm wondering how serious you are about marriage."

My heart skips a beat. "Serious about marriage?"

"Yeah." His thumb rubs over the back of my knuckles and casually plays with my ring finger. "I want to know what you really think about it. If it's something you can see yourself doing . . . with me."

I lift my hand to cup his cheek and force him to look me in the eyes. "I only want you and I want everything. The marriage, the house, the kids. I want it all."

"Even with this old man?"

I chuckle. "Especially with this old man." I press a kiss against his lips and marvel in the way he casually runs his hand up my back, sending goosebumps across my skin.

"Thank fuck your dad was a good man and gave us the guest house."

"Why's that?"

"Because I'm going to have a lot of fun fucking my future wife tonight."

"I'm going to need a ring before you can call me that," I say, my forehead pressed against his, our lips inches apart.

"It will come, lass. Patience."

"So there's nothing hiding in that pocket of yours right now?"

He chuckles and shakes his head. "Nah, I have to ask your dad for permission first then find the perfect ring. That's going to take time."

"I don't need the perfect ring. I just need you."

"And that's why I love you, and why I want the perfect ring."

I sigh and lean my head into the crook of his neck, letting him stroke my hair as we enjoy the different colors in the sky.

"But you are going to propose?"

"I am, because there's no way in hell I'm ever letting you go again."

Little does he know, even if he tried, I wouldn't let him.

EPILOGUE

Dear Diary,
 We've been through a lot, name after name, after name, and what it comes down to is . . . I'm going to act like a besotted teenager with heart beams spewing from her hormonal eyes.

I've learned a lot over the course of this year, but one of the most important things is that I have worth. Not because of the millions in my bank, not the woman by my side. Me. My ma hasn't given up chasing me for money yet, but I've stood strong and not relented once. Her comments don't have the same damaging effect any more, which is grand. A sign of healing, I've been told.

This might come as a shock to you, after everything I've written, but guess what? I proposed to Sutton, my girl. And do you know what she said?

She said yes!

Talk about instant pride filling a man's chest. It might be an odd thing to say, but I've never been more proud of myself than when the girl of my dreams looked down at me with tear-filled eyes, hands clasped over her mouth as she nodded her head, agreeing to marry me.

Me.

The fuck-up from Killarney with no future.

The frat boy from Yale with no hope.

The biggest whiskey-slugging, Guinness-guzzling eejit in New York City with no substance.

She said yes to me. I still don't know how I was able to convince her to date me in the first place, let alone marry me, but I know one thing's for sure: it has to be the luck of the Irish.

Roark

Made in the USA
Middletown, DE
20 September 2023